Nina's gaze was pulled to the Atlantean crown. *Priceless,* she had called it less than thirty minutes earlier—but now someone intended to find exactly what that translated to in the real world.

The bikers stopped and climbed off their machines, guns raised. No shouted orders, no demands, no threats. They had made their intentions perfectly clear—and another burst of fire from an MP5K as a prone security guard tried to draw his weapon hammered the point home.

"What do we do?" Nina whispered. "We can't let them steal the crown!"

"Y-yes, we can!" Boyce said, voice quavering. He raised his head as the faceless trio approached. "I'm the mayor of San Francisco. Please, take what you came for and leave. Nobody else has to get hurt." Nina scowled at him, but knew there was nothing else they could do.

The Nemesis kept reversing. Its rear bullbar clipped another display case, which toppled over and smashed. The golden trident clanged across the floor as the big 4×4 stopped behind the three men.

They regarded the crown impassively...then at a gesture from the tallest of the trio, apparently the leader, moved to the next case.

The one containing the Talonor Codex.

By Andy McDermott

The
Sacred
Vault

The Sacred Vault

Andy McDermott

BANTAM BOOKS
NEW YORK

A 2011 Bantam Books Mass Market Edition

Copyright © 2010 by Andy McDermott

Published in the United States by Bantam Books, an imprint of The Random House Publishing Group, a division of Random House, Inc., New York.

BANTAM BOOKS and the rooster colophon are registered trademarks of Random House, Inc.

Originally published in hardcover in Great Britain by Headline Publishing Group, London, in 2010, and published by arrangement with Headline Publishing Group.

ISBN 978-0-553-59364-8

Cover design: Carlos Beltram
Cover art: Blacksheep, based on images from Superstock

Printed in the United States of America

www.bantamdell.com

2 4 6 8 9 7 5 3 1

For my family and friends

The
Sacred
Vault

PROLOGUE
Italy

It was a cold, crisp mid-November evening, but Giancarlo Mistretta's mind was already on Christmas as he guided his tanker along the winding road through the Casentinesi forest. His apartment would play host to the celebrations this year; twenty-three people to cater for, maybe twenty-four if his sister's newest baby arrived earlier than expected...

He pushed his plans aside as a tight turn appeared in the headlights. Slowing the truck to a near crawl, he checked his watch. Slightly ahead of schedule—there was still one more gas station to supply before he could return to the depot, but he would be back home in Florence before seven. Then maybe he and Leany could advance their plan for a baby of their own...

He guided the tanker around the corner—then braked. A charcoal-gray BMW was slewed across the road, one wheel in the ditch. A woman in a dark suit waved for him to stop.

Giancarlo suppressed a sigh. The BMW was blocking his way. So much for getting home early. Still, he wouldn't be setting much of an example for any future little Giancarlos if he didn't help a lady in distress.

He stopped, taking a closer look at the woman. Long, glossy black hair and dark skin—Indian, perhaps? Probably in her late twenties, and quite attractive, in a businesslike way. He could almost hear Leany reprimanding him for that, but married or not, he still had eyes, didn't he?

The woman walked toward the truck. Giancarlo climbed out to meet her. "Hi," he called. "Looks like you could use some help."

She looked briefly into the woods as she advanced. Giancarlo noticed that her features were marred; only her left eye had moved, the right staring fixedly at him. The pale line of a scar ran from forehead to cheek over the socket.

A glass eye.

He glanced at the BMW. "Are you stuck? I can give you a—"

She whipped out a silenced handgun and shot him three times in the face.

Giancarlo's lifeless body slumped to the tarmac. A man stepped out of the darkness of the woods. Tall, muscular, and dressed entirely in black, Urbano Fernandez regarded the corpse with an expression of mock apology. "Poor fellow," he said. The language was English, but the accent was smoothly Spanish. "Never any pleasantries with you, are there?" he went on as the woman holstered the gun.

"A waste of time," said Madirakshi Dagdu coldly. As the unfortunate Giancarlo had guessed, she was Indian, her accent thick and stilted—English was a language in which she had only recently needed proficiency. She indicated the truck driver's body. "Dispose of that."

Fernandez snapped a sarcastic salute. "Yes, *ma'am*." He pulled on a pair of black leather gloves, pausing to brush his pencil mustache with his fingertips before dragging the corpse into the undergrowth. "You didn't have to be here at all. We don't need to be, what's the word? *Nurse-maided.*"

He knew full well what the word was, but took a certain amusement from her frown of deep concentration as she tried to translate it. "This operation is more expensive than the others," she said once the meaning had come to her. "My employers want to be sure their money is being used well."

"It will be worth every dollar," said Fernandez, dumping the body. There was no point concealing it—the area would be crawling with people soon enough. He went to the tanker. "Now go. Meet me down the road."

Madirakshi returned to the BMW without a word. Fernandez watched her, thinking it was a shame such an attractive figure was wasted on an ugly personality, then moved to the valves on the tanker's side as the car reversed out of the shallow ditch.

Even after delivering most of the day's supplies, the tanker still contained more than five hundred gallons of gas. The Spaniard turned the wheel above one of the gaping stainless-steel nozzles. Fuel gushed out. He winced at the sharp smell, backing away to avoid being splashed as he opened the valve wider. The gush became a geyser, spraying into the woods.

He climbed into the cab. The engine was still running, so he released the brake and depressed the heavy clutch to put the truck into gear, slowly following the BMW as it sped away.

Gas spewed over Giancarlo Mistretta's corpse as the tanker rumbled into the night.

• • •

A quarter mile down the road, Fernandez saw the waiting BMW's headlights. He pulled over, then hurried to the car.

Madirakshi's only greeting was a cold look. Fernandez ignored it. After tonight, there was only one more job planned, which might not even be necessary if his employers were persuasive enough—and then he would be rid of them and all the freaks in their entourage.

Even before he had fastened his seat belt, the BMW surged past the tanker, heading back up the road. A smeared pool of blood marked where the driver had been shot; Madirakshi stopped level with it.

Fernandez lowered his window. He took a Zippo lighter from a pocket and with a single practiced move flicked it open and lit it. A moment to regard his reflection in the polished metal, then he tossed the lighter into the trees.

Even before it hit the ground, the results were explosive. The highly flammable vapor rising from the pool of gas ignited, a fireball boiling upward into the trees and setting them alight. Giancarlo's fuel-soaked body was consumed by the inferno as easily as the branches. A thick trail of flames raced away down the road.

Fernandez shielded his face from the heat with one gloved hand. "Time we left. *Quickly*."

Madirakshi needed no further prompting. The BMW roared away. Fernandez looked back as the car reached the corner—to see a huge explosion rip through the forest a quarter mile behind as the tanker blew up, a seething mushroom cloud of blazing orange and yellow rising into the night sky as flaming fuel rained down around it. A moment later, the blast reached him, an earthshaking *thump* followed by a thunderous roar of air being pulled in to feed the conflagration.

"Perfect," said Fernandez. "Now for stage two."

The BMW raced through the darkened forest, heading for the city of Florence as the trees behind it turned into a wall of fire.

• • •

The banging of the chair stopped as Braco Zec pointed his gun at the young woman tied to it. "Cut that out," he said in fluent Italian. "I told you, do what we say and you'll live." He dragged the chair and its gagged occupant away from the wall, then returned to the small apartment's living room. Six other black-clad men and their equipment occupied most of the space, but he pushed through them to the window, peeling back his dark balaclava to reveal a weather-worn face, hair shaved down to a gray stubble. Deep creases across his forehead showed that he had witnessed—and endured—far more than most men of his thirty-four years.

The mercenaries had taken over the apartment that afternoon, Zec tricking the woman into letting them in by claiming to be delivering a parcel. She had been selected during the operation's exacting planning phase, being the only single occupant of any of the suitable top floor apartments on the narrow Via degli Alfani. Considering what was across the street, it was perhaps inevitable that she was an aspiring artist.

He looked out at the eighteenth-century buildings: the museum complex containing the Galleria dell'Accademia. One of Florence's top tourist attractions—and home to one of the world's most famous pieces of art.

Their target.

Zec's phone rang. Fernandez. "Yes?"

"We're here. Let us in."

The Bosnian craned his neck for a better look at the street below. Two figures passed under a streetlight, approaching briskly. Fernandez and the Indian woman. The creases in Zec's forehead deepened. To him, Dagdu's presence was almost insulting, a sign that their employer didn't trust them to carry out the job without supervision. Weren't all their previous successes, including stealing a set of Chinese terra-cotta warriors out of their museum in Xi'an, and removing one of Islam's holiest relics from Mecca itself, enough to prove their prowess? And Interpol was no nearer to catching them now than after their first "commission" eight months earlier. Fernandez's inside knowledge of how the police worked, how they thought, kept them several steps ahead.

He suppressed his annoyance—she was their paymaster's representative, after all—and went back to the hall as the entry buzzer rasped. He pushed the button, then waited with slight anxiety for them to climb the stairs. If any of the other residents chose that moment to leave their apartment, and saw their faces...

But there were no such problems. The soft clump of boots outside, then a single sharp rap on the door. Zec opened it, and Fernandez and his companion entered.

The Spaniard shared a brief smile of greeting with his second in command. "Anything to report?"

"You've made the evening news," Zec told him. "The fire's spreading—they're calling in fire trucks from every surrounding town. And," he added meaningfully, "helicopters."

"Excellent." Fernandez dialed a number on his phone. "Status?"

"Air traffic control has our flight plan," said the voice at the other end of the line. "We're ready."

"Then go." He disconnected. "Where's the roof access?" Zec pointed at a skylight. "Okay, let's get into position." He moved to address the rest of the team.

Madirakshi, behind him, looked into the bedroom. "What is this?" she snapped on seeing the prisoner.

"She won't be a problem," said Zec. "She hasn't seen our faces."

Madirakshi's expression was as fixed as her artificial eye. "No witnesses." She stepped into the bedroom. The bound woman, facing away from the door, twisted against her restraints, making panicked noises. She didn't need to understand English to recognize the dangerous tone of the new arrival's voice.

"If you shoot her, the neighbors might hear," Fernandez warned.

"I don't need a gun." She stopped directly behind the other woman, whose muffled cries became more desperate.

"Leave her," said Zec, coming into the room. "I promised she would live if she caused no trouble."

Madirakshi ignored him. She placed her fingers against her right eye socket and pressed. There was a soft sucking sound, and with a faint plop something dropped into her waiting palm.

Her glass eye, glistening wetly.

Zec had seen many horrific things in his life, but the casual way the woman removed the prosthetic still produced a small shudder of revulsion. Disgust then turned to confusion as she took hold of the eye with both hands and twisted it. There was a click, and it split into two hemispherical halves. What was she doing?

The answer came as she drew her hands apart. Coiled inside the eye was a length of fine steel wire. By the time Zec realized it was a garrotte, Madirakshi had looped it around the defenseless young woman's throat and pulled it tight.

"No!" Zec gasped, but Fernandez put a firm hand on his shoulder to pull him back. The Italian woman couldn't even cry out, her airway crushed by the razor-sharp wire. She convulsed against the ropes. The chair thumped on the floor; Madirakshi pulled harder, sawing the wire through skin and flesh. Blood flowed down the woman's neck.

Her fingers clenched and clawed... then relaxed. One last bump, and the chair fell still.

Madirakshi unwound the garrotte and turned. For the first time, Zec saw her face as it really was, a sunken hole with the eyelids gaping like a tiny mouth where her right eye should have been. Another revolted shudder, accompanied by anger. "You didn't have to do that!" he said.

"No witnesses," the Indian repeated. She took out a

cloth and ran it down the length of the blood-coated wire. The garrotte clean, she re-coiled it, then fastened the two halves of the eye back into a single sphere. *Snick.* Another practiced move, and with a small but unsettling noise of suction the prosthetic was returned to its home. "Now. You have a job to do."

"We do," said Fernandez before Zec could respond. He leaned closer to his lieutenant, adding in a low voice, "I think perhaps having a baby has made you go a little soft, Braco. If this is going to be a problem..."

"No problem," said Zec stiffly. "But I promised her—"

"Never make promises you might not be able to keep," Fernandez told him, before clicking his fingers. The men in the living room looked around as one, ready for action.

* * *

Ten minutes later, all eight mercenaries were on the apartment's sloping roof.

Fernandez peered over the edge. Below, Madirakshi left the building. Relieved to be rid of her at last, he backed up and faced his team. "Ready?"

The responses were all in the affirmative. Each man was now armed, compact MP5K submachine guns fitted with laser sights and suppressors slung on their backs. Other pieces of gear were attached to the harnesses they wore; not mere equipment webbing, but parachute-style straps able to support their body weight and more.

The Spaniard looked at his watch. Five minutes to get everyone across to the roof of the Galleria dell'Accademia, another five to eliminate the guards and secure the room containing their target, five more to prepare it—and themselves—for extraction...

Fifteen minutes to carry out the most audacious robbery in history.

He gestured to one of his men, Franco, who had already secured one end of a line inside the open skylight. At the other end was a barbed metal spear, currently loaded into a custom-built, gas-powered launcher.

Franco had already selected his target, a squat brick ventilation blockhouse poking up from the Galleria's roof like a periscope. He tilted up the launcher. Fernandez watched him closely. This was a "wildcard moment," the biggest risk in any operation. If the brickwork was too weak to take the weight, if someone heard the noise of the launch or clang of impact and looked up at the wrong moment...

At least they could minimize the chances of the last. Franco raised a thumb. Another man, Sklar, held up a string of firecrackers, lit the fuse—and flung them down the street.

There was a small square at the Galleria's southwestern corner. The fireworks landed at its edge. People jumped at the string of little explosions. Once the initial fright passed, some onlookers were annoyed, others amused by the display... but they were all looking at the ground.

"Now," said Fernandez.

Franco pulled the trigger. There was a flat thud as compressed nitrogen gas blasted the spear across the street— and a sharp clang as the spearhead pierced the blockhouse.

All eyes below were still on the firecrackers.

Franco put down the launcher and tugged on the line, gingerly at first, then harder. The spear held. He pulled a lever on the launcher's side to engage a winch mechanism and quickly drew the line taut.

Fernandez gestured to a third man, Kristoff—the smallest and lightest member of the team. The German gave the line a tug of his own to reassure himself that it would hold, then clipped his harness to it and carefully lowered himself off the roof.

The others held their breaths. If the spear came loose, it was all over.

Suspended below the line, Kristoff pulled himself across the street. The cable shuddered, but held firm. Fernandez didn't take his eyes off the spear. The crackle of fireworks had stopped, and now he could hear the crunch of broken bricks shifting against one another...

Kristoff reached the Galleria's roof.

Mass exhalation. Fernandez realized he was sweating despite the cold. Kristoff detached himself from the line, then secured it around the blockhouse.

Thumbs up.

Fernandez hooked himself to the cable and pulled himself across, followed in rapid succession by the others. He checked his watch as the last man reached the Galleria. They had made it with thirty seconds to spare.

Now for the next stage.

He took out his phone and entered another number. He didn't lift it to his ear as he pushed the final button, though. He was listening for something else.

*　*　*

In a Florentine suburb two miles to the southwest, two cars had been parked, one at each end of an unremarkable street.

Each car contained just over a pound of C-4 explosive, wired to a detonator triggered by a cell phone. The phones had been cloned; all shared the same number, ringing simultaneously.

An electrical impulse passed through the detonator—

By the time the booms reached the Galleria dell'Accademia eight seconds later, the men on the roof were already moving toward their next objectives.

They raced across the rooftops, splitting into four groups of two men each. Zec and Franco made up one team, reaching their destination first as the others continued past.

The pair dropped onto a section of flat roof where large humming air-conditioning units kept the museum's internal temperature constant. There was a small window just below the eaves of the abutting, slightly taller building. Zec shone a penlight inside. An office, as expected. A glance below the frame revealed a thin electrical cable. The window was rigged with an alarm.

He took a black box from his harness, uncoiling wires and digging a sharp-toothed crocodile clip deeply into the cable to bite the copper wire within. A second clip was affixed on the other side of the window. He pushed a button on the box. A green light came on.

Franco took out a pair of wire cutters and with a single snip severed the cable between the clips.

The light stayed green.

Zec touched his throat-mike to key it. "We're in."

* * *

Inside the museum, lights of the halls and galleries were dimmed to the softest glow. Had it been up to the curators, they would have been switched off entirely, to prevent the artworks from fading, but the security guards' inconvenient human need for illumination had required a compromise.

The Galleria dell'Accademia is not an especially large museum, so the night watch usually consists only of six men. Despite the cultural value of the exhibits to the Italian people, this seemingly small staff is not an issue: Any kind of alarm would normally result in a rapid police response.

But on this night, the police had other concerns.

Two guards entered one of the upper-floor galleries. Familiarity had turned the art treasures into mundane furniture, the monotony of patrolling the halls punctuated only by check-ins with the security office. So the unexpected crackle of one man's walkie-talkie got their attention; the next check wasn't due for twenty minutes. "What's up?"

"Probably nothing," came the static-laden reply. "But Hall Three has gone dark. Can you look?"

"No problem," said the guard, giving his companion a

wry look. That passed as excitement in their job: checking for faulty lightbulbs.

They made their way to a short flight of steps. It was immediately clear there was something wrong with the lights in Hall III, only darkness visible beyond the entrance. One guard took a flashlight from his belt, and they advanced into the gallery.

Nothing seemed out of place in the beam.

The second man shrugged, turning to try the light switches—

A pair of eyes seemed to float in the blackness before him.

Before he could make a sound, he was hit in the heart by two bullets from Zec's MP5K, the suppressor muting the noise of the shots to nothing more than sharp *tchack*s. His partner whirled—and a gloved hand clamped over his mouth, Franco's black-bladed combat knife stabbing deep into his throat.

Both bodies were hauled into the shadows. Zec pulled up his balaclava and took the dead guard's walkie-talkie. "Something's buzzing," he said in Italian, the radio's low fidelity disguising his voice. "The camera might have shorted out. Can you check the system?"

"I'll run a diagnostic. Hold on."

Zec dropped the walkie-talkie. The computer would spend the next thirty seconds checking the various cameras and alarms around the building, eventually coming to the conclusion that the camera in Hall III was malfunctioning—unsurprising, since he had shot it.

But while the computer was busy, the security systems would be down.

He keyed the throat-mike. "Two down. Go."

• • •

Fernandez and Sklar were suspended on lines hanging from the roof on the southern side of a courtyard, waiting for

Zec's signal. The instant it came, Fernandez kicked open an upper-floor window and swung inside, unslinging his gun. The Ukrainian jumped down beside him.

He and his team had reconnoitered the Galleria multiple times over the past month, and he knew exactly where he had entered the building—the upper level of the main stairwell. Right now, another team was also entering on the ground floor.

This part of the mission was a hunt—and a race against time. Find the remaining guards...and kill them before they could raise the alarm.

Fernandez knew where two of them would be—the security control room. He and Sklar hurried down the staircase. The position of the remaining two guards was another wildcard, which was why he had chosen entry points that would let his team spread out as quickly as possible. Speed and surprise were everything—it only took one guard to push a panic button...

They reached the ground floor. Fifteen seconds before the cameras came back online. Sklar hared off into the main entrance hall. Fernandez, meanwhile, shoved through a door marked PRIVATO and threaded his way along a narrow corridor.

Another door. Five seconds left. He raised his gun and kicked it open.

The guard seated in front of the security monitors looked around in surprise—

Tchack. Tchack. Tchack. The guard crashed off his chair, arms spasming in reflexive response to the three bullets that had just slammed into his skull, splattering blood across the blank monitor screens.

Shit! Where was the other man?

The diagnostic ended, and the monitors came back to life. He spotted one of his men in the Sale Bizantine, another in the Sale Fiorentine. Where were the guards?

There—in the Salone del Colosso. Sklar would be closest to them—

Both guards fell, thrashing in their noiseless death throes as a burst from Sklar's silenced MP5K cut them down. Confirmation came through his earpiece: "Two down."

Just one man left—but where?

The answer was almost comical in its obviousness. Fernandez rushed out of the control room and headed back up the passage to another door marked WC.

He opened it. A small tiled room, two stalls, one closed...

The rapid *tchack*s from the gun were louder in here, echoing in the confined space. The stall's wooden door splintered, a startled gasp coming from behind it—along with clanks of shattering porcelain and the dull thud of lead entering flesh. A trickle of water ran out from beneath the door, pinkish rivulets spreading through it.

Six guards dealt with.

Fernandez hurried back into the museum proper, turning left in the entrance hall and looking down the length of the gallery to see his target at the far end.

Michelangelo's *David*.

Possibly the most famous sculpture in the world, the Renaissance masterpiece towered above its viewers, more than sixteen feet tall even without its pedestal. During the day, illuminated mainly by light coming through the glass dome in the ceiling, the marble statue was a soft off-white, almost blending into the blandly painted walls of the semicircular chamber in which it stood. But at night, sidelit and with its surroundings in shadow, the naked figure stood out starkly, appearing almost threatening, a faint sneer of disdain visible on the young future king's lips as he prepared to face Goliath in combat.

To Fernandez, the image seemed appropriate. After all, he was the David who defeated the Goliath of the world's combined law enforcement agencies...

You haven't done it yet, he warned himself as he marched toward the statue, passing more of Michelangelo's sculptures along the way. Three of his men were already waiting at David's feet, and he heard footsteps behind—Zec and Franco. As for the last two team members...

He looked up at the dome, catching a glimpse of movement outside. They were right where they should be. Everything was on schedule.

"You know what to do," he announced as he reached the statue. "Let's make history."

"Or *take* history," said Zec. The two men grinned, then everyone moved into action.

One man ran to a control panel on one wall. It was protected by a locked metal cover, but a moment's effort with a crowbar took care of that. The others went to the statue itself. Kristoff and Franco climbed onto the plinth, their heads reaching only to David's mid-thigh. They took out coiled straps, wider and much thicker than their own harnesses, and carefully secured them around the statue's legs.

Once they were in place, Kristoff took out another coil and, keeping hold of the buckle at one end, tossed it upward. It arced over the statue's shoulder, dropping down on the other side like a streamer. Another man caught the coil and passed it back between David's legs to Franco, who ran it through the buckle, connected it to the leg strap, and pulled it tight. The process was repeated with a second strap over the other shoulder.

Kristoff quickly used the straps to scale the stone figure's chest, hanging on with one hand as more straps were thrown to him. Fernandez looked on as his plan literally took shape before his eyes. The growing web was much like the harnesses he and his men were wearing, designed to spread out the weight of the body over as great an area as possible when it was lifted.

In the case of David, that weight was more than six tons—*plus* the pedestal. But that had been planned for.

The Spaniard gestured to the man at the control panel. He pushed a button. A hydraulic rumble came from the floor.

Very slowly, the statue began to rise.

At considerable expense, the Galleria had recently installed a system to protect the *David* from vibrations, whether in the form of earthquakes, city traffic, or even the constant footsteps of visitors. Powerful shock absorbers under the pedestal shielded it from tremors—but also allowed it to be elevated for those rare occasions when the statue had to be moved. At full height, there was just enough space for a forklift's blades to slip beneath the base.

That was all the space Fernandez needed.

Zec and the other man at the statue pushed more straps, thicker still and bearing heavy-duty metal D-rings, under the base. Once that was done, they fastened them over the pedestal, then began to secure the harness to them.

Fernandez took out his phone again, dialing the first number he had called earlier. The answer was heavily obscured by noise. "We're less than two minutes out—but ATC's issued an alert about us being off course."

"We're almost ready," said Fernandez. "Just follow the plan." He disconnected, hearing knocking from the dome. One of the two figures outside gave him a thumbs-up.

Zec rounded the statue. "All set. I just hope the harness holds."

"It'll hold," Fernandez assured him. He raised his voice. "Move back!" Everyone cleared the area beneath the dome.

The men on the roof had also retreated, one of them pushing a button on a control box—

The explosive charges they had placed around the dome detonated as one.

Glass panels shattered into a billion fragments, the severed steel framework plunging down into the gallery and smashing the marble floor. The horrendous noise echoed through the museum's halls—followed by the piercing shriek of sirens as vibration sensors throughout the building were triggered.

The police would be on their way. But with attention diverted by the forest fire to the east and the car bombings to the southwest, their response time would be slowed, their numbers reduced.

And Fernandez and his men would be gone.

The two men who had planted the explosives were already rappelling into the museum as the others quickly cleared wreckage out of the way. Even over the alarms the Spaniard could hear another sound, a thudding bass pounding getting louder and louder...

The breeze blowing in through the hole was magnified a hundredfold as a helicopter surged into view overhead, the beat of its rotor blades shaking the air. The massive aircraft was a Sikorsky S-64 Skycrane, the machine's name revealing its purpose: to lift extremely heavy objects.

Like Michelangelo's *David*.

Cables dropped from the helicopter, heavy hooks on their ends clanging on the cracked marble. Fernandez and his men each took one line and pulled it to the statue. Six cables were attached to the D-rings on the base, while Kristoff and Franco scaled the pedestal again and hooked their lines to the webbing around the great carved figure itself.

Fernandez moved back beneath the hole and looked up. The Skycrane had been painted dark green to match the livery of the Italian Forest Service's fire-fighting S-64s, its radio transceiver hacked to give air traffic control the identification number of one of the real choppers. But where the Italian aircraft had giant water tanks beneath the long dragonfly spine of their fuselages, this had just a bottomless mock-up, thin aluminum concealing a powerful winch.

A wave from Fernandez, and the winch began to draw up the cables.

The men took positions on each side of the statue, hands pressed against the pedestal. The cables pulled tight, the straps creaking as they took the strain. Fernandez watched the marble figure closely, hoping his calculations were right. If the harness didn't protect the *David* from the worst stresses of the lift, this would get very messy...

The pedestal slid off the shock absorbers and ground noisily across the floor. Everyone pushed harder to keep it in a straight line as the lines tightened. They had to get the sculpture directly under the hole before they could escape. The cables scraped on the edge of the ruined dome, glass fragments and pieces of broken masonry raining down.

The Skycrane rose, the statue jerking up and swinging a foot or two before the edge of the base crunched against the marble. Fernandez waved angrily at the winch operator. Even minor damage to the statue would affect their payment.

The winchman got the message. The statue lifted again, more gently. Another two yards to go before it was in position. The men kept pushing, guiding it. One and a half, one...

The plinth thumped down on the broken floor, grinding glass to powder beneath it. Fernandez saw that the cables were more or less dead center of the circular hole. "Hook up!" he shouted.

Each man attached his harness to the D-rings. Once they were all secure, Fernandez gave another signal to the winchman.

The engine noise rose to a scream as the helicopter climbed.

Another jolt as the statue left the floor—this time for good. Fernandez and his team were lifted with it. The noise and downwash from the Skycrane were horrific, but if everything went to plan they wouldn't have to endure it for long...

More power. The statue began to twist in the wind as it rose. Fernandez had expected that; there was no way to prevent it. All he could do was hope it didn't get out of control.

Four yards up, five, the ascent getting faster. The Galleria spun around them—and then they cleared the roof. They were out!

He scanned the city as they continued to climb, the Sky-crane lethargically tipping into forward flight and turning northward. Strobe lights flicked through the streets leading to the museum. The police. Fernandez smiled. They were too late.

There was one police vehicle that concerned him, though. Off to the southwest, he saw a pattern of pulsing lights in the sky. Another helicopter.

Heading toward them.

As he'd expected, it had been called in to provide aerial support for the cops responding to the car bombs—but the Skycrane's deviation from its course and the alarms at the Galleria dell'Accademia had caused someone to put two and two together and realize that the explosions were, like the forest fire, just a diversion.

The Skycrane picked up speed, Florence rolling past below. Not quickly enough. The police chopper would rapidly catch up with the lumbering Sikorsky—and for the plan to succeed, the next stage had to be carried out without witnesses.

Fernandez looked ahead, eyes narrowed against the blasting wind. The city's northern edge was not far away, twinkling lights abruptly replaced by the blackness of woods and fields as the landscape rose into the hills. No roads; only an aircraft could pursue them.

But he had planned for that. Another member of his

team was positioned on a rooftop at the city's periphery, directly beneath the Skycrane's course.

The Sikorsky and its strange cargo swept over the urban boundary. The police chopper was gaining fast. Glaring blue-white light pinned the Skycrane from behind as the other aircraft's spotlight flicked on, playing over the green fuselage before tilting down to turn the suspended statue a dazzling white.

The police helicopter closed in—

And suddenly dropped out of the sky in a sheet of flame, spiraling down to smash explosively into the woods beyond the city.

Fernandez's man on the ground had been armed with a Russian SA-18 anti-aircraft missile, the shoulder-fired weapon homing in on the helicopter's exhaust and detonating more than two pounds of high explosive on impact.

The Spaniard smiled. The Italian air force would now be called in to hunt down the helicopter—which was exactly what he wanted them to do. Because a few minutes from now, he and his men would be putting as much distance between themselves and the Skycrane as possible.

More dark forests below as the Sikorsky descended and slowed. They were nearing their destination: an isolated road winding through the hills. He spotted a red light flashing among the trees. The last team member, waiting with the truck.

Treetops thrashed in the helicopter's downdraft as it hovered, the statue swinging pendulously for several worrying moments before settling down. The truck's trailer was directly beneath it—a standard twelve-meter container, with an open top. A metal frame of a very specific shape had been welded to its floor and covered with thick foam padding. Beside the trailer, a large object was hidden beneath a tarpaulin.

"Okay, drop!" yelled Fernandez, pulling out a clip on his harness. His support line uncoiled and fell away. He quickly rappelled into the truck, the other men following. The moment their boots hit metal, they detached the lines and stood beneath the statue. Fernandez switched on a lamp to give the winchman a clear view, then joined the others.

The statue's base was about three yards above the container's top, slowly turning. Fernandez signaled for it to be lowered. The winch whined, cables shuddering as the statue descended. The men warily reached up. An agonizing moment as the pedestal's corner clipped the container's edge, steel bending with a screech, then it slipped inside.

Hands gripping the base, eight men strained in unison to turn David in a particular direction as the great figure continued its steady descent. Fernandez gestured for the winchman to slow. The men pushed harder, the statue still at an angle. Less than two feet. Another push—

The base lined up against a length of metal pole at the end of the frame. Fernandez waved his hands. The winchman responded—and the statue landed with a bang that shook the entire container.

But the Skycrane's job wasn't done. The container was less than eight feet tall, the statue standing high above its top. The men moved to each side of the framework as the Sikorsky slowly moved forward. The cables pulled tight again, dragging the statue after the aircraft—but the bar across the container's floor stopped it.

Like a soccer player tripped by a sliding tackle, David began to fall.

In slow motion. The cables and the harness took the strain. Little by little, the giant was lowered toward the waiting frame, each section of which was shaped to support a specific part of the statue's body. Lower. Fernandez held his breath. David's sneer now seemed directed at him personally, daring him to have miscalculated...

He hadn't. The statue touched down, the foam compressing, steel creaking—but holding.

"Secure it!" he barked. Three of the men lashed the statue down, the others detaching the cables. Fernandez hurried to the container's open end and jumped out. The Skycrane increased height slightly and edged sideways, hooks banging on the corrugated metal. Inside the container, the team hauled on ropes hanging over its side—pulling up the tarpaulin so the open roof could be covered.

As the grubby blue tarp moved, it revealed the object lying on the ground. The sight almost made Fernandez laugh out loud at its sheer audacity, even though he had thought of it in the first place.

A replica of David.

It was crude, only nine-tenths life-sized, made of fiberglass where strength was needed, chicken wire and papier-mâché and cardboard elsewhere. At close range it looked like a joke, a refugee from a school craft fair. But nobody *would* see it at close range. All they would see was what they had been told to expect: a priceless national treasure suspended from a helicopter.

He and the truck driver secured the hooks to the harness around the duplicate's chest, then Fernandez signaled to the Skycrane. The helicopter's engines shrilled as it increased power, pulling the imitation statue upright, then turning away once its new cargo was clear of the truck.

Fernandez watched the helicopter go. That was the final stage of the plan: the ultimate decoy. The pilot would take the Sikorsky up to ten thousand feet, heading northeast, then lock the controls to put it into a slow but steady descent—and he and the winchman would bail out, parachuting down. When military aircraft intercepted the helicopter, they would be unable to take any action for fear of damaging the statue, leaving them impotently following until it eventually smashed down in the hills some thirty miles away ... by which time the real statue would be safely on its way to its new owner.

He laughed, unable to hold in his delight any longer.

They had done it! He really was the greatest thief in history. One more job, and the team would receive the rest of their hundred-million-dollar payment—with half of it going to its leader and mastermind. And the final robbery, in San Francisco, would be a piece of cake in comparison with what they had just achieved.

The tarp roof was secure, the rear doors closed. Still smiling, Fernandez climbed into the cab and signaled the driver to head off into the darkness.

1

New York City

Three Weeks Later

"So I'd like everyone to join me in a toast—a *belated* toast—to the marriage of two great friends of mine...Eddie Chase and Nina Wilde."

Nina leaned around her husband to speak to the gray-haired man beside him as applause filled the room. "That was a nice speech, Mac."

"Yeah," rumbled Eddie, less impressed. "You only mentioned a few embarrassing moments from my time in the Regiment."

Jim "Mac" McCrimmon grinned. "What are best men for? Besides," the bearded Scot went on, "I'd never tell any of the really embarrassing SAS stories in mixed company. Certainly not in front of your grandmother!"

Nina stood. "Okay," she said, running a hand self-consciously through her red hair as everyone looked at her, "I know it's not traditional for the, ah, 'new' bride"—she made air-quotes, raising laughter—"to speak at this point, but our lives have been anything but traditional since we met." More laughs. "So I wanted to thank you all for coming—it's great that so many of you could make it for our first wedding anniversary, and we've had some lovely cards and messages from those who couldn't be here. And most of all, I'd like to thank the man who made it all possible—my strangely charming, sometimes crazy-making, but always amazing husband." She kissed the Yorkshireman to more applause. "Anything to add, Eddie?"

"You pretty much covered it. Except for...bottoms up!" He raised his glass. "Enjoy the party!"

The DJ took the cue and put on a song—which, as per Eddie's instructions, was a version of "Por Una Cabeza." He stood, holding out a hand. "Fancy a dance?"

She smiled. "Y'know, I might have practiced this one a few times..."

"Good job too—you were bloody rubbish at it in Monaco!" He led her to the dance floor, the couple exchanging congratulations and jokes with friends along the way before taking their positions for a tango.

"Ready to dance, Mr. Chase?" said Nina.

"If you are, Mrs. Chase," Eddie replied. Nina arched an eyebrow. "All right, Dr. Wilde," he said with a playful sigh of defeat. "Just thought I'd try to have one vaguely traditional thing in our marriage."

"You're so old-fashioned," she said, teasing. "And a one, and a two, and...dance!"

* * *

"I'm actually impressed," said Elizabeth Chase to her younger brother. The DJ had switched to pop after Nina and Eddie's display, the dance floor now drawing the younger and/or more inebriated guests while the host and hostess split up to circulate. "I had no idea you were so graceful. Shouldn't you be wearing spangly trousers and dancing with celebrities?"

Her grandmother tutted at her. "Well, I thought it was very nice, Edward."

"Thanks, Nan," said Eddie. "And I'm glad you're here

to see it. And you, Holly"—he smiled at his niece—"and even you, Lizzie . . . I mean Elizabeth."

Elizabeth gave him a look somewhere between acknowledgment of the shared sibling joke and actual annoyance. Holly's expression, meanwhile, was of genuine pleasure. "It's so awesome to be here, Uncle Eddie! I get to see you and Nina—do I call her Aunt Nina now? It sounds weird—and check out New York, *and* I'm getting time off school! Mum never normally lets me skive out of anything."

"Probably for the best—mind you, I skived out of school all the time, and it never did me any harm," Eddie told her, smirking at his sister's sarcastic snort. "Anyway, it's good to have the whole family here."

"Not the *whole* family," Elizabeth said pointedly.

Eddie forced himself to ignore her. "So, who wants another drink?"

"Me!" Holly chirped, holding up her champagne glass.

"You've had enough," her mother said firmly.

"Aw, come on! I'm seventeen, I'm *almost* old enough."

"Not here, you're not," said Eddie. "Drinking age is twenty-one in the States." At Holly's appalled look, he went on: "I know, how crap is that? But if you had any more, Amy here might have to arrest you." He tugged the sleeve of another guest. "Isn't that right, Amy? I was just telling my niece about how strict you American cops are about the drinking laws."

"Oh, totally," said Amy Martin, joining the group. She regarded Holly's glass. "I mean, that's a potential 10-64D right there. I'm off duty, but I might have to call that in and take you downtown." Holly hurriedly put down the glass.

Eddie laughed and introduced the young policewoman to his family—then looked around at a commotion from the function room's main entrance. "I might have bloody known he'd cause a scene. Hang on." He crossed the room to close the doors, a task made harder by the press of onlookers trying to see inside. "Private party, so piss off!" he warned the gawpers as he shut the doors, then turned to the new arrival and his companion. "Glad you could make it. You're only an hour late."

As usual, the sarcasm went completely over Grant Thorn's head. "Sorry, dude," said the Hollywood star. "Jessica couldn't decide on a dress."

Eddie recognized his partner as Jessica Lanes, a starlet-of-the-moment famous for a couple of successful teen comedies and a horror movie, as well as her willingness to remove her clothes for men's-mag photo shoots. "Nice to meet you," he said to the blonde, who smiled blankly.

"Eddie here saved my life," Grant told her. "He's a cool dude, even though he's a Brit."

"Wow, you saved his life?" asked Jessica. "Awesome. So, you're like a lifeguard?"

"Something like that," Eddie replied, deadpan. Some-one else tried to peer into the room; he moved behind Grant to secure the doors again, whispering, "Thought you were bringing that other Jessica? You know, the dark-haired one?"

"Old news, man," Grant said quietly. "Besides, a Jes-sica's a Jessica, right?"

Eddie shook his head, then escorted the pair through the room, which had suddenly been energized by the injection of star power. Holly in particular was dumbstruck by the appearance in three dimensions of a man who had previ-ously been limited to posters on her bedroom wall. "Every-one, this is Grant and Jessica, who...well, you probably recognize."

Nan peered at the pair as Eddie completed the introduc-tions. "Ooh, I know you," she said to Grant. "I saw you on the telly. You were in an advertisement, weren't you?"

"Nan!" whispered Holly, mortified. "It was an advert for his *film*! That he was starring in! As the star!"

"Oh, that explains it. I don't watch films these days," Nan confided to Grant. "They're all so noisy and violent,

just silly nonsense. But I'm sure yours are very good," she
added politely.

Eddie held in a laugh at Grant's discomfiture. "Anyway,
I was getting drinks, wasn't I?"

He headed for the buffet tables, passing Nina along the
way. "Who's that with Grant?" she asked.

"A Jessica."

"I thought his girlfriend was the one with dark hair?"

"Keep up, love. You're a celebrity yourself, you should
know this stuff."

"I am not a celebrity," Nina said, faintly irked by the accusation.

"Right. Being seen on live TV inside the Sphinx by two
hundred million people doesn't count."

She groaned. "Don't remind me. See you later." Giving
him a kiss, she continued circulating, spotting some friends
and colleagues at one table. "Matt, Lola!" she called, joining them. "Everything okay?"

"Great, thanks," said Matt Trulli, holding up his glass.
"Top bash you and Eddie've put on. Congratulations!"

"Well, it's mostly Eddie who organized it," she told the
tubby Australian engineer. "I've been a bit preoccupied
with work—I spent most of the week in San Francisco. But
if you're enjoying it, I'm happy to take the credit!"

"You look lovely, Nina," Lola Gianetti said. Nina felt
her cheeks flush a little at the compliment from her personal assistant—though she had to admit that her cream
dress was considerably more elegant than the suits she
wore at the office or the rugged and functional clothing
preferred out in the field. "And I didn't know you and
Eddie could dance!"

"That tango looked pretty hot stuff," said Matt.
"There, er, there many single women at dance classes?"

Nina was saved from having to answer by the arrival of
another guest. "There you are, Nina," said Rowan Sharpe.
"I thought I'd never catch up with you."

"We've spent practically the past week together, Rowan," she said, grinning. "I would have thought you'd be sick of the sight of me by now."

"Oh, don't be absurd." The tall, black-haired Connecticut native was in his late thirties, and in his tuxedo looked even more dashing than usual. Lola's attention had definitely been caught, Nina noticed with amusement. "I certainly wasn't going to miss this—even if I had to fly all the way from San Francisco to be here."

"Rowan, this is Matt Trulli," said Nina, making introductions. "He used to work for UNARA, and now he's with the Oceanic Survey Organization. Matt, this is an old friend of mine, Dr. Rowan Sharpe. He's in charge of the Treasures of Atlantis exhibition."

"Oh, *I'm* in charge?" said Rowan, feigning surprise. "Funny, I thought you were. I mean, you're constantly there bossing everyone about..."

Nina gave him a little laugh. "I'm the boss, so I'm allowed to be bossy. Besides, the exhibition's really important to me. I just want things to be perfect."

"Well, you always were a perfectionist." He winked at her, then looked her up and down. "And speaking of perfection, you look absolutely incredible tonight. I'm very jealous of Eddie." He sighed, smiling. "Ah, the path not taken..."

"Knock it off, Rowan," said Nina, but not before Lola and Matt exchanged curious looks. "Rowan and I used to date," she explained. "A long time ago, when I was an undergraduate." Another look passed between them. "*Yes,* I had boyfriends before I met Eddie. Why is everybody always so surprised about that?"

"Though I'd actually known her for years," Rowan added. "I was a friend of Nina's parents—Henry Wilde was my archaeology professor. I even helped them with some of their research on Atlantis." He put a gentle hand on Nina's shoulder. "Henry and Laura would be so proud of you. You found what they spent their lives searching for."

"Thank you," Nina replied, with a twinge of sadness: Her parents had lost their lives searching for Atlantis. She pushed the thought to the back of her mind. Both the impending exhibition and this evening were about celebrating what the hunt for Atlantis had brought her, not regretting what it had taken. "But the main thing now is that the whole world can see it for themselves."

"It's a shame you can't come with me for the exhibition's entire tour. But I suppose Eddie would get rather annoyed if I took you away from him for four months."

"He might at that," said Nina, smiling. "And speaking of Eddie, I should go and find him again, so I'll see you all later."

"Have fun." Rowan held up his drink to her, then said to Matt, "So, what do you do at the OSO?"

As Matt launched into what promised to be an extremely technical summary of his work building robotic underwater vehicles, Nina continued through the room, looking for Eddie. Before she saw him, though, she encountered more very familiar faces. "Hi!"

"Nina!" said Macy Sharif in delight. The archaeology student had been in conversation with Karima Farran and Radi Bashir, the Jordanian couple respectively a friend of Eddie's from his days as an international troubleshooter-for-hire, and a producer for a Middle Eastern news network. "How are you?"

"I'm fine, thanks," said Nina, embracing her. "How are your studies going?"

"Well, you know that I used to be kind of a C student?" Macy said with a cocky grin. "Well, I'm now a...B student! B-plus, even. Sometimes."

"That's great! And you've still got another year and a half to get that A—like I said at the UN, if you want a job at the IHA when you graduate, just ask."

"I think I will. Thanks." She glanced past Nina. "Hey, is that Grant?" Nina nodded, and Macy's look became more predatory. "I'm gonna say hi. You think he'll remember me?"

"You're hard to forget," Nina assured her. Macy quickly applied another coat of lipstick, then darted off through the crowd. "He's with someone," Nina called after her.

"We'll see!"

"She's very . . . *forward,* isn't she?" said Karima.

"That's one way to describe her," Nina replied, amused.

Rad nodded. "She was just telling us in alarming detail about her night with some racing driver in Monaco. It's only the second time we've met her! I might be a journalist, but there's still such a thing as too much information."

"She's a live one, that's for sure. So how are you two?"

"Edging ever closer to getting married," said Karima, putting an arm around her fiancé's shoulder. "Next spring, we think."

"Or maybe summer," Rad added. "Or autumn." Karima jabbed him with her sharp nails. "Ow."

"That's fantastic," said Nina. "And it's so great of you to come all this way for tonight. Thank you."

The beautiful Jordanian smiled. "We wouldn't have missed it. Although I have to admit we're making a vacation of it."

"Two weeks in the States," said Rad. "We're doing a tour. I can't wait to see the Grand Canyon."

"He means he can't wait to see Vegas," Karima said knowingly.

"I'm sure you'll enjoy it," Nina told them. "Have you told Eddie that you've almost set a date?"

"Not yet," said Rad. "We only spoke to him very briefly when we arrived."

"I'll go find him. I'm sure he'll be thrilled." Nina spotted her husband talking to Mac. "Eddie! *Eddie!*" Mac looked around at her, but Eddie didn't react. "Deaf as a post in his old age."

• • •

"Your wife's calling for you," Mac said.

"Hmm?"

"Your wife. About five-five, red hair, very pretty, famous archaeologist?"

"Oh, *that* wife." Eddie glanced back, but the people surrounding Grant and Jessica blocked his view. "I didn't hear her."

"Trust me, that's an excuse you'll only get away with once." Mac gave him a wry smile, which faded at the lack of response. "Something wrong?"

"No, nothing." said Eddie a little too quickly, looking around the room. Mac raised an eyebrow, but he didn't comment further. "Pretty good turnout. Pity not everyone I invited could make it, but I suppose you can't expect everyone to fly halfway around the world for cheese and pickled onions on sticks."

"Yes, a shame," Mac agreed. Another smile, this time decidedly cheeky. "I was rather hoping to catch up with TD…"

Eddie groaned in only partially feigned dismay at the thought of his former commanding officer and the far younger African woman together. "Behave yourself, you dirty old sod. Christ, I can't think what she ever saw in you."

"Oh, I imagine things like charm, chivalry, wisdom… Perhaps you've heard of them."

"Tchah! I ought to kick out your tin leg for that." He swung his foot at the older man's prosthetic left limb, stopping an inch short.

"Well, if you think you need to even the odds…" They both chuckled, Mac raising his glass. "Anyway, here's to a successful marriage, Eddie."

"Thanks." They clinked glasses.

"So how's domesticity treating you so far?"

"Sort of normal. But we need one of those signs saying how many days it's been since we last had someone try to blow us up. We're up to about five months at the moment."

"Let's hope you break your record by a long, long way." Behind Eddie, Nina approached, calling his name again. Mac deliberately raised his voice so she would catch it. "Although I expect you'll soon start missing being shot at."

"He'd damn well better not," said Nina as she reached her husband, taking him by surprise. "Didn't you hear me?"

He shrugged. "It's a bit noisy in here."

"So what are you two old warhorses talking about?"

Eddie looked offended. "Oi! Less of the *old*."

"We were just having a toast to a happy marriage," said Mac. Nina beamed at Eddie and put an arm around his waist. "And Eddie was also saying how glad he was that so many people made the time to come tonight."

"I know," she said, looking around at the guests. "Isn't it great? Although I'm a bit disappointed that Peter Alderley didn't even reply. What did he say when you gave him the invitation?"

Mac blinked. "Invitation?"

"Yeah. I put it in with yours because I didn't know his address."

The Scot was still puzzled. "I didn't get an invitation for Peter."

"You didn't..." Nina gave her husband a look of deep suspicion. "Eddie? What did you do with Peter's invitation?"

"Oh, that," Eddie said nonchalantly. "It dropped out of the envelope before I licked it. And then it somehow...fell down a drain."

Nina pulled away from him. "Eddie! I can't believe you did that! Especially after everything he's done at MI6 to help us."

"Alderley's a tosser, and he can't stand me anyway."

"That's not the point!"

"Is Eddie causing trouble again?" said Elizabeth, joining them. "Somehow I'm not surprised."

"Afraid so." Nina sighed.

"Nan's getting tired, so it'd be best if she went up to her room," Elizabeth told her brother. "But she'll want to say good night to you before she goes."

"Well, yeah," said Eddie, smirking. "Since I'm her favorite grandchild, an' all."

"God knows why. But come on over. You too, Nina, so she can have all the family together." She led them across the room, adding a sharp aside to Eddie as Nina detoured to put down her glass: "Almost."

"Right. Weird cousin Derek's not here, is he?" said Eddie.

Elizabeth had no intention of giving up. "You know exactly who I mean."

"Oh, don't fucking start," he muttered.

"You haven't spoken to Dad for over twenty years, Eddie. His son's got married, for God's sake. I'm not saying you should have some big Hollywood tearful reconciliation in front of everyone—"

"Good, 'cause that's not going to happen."

"—but you could at least phone him."

Eddie's face was a cold mask. "Why? I've got nothing to say to him."

"And what if you and Nina have kids? Are they going to grow up never knowing their grandfather? He's not getting any younger. Nor are you, for that matter."

"Tell you what," he said, irritation breaking through, "how about we end this discussion before it pisses all over, you know, the special day?"

"Just think about it, Eddie," Elizabeth said as they reached Holly and Nan, waiting near the doors.

"Already have, a long time ago. Hi, Nan!"

"Come here, Edward!" said Nan, and he bent to hug her. "Oh, my little lambchop. Married again!" She wagged a finger in mock reproach. "I'm still cross that you didn't invite me to the actual wedding, though."

"We didn't have time, Nan," said Eddie as Nina caught up. "It was a bit rushed."

"Yeah, sorry about that," said Nina. "You forgive us?"

"Of course I do," said Nan. "Come on, let me hug my granddaughter-in-law."

"You want me to walk you up to your room, Nan?" Eddie asked.

She waved a hand at him. "Oh, don't be silly! You should be enjoying your night, both of you. Holly can take me."

Holly shot a stricken glance toward Grant, from whose company she had just been forcibly removed, promoting her mother to sigh and step in. "It's okay, Nan, I'll take you. No more champagne," she added sternly to Holly.

"We're off to San Francisco the day after tomorrow," Eddie said to Nan as Elizabeth ushered her to the doors, "but we'll see you again before we go."

"It's been so lovely to see you both," said Nan. "And I hope you have an absolutely wonderful marriage. In fact, I know you will."

"Thank you," Nina said. Nan gave them a last wave as Elizabeth escorted her out. More people were lurking outside; news of Grant and Jessica's attendance had spread through the online social networks. The moment the doors closed again, Holly made a beeline back to Grant's group, where she found herself in competition with both Jessica and Macy for his attention. Nina turned to Eddie. "What were you and Elizabeth talking about?"

"Nothing important."

She knew him better than that. "Family matters?"

"Only one part of the family."

"Three guesses which?"

"Like I said, nothing important." Keen to change the subject, he gestured across the room. "Oh, hey, there's Rowan." He waved him over.

"Careful, Eddie," said Nina teasingly as Rowan approached. "He might charm me away from you."

"Anyone who takes you away from me'll regret it," Eddie rumbled before giving the taller man a faintly insincere smile. "Hi, Rowan. Glad you could make it."

"Glad to be here!" Rowan replied. "Sorry to have monopolized Nina recently."

"Yeah, it'll be good to finally have some time alone with her tonight. That's if she doesn't bring a big bloody bundle of work home with her."

"Yes, she always has been rather obsessive when it comes to Atlantis, hasn't she?" said Rowan. "While we were setting up the exhibition, she wouldn't even take time out for a tour of San Francisco. She's a real slave driver."

"Tell me about it," said Eddie. He grinned at his wife, who was struggling not to rise to the bait as the teasing was turned on her, and attempted a falsetto New York accent. "'Eddie, can you move these boxes? Eddie, can you jam this booby trap? Eddie, can you kill these bad guys?'"

"I don't sound like that," Nina objected. She looked at Rowan. "Do I?"

He winked at her. "Not at all. But I'd just like to say, Eddie, you're a very lucky man. Congratulations. To both of you—Nina's lucky charm obviously works for other people too."

Nina touched her pendant, made from a broken scrap of what had turned out to be an Atlantean artifact discovered on an expedition with her parents as a child. "Let's hope it keeps on doing that, huh? I'd like the Treasures of Atlantis exhibition to be a huge success."

"It will be—and it won't have anything to do with luck, Nina. It'll all be down to you."

"And you too."

"Thank you." Rowan smiled, then kissed her.

"Oi, oi," said Eddie, nudging Nina away from him. He gestured across the room. "Want to dance?"

The DJ was playing Ricky Martin's "She Bangs." "This isn't really tango music."

"So, we'll improvise. Come on."

He led her to the dance floor. Nina put her arms around his waist. "Thanks for doing all this."

"Hey, any excuse for a booze-up."

"Sentimental as always, huh?" But she could tell that under his bluff exterior, the broken-nosed, balding Englishman was enjoying the celebration as much as she was.

2

A few hours later, the party was over, and Nina and Eddie returned to their apartment on Manhattan's Upper East Side. "God, I'm exhausted," said Nina, stifling a yawn as she entered. "And there's still loads to do tomorrow." She dropped heavily onto the couch and kicked off her shoes.

"Well, at least you don't have to deal with it on your own," Eddie said.

She smiled at him. "Aw, thanks, honey."

His tone became sarcastic. "I didn't mean me. I meant your boyfriend, Captain Perfect. He'll give you a helping hand...and try to cop a feel with it."

"Oh, *Eddie*! You're not really jealous of Rowan, are you?"

He grinned, exposing the gap between his front teeth. "Don't be daft. I'm just taking the piss." A beat. "Mostly."

"You don't have anything to worry about. Rowan and I broke up a long time ago." She thought about it for a moment. "God, it's been twelve years. I was only twenty. I can't believe how much has happened since then."

"And how old was he?"

"Twenty-six."

"So he was a cradle snatcher?"

"And what does that make you?" she asked with a smile. "You're the same age as Rowan."

"Yeah, but you're older now. Half the man's age plus seven years, that's how old the woman has to be to stop the bloke from being a creepy perv."

"He was twenty-six, I was twenty. Do the math."

He worked it out. "Bollocks! Although, hang on," he continued as she laughed, "how old were you when you *started* going out?"

"Nineteen."

"Ha!"

"And Rowan was a year younger as well."

Another few seconds of mental arithmetic. "Definitely on the dodginess borderline. Anyway, I still think he's got his eye on you."

"Only as a friend, Eddie." Her mood became one of reverie as her husband sat beside her. "He was a great friend, actually. He helped me through a really tough part of my life, when my parents died. I honestly don't know what I would have done without him. Or what I'd be doing now."

"What do you mean?"

"I almost gave up on archaeology. I mean, it got my parents killed—if they hadn't been obsessed with finding Atlantis, they'd still be alive. I almost dropped out because for a while I didn't want anything more to do with it. Rowan changed my mind. So I stayed on, got my degree and then my PhD, and, well, here I am."

Eddie shook his head with a wry expression. "Can't imagine what you'd be doing now if you weren't an archaeologist."

"I dread to think. I once had a summer job in an office and I hated every minute of it. And what about you? Where would you be if you hadn't met me?"

"Christ knows. Running around the world getting into trouble, probably."

"Oh, so no change there."

"Ha fuckin' ha. I'd still be doing the same kind of work as I was then, though. It's what I'm best at." He looked at a shelf across the room.

Nina followed his gaze. "Thinking about Hugo?" she asked softly. The shelf contained mementos of their pasts; propped against a Cuban pottery figurine of Fidel Castro was a photograph of Eddie and another man, who had a long face and a prominent nose.

"Yeah," said Eddie. "Wish he could have been at the do tonight." Hugo Castille, his friend and comrade from his troubleshooter days, had been killed during the hunt for Atlantis. "Other people too. Like Mitzi." He shook his head. "Shit, maybe I'm getting old. Starting to lose more friends than I'm making."

She gave him a sympathetic look. "You've made a friend of everybody you've helped, Eddie. And there have been a lot of them. Trust me, I'm one of them."

"Thanks, love." He kissed her cheek. "So I've kind of got Rowan to thank for us getting together? I suppose that makes him an okay bloke."

"High praise indeed, coming from you." Another reminiscent smile. "You know, when I was a teenager and he was helping my parents as a grad student, I had *such* a crush on him..."

"Yeah, I really needed to hear that."

She stroked his face. "Don't worry. I made my choice. And I think it was the right one. Usually..."

He swatted at her playfully as he stood and headed for the kitchen. "I'm going to put the kettle on. You want anything?"

"No thanks," she called after him. "Just a decent night's sleep. The exhibition opens in two days, and there are still a hundred and one things I need to sort out."

"What?"

"I said, there's loads still to organize. I'll be on the phone all tomorrow. Oh, the joys of management." She leaned back, then remembered something. "Eddie?"

No answer. "Eddie!" she said, more loudly.

He appeared in the doorway. "Yeah, I heard you. What?"

"Actually, it's about you hearing me. Or not. Is everything okay?"

"Why wouldn't it be?"

"Because a couple of times at the party you didn't hear me—even when I was right behind you. And I've noticed it a few times recently. Maybe you should see a specialist, get your hearing tested. After all," she said, lightly humorous, "you've been close to a lot of loud bangs over the years."

A conflicted look crossed his square face, immediately making her regret her levity. She sat up, concerned. "Eddie, what is it?"

He sat beside her. "The thing is . . . I *did* see a specialist."

"What? When?"

"About two months back. I'd been having trouble on and off since that bloody room in the pyramid with the big pipe-organ thing." Nina remembered it all too well, an ancient booby trap deep within the Pyramid of Osiris designed to deafen intruders with an unbearable blast of sound. "So I made an appointment to have my ears checked out."

"Why didn't you tell me?"

He shrugged; not dismissively, but in a kind of resignation. " 'Cause I thought it'd go away on its own. It always did before—like you said, I've heard a lot of loud bangs. Only this time . . . it didn't."

"What did the specialist say?"

He stood and went into the study, returning with a manila envelope. "Let's see," he said, taking out a sheet of paper. " 'Permanent threshold shift due to repeated damaging levels of noise exposure...sensorineural hearing loss to a moderate degree in the high frequencies...' In other words, my hearing's fucked."

Nina felt suddenly cold, the happiness of the evening evaporating. " 'Permanent'?"

He held her hands to provide reassurance. "It's not like I've gone stone deaf, and he said it wouldn't get any worse for now. It just means I can't hear as well as I used to, and it's worse with high-frequency sounds, like voices. Well, women's voices, basically."

She wasn't sure how to respond. "Oh God. Eddie, that's..."

He smiled crookedly. "You'll just have to nag me in a deeper voice if you want me to hear you."

Nina wasn't amused. "Why didn't you tell me?"

"Well...you know what I'm like. Not big on owning up to being less than one hundred percent at anything."

"Yeah, I've noticed." She managed a slight smile.

"Tchah. But yeah, it's made me think a bit. If one thing starts going, then what's next?"

"Is that why you've been spending so much time at the gym? Fending off the inevitable ravages of age?"

"Oi!" he protested. "Thirty-eight's not old. And I'm still in top nick—going to the gym's just a way to keep from getting a fat arse from sitting in an office all day. You should come with me."

"Are you saying *I've* got a fat ass?"

He made a show of examining it. "Your arse is a thing of beauty. And women always look better with curves anyway."

"You *are* saying I've got a fat ass!" They exchanged smiles, then Nina's face became more serious. "So what are you going to do?"

"Not much I can do. It's not like when I trained back up after breaking my arm—I can't lift weights with my ears. I just need to stay away from loud noises." A rueful look.

"It's funny—the doctor asked me if I'd been near anything loud in the past few years. I was thinking, Christ, where do I start? Underneath a jet while it was taking off, running out of an exploding power station, having a stealth bomber drop bunker-busters on me..."

Nina patted his shoulder. "Y'know, I'm more than happy for us to have a quiet life."

"I suppose..."

She snorted. "Oh Jesus—you really do miss the action, don't you?"

"No, no," he insisted. "Well, a little bit. I mean, it's sort of what I do, innit?"

"Perhaps, but I wish it didn't go to such extremes. Exotic travel, amazing historical discoveries—that's the kind of excitement I'd be happy with. No need to add tanks and bombs and machine guns as well!" She kissed his cheek. "You looked after me during everything we've been through in the last four years. You can take things easy from now. You deserve it."

"Aye, well..." He returned the kiss. "Just so long as things don't get boring."

"I'll try to find a happy medium." She kissed him again and stood. "Come on, let's go to bed. I'm sure we can find something exciting to do there."

"I've got some ideas, but you always call me a pervert when I suggest 'em!" He had started to follow her across the room when his phone rang. "God, who's this?" he muttered, fishing it from his pocket. "Hello? Oh Nan, hi. I thought you'd gone to bed?" He listened, tapping a foot with mild impatience as his grandmother ambled toward her conversational destination. "What? No, Nan, you have to pay extra for the movie channels. That's why you can't see them. And trust me, you won't like any of Grant's films anyway."

"I'll be in here," said Nina, smiling as she entered the bedroom.

Eddie gave her a resigned shrug. "No, Nan, no—you definitely don't want to watch *those* channels! Just go to bed, okay? Yeah, yeah, we'll see you tomorrow. Okay, Nan, night. Night-night. Bye." He ended the call. "Bloody hell. Can't even get any time to ourselves in our own home."

"Only a couple more days and we'll finally be able to have a nice, relaxing break," she assured him.

* * *

As Nina had gloomily predicted, a large part of her next day was spent on the phone. The Treasures of Atlantis exhibition, displaying a plethora of ancient artifacts the International Heritage Agency had recovered from the sunken ruins of Atlantis, was about to begin its four-month tour of sixteen cities in fourteen countries. Even delegating much of the organization to Rowan Sharpe and others, the IHA's director was finding it a major—and draining—addition to her workload.

"Oh God," she sighed, rubbing her eyes at the conclusion of one especially long call. "Next time I have to work with the Secret Service, please just phone them anonymously and tell them I'm a communist or something, so they'll blacklist me and I'll never have to deal with them again."

"Clearance hassles?" asked Eddie, who had been sitting with his feet up on her desk, waiting for her to finish.

"You're not kidding. Interpol suggested that the UN ought to beef up the exhibition's security because everyone's paranoid after Michelangelo's *David* got stolen, but now the Frisco city council's complaining because they don't want to pay their half of the extra costs, *and* the Secret Service threw a fit because they have to vet the extra staff. Plus, the mayor's office keeps adding to the VIP list because obviously everybody wants to meet the president, and the Men in Black need to clear all the new guests too. And for some reason, they've decided it's all my fault."

"It's tough at the top."

"Damn right. And get your feet off my desk." Nina glowered at the offending extremities until they returned to the floor. "Is everything ready?"

He nodded. "The flights and hotel are all confirmed, and Lola's going to bring those Egyptian reports you needed to check. Oh, she says she needs higher clearance to get them, though. The Egyptian government wants some stuff kept classified. They're down in secure storage."

She made a sour face. "The only way that'll get approved before we fly out tomorrow is if I go and stand on the security supervisor's desk until he signs it off. She can just use my clearance, she's got the code."

"Christ, you don't even let me use your security code."

"She's my PA, not my husband. It's a whole different degree of trust." She smiled at his exaggeratedly offended expression. Her phone rang; she picked it up. "Hi, Rowan! Back in San Francisco, then? Are you wearing flowers in your hair?"

Eddie watched her face fall as her old friend spoke. "I'll wait," he said, putting his feet back on the desk.

Nina flapped an irate hand to shoo them off. "Okay, I'll talk to them," she said, exasperated, after some time. "I'll see you there tomorrow. Bye." She hung up and buried her face in her hands. "Ugh."

"Problems?"

"Of course. The mayor's changed the VIP list again. Which means the Secret Service will be calling to yell at me in about five minutes."

"You want me to tell 'em you're a communist?"

"Don't tempt me."

"Still," Eddie said reassuringly, "after tomorrow it's out of your hands and you can stop worrying about it. You just have to fly to Frisco, show off all the stuff from Atlantis, meet the president...then you can finally get back to what you really love. Digging bits of old junk out of the ground."

It was her turn to look offended. "Ha ha. Although it *will* be good to get back to some real archaeological work." She glanced at a display case in one corner. "Maybe I'll finally figure out where Prince came from."

Eddie grinned, going to the case. "Prince. That still makes me laugh." He peered at the small purple figure within. The statuette, crudely carved from an oddly colored stone, had been discovered inside the Pyramid of Osiris, but it bore no resemblance to any known artifact from ancient Egypt, and even after five months of analysis nobody at the IHA was any nearer to identifying its origins. "Tell you what, give me a hammer drill and ten minutes alone with him, and I'll find out everything he knows."

"I don't think that approach would get through the peer-review process," Nina joked, then she became pensive.

"What's up?"

"Just thinking about the president," she said. "I don't know what to expect. I mean, the guy was Dalton's vice president. He might not be too happy that we forced his boss to resign."

"Are you kidding?" said Eddie. "He became the most powerful man in the world because of us. We ought to be on his bloody Christmas card list. Anyway, I thought him and Dalton couldn't stand each other."

"It was something of a party-unity ticket, I suppose. I'm still worried, though."

"If he had any problems with us, the Secret Service wouldn't let us within a mile of him."

"You've got a point. But I'll be glad when it's all over."

Eddie rounded the desk, leaning over the back of her chair to give her a shoulder massage. "You just need to chill out, that's all. Think of it as getting a free trip to San Francisco. How bad can it be?"

Nina tipped her head back to look up at him. "Isn't that normally what one of us says just before something explodes?"

Eddie laughed. "Come on. What are the odds of that?"

3
San Francisco

The Halliwell Exhibition Hall in the city's Civic Center district was wreathed in fog, streetlights beyond the glass façade reduced to indistinct UFO-like glows. San Francisco's notoriously changeable weather had gone from clear, if cold, to completely smothered in barely an hour.

In some ways, Nina wished the fog had descended earlier. That way, Air Force One's landing might have been delayed, forcing President Leo Cole to change his itinerary. The official opening of the Treasures of Atlantis exhibition was, she was sure, the least important of his three engagements of the night before he embarked on a tour of the Far East prior to the upcoming G20 summit in India. But he was here, accompanied by his family, his political entourage, the press corps, and what seemed like several hundred Secret Service agents, impassive eyes constantly sweeping the room.

The speeches had been made—first by Nina, then the mayor of San Francisco, and finally the president himself—and now Cole and his family were being given a personal tour of the exhibits by Rowan Sharpe and Nina. "And here," she said, indicating one of the display cases, "we have an artifact recovered from the Temple of Poseidon: a golden trident."

Cole nodded appreciatively. "A solid gold weapon. I guess Atlantean defense contractors weren't that different from ours!" Sycophantic laughter came from his retinue.

Even though she knew he was joking, Nina felt compelled to correct him. "It's not actually *solid* gold—it wouldn't be much use as a weapon if it were. It has an iron core for extra rigidity. Although it's purely ceremonial, of course."

"Of course," said Cole politely. "And what about this?" He indicated the neighboring case, which held a large book, some eighteen inches tall and almost a foot wide. It was open, revealing its most unusual feature—the pages were not paper, but sheets of reddish gold metal, scribed with dense text in the ancient language of the Atlanteans.

"We call it the Talonor Codex," said Nina. "It's not the most valuable artifact the IHA's recovered from Atlantis in purely monetary terms—although it's made from orichalcum, a gold alloy, so it's worth a lot in its own right. But its contents are what make it really valuable."

"Talonor was one of Atlantis's greatest explorers," Rowan went on. "On one of his expeditions he visited South America, and on another he rounded Africa, crossed the Arabian peninsula, and even reached India. The codex is his journal, an account of all the places he visited and peoples he encountered."

"Our researchers at the IHA are working to translate the entire text," Nina added.

"Impressive," said Cole. The book was supported by a stand; he circled the case to look at the cover, noting a round indentation about six inches across in the metal, then moved on. "Now, this looks valuable."

Rowan nodded. "It is—it's our crown jewels, literally."

"It's beautiful," said the first lady. "How much is it worth?"

"It's hard to say," Nina replied as everyone gazed at the object behind the toughened glass. It was an ornate crown, made from gold and orichalcum with silver trim. The metalwork was adorned with precious stones, which glinted enticingly under the lights. "In purely material terms, maybe three million dollars. But as a cultural artifact, the crown of the ruler of a lost civilization . . . who can say? It's literally priceless."

"Then I hope your security's up to scratch," the president joked. More laughter. "This is an incredible exhibition, Dr. Wilde."

"Thank you, Mr. President." She felt relieved. Maybe her concerns about the big, jowly former lawyer had been unfounded.

"It's good to see that all the funding the US government has put into the IHA is finally producing some visible returns," he continued, squashing Nina's optimism like a bug. "After all, these are turbulent economic times. The American taxpayer needs to know the money is being spent wisely."

"Well, I'm not American, but I pay taxes here," said Eddie, moving closer to Nina, "and I think the IHA's pretty good value. Especially as it does all kinds of useful stuff that most people don't hear about. Mr. President," he added.

Cold looks came from the presidential entourage, but Cole gave him a smile; one that didn't quite reach to his eyes. "Of course it does, Mr. Chase. By the way, it's interesting to meet you and Dr. Wilde at last. My predecessor was very well acquainted with you both."

"Hopefully we, ah, lived up to your expectations," said Nina, feeling a nervous knot form in her stomach. That Cole's reply was just another empty campaign smile only made it tighter.

Instead, he turned to his followers. "A great exhibition, wouldn't you agree? Let's hear it for Dr. Wilde and the IHA." There was a ripple of polite applause. "Now unfortunately, I have to move on to my next engagement— keeping a roomful of lawyers waiting for their five-hundred-dollar-a-plate dinner is a surefire way to get sued!"

The group's laughter as he led it away seemed genuine this time, lawyer jokes always universally appreciated. The Secret Service followed, moving toward the main entrance in unison as if someone had tilted a tray of ball bearings. Someone loudly announced that the President was departing, and the other guests broke off from their conversations to applaud him as he left. Nina joined in, though Eddie's response was more of a slow hand clap.

"I didn't like what he was implying about the IHA," said Nina to her husband, concerned. "You think he's going to cut our budget?"

"Who knows what any politician's thinking? Except for *I want more power,* obviously."

"I assure you, we're not all like that," said a voice behind them. Nina winced a little when she realized to whom it belonged: Roger Boyce, the mayor of San Francisco.

"I'm sure you're not, Mr. Mayor," she said. She had been introduced to Boyce before the president's arrival, and knew a little about him by reputation: the latest in a long line of Democratic incumbents, and by all accounts a fresh-faced poster boy for political correctness. He was accompanied by a group of people who, Nina guessed from the number of outfits that cost more than her monthly salary, were the VIPs whose invitations had caused her so much hassle the previous day. "Eddie was only joking. Weren't you?"

"Uh-huh," said Eddie, without conviction.

"Oh, no offense taken," said Boyce breezily. "It's all part of the job. You won't last long as mayor if you're thin-skinned! But hey, I wanted to thank you and Dr. Sharpe for doing such a terrific job with the exhibition. I'm sure it'll be a huge hit when it opens to the public tomorrow. Just a shame it can't stay here for longer."

"Fifteen other cities might get mad if it did," Rowan said. "But I think it'll get the tour off to a great start."

"Well, what better place to start anything than San Francisco?" asked Boyce, gesturing at the fog-shrouded street beyond the windows. Nina almost replied *New York,* but suppressed the urge. "Have you had a chance to check out our city?"

"Not yet," said Eddie. "Looking forward to it, though. I want to drive too fast down that twisty street, and see where all those great car chases were filmed—*Bullitt, The Rock*..."

"There's more to San Francisco than car chases," Nina chided, sensing Boyce was unhappy at hearing his community reduced to a backdrop for Hollywood blockbusters. "We'll be visiting places that are actually interesting too."

"Happy to hear it." The mayor turned to his companions. "Anyway, if I may, I'd like you to meet some very special guests."

He made the introductions; the VIPs were a mix of leaders of impeccably liberal special-interest groups, entrepreneurs from Silicon Valley, and foreign businesspeople being wooed by the mayor in the hope they would bring jobs to California in general, and San Francisco in particular. "And this is Pramesh Khoil and his wife, Vanita," he said of the final couple. "Mr. Khoil owns some of the fastest-growing technology and telecom companies in India—and is also the inventor of the Qexia search engine."

"Oh, Qexia? 'Just ask,' right?" said Nina, repeating the slogan from Qexia's TV commercials as they shook hands. On the surface, Khoil was extremely unassuming, with a round face as smooth as a sea-worn pebble behind wire-rimmed glasses, and tending toward a plumpness that his tailored Nehru jacket could not hide. Even had she not been wearing heels for the occasion, he would only have been fractionally taller than her. She guessed him to be in his early forties. "You invented Qexia? A friend recommended it to me—I use it almost all the time now."

"We will become the world's top search engine within two years," said Khoil matter-of-factly. His English was very precise but oddly accentless, flat and vaguely robotic. "I am very pleased to meet you, Dr. Wilde."

"We were hoping to discuss the exhibits," said Vanita. Unlike her husband, she had a distinct, melodious accent, and was considerably more striking, wearing a traditional Indian sari of exquisitely decorated silk and bedecked in jewelry, most prominently a pair of large golden earrings. She was about the same age as Khoil and undeniably beautiful, but in a sharp, bird-like way, her nose thin and angular.

"Just ask, to coin a phrase! Dr. Sharpe and I will be happy to answer any questions," Nina said, addressing the group.

As she'd expected, the majority of questions were about the crown. But the Khoils were more interested in another artifact. "The Talonor Codex," said Khoil, bending for a closer look. "How much of it has been translated?"

"About ninety percent, so far," said Nina. "Dr. Sharpe has been in charge of the translation work. The last ten percent is the tricky part, but our knowledge of the Atlantean language is growing all the time."

"Have you considered using crowd-sourcing to speed up the process?"

Nina was surprised by the question. "Er, not really. It's not how we work."

He regarded her owlishly. "Dispersing the project throughout a network would be quicker than concentrating it among a few people. Aggregating a larger number of results would also reduce the probability of individual error. My company can provide suitable software—for a very reasonable fee."

"Archaeology isn't really like computer science," said Nina. "Besides, we want to keep the translation work in-house for security reasons. The codex describes a lot of places visited by Talonor, which are all potential sites of great archaeological importance. If we made it publicly available too soon, they could be raided before we had a chance to examine them."

"But some pages have already been made available on-line by the IHA."

"That was my predecessor's decision, not mine," said Nina, acid in her voice at the thought. "One I reversed as soon as I was appointed director. I rate science higher than publicity."

"Both have their place. And you are no stranger to publicity yourself."

"Not always intentionally, I can assure you. But that's why we chose to display these particular pages of the codex." Nina indicated the scribed metal sheets. "Pictures of them had already been released."

"But it is these pages that caught my interest." For the first time, a hint of emotion—excitement—came into Khoil's mechanical voice as he pointed out the bottom half of the second page. "This text here—it is not Atlantean, but Vedic Sanskrit." He looked at Nina. "The language of ancient India."

"Yes, I know. It was in use up to about six hundred BC, when it was replaced by Classical Sanskrit, but nobody was sure how long it had been used before that—until now, anyway. Atlantis sank around nine thousand BC, so for Talonor to have encountered the language it must have existed before then."

"And so must Indian civilization." Khoil circled the display case to examine the impression in the book's thick cover. "A civilization based on the teachings of the Vedas... which are still followed today. Making Hinduism the world's oldest surviving religion." He smiled, the expression oddly out of place on his placid face. "And increasing the likelihood of one of its schools being the only true religion, wouldn't you say?"

"I try not to get involved in religious debates," Nina said firmly. The conflict between archaeological discoveries and dogma had nearly gotten her killed on more than one occasion.

Khoil put his face almost against the glass as he peered intently at the indentation. Standing nearby with Vanita, Eddie felt compelled to break the silence. "So, Mrs. Khoil," he said, "how did you meet your husband?" She gave him a dismissive look, not interested in small talk. He took that as a challenge. "What first attracted you to the billionaire Pramesh Khoil?"

Vanita bared her teeth in response to the little joke. "Do you think I'm some kind of gold digger?" she snapped.

"No, that's not what I meant," said Eddie hastily. "It was just—"

"I got my doctorate in psychology before Pramesh even started his company! Did you assume that because I'm a woman I'm some passive and subservient adjunct to my husband?"

"No, I think he assumed that everybody appreciates his, uh, *distinctive* sense of humor," Nina said quickly. The mayor was looking horrified that a faux pas had been committed on his watch. "There wasn't any offense intended."

Eddie nodded. "Yeah. If I'm *trying* to offend someone, I don't muck about."

"Honey, not helping," Nina said through gritted teeth. She turned back to Vanita. "We're both very sorry for any misunderstanding."

The Indian woman maintained a tight-lipped silence, but her husband spoke up instead. "We accept your apology, Dr. Wilde. Now, we were discussing the Talonor Codex. Are you sure the IHA would not be interested in using my company's software to assist with the translation work?"

He wasn't just a genius programmer, but also a determined salesman, Nina thought. "No, but thank you for the offer. As I said, only a few people have access to the full text for security reasons."

"You misunderstand me. I am not suggesting that you give it to strangers. No, I am offering the services of Qexia."

"I'm not a computer expert," Rowan said, puzzled, "but I don't see how putting the text into a search engine would help with the translation."

"It is more than just a search tool. It is a system of analytical algorithms, a deductive computer." Khoil was becoming impassioned again. "When you use Qexia to find information on a particular subject, you see not a list but a 'cloud' of interlinked results, yes? The relative importance of each result is not decided solely by a count of its connections to other webpages, like some inferior search engines." He glanced at one of the Silicon Valley bigwigs, who scowled. "Qexia analyzes each page, finds connections to other pages through deductive logic based on its profile of the user. It can apply the same principles to translation. The more data it has, the better the results. Give it all the information you have on the Atlantean language, and it will provide a full and accurate translation."

"Computer translations?" said Eddie. "They always come out like the manual for a cheapo DVD player. 'Having the insertions of disk in tray slot...'"

Khoil prickled at the implied slight on his technology. "Qexia is much better than that." He faced Nina. "It will even make part of your profession obsolete. There will be no need to waste years piecing together scraps of data in order to find an archaeological site. Such as Atlantis." He gestured at the exhibits. "It took you how long to deduce its location? Years? Given the same data, my software could have found it in days. Perhaps even hours. Then all you would need would be strong arms to do the digging."

Now it was Nina who bristled. "There's more to archaeology than just assembling data," she said scathingly. "You need a broad base of knowledge in areas that might seem unrelated. When I worked out Atlantis's location, I didn't have all the facts, so I had to fill in the gaps based on my own experience—and intuition. A computer can't do that."

"We'll have to agree to disagree, then," said Vanita, joining Khoil. "I know the power of Pramesh's software. It will change the world."

"So you are definitely not interested in my offer, Dr. Wilde?" Khoil asked.

"I'm afraid not," said Nina. "If nothing else, it'd take all the fun out of the work."

He shrugged. "As you wish. But I am sure the codex will—" He broke off at the approach of a woman holding a cell phone. She was Indian, dressed in a formal and slightly staid business suit, an employee rather than an executive. Her long dark hair was styled to cover, but couldn't fully conceal, a scar slicing down her forehead over her right eye. "Yes, Madirakshi?"

"The call you were waiting for, Mr. Khoil," said the woman.

"My apologies, but I must take this," Khoil told Nina. He stepped away, Vanita and Madirakshi following as he answered the call. "Yes? No, no change. As we discussed, yes."

"Bloody hell, I didn't have any trouble hearing *her* voice," muttered Eddie, regarding Vanita. "And Christ, he sounds like he learned English from a Speak and Spell."

"Is everything all right, Dr. Wilde?" asked Boyce, with a hint of anxiety.

"Fine. Just a minor misunderstanding."

"Happy to hear it!"

Another VIP asked Nina a question about Atlantis as

Khoil ended his call and he and Vanita returned to the group, their assistant briskly departing. Eddie watched her go; now that the presidential entourage and the Secret Service agents had left, the exhibition hall was noticeably less crowded. A clear social hierarchy was visible as a result: Boyce's bodyguards and the building's own security staff at the very edges of the room, with groups of PAs and secretaries and business underlings orbiting the center where their bosses schmoozed and networked. The woman, Madirakshi, joined three Indian men in a far corner, one of them a bearded giant standing head and shoulders above the others.

He looked toward the high windows as Nina continued talking. There was a plaza outside, headlights dimly visible on the foggy street beyond. He hoped conditions would improve tomorrow; there wouldn't be much point touring the city if they couldn't see it...

He stiffened, suddenly alert as he registered that something wasn't quite right. It was the headlights. They were pointing directly at the windows.

But the street ran *past* the exhibition hall, not toward it—

The headlights moved.

Coming at him.

"Mr. Mayor!" he barked to Boyce. "Get security, there's—"

The windows exploded under blasts of gunfire.

4

Everyone down!" Eddie yelled, covering Nina with his body. Shattered glass spilled across the polished floor. The hall filled with panicked screams—which were quickly drowned by the roar of engines.

Several motorcycles charged into the room, their riders sheathed in black leather, faces hidden behind mirrored visors. More gunshots crackled as the riders spread out across the hall, firing MP5Ks in sweeps just above the guests' heads to force them to the floor—then aiming lower to pick off specific targets. Blood-spattered bodies tumbled, the hall's security personnel and the mayor's bodyguards cut down.

Another engine, louder, a vicious snarl. A vehicle smashed through the remains of the windows and made a sweeping 180-degree hand-brake turn, swatting aside people unlucky enough to be in its path and demolishing a display case. It resembled a Range Rover, only hugely bulked up and steroidal, thick bullbars protecting its front and rear and oversized tires bulging beneath its heavy-duty suspension. A Bowler Nemesis, a powerful off-road racing vehicle that could outpace many sports cars—and do so over the most punishing terrain.

The bikes were also off-roaders, Eddie saw. The attackers had a getaway plan that would take them somewhere no police car could follow.

The Nemesis backed farther into the hall, people on the floor scrambling out of its way. Some of the bikers dismounted, guns covering the crowd, while three rode toward Eddie and Nina's position.

Nina's gaze was pulled to the Atlantean crown. *Priceless,* she had called it less than thirty minutes earlier—but now someone intended to find exactly what that translated to in the real world.

The bikers stopped and climbed off their machines, guns raised. No shouted orders, no demands, no threats. They had made their intentions perfectly clear—and another burst of fire from an MP5K as a prone security guard tried to draw his weapon hammered the point home.

"What do we do?" Nina whispered. "We can't let them steal the crown!"

"Y-yes, we can!" Boyce said, voice quavering. He raised his head as the faceless trio approached. "I'm the mayor of San Francisco. Please, take what you came for and leave. Nobody else has to get hurt." Nina scowled at him, but knew there was nothing else they could do.

The Nemesis kept reversing. Its rear bullbar clipped another display case, which toppled over and smashed. The golden trident clanged across the floor as the big 4×4 stopped behind the three men.

They regarded the crown impassively...then at a gesture from the tallest of the trio, apparently the leader, moved to the next case.

The one containing the Talonor Codex.

Through her fear, Nina felt a moment of shock. *That* was their objective?

Rowan's reaction was a more exaggerated version of her own. "No, you can't take it!" he cried, springing up—

The leader shot him.

A bullet hit Rowan's upper chest, slamming him back down with a spurt of blood. His head cracked against the floor.

"Rowan!" Nina screamed. Eddie forced her down as she tried to crawl to him. Her friend was still alive, feebly writhing, but blood was running down his shirt.

The leader fired a single shot at the case. The toughened glass splintered, crooked cracks radiating from the bullet hole, but didn't entirely break—until a blow from the butt of his MP5K finished the job. He lifted out the codex, cradling the heavy book in his arms as another man approached the Nemesis and raised its hatchback. There was a large metal box inside, lined with foam rubber. He lowered the ancient artifact into it, then closed the case and slammed the hatchback shut. The off-roader's engine revved.

The bikers closest to the broken windows rode out into the fog. The Nemesis bulled its way through the scattered debris and terrified guests after them.

The trio who had taken the codex mounted up. Two of them set off without a pause; the leader glanced back at Nina's group before moving—

Eddie dived, landing by the golden trident. He snatched it up and leapt to his feet, flipping it around so the three spearheads were pointing backward.

Nina rushed to Rowan. "Somebody help me!" she cried, pressing her palm against the wound to try to stanch the bleeding. He groaned.

The Nemesis and the first two bikers reached the windows, crunching over the glass. The leader followed—

Eddie hurled the trident. It flew across the hall like a gleaming javelin, spearing down at its target...

Not the rider, but his bike.

The shaft shot between the rear wheel's spokes to be slammed against the forks, instantly locking the wheel. The rider was thrown off as the bike crashed to the floor.

Eddie ran at him. Catch the leader, and this would be over—

The raider rolled, catlike, back on his feet in a moment—and drew his gun.

Eddie hurled himself behind one of the surviving display cases as bullets sprayed across the room. They smacked into the thick glass, crazing and cracking it—then the onslaught stopped. The gunman dropped his weapon. Out of ammo.

Engine snarl. The Nemesis's driver had heard the gunfire and quickly reversed back into the hall. The rider ran to the vehicle and jumped in.

A siren grew in volume outside. Somebody on the street had called 911, the police responding rapidly to an incident at the mayor's location—

More gunshots as the bikers opened fire on the approaching cops. Staccato clangs of lead striking steel and cracks of glass, then the police car veered across the plaza, coming to an abrupt stop against a concrete planter. The siren fell silent, strobes flicking eerily through the fog.

The Nemesis surged away with a V8 bellow.

Eddie ran to the abandoned bike and yanked the bent trident out from the wheel. He pulled the vehicle upright. It had stalled; he jumped on and slammed his heel down on the long kick-start lever. The engine rasped to life. He twisted the throttle, pulling the front wheel around.

"Eddie!" Nina yelled across the hall. "What're you doing?"

"Going after them!"

"No, wait—"

Too late. He powered through the opening, turning hard to head after the fleeing Nemesis. The bike's taillight vanished into the fog.

One of the guests, a balding, middle-aged man, hurried over to Nina and Rowan. "I'm a doctor," he told her. "Please, move your hand—I need to see the wound."

Nina reluctantly lifted her hand from Rowan's chest, cringing as a thick crimson gush pumped from the hole. "Will he be okay?"

"I don't know," said the doctor, quickly assessing the damage before putting his own palm firmly over the injury. "It missed his heart, but it might have punctured a lung."

"I've called for an ambulance," one of his companions reported, waving a cell phone.

Anguished, Nina looked between the injured man and the broken window through which her husband had just disappeared. Rowan read her expression. "Nina," he gasped, his breathing hoarse and labored. "Go help Eddie. Get—get the codex back."

"But I can't leave you!"

"I'll be okay." He forced a once very familiar smile through the pain. "Go on. Bring me some chocolates at the hospital. Dark ones."

Nina gripped his hand. "As if I'd forget what you like." She squeezed it more tightly, then, after a moment of hesitation, let go and stood. Rowan winked at her. Reassured, however slightly, she turned. Through the broken window, the police car's blinking strobes caught her attention. "Mr. Mayor!"

Boyce struggled upright, shaking with adrenaline and fear. He looked around at Nina's insistent shout. "W-what?"

Nina grabbed his arm and pulled him toward the plaza. "There's a police car outside—tell them to put up roadblocks. Now!"

He was still too shocked to think straight. "But—I can't just order them to do things—"

"You're the goddamn *mayor*!" Nina reminded him as they reached the police cruiser. It was a Dodge Charger, a powerful four-door sedan in SFPD black and white—but both officers inside were slumped over, unconscious or dead. "Dammit!"

"My God," gasped Boyce, recoiling at the sight. "Now what do we do?"

Nina looked in the direction Eddie had gone—and made a decision. "We follow them. You can guide the cops to block them." She opened the driver's door. The man at the wheel was dead, hit by several bullets. Suppressing her revulsion, she unfastened his seat belt, then dragged out the body.

Boyce gawped at her. "You can't do that! It's—a crime scene or something!"

"Just get in! No, in the front!" she shouted as he opened the rear door. "I need you to use the radio!"

The other cop was also dead, a bloody hunk of skin and bone hanging off his temple. Shuddering, Nina released his seat belt as Boyce ran around the car. "Don't look at his face, just pull him out," she ordered.

The mayor tried to follow her advice, but couldn't help glimpsing the wound and had to stifle a yelp of disgust. However, he reluctantly manhandled the body out of the car, calling to someone inside the exhibition center to watch over the dead men.

"Come on!" said Nina impatiently. Boyce climbed in beside her. She put the Charger into reverse. Metal and plastic graunched where the front bumper had jammed against the planter, then ripped free. She powered into the fog. "Get on the radio."

• • •

At the wheel of the Nemesis, Zec flipped up his visor to look anxiously at Fernandez. "Are you okay?"

The Spaniard kneaded his bruised shoulder. "I think so. Thanks for coming back for me."

"I was hardly going to abandon you, Urbano. You

haven't paid us the rest of our money yet!" He smiled, but Fernandez was not amused. "Who was it? A guard?"

"No, one of the guests. Bastard! If I see him again, I'll kill him."

Zec's side mirrors revealed something approaching rapidly from behind. "This is your chance."

"What?" Fernandez glared at the mirror. A single headlight pierced the murk—one of the team's powerful Honda XR650R dirt bikes. *His* Honda. "He's chasing us!" he said in disbelief.

"What do we do?"

"Follow the plan—get onto Taylor Street and head up the hill. Where's the radio?" He searched for Zec's walkie-talkie. "Go faster!"

* * *

The fog had turned the streets damp and slippery, and the Honda's high, gawky stance made Eddie feel even more unsteady. But he was quickly getting the feel of the off-roader.

The Nemesis accelerated, the shrill whine of its supercharger echoing off buildings as it barged past a car, which braked and skidded. Eddie cursed, swerving around it. Was his bike fast enough to catch the 4×4?

Only one way to find out. He twisted the throttle harder.

* * *

"Yes, I really am Mayor Boyce!" said Boyce into the radio handset. The dispatcher at the other end of the line had plenty on her plate with the rash of 911 calls, and she was unimpressed by the crazy guy commandeering police frequencies and claiming to be the mayor. "Look, just get ambulances to the Halliwell building, and set up roadblocks, right now! There are armed robbers escaping on motorbikes and some sort of big SUV, and they've killed several people, including two police officers."

The woman was immediately more attentive. "There are officers down?"

"Yes, two men were shot! We're in their car chasing the, ah, the perps—we're on..." He scoured the surroundings for landmarks. "I don't know which street, it's too foggy."

"Which car are you in? What's its number?"

Boyce hurriedly searched for any identifying signs, spotting a plaque on the dashboard. "Car Six Forty-three."

"Hold on, I'm checking its LoJack tracker... Car Six Forty-three is heading eastbound on Eddy Street, approaching Leavenworth."

"Yes, that's us," Boyce told her. "We're a couple of blocks behind the robbers—we'll guide you to them. Just stop them before they can get away!"

"We're on it, uh... Mr. Mayor. Units are responding. Take no unnecessary risks."

"Bit late for that," Nina muttered. A stalled car materialized from the murk ahead of them, forcing her to make a hard turn to avoid a collision. "This is like a damn obstacle course! Where's the siren?"

* * *

The bike twitched under Eddie, the knobbly off-road tires fighting for grip on the wet tarmac. "Shit!" he gasped, risking a millisecond glance at the speedometer. He was doing over sixty down the three-lane street, and the Nemesis was still pulling away.

Noise from ahead, tire squeals and blasting horns. The twin red eyes of the Nemesis's taillights disappeared around a corner, turning left to head north.

Other lights were strewn across his path where cars had skidded and collided as the bikes and the Bowler tore through the intersection. He braked, pumping the levers to stop the wheels from locking. The Honda shimmied and writhed. One foot down for balance, the sole of his shoe scraping on the road, he angled between two dented cars to make the turn. He was just about able to make out a sign on the corner: TAYLOR ST.

The road led uphill, the rising line of streetlights telling him it got steeper ahead. The incline wasn't affecting the Nemesis, though—the red eyes were smaller, fainter, pulling away.

* * *

"I don't know who he is," Fernandez said into the radio as the Nemesis powered up Taylor Street, swinging across all three lanes to overtake traffic, "and I don't care. Just take him out!"

Ahead, the lights of the team's bikes danced like fireflies as they dodged obstacles. Two of them flared, the Hondas and their riders materializing from the fog as they braked.

Fernandez watched the mirror as the Nemesis overtook them, the bikes falling back to intercept his pursuer.

* * *

Eddie was forced to swing wide to avoid a car pulling out of a parking space. He glanced back at the near-hit before returning his full attention to the road. Where was the Nemesis?

Twin red lights, not far ahead—

They split apart.

Bikers!

They had slowed, waiting for him to catch up. One went to each side of the street, a pincer movement to trap him.

Another intersection flashed past, an angry horn Dopplering away behind. The bike to Eddie's right was closer. He drew almost level, seeing the rider's blank mirror-mask looking across at him.

Left hand reaching for something—

Eddie swerved sharply away as the rider drew an MP5K. He ducked as fire burst from its muzzle. A crash of glass came from the sidewalk as the bullets shattered a window.

But he couldn't retreat any farther, blocked by a line of parked cars—and the other bike was directly ahead, pinning him in the gunman's sights.

Another intersection—

Eddie made a hard left turn, slipping between two cars waiting at the junction and riding up onto Taylor Street's sidewalk. A pedestrian ahead—he jerked the handlebars, passing so close that his arm brushed against her.

The second biker dropped back to get a better firing angle. Head low, Eddie shot past another startled pedestrian. A green glow in the mist ahead—traffic lights at a crossroads. The biker would have a clear shot as he crossed the junction.

A shape in the fog, a man with an umbrella—

Eddie snatched the umbrella from his hand as he passed. The slipstream immediately snapped it inside out as he held it up to the wind. It flapped behind him like the broken wing of a bat.

Intersection—

Eddie swung back onto Taylor Street proper, crossing directly in front of the other bike. He whipped the ruined umbrella into the rider's face. With his helmet and heavy leathers as protection, its flimsy spokes and fluttering fabric couldn't hurt him...

But it could block his vision.

Only for a second, as he raised his gun hand to bat away the obstruction—

Eddie didn't even need that long. Braking fiercely, he swerved to shoulder-barge the other man into a parked van.

There was a huge bang as the Honda came to an abrupt stop, its rider flipping over the handlebars to slam spread-eagled against the van's flat back. He hung for a moment like a pinned butterfly, then dropped twistedly onto the mangled bike.

Eddie didn't look back—the noise of impact was enough to tell him he had nothing further to worry about from that quarter.

The dead biker's comrade was another matter. He swept toward Eddie, gun at the ready.

* * *

"They're heading north on Taylor!" Boyce breathlessly reported as Nina turned and accelerated up the hill, the siren encouraging confused drivers who had become embroiled in the chase to move out of their way.

"Roger that, Mr. Mayor," said the dispatcher. "Units are moving to intercept."

"Where does this road go?" Nina asked.

"To the top of a big hill...and then down again," said Boyce, checking his mental map of the city. "But they could be going anywhere from here."

Nina wasn't sure about that. The robbers had a reason for taking this particular route. But she didn't know San Francisco's geography, so it eluded her. All she could do was keep following and hope the SFPD would trap them.

* * *

Over the snarl of the Bowler's engine, Zec heard sirens ahead—distant, but closing. "What if they beat us to the top?"

"Make sure they don't," Fernandez told him. Zec got the message and pushed the accelerator harder. The Nemesis overtook a crawling Volkswagen Beetle and powered up a steep section of the hill, an intersection approaching fast—

The blocky bulk of a cable car loomed through the fog to their right on a collision course.

"*Srati!*" yelled Zec as the Nemesis shot over the hill

crest and went airborne. The cable car's driver saw its headlights just in time and yanked the brake lever, sparks flying from the metal wheels. The 4×4 flew across the vintage tram's track, clearing it by an inch before crashing back down. Fernandez gasped in relief.

Behind, the cable car screeched to a stop in the middle of the crossroads, blocking the street.

* * *

Eddie and the biker ducked and swerved in a deadly two-wheeled dance. The MP5K spat fire; Eddie heard—and felt—a burst of bullets crack past as he veered back across the street.

The other man tried to cut behind him. Eddie braked and swung the other way. If the raider got on his tail, it would expose him to an attack from behind. But if he slowed too much, he would make himself an easy target.

The road ahead steepened sharply, the front forks of both bikes compressing with a *whump* as they hit the incline. The other rider, tracking Eddie, was less prepared for the impact. His bike lurched.

Eddie saw his chance.

He blasted past the other man, racing up the hill. A VW was in one lane at the top; he moved to pass it. He needed to open up a gap on his enemy and catch the Nemesis. If he got close enough to the 4×4, it might deter the other man from firing.

An intersection was just ahead—

And a cable car right in his path!

5

There was no way Eddie could turn fast enough to avoid the tram—and if he stopped, his pursuer would kill him.

If he couldn't go *around*—

He twisted the throttle as far as it would go and aimed at the sloping rear of the Beetle, pulling the bike into a wheelie. The Honda slammed into the back of the Volkswagen—and continued up over it. The rear window shattered, metal buckling under the bike's weight, but Eddie was already clear, flying skyward...

Over the cable car.

The biker was less lucky, not seeing the tram through the fog until it was too late—

He smashed into its side at more than sixty miles an hour.

The XR650R disintegrated into a mangled scrap as it hit the tram's heavy steel chassis. Its rider was thrown through antique wood and glass panels, bursting from the cable car's other side to crash down in the intersection of Taylor and California streets—minus an arm, which spun past and bounced along the road.

A painful impact pounded up Eddie's spine as he landed. He swerved violently to avoid the severed arm. Headlights loomed in his path. This section of Taylor Street had two-way traffic, increasing the risk of a head-on collision. He yelled and swung to the right, bringing the bike back up to speed after the retreating lights.

* * *

"Car Six Forty-three, Six Forty-three," said the dispatcher. "LoJack shows you on Taylor approaching Pine, please confirm."

"This is the mayor," said Boyce into the handset. "I confirm."

"Be advised of a traffic incident at California and Taylor, use caution. Units are setting up roadblocks ahead of you. Other units about to enter pursuit from both sides of Washington."

"Excellent work, dispatch, thank you," said Boyce, voice switching effortlessly from panicked passenger to patronizing politician.

"What does that mean?" Nina asked.

"It means," he said with rising excitement, "they're completely boxed in. We've got them!"

* * *

The Nemesis shot across the junction of Taylor and Washington. Zec glanced nervously to his right, seeing red and blue strobe lights cutting through the fog toward him. Another SFPD cruiser was powering down the hill to the left, farther away.

"Just stay ahead of them," said Fernandez, voice tense but confident. "Only four more blocks..."

* * *

Eddie heard multiple sirens ahead, getting louder. If they could cut off the Nemesis—

No such luck. Flashing lights swept out of a street to the right behind the speeding off-roader.

He eased off slightly, considering his options before deciding to keep going. The cops might be able to stop the Bowler—but they would still need to be warned about the other bikers. If they turned and came back to rescue their leader, it could be a bloodbath.

Twisting the throttle again, he followed the police car through the intersection—

"Fuck!" He hauled the Honda hard over to avoid a second police car that screeched around the corner to his left, almost scooping him up as a hood ornament.

"You on the bike!" a voice boomed from the cruiser's loudspeaker. "Pull over, right now!"

"Not me, you dozy twats!" Eddie shouted, jabbing a hand at the cars ahead. "Go after *them*! I'm the good guy!"

They couldn't hear him—and in hindsight, he realized that making a gesture which could easily be mistaken for flipping the bird had probably been a bad move. "I said pull over, smart-ass!" the cop growled.

"Buggeration and fuckery," he muttered, going faster.

* * *

Nina swung the Charger around the stationary cable car, Boyce regarding the hole smashed through the historical vehicle with dismay. A small crowd of gawpers in the road scattered at the police car's approach, revealing a leather-clad body lying on the tarmac. She swerved away from it—seeing a smaller object through the fog too late to avoid running it over.

"What was that?" demanded Boyce.

"Uh—I think a bad guy left his parts in San Francisco," said Nina, cringing. The mayor gave her a dirty look.

"All units, all units," said the radio, "high-speed pursuit

heading up Taylor toward Broadway. Roadblocks now in position, further units moving to intercept."

Boyce stared ahead. "If they keep going on Taylor, there's no way they can escape."

"They *must* have something planned," Nina said as she accelerated. "Why would they be using dirt bikes and a big-ass dune buggy unless they were planning to go off road?"

"There's nowhere they can do that on Taylor Street," said Boyce confidently—then his face fell. "Except for Coolbrith Park..."

• • •

The bikes leading the pack slowed as they approached the summit, the Nemesis quickly catching up. Ahead, Taylor Street dropped away sharply, a steep hill leading down to the intersection with Green Street—where a roadblock was waiting. For a two-block stretch, there were no other exits.

For cars, at least.

But running eastward was a small park. Named for California's first poet laureate, the tiered slope was a little oasis of greenery amid the surrounding condominiums, carefully tended flowers and bushes adding to the idyll...

Which was shattered as the bikes roared off the road, some of them taking the clear but bumpy route down the steps flanking the park while others simply plowed through the vegetation, knobbly tires ripping up soil and grass.

Behind them, Zec slewed the Nemesis into a skid that left it pointing at the park entrance. He quickly engaged the low-range gearing, then used the 4×4's high clearance and oversized wheels to mount the tall curb. The Bowler tore through a flower bed and continued rapidly down the slope, all four wheels clawing for grip.

The first police car reached the hilltop and slithered to a halt, but there was no way it could follow. A cop jumped out and drew his gun, about to fire after the disappearing vehicle—

"'Scuse me!" cried Eddie as he whipped past, swatting the gun out of the officer's hand to avoid getting a bullet in the back.

Dodging trees, he bounded down the park's tiers in the wake of the Nemesis as it smashed through the foliage—then heard a loud bang, followed by the roar of its engine speeding away. The robbers had reached another road. Not knowing what to expect, Eddie braced himself as he brought the bike through the flattened bushes—and found himself briefly in free fall, riding off the edge of a terrace. A slam of impact, then he was back on tarmac on Vallejo Street.

He could still hear sirens—behind him. For now, the robbers' plan had succeeded. They had shaken off the police.

But they hadn't lost all their pursuers. Eddie revved the engine, racing downhill after the Nemesis.

* * *

A radio report confirmed Boyce's fear: The raiders had driven through Coolbrith Park, leaving the police with no choice but to take the long way around to catch up.

Nina had no intention of letting them escape that easily. "Which way to intercept them?"

"They're going east, so right," Boyce told her. An intersection ahead; she turned the wheel sharply to make the turn. "No, not *this* right! It's a one-way—"

A single headlight in their path—

They both screamed as Nina swerved onto the sidewalk to dodge the cable car clanking up Jackson Street. The Charger's side scraped a wall, sending up a shower of sparks and smashing the wing mirror as the tram rumbled past.

"Okay," Nina gasped as she straightened out, "you tell

me things like that *before* I turn from now on, okay?" A car was also coming up the hill, but the strobes and siren prompted it to dart out of her way. "You know the city—where are they going?"

Boyce had gripped the shotgun rack for support, and forced himself to release his clenched hands. "I—I don't know. If they want to get out of the city, the only routes from here are the Bay Bridge or the Golden Gate—but they're not heading toward either of them."

"So what's in the direction they're going?"

"Just the marina. We're less than a mile from it."

"They must have a boat," Nina realized. She indicated the radio. "Tell the cops they need to get to the water-front!"

* * *

The robbers followed a zigzagging course across the city grid before heading east again, now speeding up Union Street. The road ahead rose steeply as it climbed the western flank of Telegraph Hill, a park topped by the white pillar of Coit Tower at its summit.

Fernandez checked the mirror. The Honda's headlight was still behind them in the fog, an irritating gnat that just wouldn't go away. The Spaniard had been over every inch of the route before; he thought for a moment, then picked up the radio to issue a command.

* * *

Even the mighty XR650R was laboring on the incline, but Eddie saw the hilltop ahead. The Nemesis crested it, engine growl fading. He eased off on the throttle, not wanting to make a flying leap into the unknown when he reached the summit.

The fog was lighter on the hill's eastern side, the lights of the Bay Bridge dimly visible in the distance. The road forked, to the right making a ninety-degree turn, the left route continuing a short way downhill before doing the same.

No sign of the Nemesis. Which way had it gone?

Eddie could still hear the raw snarl of its engine somewhere below. He went left. Lights blinked ahead, warning of construction and remodeling work on a house built on the steep hillside. He turned the corner—

And rode into a storm of gunfire.

Bullets blazed from an MP5K, a biker stationary in front of a smashed fence at the road's end. Eddie glimpsed the Nemesis disappearing down the steep wooded hill beyond it—but the only thing on his mind was staying alive. No time to turn and retreat.

He twisted the throttle—and crashed the bike through a barrier, flashing lights scattering as he ripped through plastic sheeting into the house.

The raider tracked him, plaster and lath no obstacle for 9mm submachine-gun rounds. Debris stabbed at his face and hands, tools and paint cans scattering under his wheels.

The bullets got closer. As did the far wall—

He didn't stop.

Another sheet of plastic burst apart as he plowed the Honda through it into open air, the hillside whirling below him...

He landed with a painful slam on the roof of another house, the next in a steeply stepped terrace running down the hillside. But he knew even as he clenched the brake levers that he was going too fast to stop before the edge.

Falling—

A hard landing on another house. The tires tore at the roofing felt, skidding, but he still couldn't stop...

"Shiiiiiit—"

Eddie hit the last roof, finally halting less than a foot from the edge. He looked down at the treetops below, suppressing a shudder.

Noise to his right, glimpses of lights bouncing down the hill through more trees. He projected their course to a street at the foot of the hillside. Above, police sirens wailed in useless confusion as the cops arrived and once more found themselves with nowhere to go.

Eddie surveyed the rooftop. Where could *he* go?

A balcony jutted from the wall below, giving the house's occupants a panoramic view of the bay. Steeling himself, he blipped the throttle and rode the bike off the edge of the roof, dropping onto the balcony with a bang that shook the extension so hard he was afraid it would tear from the wall.

But it held. Relieved, he turned his head to see that the house was occupied, a man and woman goggling at him from an expensive sofa.

He knocked on the glass. The couple looked at each other, then the man hesitantly slid open the door. "Hello?"

"Evening," said Eddie. "Can I come through?"

Another uncertain exchange of glances, then the man stood back. Eddie guided the bike inside. "If you need to get the carpet cleaned," he said, noticing he was leaving a dirty track, "bill the International Heritage Agency. Tell 'em Eddie said it was okay."

"I'll...I'll do that," the man said. The woman opened a door, guiding him into a hall. A second door led outside. Steps headed back up to the road above, but Eddie realized he could cut across the steep hillside to reach the path the robbers had followed.

He looked down the hill. The lights were almost at its foot. Thanking his hosts, he hauled the Honda around and started after them.

• • •

The bikes reached the bottom of the slope. A tall chain-link fence separated the rough ground from Sansome Street, but Fernandez had prepared the way by cutting the padlock securing a gate. The lead Honda bashed it with its front wheel and the gate flew open. The other bikes streamed through. The Nemesis's exit was less subtle, Zec simply smashing down the entire fence.

Fernandez glanced back up the hill. No sign of the pest. He smiled, checking the street to the north. They had a clear run to the marina, and the police would have to go many blocks out of their way to round the natural barrier of Telegraph Hill.

"Almost there," he told Zec triumphantly as the Bosnian sent the Nemesis surging up the street after the bikes. "A nice easy end to your last job, eh?"

"We're not clear yet," Zec pointed out.

Fernandez smirked. "You always were a pessimist, Braco. Smile! You'll be home with your wife and boy soon enough. And *rich*!" Over the engine noise he heard a siren, but it was some way behind them. "Who can stop us?"

* * *

Nina turned north. The fog was thinning, letting her speed up as she cut through the traffic, siren blaring.

Boyce was on the radio again. "This is the mayor. We're on Sansome—where are those officers?"

"Units on Calhoun Terrace have lost contact, repeat, lost contact," the dispatcher reported.

"Where's that?" Nina asked.

Boyce pointed up and to her left. "Top of the hill. There's a six-block stretch without any streets; it's too steep."

"Not if you're driving an off-roader. How far to this marina?"

"Nine or ten blocks."

No way of knowing how far the robbers were ahead. All Nina could do was go even faster.

* * *

Eddie's Honda slithered down the last few feet of the slope, weeds crunching under its wheels. The headlight picked out a mangled chain-link fence. He rode over the flattened barrier, getting his bearings. A siren was coming from the south...and a familiar V8 growl fading to the north.

Revving the engine, he set off in pursuit.

* * *

The Nemesis reached the Embarcadero, the long, broad road running along the edge of San Francisco Bay. The marina was just a few hundred yards away. The bikes were already there, pulling onto the boardwalk. Fernandez pointed for Zec to follow.

Two powerful speedboats waited at a jetty. All they had to do was unload the codex, get aboard, then make a fast escape across the bay, one boat heading eastward for Oakland while the other made for Marin County to the north. The fog was an unplanned bonus—it would make the vessels even harder to follow, the treacherous conditions grounding the SFPD's helicopters. No need to use any expensive missiles tonight.

Zec swerved the Nemesis onto the boardwalk and skidded to a stop. Fernandez jumped out. Most of his men had already run to the boats; one hung back, waiting for him. "Braco and I will unload the case," he said, flipping up his visor. "Make sure nobody interferes." He gestured at the biker's MP5K; the man's helmet bobbed in acknowledgment. "Braco, come on."

The Spaniard and his second in command ran to the back of the Nemesis. The case containing their prize lay inside, scuffed but otherwise undamaged by its roller-coaster ride across the city. They lifted it out—

Engine noise, approaching fast. The strident rasp of a Honda XR650R.

"I don't believe it!" said Fernandez, exasperated. An all-too-familiar single headlight was racing straight for them. He called to the remaining man as he and Zec carried the case to the jetty. "Kill that bastard!"

The biker took up position between the Nemesis and the approaching motorbike, readying his gun.

* * *

Eddie spotted the lights of the stationary Nemesis by the waterfront. Figures faded into view through the murk as he approached.

One was in a firing stance—

Another burst of bullets seared at him.

He dropped as low as he could as a round cracked against the Honda's front fairing, blowing out the headlight and spitting fragments into his face—and another shot tore into the front wheel. The tire exploded, rubber flapping as it sheared off the steel rim. The handlebars were wrenched from his grip as the bike went into an uncontrollable slide.

Eddie threw himself off. He yelled in pain as he hit the boardwalk and skidded across the wet wood, clothes ripping. The Honda tumbled onward...

Straight at the Nemesis.

The gunman tried to jump out of the way—

Too late. The bike slammed him into the parked 4×4 with backbreaking force. The Honda's fuel tank ripped open on the Nemesis's rear bullbar, metal sparking against metal.

The bike exploded, the blast kicking the Nemesis's back end up into the air—just as the off-roader's own far larger fuel tank detonated. A fireball surged across the boardwalk, the blazing Nemesis flipping end over end over the waterfront railings to smash down on top of one of the speedboats, crushing the men inside it down into the marina's dark waters.

The explosion knocked Zec off his feet and sent Fernandez reeling. The case fell. It landed on the jetty's edge, wobbling precariously on the brink. Fernandez lunged for it—

It dropped off the edge, hitting the water with a flat splash. For a moment it seemed it would float . . . then the sea swallowed it.

Fernandez looked down at the ripples in horror. So close to success, literally seconds from escape—and now the treasure was lost! Jaw set in anger, he spun to find the man who had ruined everything.

Roaring like a charging bull, Eddie tackled him to the dock.

Aching from his hard landing, suit and skin torn, singed by the fireball, the Englishman was driven by fury. His opponent was still wearing his crash helmet, but there were plenty of other places he could land a painful blow— as Fernandez discovered an instant later when he was punched hard in the groin.

"You fucker!" Eddie snarled, slamming him down hard on the planks. "Teach you to fucking shoot at me, you gimp-suited bast—"

Zec's boot smashed into his side, knocking him off the fallen raider. Eddie landed on his back, winded. Zec kicked him again, then pulled Fernandez to his feet—

A shotgun blast boomed from the street.

Searing lead shot ripped through Fernandez's leathers and burned into his upper back. The Spaniard howled, falling again, convulsing in agony. He had shielded Zec from most of the blast, but the Bosnian still took several pellets to one arm. Zec staggered backward, clutching the wounds.

Nina's police car crashed onto the boardwalk, Boyce leaning from the window with the shotgun in his hands.

"Eat that, you cocksuckers!" he howled, racking the slide.

"Aim higher!" Nina told him. "Don't hit my husband!" The mayor fired again. "Higher! Aim *higher*, idiot!"

Zec hesitated, looking at Fernandez, then dived into the remaining speedboat as another burst of red-hot buckshot seared through the mist. "Go!" he bellowed at the man at the controls.

"But Urbano—"

"There's nothing we can do! Get out of here!"

The boat surged away, huge plumes of froth spraying up from its twin outboards. "Yee-hah!" whooped Boyce, firing again. "Yeah! Run, you bastards! Get the fuck out of my city!"

"Is this what you're like at city council meetings?" Nina braked hard, stopping the police car at the end of the jetty. She jumped out and ran to Eddie. Boyce leapt from the car and kept firing after the departing boat until the shotgun was empty. "Eddie! Are you okay? Eddie!"

He painfully raised his head, trying to smile but managing only a grimace. "Yeah, I'm okay . . . but I've got a fucking huge case of road rash."

"Oh, thank God." She knelt to support him. "What happened to the codex? Did they get away with it?"

"No."

She surveyed the jetty, seeing no sign of the case. "Then where is it?"

He held out a shaking hand and pointed down into the water. "Hope it's rustproof."

Boyce came over, looking at once flustered and exhilarated. "Damn. That was . . . wow. I've never fired a gun before."

"Fun, was it?" Eddie asked.

"Ye— I mean, no, of course not! Guns are a menace to a safe and civil society. Obviously." His expression became sheepish as he forced himself back on message.

More sirens approached, other police cars finally catching up. Officers hurried across the boardwalk, guns drawn. "Mr. Mayor!" one of them shouted. "Are you okay?"

"I'm fine," he said, pointing at the wounded Fernandez. "Arrest this man—he's one of the gang who just robbed the Atlantis exhibition and killed several people, including two police officers. And his associates just left this dock in a speedboat—get units after them immediately." He indicated Eddie. "This man also needs medical attention. No, don't arrest him!" he added as the cop took out a set of handcuffs.

"Do I look like a bad guy or something?" Eddie complained.

"You've looked better," Nina told him, before addressing Boyce. "Mr. Mayor, we need divers here as soon as possible. The artifact they stole is in the water."

"You heard her," said Boyce, nodding.

"Yes, sir." The cop raised his radio, then gave him a questioning look. "Uh, Mr. Mayor?"

"What?"

"The shotgun, sir?"

"Oh. Right." Boyce hurriedly handed him the empty weapon. The cop took it and barked instructions into his radio. Nearby, Fernandez let out a choked moan as two other officers roughly pulled him to his feet and cuffed his hands behind his back; a suspected cop-killer would not get kid glove treatment in even the most liberal city.

Another siren sounded in the distance, a different wail— an ambulance. "Okay, let's get you to a hospital," Nina said to Eddie, standing. "And then I can see how Rowan's doing."

"Typical," Eddie snorted, forcing himself to his feet. "You're more worried about your ex-boyfriend."

"Hey, I did mention you first..."

He managed a half smile, then became more serious. "How is he? I didn't see what happened after he got shot."

"One of the guests was a doctor. He thought Rowan might have a punctured lung, but seemed to think he'd be okay."

"Good." The ambulance came into sight, strobe lights pulsing. Eddie watched it approach, gingerly feeling the torn backside of his trousers. "Hope they've got a pair of tweezers, " 'cause I've got an arse full of splinters!"

Nina grinned and patted him lightly on the butt, getting an annoyed grunt in response, then helped him to the ambulance.

* * *

Eddie's injuries fortunately turned out to be comparatively minor, a collection of cuts, grazes, and bruises that looked far worse than they actually were. Once assured that he would be all right, Nina left him to be patched up in the emergency room while she went in search of Rowan Sharpe.

He had been taken to an operating theater so his gunshot wound could be treated. She couldn't help but be worried, but the nurse's assurance that he had been stable and conscious when he was moved out of the ER assuaged her concerns a little.

The route from the ER to the surgical waiting area took her past the hospital's main entrance—and its gift shop. Remembering her promise to Rowan, she smiled and popped in to make a purchase before continuing on her way.

A familiar face was already in the waiting area: the doctor who had provided first aid at the exhibition center. "What's happening with Rowan?" asked Nina after they had exchanged brief greetings. "How long has he been in there?"

"About thirty minutes," said the doctor. "The bullet wound was a through-and-through, fortunately—clean entry and exit. He was very lucky, actually. It only scraped his lung. Another inch to the side..."

Nina shuddered, not wanting to think about it. "But he'll be okay?"

"His chances are good, I'd say. There was a fair amount of muscle damage, though, so he'll be in pain for some time."

"I know how that feels," said Nina, absently touching her right thigh, where she had once received a bullet wound of her own. The doctor continued describing Rowan's good fortune at having avoided significant damage to any major organs, but she was now only half listening. The main thing was that he would be all right.

After twenty minutes, the doors to the operating theater opened and Rowan, lying on a gurney, was wheeled out. At first Nina thought he was unconscious, but as he passed his eyes flickered open and met hers. One eye closed again... in a wink. "Thank God," she whispered.

About ten minutes later, a nurse came to find her. "Dr. Wilde? Dr. Sharpe is asking for you."

Nina jumped up and followed the woman to a recovery room. Rowan lay in a bed, a pale, fragile figure hooked up to wires and tubes. A monitor beside the bed silently recorded the slow pulses of his heartbeat. "Rowan? How are you feeling?" She felt almost embarrassed at asking such a dumb question, but it was all she could think of.

"Hey, Nina." His voice was little more than a whisper behind a transparent oxygen mask. "So that's what getting shot feels like? You didn't tell me it hurt so much."

"Can I touch him?" Nina asked the nurse, getting a nod in reply. "Jerk," she said, rapping his knuckles. "God, I was so worried about you."

"So was I!" He tried to laugh, which turned into a cough. The nurse gave them both a scolding look, and checked the monitor before leaving the room. "What about the codex?"

"They didn't take it," Nina said, tactfully deciding not to concern him with the news that it was currently on the bottom of San Francisco Bay. "Eddie stopped them."

"Great. I think you've...found quite a good husband. Obviously not the best you *could* have done, but..."

"Oh, stop it."

He smiled, then turned his head slightly to look down at her neck, weakly raising one hand to indicate her pendant. "Just goes to show that thing...really does bring you good luck."

"Seems like I need a lot of it."

"I'm just glad some of...your luck rubbed off on me tonight." His gaze moved down to her hands. "Did you... bring me something?"

Nina held up a bag of chocolates. "Dark. I remembered. Wouldn't want to give you hives."

"Yeah, as if I don't...have enough to worry about!" Another smile—then he frowned sharply.

"Are you okay?" Nina asked. "Shall I get the nurse?"

"No, I'm fine, just...a headache. Think I took a knock when I fell down. Didn't notice at the time because of the whole...getting shot thing..." Another twinge, more pronounced. "Ow, jeez. That really is...one hell of a headache. Got any Tylenol?"

The peaks on the heart monitor were closer together, rising higher. "I'm getting the nurse," Nina said, worried.

"No, I'm okay, I—*nghh*!" His whole face twisted, body flinching. An alarm trilled on the monitor, Rowan's heartbeats no longer silent as the machine recognized dangerous activity.

Nina jumped up and threw open the door. "Hey! I need help in here, quick!"

A doctor and a nurse ran in, the nurse checking the readings on the monitoring equipment while the doctor examined his patient. "It's not his breathing," the nurse reported.

"Pupils are dilated, left eyelid drooping...," muttered the doctor, shining a penlight into Rowan's eyes. "Dammit! We need to get him back to the OR, right now—get Dr. Kyanka down here."

"What's happening?" Nina asked desperately as the nurse hurried to the room's phone. "I thought he was all right!"

"He was. We treated the gunshot wound—this is something else, looks like a cerebral aneurysm."

"What? Oh, my God!"

The nurse slammed down the phone. "Dr. Kyanka's on his way." Another nurse burst into the room to help her move the patient.

Nina watched, helpless, as the pain-stricken Rowan was rushed away. "Help him, please!"

"We'll do what we can," said the doctor as he charged after them down the corridor. But his grim expression filled Nina with terror.

* * *

Bandaged, limping slightly on a stiff leg, Eddie made his way through the hospital. He was mildly irked that Nina hadn't returned to the ER; Rowan's injuries were far more severe than his own, yes, but a bit more support from his wife would have been nice.

He arrived at a small waiting area and saw Nina hunched in a chair. "There you are!" he called. "So you'd rather hang about waiting for your ex-boyfriend than watch your husband have splinters tweezed out of his arse..."

He trailed off as she looked up at him, eyes red and puffy, cheeks streaked with tears. There was only one possible cause for her distress. "Oh, shit," he said, quickly sitting beside her and holding her hands. "Are you okay? Is Rowan..."

"He—he didn't make it," she said, throat raw. "He was

okay, they treated the bullet wound, but then he, uh..."
Her voice began to quaver. "He had a ... burst blood vessel
in—in his brain..." She broke down, sobbing.

"I'm sorry," said Eddie, knowing all too well what it
was like to lose a friend. He wrapped his arms protectively
around her and held her close as she wept.

6

New York City

The recovered Talonor Codex rested on Nina's desk. Around it lay dozens of photographs and page upon page of printouts—the IHA's reference images and translations of the ancient document.

None of them were helping. Nina had gone through the translations twice already that morning, but even as she began a third reading she suspected it would prove equally unenlightening. Talonor had been methodical in the accounts of his travels ... meaning the sheer amount of information was overpowering. How could she pick out what she was looking for in a journal that spanned three continents?

But no matter how much she tried to focus her mind on her task, no matter how many times she re-read the ancient text, she was unable to escape a constant, gnawing guilt. She knew that she was using work as a way to avoid thinking about the events in San Francisco, the analytical part of her mind attempting to box up and shut away the emotional. But the attempt was doomed to failure. The codex itself was a reminder, a *symbol* of her loss. Rowan Sharpe had died because of it.

That thought tore open the box. Its contents flooded her mind, memories of Rowan from throughout her life. As a colleague, as a friend...as a lover. But the one that hit her the hardest was the image of him with her parents when she was a teenager with a puppy-dog crush, all of them working together to solve the riddle of Atlantis.

That riddle had taken the lives of her parents. And now, fourteen years later, even though she had solved it...it had taken Rowan too.

Her eyes stung with tears.

Eddie entered the office, walking rather stiffly. "Ay up," he said in casual greeting—then he read her expression, his own filling with concern. "You all right?"

"No," she admitted, trying and failing to hold back a sob as she wiped her eyes. He crouched beside her, putting an arm over her shoulders. "Oh, God, Eddie. Rowan's dead, and it's all my fault..."

"It's *not* your fault," Eddie said firmly. "Why d'you say that?"

"Because...because I brought him into all this. I hired him to be in charge of the exhibition. If it hadn't been for me, he'd still be alive..." She broke down, hands to her face to cover her grief and shame.

"Nina, look at me. *Look*." He slowly pulled her hands down so he could meet her eyes. "I know I got a little bit jealous of Rowan, but it wasn't serious. He was a good guy. But you didn't kill him, okay? You have to tell yourself that. It was like..." He paused, recalling the impact of a loss of his own a year and a half earlier. "Like when Mitzi died when we were looking for Excalibur. I blamed myself for that when it happened. You remember?"

"Yeah."

"But...but I realized as time went on that *I didn't kill her*. Just because she was there with me didn't make it my fault that she died—I didn't pull the trigger. And I know this'll sound harsh and horrible right now, but it's the same for you. You didn't kill Rowan. And you didn't *get* him killed either."

"But he would be all right if—"

"You *didn't*," he repeated, more forcefully. "Okay? And they arrested the guy who did. They've got him. He did it, not you. Don't blame yourself for it. That's what I did with Mitzi, and . . . well, you remember. Things went bad for a while. I don't want you to have to go through the same thing that I did."

"I can't help it," she said. "And . . . and I know I should talk to his father, tell him what happened, but . . . I can't face it. The hospital told him, he knows that Rowan's dead, but . . ." Tears rolled down her cheeks, her voice dropping to a whisper. "What if he blames me? If *I* think it's my fault, what if he does too?"

Eddie held her more closely as she buried her face against his shoulder. "Hey, hey," he said, stroking her hair. "He won't blame you, because you didn't do anything wrong."

"I . . . You're right, I know. I know that, in my head. But I don't *feel* that."

"It's tough, I know. Believe me, I bloody know that! But you'll get through it, and you'll stop blaming yourself. I know that too. Look, you don't have to do anything right now. You should go home."

Nina lifted her head and wiped her eyes again. "No . . . no, I'd rather keep working. An Interpol officer's coming in to see me later. If I can figure out why the raiders wanted to take the codex rather than anything else, it might help them find out who was behind the robbery—and the thefts of all those other treasures." She sat upright, taking a long breath as she forced herself back into a business-like mind-set. "I'll be okay."

"You sure?"

A halfhearted smile. "As much as I can be."

"That's my girl." Eddie kissed her, then stood and

stepped back to regard the contents of her desk. "So what have you worked out so far? Sussed it all out yet?"

"Not yet," she said with a sigh. "Maybe I should have taken that guy Khoil up on his offer to translate it."

"So what have you got?"

"Mostly that as an explorer, Talonor's a name that should be up there with Columbus and Cook and Marco Polo. The codex only covers one of his expeditions, but we know that he visited South America as well—he discovered the site that would become the Atlantean settlement we found there. There might have been other expeditions too; we just haven't found his accounts yet."

Eddie flicked through a few pages. "Is the translation accurate?"

"As far as we know. Why?"

"Just that I recognize the way it's written. It's like a military report, a tactical assessment—just the facts, ma'am. When he reaches somewhere, all he says about it is how many men old enough to fight live there, what the landscape's like, and where the high ground is, that kind of stuff. This Talonor bloke wasn't an explorer—he was a scout."

"The Atlanteans were conquerors," Nina reminded him. "I suppose knowing a potential target's strength was more important than their cultural heritage." She remembered something and searched through the papers. "Although... here. He took more of an interest than usual in one group of people."

"Which ones?"

"Some Hindu priests. He met them in the Himalayas when he was traveling up the Ganges. Afterward, he carried on about a hundred miles northeast into Tibet and discovered the Golden Peak—the other major Atlantean site."

"Yeah, we had a lot of fun there, didn't we?" said Eddie,

with a hint of sarcasm. "So what about these priests? Were there Hindus around that long ago?"

"Hinduism's been around for a long time—much longer than any of the Abrahamic religions. Even before we found the codex and confirmed from this"—she opened the codex to the pages that had been on display in San Francisco and indicated the section of Vedic Sanskrit text— "that the ancient Hindus were contemporaries of the Atlanteans, there was evidence that the religion existed at least as far back as three thousand BC. And the epic Hindu texts described a civilization that went back even farther."

"They weren't talking about the Veteres, were they?"

"I don't know." Nina gave him a slightly pained look at the mention of the long-dead race she had unearthed a year earlier. "But let's not go shouting about the possibility, huh? We already had fanatics from three religions trying to kill us over it—I don't want to add a fourth."

"I'll keep it to myself," he assured her. "What did Talonor say about 'em, then?"

Nina read from the translation. "It says, 'We were guided away from the river at latitude one north'—that's using the Atlantean scale, obviously—'to a great temple. Though the inhabitants were not hostile, they were well prepared to defend their holy mountain...' He goes on about how hard it would be to mount an assault because of the terrain, so you were right—it's a tactical report. Anyway, 'The priest granted me the honor of entrance, where he showed me an image of their god—whom I recognized as the great Poseidon from the trident he held, though these men know him by a different name.' Then he wonders if these people are cousins of the Atlanteans with a common mythology—which is actually an interesting theory. I might have to look into that..." She trailed off, musing over the idea.

Eddie whistled sharply and tapped the codex. "One thing at a time, love."

"Right, sorry. Where was I? 'The priest was intrigued by my thoughts. He told me the knowledge of Poseidon might contain an answer, but because the texts were kept elsewhere for protection, I would have to wait to see them. When I asked how long, the priest said it would take one day for his acolytes to reach the sacred vault, but only one hour to return. When I asked how this was possible, he smiled and told me Poseidon had many secrets.' "

"What, did they teleport or something?"

"No idea." Nina flicked through the translation. "But yeah, Talonor decided to stay, and a day later they came back with some stone tablets—which were written in Vedic Sanskrit." She indicated the text inscribed on the orichalcum sheet. "This section here is a copy of part of Poseidon's knowledge...wait a minute!" She snapped her fingers as disparate elements suddenly meshed together perfectly in her mind. "I'm a dumb-ass. Why didn't I realize it before? It's not Poseidon at all. It's *Shiva*. He's often depicted using a trident as a weapon."

"Shiva?" Eddie asked.

"One of the Hindu gods."

"I know *that*. I meant, which one? What's his gig?"

"Oh, nothing much," said Nina. "Just the Destroyer of Worlds."

He frowned. "So he's a bad guy?"

"No, not at all. Hinduism's based around the idea of cycles, everything going through a never-ending process of birth, life, death, rebirth—even the entire universe. Shiva's the god who ends each cycle through an act of destruction...but by doing that, he enables the next cycle to be created. He's one of the most important figures in Hindu mythology. We translated it as Poseidon because Talonor was imposing his own beliefs on another culture—typical Atlantean arrogance. So when he described the priest talking about the knowledge of Poseidon, what he really meant was the knowledge of Shiva. And in Vedic Sanskrit, the word for knowledge is *veda*—but *veda* has another meaning. The Vedas are some of the oldest Hindu sacred texts, dating back to at least-fifteen hundred BC—but these... Shiva-Vedas would be much older. And they were kept in this vault...the Vault of Shiva."

Eddie turned to the next page of the codex, on which was scribed more Vedic Sanskrit text before it reverted to the Atlantean language. "What does the rest of this say?"

Nina checked another sheet. "It's mostly about the cycles of existence. Destruction and creation. Talonor must have liked the idea." She went back to the transcript of the Atlantean text. "The priest also showed him the key to the Vault of Shiva—which is this thing, right here." Closing the codex, she indicated the impression in the orichalcum cover.

Eddie looked closely at the indentation. The width of a spread hand, it had at its center an ornate relief of a man's face, lips curled in an enigmatic smile. Five smaller faces encircled him, all female. "The priests must've been pretty trusting to let him stamp a copy of their key. What if he'd decided to rob the place?"

"According to the text, they said that even if he found the vault, he'd never get in, because 'only those who know the love of Shiva' can use the key," Nina told him. "They seemed very sure of that."

"They'd have been a bit less cocky if dynamite had been invented back then. Who are the women?"

"Goddesses. Shiva's wives, I suppose."

"He had five wives? Thought he was a Hindu, not a Mormon."

"He didn't have them all at the same time." Nina indicated two of the faces. "I don't know off the top of my head who they all are, but these are Shakti, the goddess of feminine power, and Kali, goddess of death."

"Oh, I know who Kali is," said Eddie, grinning. "From *Indiana Jones and the Temple of Doom*, right?"

Nina winced. "Yes, but if you're ever talking to a devout Hindu, please don't say that! I was once talking to an Indian scholar about the portrayal of archaeology in the media and mentioned Indiana Jones, and he wasn't happy. Kali's not a goddess you'd want to get on the wrong side of, but she's definitely not evil either, and he was kinda pissed that the first things a lot of Americans think of in regard to his religion are human sacrifice and chilled monkey brains." The phone rang.

It was Lola. "Dr. Wilde? The Interpol officer you were expecting is here."

"Oh, good. Show him through, please."

Lola entered, followed by a tall man in a pale blue suit. "Dr. Wilde? This is Mr. Jindal."

"Hi, come in," said Nina, standing to greet him. As she had expected from his surname, the international police agent was Indian; mid-thirties, with angular yet handsome features and black hair styled almost into a quiff. "I'm Nina Wilde; this is my husband, Eddie Chase."

"Ankit Jindal, Interpol senior investigator," said the new arrival, shaking their hands and giving them a beaming white smile. "Pleased to meet you." Unlike that of the respectively robotic and uptight Pramesh and Vanita Khoil they had met two days earlier, his accent, while still distinctly Indian, was relaxed and warm.

"I won't mention Indiana Jones," Eddie whispered to Nina, who held in a faint grin.

Jindal looked at the artifact on Nina's desk. "The Talonor Codex?"

"That's it," she said.

He nodded appreciatively. "I'm glad it survived unharmed. I can't say that about all the treasures the Cultural Property Crime Unit recovers."

"So how can we help you, Mr. Jindal?"

"The first thing I wanted to do was give you some good news in person: We've identified the leader of the raiders. Urbano Luis Fernandez, Spanish, former member of the Grupo Especial de Operaciones—the Spanish police's special operations unit."

"Pretty big career change," said Eddie.

"It's how he evaded capture for so long—he knows all the tricks. But we have him now, thanks to you."

"So what's going to happen to the son of a bitch?" Nina asked. An uncharacteristic hardness crossed her face. "He can fry as far as I'm concerned."

"He might. Although we don't know where. A lot of diplomacy was needed to persuade the US government to turn him over to Interpol. He's wanted in at least twelve countries, and they all want to put him on trial for the theft of their cultural treasures—and the murders of the people they killed taking them."

"I can imagine. Michelangelo's *David* versus the terracotta warriors? The Italians and Chinese must be practically at daggers drawn over who gets their hands on him first, for a start."

"More than that. This has to remain classified," Jindal said, giving them both warning looks, "but there have been other robberies that haven't been revealed to the public—either because it would be politically embarrassing, or because it could actually be dangerous. One of the stolen items is the Black Stone from Mecca. The Saudis have replaced it with a replica, but if that is discovered there'll be chaos."

"You're not kidding," said Nina, shocked.

"The what?" Eddie asked.

"The Black Stone was supposedly put in place in the Kaaba Temple by Muhammad himself," she explained.

"It's a key part of the hajj, the Islamic pilgrimage—if it's revealed as a fake, the entire country will explode."

"Just what we need in the Middle East right now."

"Which is why we're trying as hard as we can to get Fernandez to name his employer, so all the stolen treasures can be found and returned," said Jindal. "But he's not talking. Which is another reason I wanted to see you—you might be able to help us. More specifically, Mr. Chase might."

"Me?" said Eddie. "How?"

Jindal took documents from his briefcase and laid them on Nina's desk. Each had a photograph attached. "These are three of the raiders who were killed in San Francisco. They're all different nationalities: Nicaraguan, Ukrainian, Portuguese. But what they have in common is that they are all known mercenaries."

"Mercenaries, eh?" Eddie took a closer look at the photos, but didn't recognize any of the faces. He glanced sidelong at Jindal. "Been reading up on me, have you?"

The Indian smiled. "I hope you're not offended."

"Nah, it's just that it's been a while since I was in that line of work. And I never really thought of myself as a merc. More like a troubleshooter."

"Oh, yeah," said Nina. "You see trouble, you shoot it."

"Hey, you weren't complaining at the time! So, who are these guys?"

Jindal tapped on each picture in turn. "Ramon Maltez Espinosa; Gennadi Sklar—"

"Sklar?" Eddie interrupted.

"You know him?"

"Never met him, but I know the name. Worked in Africa, mostly...Harare, that's where I heard about him."

"You were in Zimbabwe?" Nina asked. However much she thought she knew about her husband's past travels, he still always had the ability to surprise her.

"About six years ago," Eddie told her. "Don't plan on

going back—I'm not popular there. But this bloke Sklar, that's where I know his name from."

"Small world."

"You get to know most of the people in the business after a while. The professionals, at least—the ones who're good enough not to get killed." He turned to Jindal. "This Fernandez, for jobs like the ones he's been pulling, he'd be after the absolute best people he could get. And there's not that many middlemen he could go through to find 'em."

"I doubt they'd be willing to talk to Interpol, though," said Jindal.

"Maybe not, but they might talk to me. Somebody'll know something—maybe even who's paying Fernandez. And I wouldn't even need to go to them—just thinking that I could might be enough to get Fernandez to open up."

Jindal considered it. "We've been trying to work out a deal, but so far he's refused everything. Perhaps a stick to go with the carrot might encourage him to talk..." Another moment of thought. "Would you be willing to fly back to Lyon with me? Not just for this—your firsthand account of events, and any help you could give us concerning Fernandez's mercenary connections, would be very useful. But if we can't persuade him to accept a deal, then perhaps a threat would be more effective. Not a physical threat," he hurriedly added.

Eddie grinned. "Never crossed my mind. But I'm up for it." He turned to Nina. "That's if you're okay with it. If you don't want to be on your own..."

She took a moment to reply. "I'll be okay. Especially if your going helps nail this bastard."

"Are you sure?"

"Positive," she insisted. "If it leads to catching whoever's behind this, I'm all for it."

"Excellent," said Jindal, nodding. "I'll arrange the flight." He looked at the ancient volume again. "As for the codex itself...have you found any reason why whoever was paying Fernandez wanted him to steal it?"

"I think I might have," said Nina. She explained her deduction about the link between the Atlantean god Poseidon and the Hindu god Shiva, opening the codex to the pages that had been on display to illustrate her point. "If this Vault of Shiva still exists, then its contents would be an incredible archaeological find."

"Big enough to kill for?" Eddie asked.

Jindal looked thoughtfully at the ancient words. "The Vedic Sanskrit text, the Indian connection, was one of the reasons why I pushed to get this assignment. There is a big black market for ancient Hindu artifacts—and yes, people are willing to kill for them, unfortunately. But this would be on a much larger scale than anything I've dealt with before."

"How long have you been with Interpol?" Nina asked.

"About three years. I used to be a detective with the Delhi police—finding art thieves was my specialty, and since a lot of cases involved international trafficking it made sense to transfer to Interpol when the opportunity arose."

"Sounds like a cool job," said Eddie. "Travel, busting bad guys, recovering stolen treasures..."

"It has its moments—though I don't think it compares to what you do." He noticed the display case. "Is that the Egyptian artifact?"

"You know about it?" Nina asked, slightly surprised that he was aware of the small purple figurine.

"Yes—the Egyptians asked to check Interpol's database to see if it matched anything stolen or recovered. It didn't, so I suppose they then gave it to the IHA in the hope that you'd be able to identify it."

"No luck so far," Nina admitted. "But we'll keep on trying—at least until the Egyptians get fed up with waiting and ask for it back!"

The three shared a small laugh, then Jindal gathered up his documents. "Thank you for your help, Dr. Wilde. And Mr. Chase, I'll call you as soon as I confirm the flight." He said his good-byes to the couple, then departed.

"Better go home and pack my toothbrush," said Eddie.

"Do you think you'll be able to get this Fernandez to talk?" Nina asked.

A cat-like grin. "If they give me five minutes with just me, him, and something sharp."

"I doubt Interpol would approve... but in this case, I wouldn't be opposed." She carefully nestled the codex into the padding inside a large steel case and closed it. "But until we actually find out who's behind the robberies, we need to keep this safe. Can you carry it for me?"

"Half the time I think you only married me to have someone to lug heavy objects about," Eddie said in jocular complaint as he picked up the box—whereupon his tone became genuine. "Ow! Bloody hell."

"Are you okay?"

"Yeah, fine." He put a hand to his ribs. "Bit of a twinge, that's all."

"There are some painkillers in my desk."

"No, I'm okay," he insisted. "Just that my side feels like someone's sandpapered it."

"It looked like it too. Sure you're all right? I can get someone else to take it to the vault."

"Nah, I've got it." He hoisted the case again. "Although I bet librarians were bloody glad when someone got the idea to make books out of paper rather than metal."

They took an elevator down to the Secretariat Building's lowest basement level. Most of the floor was occupied by a data center, computer servers handling the terabytes of information flowing through the UN, but their destination involved a more physical form of storage.

A familiar face was at the entrance. "Hey, Lola," said Nina, seeing her assistant chatting to one of the guards at the security station, a tall young Haitian called Henri Vernio.

"Oh! Nina, hi." Lola blushed, as if she had been caught in the act; Nina wondered if she was dating the man. She indicated a little cart stacked with folders. "I was just getting these for you."

"Thanks," said Nina, teasingly adding: "No rush."

"I was, ah, on my way back upstairs anyway," Lola said, giving the disappointed guard a quick good-bye before scurrying off with the cart.

Nina smiled, then turned to the other guard, Lou Jablonsky, an overweight Brooklynite ex-cop. "We're putting the Talonor Codex back in the vault."

"Sure thing, Dr. Wilde," said Jablonsky. He began to enter their details into his computer. "Hey, Eddie. You okay? Lola told us you got pretty banged up in Frisco."

"Yeah, I'm fine," Eddie replied. "Except it looks like someone used a cheese grater on my arse."

Jablonsky grinned. "Some weirdos pay good money for that. Okay, if you'll follow me..."

The high-security vault was only one part of the secure archive; most of the space was occupied by labyrinthine ranks of lockers and filing drawers, with a reading area in one corner where researchers could examine classified material without the extra bureaucratic hassle required to remove it from the room. Cameras on the ceiling watched every square foot of the climate-controlled chamber. The entrance to the vault itself was a large stainless-steel door in direct line of sight of the security station. Jablonsky inserted a keycard into a slot on the door and looked back at Vernio, who put a card of his own into another reader and entered a command on the computer.

A warbling alarm warned anyone near the vault to stand back as the thick door unlocked and swung slowly open. Nina waited until Jablonsky gave her a nod, then went inside, Eddie carrying the case in after her. The interior was a cramped circular room, the wall lined with more steel-doored lockers of various sizes. A computer terminal was set into a small pedestal-like desk at the center, the screen displaying the combined weights to the gram of the visitors and what they carried: the floor around it was pressure-sensitive, another security system to ensure nothing was smuggled out. "Christ," Eddie said, looking up at the ventilation grille in the ceiling. "It's always so bloody cold in here."

"It's nice in the summer, though," Nina reminded him. She sat at the desk and entered her security code. A panel on the desktop lit up, and she placed her right hand flat on it. A brighter line of light moved down the panel's length—a palm-print scanner. A red LED above the handle of one of the largest lockers turned green.

Eddie slid the case inside, then closed the door. The LED went back to red. "Okay, sorted." Jablonsky, who had been watching from the entrance, waited until the visitors left the vault, then removed his card. More warning trills, and the door closed. Eddie gave the barrier a satisfied look. "Let's see anyone break into *that*."

"Hopefully nobody'll be trying," said Nina as they returned to the security station and signed out. "Well, if you're jetting off to France, I think I'll take some work home for the evening. See if I can figure out anything else from those translations."

"And people say you don't know how to live it up."

Nina narrowed her eyes. "Who says that?"

"Not me," he replied quickly.

They entered the lift. Eddie reached up to push the button for the IHA's floor—and barely held in a pained grunt. He rolled his shoulder, trying to knead out the stab of pain in one of the muscles. "Fuck."

"Are you really sure you're all right?" Nina asked. "If you don't feel up to traveling—"

"Course I'm up to it," he said sharply. "It's not like I'm crippled. I've had worse."

"And are you sure you don't want any painkillers?"

Eddie hesitated before replying. "Yeah, I'm fine. More or less." He gingerly touched a particularly sore spot on his backside. "Might need an extra cushion for the flight, though."

7
France

"Has he said anything?" Nina asked.

"Not so far," Eddie told her. They were on opposite ends of a transatlantic call, she at the United Nations in New York, he in Jindal's office at Interpol's headquarters in Lyon. He was tired, from both a day spent working with the investigators and jet lag, but hopefully the prisoner he was about to see would be more exhausted—and therefore likely to let something slip in the next round of questioning. "Kit's going to let me watch the next interrogation in a few minutes."

"Kit?"

"Jindal. Short for Ankit."

Her voice became teasing. "Oh, you're on first-name terms already? That's so sweet!"

"We were on an eight-hour flight, and you know me, I can't keep my gob shut for eight *minutes*. Anyway, I'll be watching from behind the glass, just like in a cop show. They're going to try to make a deal so he'll give up whoever hired him—we'll see what he says."

"A deal. God." Anger entered her voice. "I wish there were some other way."

"So do I. I don't want that bastard to walk free any more than you do. But it might be the only way to recover all the stuff he stole."

"I suppose...," she admitted reluctantly.

"At least we don't have to worry about him nicking the codex anymore." He looked around as Kit entered and gestured for him to follow. "Got to go—they're about to start."

"Okay," said Nina. "See you soon. Love you."

"Love you too. Bye." He disconnected and followed Kit from the room. "Don't suppose he's cracked already, has he?"

The Indian shook his head. "I'm afraid not. But our lawyers have come up with an offer, so we'll see if he takes it." They reached the elevators, then rode up to the Interpol building's seventh floor. A steel-barred security gate was opened for them once their identities had been confirmed by a guard, and they entered the interrogation area.

Kit led Eddie into a darkened room. A lanky female officer in her forties was checking a video camera. "Eddie, this is Renée Beauchamp," said Kit. "She'll be conducting the interrogation with me."

Eddie shook her hand. "Good cop, bad cop, eh?"

"We are both good cops," she said with a small smile as she gave a folder to Kit. "This is the agreement—it's as we discussed. All he has to do is sign it."

"What're you offering him?"

"In exchange for testifying against his employer, and providing all the stolen treasures are safely returned, he will get reduced charges and trial in only a single country—of his choosing. Since the Chinese have said he will get the death penalty for stealing the terra-cotta warriors, and the Saudis would almost certainly have him secretly executed to cover up the theft of the Black Stone, I think he will respond favorably."

Eddie regarded the interrogation room's occupant

through the two-way mirror. Fernandez, though bruised and with his hands cuffed behind his back, didn't seem worried. If anything, he appeared almost smug. "Find out in a minute, I suppose."

Eddie sat and looked on as the two Interpol officers entered the interrogation room, uncuffing Fernandez before facing him across a table. The Frenchwoman spoke first, explaining the terms of the deal. Fernandez sat in silence until she finished, a smirk curling the corners of his mouth.

"Thank you for that," he said at last, "but now, here is *my* offer. In return for total immunity from prosecution, signed by every country in which I am *alleged*"—the smirk widened—"to have committed these crimes, and also being granted a new identity and witness protection in a country of my choosing, I will give you the name of those who I *believe*"—he raised a finger theatrically—"are in possession of the missing treasures. Until I get that, I have nothing more to say."

"You seriously expect us to arrange full immunity?" asked Kit.

"As I said, I have nothing more to say." Both cops shot more questions at him, but his only response was a self-satisfied silence. After a few fruitless minutes, they gave up, handcuffing him back to the chair before returning to the observation room.

"Well," said Kit, "that didn't go as well as I hoped."

Beauchamp sighed. "The arrogance of the man! How can he not see that this is his only chance?"

Kit regarded Fernandez through the mirror. "He must be very scared of his employer to make such big demands in return for giving him up."

"Is Interpol likely to meet them?" asked Eddie.

"It's not really up to us. It depends how desperate the countries involved are to get back their national treasures. Even the Saudis might agree to his terms if they can recover the Black Stone without anyone knowing it was stolen."

Eddie looked at the prisoner for a long moment. "I've got an idea," he said at last. "I'll need to go in there, though. Alone."

"I am not sure that would be wise," said Beauchamp doubtfully.

"I won't lay a finger on him, if that's what you're worried about. Honest!" He held up his hands. "I'll just try a different angle. Something he might respond to better."

Kit also appeared unconvinced. "It isn't exactly standard procedure..."

"It isn't exactly a standard case either. Come on, let me try. Worst that can happen is that he tells me to piss off."

The two Interpol officers exchanged looks, then Kit nodded. "All right. But we'll be watching from here."

"I'll try not to block your view with all the blood on the glass. Kidding!" Eddie added as he opened the door.

He went into the neighboring room. Fernandez looked up at him with a flash of recognition, then concern.

"Yeah, it's me again," said Eddie with a cold grin. "Thought I'd pop in for a chat. Maybe finish what I started in San Francisco." He slapped a fist into his open palm, then sat facing the Spaniard across the table.

Fernandez glanced at the mirror. "Not quite standard Interpol procedure."

"I don't work for Interpol."

"So who do you work for?"

"Doesn't really matter. What I'm interested in is, who do *you* work for? See, when someone tries to kill me *and* my wife, I take it personally. Not very professional, I know, but I'm an emotional sort of bloke. And you really don't want me to be pissed off at you."

"Professional?" said Fernandez, raising an eyebrow. "You're not a cop, and you don't seem the intelligence type, so...a mercenary?"

"Ex. Settled down now."

A faint smile. "You never really leave. However hard

you try, if you are a natural fighter, you always get pulled back in. And I can tell you are a natural fighter. What is your name, by the way? I prefer to know who I am being threatened by."

"Chase. Eddie Chase."

Another flick of an eyebrow, this time at a memory. "Chase...Algeria, yes? About seven years ago? You blew up the warehouse of Fekkesh, the arms dealer."

"Might have done."

"And Fekkesh himself did not fare much better. I heard that he lost his—"

"I'm not here to talk about me," Eddie interrupted sharply, deciding Interpol didn't need to hear the details of a mission that, while justified, had not been entirely legal. "Let's talk about you. And your dead mates. Especially Gennadi Sklar. Used to work out of Zimbabwe, didn't he?"

The tiniest twitch of Fernandez's eyes revealed his unease that Eddie knew the background of his late associate. "He worked from many places," he said dismissively, trying to cover the fact. "It is part of the job, as you know."

"But he *mostly* worked from Zimbabwe. Which means he would have been getting jobs through Strutter. Been a while since I've seen him, but I'm sure he'd remember me. Now, I don't like Harare, it's a shithole, and Strutter's a scumbag, but if I had a couple of drinks with him I bet I could catch up on the grapevine very quickly. Who's where, doing what...and for who."

Fernandez's discomfort was now far more evident. "Everybody knows something," Eddie pressed on, "and they'll tell me stuff that a cop'd never find out. I might have been out of it for a while, but I'm still part of that world— and it's a small world. Lots of little bits of information floating about...all I've got to do is put them together, and I'll know who hired you."

"Nobody will ever tell you that," Fernandez insisted, but perspiration had started to bead on his thin mustache.

"I dunno, I can be pretty persuasive." He leaned forward, gaze hard. "If I find out who your boss is, then any deal Interpol's offering you goes straight out of the window. They won't need you anymore. And then you, mate, will be fucked. You want to go on trial in China? Or Saudi Arabia? Hell, you killed two cops in California—they've still got the death penalty there." He stood. "If I were you, I'd think about it. But do it quick. I've got a plane to catch."

He left, returning to the observation room. The two investigators were waiting for him, both seeming impressed. "Could you really find out who hired Sklar in Zimbabwe?" Kit asked.

"In theory," said Eddie awkwardly. "Only I wouldn't be the best person to send, 'cause, er...I've got a death sentence on me there."

"What?" said Beauchamp, shocked.

"Yeah. A while back I helped some people who were high on the government's shit list get out of the country. Only problem was, it got me added to the list as well. So I don't really want to go back there."

"I can see why," Kit said. "But hopefully, you won't need to." He gestured toward the prisoner. "Fernandez definitely seems to be considering what you said."

"Then we should let him sweat for a while," Beauchamp said. "Very good work, Mr. Chase." She turned to Kit. "I will brief the director. You look tired—both of you do. You should get some rest."

"It's been a long day," Eddie agreed. He checked his watch, finding that it was after nine o'clock at night. He stifled a yawn. "Think I'd better get to the hotel."

"I'll show you out," said Kit. All three exited the observation room, then the two men made their farewells to Beauchamp and headed for the elevators.

As they approached the security gate, their attention was caught by a uniformed female officer on the other side.

Eddie guessed she was Indian, her black hair held up in a severe bun. She seemed to be having trouble, inserting her ID card twice before the system recognized it. The guard opened the gate and she marched through, not giving Eddie or Kit the slightest look. The reverse wasn't true, both men turning their heads to track the attractive, if stone-faced, officer as she passed.

"Hey," said Kit, "you're married."

Eddie shrugged jokingly. "Can't be sued for looking."

"Would you say that if Nina were here?"

"Yeah, probably. It's fun winding her up." They went through the gate. "Oh, I left my jacket in your office."

"No problem." Kit pushed a button to summon the elevator.

* * *

Fernandez looked up as the door opened, concealing his surprise at the sight of the new arrival. "I didn't expect you so soon."

Madirakshi Dagdu regarded him impassively with her one good eye, its artificial counterpart cold and glassy. "Have you told them anything?"

He snorted. "Of course not! They've said nothing worth replying to. Asking the same questions over and over, offering their pathetic little deals for my cooperation."

"Which you turned down."

"Obviously. Or I would not be sitting here chained to a chair, would I? Now get me out."

She nodded and moved behind him. "By the way," she said, "before I came in, I checked the next room to make sure it was empty. I saw a video camera."

Disquiet entered his voice. "You switched it off, I hope?" he asked.

"Yes." A faint wet, sucking noise behind him. "And then . . . I watched the recording."

Fernandez suddenly remembered the sound from the apartment in Florence. "No, wait, I only—"

The garrotte wire lashed around his throat and pulled tight.

* * *

Eddie retrieved his leather jacket. "What hotel've you booked me into?"

"The de Ville, across the river. You should see the Festival of Lights while you're here, by the way—there's a big show in the Place des Terreaux. It's only a few minutes from the hotel. Very impressive."

"I'll see how knackered I feel when I get there." He pulled on the jacket, grimacing as his stiff muscles protested at the movement.

"Are you okay, Eddie?" Kit asked.

"Yeah, I will be. Got pretty bashed up, that's all."

The Indian grinned. "Lots of new scars you can use to impress the ladies."

"My lady's seen all my scars already…" He trailed off, the jokey discussion unexpectedly triggering connections in his mind. A scar…

"What is it?"

"That woman who went into the cells while we were coming out—she had a scar on her face."

Kit looked puzzled. "I didn't notice."

"You weren't looking at her face. But I've seen it before…" He frowned, thinking—then his eyes widened. "San Francisco! Shit, she was there just before we were attacked! She was with the Khoils."

"Pramesh Khoil?" asked Kit, surprised. "The Qexia man?"

"You know him?"

"Everyone in India knows him—he's our Bill Gates. Are you sure it was the same woman?"

"Positive—and now she's been in the same place as Fernandez twice." Realization dawned. "She might be trying to bust him out! Come on!"

They ran from the office, hurrying to the elevators. Eddie jabbed repeatedly at the call button before losing his patience and barging open the stairwell door, clattering up the stairs with Kit right behind.

Seventh floor. They raced for the security gate, getting startled looks from Interpol personnel as they ran past. Another frustrating delay as they waited to have their IDs checked, then they rushed to the interrogation room—

The woman had been there, all right—but not to free Fernandez. He was still cuffed to the chair, but now his head lolled horribly, mouth no longer curled in a smirk but gaping in breathless terror. His neck had been sliced open almost from ear to ear, dark blood still flowing from the deep wound.

"Shit!" Eddie gasped, pushing past the startled Kit and running back to the gate. "That woman—black hair, scar down one eye—where is she?"

"She left just before you came back," said the guard, confused. "What's going on?"

"What's going on is that she just strangled one of your fucking prisoners!"

Kit ran up. "I want a full security alert—lock down the building! Nobody gets out until we find this woman. Now let us through!"

"Yes, sir!" The guard hurriedly opened the gate, then picked up a phone to raise the alarm.

"How many ways are there out of here?" Eddie demanded as they pounded back along the corridor.

"The main entrances are on the east and west sides, and then there are the fire exits, the underground car park..."

"She won't be trying to get away on foot." Interpol's headquarters were close to the southern bank of the River Rhône, a nearby lake limiting possible escape routes. They reached the elevators; one had stopped at a basement level.

Eddie hammered at the call buttons again before going for the stairwell.

A siren blared as they reached the third floor. "Lockdown, lockdown," said a man over the PA system. "Security personnel, seal off designated exits. All other personnel, remain where you are." The message was repeated in other languages as they continued their descent.

Basement level. Eddie kicked open the door—to find a uniformed man sprawled in front of the elevators in a pool of blood. The holster on his belt was empty.

"She shot him with his own gun," he told Kit, dropping into concealment behind the parked cars and signaling for him to do the same. "Which way's the exit?" Kit pointed. "Okay, you get more people down here—I'll try and find her."

"Be careful, Eddie," warned Kit on his way to the emergency telephone by the elevators.

"What do you bloody think I'm going to be?" Hunched low, he checked for any signs of movement before scurrying toward the exit. A door slammed, but the echoes of the car park made it impossible to tell where. He weaved through the ranks of vehicles to a concrete ramp leading up to ground level. Yellow-and-black striped barriers blocked both exit lanes.

Still no movement. Maybe she *was* trying to get away on foot, doing the unexpected...

"Eddie!" Kit called. "The guards are on their way!"

The shout spurred their quarry into action. A big Citroën C6 peeled out of a bay and sped toward the exit—then swerved at Eddie.

He dived onto the hood of a Renault Clio as the Citroën ripped off the smaller car's bumper, then crashed into one of the security barriers. The windshield cracked as the obstacle rode up the car's hood, but the C6 had built up enough momentum in its charge to smash through, the broken barrier clanging to the concrete.

Eddie ran back to Kit. An elevator disgorged a trio of armed guards. "We need a car!" he told them. "Someone give me your keys, quick!" One of the men fumbled in a pocket. Eddie snatched the keys from him and pushed the button on the remote. Lights flashed a few rows away. He ran for the vehicle, an aging, dented little Volkswagen Polo—not his ideal choice to pursue a large and powerful executive cruiser, but all that was available.

He started the car and pulled out. By now, Kit had issued orders to the guards and run to the main lane, waving him down. Eddie skidded the hatchback to a stop. "Come on, get in!"

"I don't have a gun!" Kit protested as the Englishman set off again.

"You've got a *phone,* haven't you? Call the Lyon cops and get them to set up roadblocks!"

The car reached the ramp and raced up to ground level. The road curved away from the Interpol building to join a street to its south. Eddie braked hard at the junction, not sure which way to go until he saw flashing hazard lights to the right—the fleeing Citroën had hit another car. He swung past the stricken vehicle and headed southwest, parallel to the river. They passed a bridge over the Rhône, but more signs of collision and chaos told him the C6 had turned south.

Kit shouted instructions in French into the phone. "There's a unit in front of us," he reported. "It's going to cut her off."

Eddie spotted the C6's distinctive vertical taillights carving through the traffic about a hundred yards ahead. The Citroën sideswiped another car, which spun out—he veered onto the wrong side of the road to avoid the scrum of vehicles skidding to a stop behind it.

Flashing lights, a police car shot out of a side road onto the boulevard. Madirakshi braked hard, the C6 fishtailing to duck down another street to the right. The cops followed, Eddie turning in after them. He crashed down through the gears, trying to recover speed as quickly as possible. Ahead, the police car closed on the Citroën.

Vertical brake lights flared—

The cops crashed into the C6's back. Glass shattered, the big car's mangled hatchback flying open—but the pursuers came off worse. The police car veered off course and hit a lamppost head-on, folding around it with a shattering crunch that echoed through the street. Kit gasped what Eddie assumed was a Hindi obscenity.

One of the C6's rear lights was still working, a single red slash speeding away. Eddie followed, sounding the horn. A narrow miss at a crossroads as the Polo swerved wildly to avoid a van cutting across their path, then back in pursuit. The closely packed apartment buildings, candles flickering in their windows, gave way to open space. They were back at the river, multicolored searchlights waving skyward on the far side where the waterfront buildings were illuminated in every color of the rainbow.

Eddie had no time to appreciate the sight. Madirakshi was heading for a bridge. He realized her plan: to disappear among the tourists flocking to see the spectacle of the Festival of Lights.

Another police car tried to block her path across the bridge. She didn't slow, deliberately aiming for its back end and smashing it out of the way. The crumpled police car whirled like a top, spinning onto the pavement and scything down a pedestrian.

Kit gasped again. "People are getting *killed*—we've got to break off!"

"No, wait!" They were gaining quickly on the Citroën; the second crash had caused serious damage. "She's slowing down. We've got her!"

The struggling C6 cut straight across the avenue at the far side of the bridge, more people scattering as the woman drove onto a broad footpath. Horn a constant wail, the

Polo followed in the wake it had cleared through the crowd.

A large plaza opened up ahead, more tourists heading to the city's heart. Two people were knocked down by the Citroën as Madirakshi swerved onto a swath of lawn, but her car was in its death throes, steam billowing from the hood. She braked and skidded in a shower of earth and torn grass, plowing the car into the crowd. Screams filled the plaza.

Eddie stopped the Polo, jumped out, and saw her sprint into the shocked onlookers. He raced after her, Kit following. "Place Louis Pradel, *vite*!" the Indian said into the phone, before yelling "Police!" and gesturing furiously for people to clear the way.

More shouts of protest and alarm as Madirakshi clawed through the crowd told Eddie the direction she was heading. The narrow street he entered was illuminated by a canopy of lights overhead, thousands of tiny bulbs sparkling like stars. He couldn't see his target in the crush of gawkers. If she doubled back, he could pass three feet from her and never realize—

A high-pitched shriek just ahead. She had knocked down a child. An enraged man yelled after her, her police uniform deterring him from violent retaliation. Eddie and Kit pushed past him—but the father grabbed the Interpol officer and yanked him backward. No uniform, no deterrent. The man hurled him to the ground, about to kick him in the face—

Eddie smashed a punch into the furious father's jaw, knocking him down. The fallen child screamed again. No time for apologies. He pulled Kit upright.

Where was the killer? He pushed forward, the street opening out into another large plaza—the Place des Terreaux. Any more yells from irate tourists would be drowned out by the carnival clamor of one of the Festival of Light's main attractions; the square was crammed with people.

Eddie blinked in momentary confusion at the sight, its sheer visual impact like a slap to his eyes. The surrounding buildings were acting as massive projection screens, turning the city into a kaleidoscopic, almost psychedelic explosion of colors. The images were constantly changing, one moment perfectly matching the ornate façades and picking out each window frame in dazzling hyperreal shades, the next swirling into motion as giant animated characters danced above the crowd.

There were other displays within the square itself. A towering sculpture spiraled toward the cold night sky, neon lights blinking in sequence to create the illusion that it was rotating. Next to it a surreal figure, a ten-foot-tall hollow man composed of pea-sized balls of light, performed acrobatic motions above a tall pedestal. A hologram; the constant crackle where intersecting laser beams from below literally set the air alight was audible even over the booming music and crowd noise.

A loud *whoosh* and a cheer came from nearby. Eddie saw flame dispersing from a fire-eating act. No sign of Madirakshi, and the constantly shifting light from the enormous projections made it near impossible to pick out any particular person.

"Do you see her?" Kit asked, catching up.

"No." He spotted a drainpipe on a nearby building and pushed his way to it. Climbing a few feet gave him enough height to see over the surrounding crowd. He scoured the milling heads, searching for anyone in a hurry—

There! Closer than he expected—she had apparently also been taken aback by the spectacle, hesitating at the plaza's entrance before moving diagonally across the square near the fire-eater. Eddie pointed, then jumped down and joined Kit, shoving through the throng after her.

A startled woman yelled in French not far ahead. For a

moment the crowd in Eddie's path parted, giving him a glimpse of the police uniform. He was twenty feet behind her, less. Another *whump* of fire, people instinctively flinching away from the billowing flame as they applauded. Madirakshi changed direction, the retreating wall of people blocking her path.

She was an arm's length away—

Eddie grabbed at her, fingers tugging her sleeve before she twisted away. He elbowed through the crowd after her to find himself in an oval space among the bustle. The fire-eater, a big man in Arabic-style clothing, looked around in surprise, a burning torch halfway to his mouth. The woman glared back at Eddie with her good eye, the prosthetic staring blankly ahead.

A stand near the fire-eater held other lit torches for his act—and a container of paraffin. She hurled the plastic bottle at her pursuers. Eddie darted aside, but it bounced off the younger man, splashing his arm.

She threw the torches.

The spilled fuel ignited. The crowd screamed and pushed back, people stumbling and causing a chain reaction as others tripped over them. A trail of flame rushed across the open space. Kit jumped away, but his sleeve was already alight. He swatted at the fire, trying to shrug off the garment. The fire-eater's assistant scrambled for an extinguisher.

Madirakshi took advantage of the panic to dive back into the crowd. Eddie ran after her.

Neon flashed ahead, the shrill mosquito buzz of the holographic display getting louder. Behind, he heard the gushing hiss of the fire extinguisher. Madirakshi's black bun had become partially unfastened in her flight, long black hair flapping behind her like a horse's tail.

Eddie reached out, grabbed it, pulled. She shrieked, then spun.

The stolen pistol was in her hand—

He ducked as she fired, the bullet hitting a man behind him and showering his companions with blood.

Eddie sprang up before she could fire again, slamming his shoulder into her abdomen. She reeled. Metal clattered against pavement as the gun was knocked from her hand.

He grabbed for the fallen weapon, missed, tripped as someone ran into him, and found himself among a forest of trampling legs. A man stumbled over him, stamping on his hand. Eddie yelled and struggled to stand, realizing through the sharp pain that he had lost sight of Madirakshi. He looked from side to side. No sign of the police uniform—

Something lashed around his neck from behind.

Eddie's hand flashed up reflexively just as the garrotte pulled tight, crushing his fingers against his Adam's apple. Choking, he tried to push the wire away, but it cut painfully into his flesh, blood oozing out. A knee crunched into his back. He struggled for breath as the wire drew tighter, sawing at his throat—

Kit hurtled from the panicked crowd and tackled her. She lost her grip on one end of the garrotte as all three fell. He tried to pin her, but she elbowed him viciously in the face and jumped back up, about to run again—

Sirens howled all around the square, a voice booming orders through a megaphone. The Lyon police were sealing off the Place des Terreaux.

Eddie got up. "There's no way out!" he gasped. "If you give up now, I *might* not match your other eye up."

To her other side, Kit was also recovering. Madirakshi glanced between the two men, eyeing up possible escape routes—and finding none, blocked by the towering neon display and the pedestal beneath the holographic dancer. "We can make a deal," said Kit. "Testify against your employer, and we—"

She was uninterested in deals. Instead, she ran to the neon sculpture—and started to climb it.

"Get round the other side, cut her off!" Eddie told Kit, but even as he spoke he realized she had no intention of jumping down. She kept climbing the ladder-like central frame, the spinning lighting effect seeming to sweep her aloft. What the hell was she doing?

The answer hit him as she reached the pinnacle, more than thirty feet above. She *wasn't* planning on coming down. Alive, at least.

"No, wait!" he shouted—

Too late.

She thrust her hands into the wiring.

The neon flickered, sparks sizzling from the sculpture's summit as thousands of volts surged through her. People screamed at the sight. Smoke coiled from Madirakshi's body as she shuddered uncontrollably, the vibrations shaking the whole tower...

Something broke loose. With the searing lightning-crack of an electrical short, the display went dark, and the woman fell away.

For a moment, it seemed as though the hollow man was trying to catch her... but he was just an illusion. High-powered lasers seared across her back as she dropped toward the holographic generator, uniform and hair bursting into flames before the blazing corpse smashed down spread-eagled on the pedestal. The operator hurriedly shut off the lasers, but the body continued to burn, rising smoke glowing in every color imaginable as it passed through the beams of the giant projections.

8

New York City

"What happened to her?" Nina asked, wondering if she had misheard Eddie over the crackly international phone connection.

"She electrocuted herself and fell on a hologram that set her on fire," he repeated. "Probably not what the local tourist board had in mind for their Festival of Lights... Anyway, she was dead set—literally—on not being caught."

"I've heard of loyalty to your employer, but jeez," she said. "And Fernandez is dead?" The thought was not exactly heartbreaking.

"Yeah. She practically sliced his head off. We just got a preliminary report on her body—that glass eye of hers was a fake."

Despite the grim situation, Nina couldn't help but smile. "They usually are."

"Ha fuckin' ha. I mean, it was a trick eye—there was a garrotte wire inside it. Someone's been getting ideas from *Last Action Hero*. And by someone, I mean Pramesh Khoil."

For the second time in less than a minute, she was astonished. "Are you serious?"

"I saw that woman in San Francisco—she brought Khoil a phone just before we got attacked. So unless she was doing some really violent moonlighting, it's a good bet that he's connected with this. My guess is that he had Fernandez killed to stop him grassing."

Thinking back, she remembered the woman. "Maybe the phone call was to tell Fernandez to carry out the raid," she mused. "His Plan A was to ask me for full access to the Talonor Codex—but when I said no, he already had Plan B all ready to go."

"Just steal the thing."

"Right. So what happens now?"

"Kit's going to India to check out the Khoils—he's willing to take my word that this woman's the one from Frisco, and he thinks that makes them worth investigating."

"And if Interpol finds the Khoils really are behind everything?"

"Dunno, but I wouldn't want to be in their shoes. Probably be a race between the Saudi General Intelligence Directorate and Chinese External Security to see who can kill 'em first for nicking their country's treasures."

"What about you?"

He yawned, almost setting her off in sympathy. "Doesn't look like I'm going to get much sleep tonight. I've got to finish giving my statement to Interpol, then I'm flying back to New York."

"What time is it there now?" She looked at her watch; it was past seven in the evening.

"After one in the morning. When are you finishing work?"

"I'm almost done. I had a fun day explaining to Sebastian Penrose and some State Department people how the director of the IHA got embroiled in another gun battle. You know, I really hoped we'd left this kind of thing behind us."

"No such luck, eh?" He yawned again, then grunted in discomfort.

"Are you okay?"

"Yeah, just got a sore neck where she cut me."

"What? She cut you?"

"Remember that garrotte? She got the drop on me with it. I'm okay, though."

Nina's concern grew. "And how did she get the drop on you?"

"It wasn't 'cause of my hearing," he said, irritation clear in his voice.

"I didn't say it was."

"You were thinking it, though. Christ, this is why I didn't tell you about it before."

Now she too was annoyed. "I was just, y'know, *worried* about my *husband.* Jeez!"

"Okay, okay, sorry. I'm just tired, that's all. Think I need another coffee or six." A further yawn. "I'll let you go. I'll give you a call from the flight, or when I get to JFK."

"Have a good trip," she said. "See you soon."

"You too. Bye."

She ended the call and stretched out in her chair. While her day had hardly been as physically exhausting as Eddie's had unexpectedly become, she still felt drained by the meetings and bureaucracy, and desired nothing more than to collapse into bed.

She finished her last few items of paperwork, then headed out, taking the elevator to ground level and ambling across United Nations Plaza toward First Avenue. Normally she would walk the four blocks to Grand Central Terminal and take the subway, but tonight she just wanted to get home quickly. A cab, then. As usual, the streets around the UN were choked with yellow cabs, but finding one for hire was the tricky part...

The roof light on one parked nearby came on. That was

a stroke of luck; the driver must have just finished his break. She walked toward it, increasing her pace when she realized she was in competition with a middle-aged man. He saw her speed up and broke into a clumsy jog, both of them reaching the cab simultaneously.

The man grabbed the rear door handle. "Sorry, lady."

"Hey!" Nina protested. "I saw it first."

"Seeing it doesn't count." He opened the door.

The driver rapped on the bulletproof screen between the front and rear seats. "The lady was here first." His accent was Eastern European, gravelly.

The man started to climb in. "Just take me to East Nineteenth Street."

"Hey!" Another bang on the screen, this time with a clenched fist. "I said, the lady was here first. Get the next one, eh?"

After a moment's hesitation, the man retreated. "I—I'll have your medallion for this," he bleated, then huffed sarcastically at Nina. "Enjoy your ride."

"I'm sure I will," she replied with a little smile. She got in, nodding to the driver. "Thank you."

She could see why her rival had backed off—the cabbie was imposing, hard-faced, and heavily built, with hair shaved to a stubble. "No problem. So, where to?"

Nina gave him the address and sat back as the cab moved off, thinking. Could Pramesh and Vanita Khoil really be involved in the thefts? They certainly had the money to finance Fernandez and his men. But it would be a collection they could never show off to anybody—and how did the Talonor Codex fit into it? It was valuable, yes, and historically important, but hardly on the level of Michelangelo's *David* . . .

A sudden wave of guilt washed over her. Thoughts of the codex inevitably led to Rowan, bringing back not only her feelings of grief, but also the reminder that she had yet to speak to his father. She had been busy, sure . . . but had that just been a way to avoid something of which, she was forced to admit, she was afraid?

She had to talk to him, she knew, however much she dreaded it. She was about to take out her phone, then decided that a cab wasn't the best place for what would undoubtedly be an emotional call. *More procrastination,* an accusing voice said inside her head, but she needed calm, quiet, time to gather her thoughts—

The cab braked sharply, jolting her back to the present. It had turned onto one of the crosstown streets—but there was no traffic ahead. So why were they stopping?

The door to her left opened, a huge bearded man squeezing in beside her.

Shit! She was being mugged!

Grabbing her bag, she slid across to the other side—

The right-hand door opened as well, a smaller, skinny man pushing her back. She was sandwiched between the two intruders. Both were dark-skinned—Indian? The cab set off again. The driver hadn't reacted—he was in on it.

But if they thought she was going to surrender meekly, they were wrong.

One hand fumbling in her bag, she drove the point of her other elbow against the smaller man's cheekbone, snapping his head back. The big guy reached for her with a rough, hairy hand—as she pulled out a can of pepper spray and squirted it in his face.

He recoiled, eyes clenching shut—but in more of an instinctive flinch than the agonized thrashing she expected. Her own eyes stung horribly as the vapor reached her in the confined space. She tried to move away, but the second man was still pressed against her. Another swipe with her elbow—

His hand clamped around it, stopping the motion as if Nina had just hit a brick wall. Startled, she tried to pull away, but the grip tightened and held her arm firmly in place. The smaller man was a lot stronger than he appeared. Fear rising, she looked at him.

A shark's mouth grinned back at her from below malevolent dark eyes. His front teeth were filed to ragged points. He opened his mouth wide, leaning closer—

Nina screamed as he bit deeply into her upper arm. She tried to blast him with the pepper spray, but the big guy had already recovered, barely affected by the hot capsaicin, and swallowed her hand in his own, squeezing hard until her joints crackled agonizingly against the can.

"Don't struggle, Dr. Wilde," said the driver. They knew who she was! It wasn't a mugging, but a *kidnapping*.

The shark-mouthed man opened his jaws, Nina's blood running down his chin. "Jesus *Christ!*" she gasped. "What do you want?" The bearded man released her hand, and the dented can clattered to the floor. In the flickering light of passing streetlamps, she saw that his lips were heavily scarred by what looked like burns, his cheeks oddly hollow.

"You'll find out soon. Here." The driver pushed a paper bag through the cash slot in the screen. The big man took it and tore it open; Nina saw that it contained a small bottle of antiseptic and several Band-Aids. "I wouldn't want you to get an infection."

"Thanks for caring," Nina growled bitterly, snatching the bag from her captor.

* * *

The cab headed north into upstate New York. The drive took well over an hour, Nina losing track of where they were once they left the main highway.

Their final destination was a private airfield. The cab stopped beside a business jet, its engines already whining. Her captors pulled her roughly from the taxi and took her to the plane's steps.

A figure appeared in the hatch. Nina recognized him immediately. "Funny," she said defiantly. "I was just thinking about you."

Pramesh Khoil's smooth, bespectacled face was as blank as it had been in San Francisco. "Hello again, Dr. Wilde." He looked to the larger of the two Indian men holding her. "Bring her aboard. Was she any trouble, Dhiren?"

She expected the big man to speak, but instead he responded with a gurgling grunt. Horrified, she realized the meaning of the facial scars and his sunken cheeks—he had no tongue. It had been burned out of his mouth. The other man said something in Hindi, his filed teeth giving his voice a wet, lisping quality.

"Thank you, Nahari," said Khoil. He stood back as they shoved Nina into the plane. She blinked at the change of lighting, looking down the luxuriously appointed cabin to see Vanita Khoil coldly regarding her from one of the plush seats. Another Indian man, square-jawed and wearing a black turtleneck, stood beside her, his alert stance that of a bodyguard.

"What do you want me to do now?" asked the cab-driver from outside.

"Follow the plan, Mr. Zec," Khoil told him. "Dr. Wilde, your keys."

"What? Hey!" The sharp-toothed man rummaged in her bag and handed her keys to Khoil, who tossed them to the Slav.

"Wait for Mr. Chase at their home," said Khoil. "I am sure he will ask to speak to his wife."

"What do you want with Eddie?" Nina demanded, covering her rising fear with anger.

"Your husband is going to get something for us," said Vanita, voice as icy as her expression. "The Talonor Codex."

Nina gave her a mocking look. "Dream on. You know that Interpol already figured out you were behind the robbery in San Francisco, don't you?"

"They may suspect," said Khoil, dismissing Zec without a further word. A crew member closed the hatch. "But they will find no proof. Not until it is too late to matter."

"So why do you need Eddie? If you want the codex, why not just make me get it for you?"

"It would be too easy for you to raise the alarm. Besides, with you as our hostage, Mr. Chase will be more malleable than you would be in the reverse position."

"You think you know us?" she sneered.

"Qexia knows you. All information about you and your husband has been collated and analyzed. Mr. Chase is more predictable than you, hence more controllable. His concern for your safety will ensure his compliance with our demands."

"He's controllable, huh? I'll tell him that when he calls—I'm sure it'll give him a laugh."

"Bite your tongue," Vanita snapped, her dangling earrings swinging. "Pramesh, take us home. I have had enough of this country."

"As you wish, my beloved." Khoil turned and entered the cockpit. Nina expected him to issue orders, but was surprised to see him sit in the pilot's seat and don a set of headphones.

"Back there," ordered Vanita, jerking a dismissive thumb toward the rear of the cabin. The two men holding Nina pulled her with them. "Chapal, the drug."

"*Drug?*" Nina cried, seeing the man in the turtleneck raise a gun-shaped device—a jet injector, used to administer drugs without a hypodermic needle. She struggled and kicked, but her captors had too firm a grip.

"I would advise that you take the drug, Dr. Wilde," Khoil called from the cockpit. "Otherwise Mr. Tandon will be forced to use his martial arts skills to render you unconscious. I understand it is excruciatingly painful."

The man in black gave Nina a broad, menacing smile. "There are a hundred and eight *marma* pressure points on the body. Twelve are instantly fatal when hit by a *varma ati* master."

"Let me guess," said Nina unhappily. "You're a master."

"Oh, yes. But the deadly points are very close to ones that cause unconsciousness or paralysis. If you struggle, even I could hit the wrong one." The smile broadened. "Would you prefer the drug?"

She clenched her jaw, reluctantly accepting defeat. For now. "Just ... get it over with."

Tandon pressed the injector's nozzle to her neck and squeezed the trigger. There was a sharp hiss of gas, and she jerked in pain as the drug was blasted through the pores of her skin. For a moment, nothing seemed to happen ... then her legs turned to rubber. The two men hauled her to a seat. The engines' whine rose to a shrill roar as the plane prepared to take off.

"You guys are gonna be ... *so* screwed ... when my husband catches you," Nina managed to say before her surroundings swirled away into a dark void.

* * *

His bruised muscles now tense and stiffened by the long flight, Eddie took a cab back into Manhattan. He tried to phone Nina, but was diverted to voice mail at the apartment, in her office, and on her cell phone. Slightly annoyed, he called Lola.

"Afternoon, Eddie," came the reply. "How was France? Did you see the Festival of Lights? I've heard it's beautiful."

"It was ... bright," he settled on. Nina obviously hadn't updated her on the previous night's events. "Listen, do you know where Nina is? I can't get hold of her."

"I'm not sure—I haven't seen her today. She must be in another UN committee meeting."

"Stuck in a plane or stuck in a meeting? Not sure which is worse."

"At least on a plane you can watch a movie. Anyway, I'll tell her you called when I see her."

"Okay. Thanks, Lola."

Finally reaching home, he lugged his bag to the apartment. "Nina, you in?" he called as he opened the door. No answer. He dumped his luggage and headed to the kitchen for coffee.

A man was sitting in one of the lounge chairs, pointing an automatic at him. "Don't move, Mr. Chase."

Eddie assessed him in a flash. Eastern European accent, probably Bosnian; big, well muscled, a face that had seen a lot of action. Definitely ex-military.

One of Fernandez's men? Here for revenge?

Even though his travel-induced lethargy had been instantly blown away by a surge of adrenaline, he feigned tiredness. "Who're you—and where's Nina?"

"Safe, for now. My employers want you to get something for them. Do it, and she will be released."

"Your employers? The Khoils, at a guess."

That surprised the man, but he quickly recovered, indicating a cell phone on a table. "Yes. They want to talk to you. The number is already entered."

Keeping a wary eye on the gun as it tracked him, Eddie picked up the phone and pushed the call button. The screen lit up, giving him a glimpse of the number before it was replaced by an animated DIALING... icon: from the unusual prefix code, 882, he realized he was being connected to a satellite phone.

A click, the ghostly echo of the signal being bounced off an orbiting relay...then a calm voice. "Hello."

"All right, Khoil, you fuckwit," said Eddie, recognizing Pramesh Khoil's flat, precise tones. "What d'you want?"

A brief pause, the time lag of the satellite transmission. "There is no need for rudeness, Mr. Chase."

"I can do violence instead."

"Your macho posturing is exactly what I predicted. I am

not intimidated. Now listen carefully. As Mr. Zec has informed you, we have taken your wife hostage."

"Zec?" Eddie glanced at the man in the chair, the unusual name echoing faintly in the recesses of his memory.

"We want you to obtain the Talonor Codex and deliver it to Mr. Zec. If you do this, your wife will be released. If you do not, she will be killed. Today is Tuesday; you have until the end of Thursday."

There was a background noise that was all too familiar after the last several hours: jet engines. Khoil was on a plane, which probably meant Nina was too... "You've fucked up, you know."

"Pardon?"

"I can't get the codex for you. Nobody can, except Nina. You need her handprint to open the vault. And since I'm guessing you're flying her *away* from the vault, well..."

"I am aware of the vault's handprint scanner. Your wife's hand will be provided to you."

Cold clutched at Eddie's heart. "If you've fucking cut off her hand I promise you I will hunt you down, and cut off *your* fucking hand, and use it to pull your fucking *heart* out through your arsehole!"

"Fantastical threats are not necessary—you misunderstand me. Your wife's *handprint* will be provided."

"It will, will it? Let me talk to Nina."

Khoil spoke to someone in Hindi. There was a faint hiss, followed by a nauseated groan.

Eddie knew who had made it, and felt a rush of relief. "Nina!"

"Ohh...Eddie?" she said, groggy and confused. "What's...oh, shit. Eddie, these assholes have kidnapped me—they drugged me!"

"You're gonna be okay. I'll take care of it."

"Eddie, they want you to steal the codex for them. You can't let them get it."

"If it's how I get you back, then yeah, I can."

"No, absolutely not! I don't know why they want it, but it's got to be for something bigger than just its monetary value. It's—"

"Shut that red-haired witch *up*!" said a woman's shrill voice. Vanita Khoil. The sound of a scuffle came over the phone.

"Nina!" Eddie shouted. "Khoil, put her back on!"

There was another hiss. "Son of a *bit*...," said Nina, her cry trailing away to nothing.

"She is not hurt, only unconscious," Khoil said, retrieving the phone. "If you obtain the codex for us, you will have her back. If you do not, or if Mr. Zec tells me you have tried to contact the authorities—or he does not check in, for any reason—we will kill her. Now give him the phone."

Raging impotently, Eddie did as he was told, then paced the length of the room. Zec listened to Khoil, finally saying, "Understood," and ending the call.

Eddie rounded on him. "So how the fuck am I supposed to get the codex out of the vault? I can't just walk out with the thing under my arm."

"Not my problem," said Zec, standing. "My job is just to deliver it to Khoil—and make sure you don't try anything stupid."

"I'm not stupid enough to risk Nina's life over some old book. You'll get it—fucked if I know how, but I'll work something out." He turned away again, pacing back down the lounge...until his gaze fell on the photo of his late friend. "Zec! Hugo Castille said he once worked with a guy called Zec, in Bosnia. That you?"

Zec glanced at the picture. "Yes. I saw the photograph. Our profession is a small world, no?"

"It's not my profession anymore. But Hugo wouldn't have worked with you if you weren't a good bloke. So why're you working for this arsehole Khoil?"

"Why does a mercenary work for anyone?" Zec asked

rhetorically. "I was Urbano Fernandez's second in command. Khoil asked me to take his place."

"You know Khoil had Fernandez killed, right? That lass with the glass eye almost sawed his fucking head off." Zec seemed disquieted by the revelation, but said nothing. "That's it? No loyalty to your mate, just take the cash from the people who killed him? I guess Hugo was wrong about you."

"I need the money," said Zec, annoyed. "I have a family now, a son—I want to give them a good life, somewhere better than Sarajevo." He realized he had perhaps opened himself up too much, and the inexpressive mask slammed back down. "But the only thing you should think about for the next two days is how to get the codex."

"Oh, yeah, that'll be a doddle, getting something the size of a bloody paving stone out of a top-security vault without anyone noticing." He gazed at the picture of Hugo for a long moment, then turned back to the Bosnian. "I'll need some help."

9

India

Nina awoke to find herself in a palace.

She had expected the plane, or a cell. But she was lying on a four-poster bed draped in fine silk, in an airy room decorated by colorful friezes on the walls and ceiling. The doors and shuttered windows were all arched, the style distinctively—almost stereotypically—Indian.

There was an odd feeling of artificiality to the place, as if she were in an Indian-palace-themed hotel room rather than the genuine article. She went to a window, where bright daylight flared through the slats. Expecting it to be locked, she tried it anyway and was slightly surprised when the shutters parted to reveal an expansive sweep of immaculate lawns and gardens below. She could see other parts of the building; it was indeed a palace, domes topping the pillared white walls. Again, there was the too-clean, too-perfect sense of its being a theme-park replica.

"Dr. Wilde," said Khoil's voice from behind her, making her start. "Good morning."

The room had changed, a section of wall silently sliding open to reveal a giant screen. The Indian's bespectacled face, three feet high, regarded her from it. She realized she was under observation, a lens glinting below the display. "Mr. Khoil," she said tartly. "Been watching me sleep, have you? I didn't realize you made your fortune through webcams."

He ignored the barb. "The room has a motion sensor. The house computers alerted me the moment you woke. Welcome to my home."

"Yeah, I'm so glad to be here." If her sarcasm had been any more acidic, it would have blistered the screen. "Where exactly am I?"

"My estate, east of Bangalore. It combines styles of the Mysore, Kowdiar, and Laxmi Niwas palaces, only updated with modern architectural elements. And integrated with the most advanced technology, of course."

"Well, of course. So are you just going to lecture me from your telescreen like Big Brother, or . . ."

"You may 'freshen up,' as you Americans say, then you will be driven to us."

"Driven?" Nina raised an eyebrow. "Just how big is this place?"

"The main building has a hundred and sixty-five rooms over five floors," said Khoil, taking her question literally. "But we are not in the palace at the moment; we are at the sanctuary."

"Sanctuary? For what?"

A faint smile on the blank face. "Tigers."

* * *

Tandon, politely menacing, collected her from her room after she had showered. He took her to an elevator, which brought them to a large underground garage beneath the palace. Dozens of cars lined the space, from a nineteenth-century Benz Motorwagen tricycle to a brand-new McLaren supercar in gleaming gold. It was an odd mix of vehicles, a little British Mini beside the rocketship bulk of a 1959 Cadillac, a record-setting Bugatti Veyron hunched next to a minuscule Tata Nano. Some facet of each vehicle's design had apparently made it worthy of inclusion in the billionaire's collection.

The vehicle Tandon took her to was less impressive than any of the gleaming exhibits, however: an electric golf cart. They drove up a steep ramp into the open, following a tree-lined drive. About half a mile north of the palace was a huge enclave, encircled by a high concrete wall topped with chain link and razor wire. A runway ran along one side of the enclosure, the long black strip showing Nina just how far the boundaries of the Khoils' estate extended. The jet sat outside a hangar, the structure's doors partially open to reveal a small, strange-looking aircraft. Its matte charcoal-gray fuselage, a propeller at its rear, seemed too narrow to carry any people—even a pilot. Then the jet obscured it as they passed.

Abutting the wall was a two-story building, an architectural sibling of the palace. Tandon took her to the upper floor. The sanctuary spread out before her through a glass wall. The view was dominated by a leafy tree canopy, though she could also see a more open area of grassland and bushes. Sunlight shimmered off a lake near the enclave's center.

"Dr. Wilde," said Khoil from one side of the large room. The tycoon was seated at a control station, a bank of monitor screens before him. The biggest showed a view from the upper branches of a tree. Beside him stood Vanita, bent over a control panel with her body language suggesting tension and concern—though the look she gave Nina was one of utter disdain. The tongueless giant and the shark-toothed man waited nearby, eyes locked on the new arrival. "Welcome to the sanctuary."

"Impressive," said Nina. "You must really like tigers."

"They're magnificent animals," Vanita said, passion clear in her voice. "And they're being slaughtered by poachers. Two of the country's reserves had every single tiger in them killed in the last few years."

"So you set up your own?"

She smiled coldly. "Any hunter who tries to harm my tigers will regret it."

A voice crackled over a loudspeaker: "Ready at station three."

Khoil acknowledged via a headset. He examined a map on one screen, colored markers slowly moving across it. "She has taken the bait," he told his wife.

Vanita regarded the monitors excitedly. "Show me."

He tapped a keyboard. One of the secondary screens flicked to a new view. "Come and watch, Dr. Wilde. You may find this interesting."

Despite herself, Nina couldn't help but be intrigued. Tigers had been a favorite animal of her childhood, even if the closest she had ever been to one in real life was at the Bronx Zoo. The combination of sleek beauty and power was appealing to many children, of either sex; Vanita had obviously carried that fascination into adulthood.

On the screen, a squat concrete bunker, partially camouflaged by vegetation, rose from the ground in a clearing. Adjoining it was an open-topped cage—in which stood a goat, tethered to a pole. Over the speakers she heard a faint bleat. "What are you doing?"

"One of the tigers injured her paw," said Vanita. "We need to bring her inside so our vets can treat her."

"We have three tigers, two female and one male," Khoil added. "They keep to their own territories, so we have several stations linked by tunnels where we can enter the sanctuary and provide them with live prey."

Nina gave the goat a sympathetic look. "Sorry, Billy."

The billionaire turned back to the controls. The image on the main screen shifted as the camera moved. Nina saw that it was airborne, slowly descending into the clearing.

Khoil touched a button, and a crosshair was superimposed over the center of the screen. "Lower the cage."

A metallic rattle came over the speakers as the cage dropped into the ground, leaving the goat standing on a metal platform. Vanita indicated one of the markers with a long red nail. "She's getting closer! Pramesh, let me see."

Khoil obediently adjusted the controls. The camera panned left, tilting downward to show a patch of bush at the edge of the clearing. "Each tiger has a tracker implanted," he explained to Nina. "We can locate them to the meter. This one will come into view . . . now."

For a moment, Nina saw nothing. Then she spotted a slight movement in the undergrowth—and suddenly what she had taken to be patches of light and shadow took on graceful yet deadly form.

A Bengal tiger, three hundred pounds of muscle, teeth, and claws standing over three feet high and eight feet long. Even with a wounded paw, the animal moved with silent, precise purpose.

"We would not normally tie up the goat," said Khoil as Nina watched, unable to look away from the spectacle. "We want the animals to keep their hunting instincts."

"Move the drone back," Vanita warned sharply. "If she hears it, it might scare her away."

"The *vimana* is eight meters away. The rotors are inaudible past six meters." But the camera retreated slightly after she glared at him.

The goat finally saw the danger. Bleating in fear, it tried to run, but was jerked to an abrupt stop by the tether. The tiger responded, a black-and-orange explosion of action as it sprang across the clearing faster than Khoil's camera could follow. By the time it caught up, the tiger had already reached its prey, slamming the goat against the side of the bunker and biting down hard on the unfortunate ungulate's throat. Blood gushed over the gray concrete. Even with a lethal wound the goat was still struggling; the tiger lashed out a paw, claws tearing open its abdomen and spilling its innards across the ground. Nina winced.

Khoil worked the joystick controls. The drone descended toward the scene, crosshairs moving over the tiger's body.

"Don't hurt her!" Vanita warned.

"I won't, my beloved," Khoil replied, a hint of impatience in his flat voice. The camera drew closer.

The tiger looked up, a noise catching its attention—

He pulled a trigger on one of the sticks. A flat *whap* came over the speakers, the image jolting backward. When it settled again, the tiger had released the goat and was trying to run back into the jungle—but only got a few yards before drunkenly flopping to the ground. A silver dart protruded from its flank.

"She is down," Khoil reported into the headset. "Bring her inside." On the smaller monitor, the platform lowered into the ground. After a short pause it rose again, several men in white overalls stepping off and moving cautiously to the fallen predator.

"Is she all right?" Vanita demanded. One of the men felt the tiger's body, then gave the hovering camera a thumbs-up.

"She will be fine," Khoil assured her. He pushed a button. The words AUTO RETURN flashed up on the big screen, the camera swinging around of its own accord and ascending above the treetops. "Now, Dr. Wilde," he said, standing, "we can talk. I suspect it will be pointless, but Qexia projected a twelve percent probability that you might be persuaded to work with me."

Nina shrugged. "Sounds like your projections have a thirteen percent margin of error, but go ahead."

As he had earlier, Khoil missed the subtext and took the remark literally. "Less than five percent, actually. But you are undoubtedly wondering why we want to obtain the Talonor Codex."

"It'd crossed my mind."

"Mr. Zec has sent me scans of all the IHA's research and translations from your apartment. They confirm everything I had hoped—that the codex contains the information needed to reveal the location of the Vault of Shiva."

"So you think it's real?"

"As real as Shiva himself." Seeing her skeptical look, he continued: "You are surprised that a computer billionaire could also be a devout believer? This is India, Dr. Wilde. The gods are all around us, as important a part of daily life as water. Vanita and I are both Vira Shaivites—'heroes of Shiva,' Following Shiva has brought us great wealth and power, and we want to show our gratitude by fulfilling the great lord's plan for the world."

"What plan?" Nina asked, but they were interrupted by a buzzing sound as something flew into the room through an open window: a black-and-silver flying machine about two feet across its front and slightly longer. It was triangular, a cylindrical shroud at each corner containing fast-spinning rotors. "What's that?"

"One of my *vimanas*—the name in the ancient Hindu epics for the flying machines used by the gods. They are described as flying chariots, mechanical birds, even floating palaces...the products of a great civilization now lost to time." The little aircraft made its way to a stand at one side of the room, hovered above it, then lowered itself down. As the buzz of its engines faded, Khoil walked to the drone, Nina—and the three bodyguards—following.

She saw that slung beneath its body was a dart gun, a camera lens above it. "That's how you tranqued the tiger? Cool little toy." The gun had a conventional trigger, pulled by a mechanism protruding from the drone's belly. It had a magazine holding two more of the darts, which were fired by a small bottle of compressed gas.

She leaned closer. The amount of tranquilizing agent needed to take down an animal as large as a tiger could be potentially lethal to a human. If she could reach the trigger mechanism...

"Vanita has her pets; I have mine. I grew up under the flight path of Bangalore airport, and when I was a child I thought the airliners were the *vimana*s my father told me about when he read from the Vedas and the Mahabharata. I actually wanted to be an engineer, to build aircraft, but then I discovered computers." Khoil became noticeably more animated as he warmed to his subject. "But it is still an interest. I own a large stake in one of India's military aircraft manufacturers, and I designed this drone myself. Getting a high thrust-to-weight ratio in a small frame was—"

"Pramesh," his wife scolded from the control station, "if you *must* talk to her at all, at least do her the courtesy of staying on topic."

Khoil's expression dropped back to its usual blankness. "But, yes, the Vault of Shiva. I do believe it is real, and I also believe it contains the means to advance the world into the next stage of existence—the words of Shiva himself, the wisdom of a god." Nina looked at him for a long moment. "You doubt me."

"It seems...far-fetched. To say the least."

"Why? Your own translations say the priests showed Talonor stone tablets from the vault. The Shiva-Vedas, the words of the god."

"Which doesn't mean they were literally carved by Shiva himself."

"I am not saying they were. But what is important is what they say...and when they were made. Dr. Wilde, have you heard of the *yugas*?"

"Well, you just jogged my memory, so yes—they're parts of the cycle of existence in Hindu mythology."

"Correct. There are four stages in the current cycle: the Satya Yuga, the Treta Yuga, the Dvapara Yuga, and finally the Kali Yuga. The Kali Yuga is the last, and most debased, part of the cycle, farthest from the golden age of the Satya Yuga. It is also the *yuga* the world is in now."

"But that's a theme with practically every religion," said Nina. "The present is always the worst time there's ever been, and things were invariably better in the past. It's either rose-tinted nostalgia, or 'proof' that things have descended into sin and decadence—and the only way out is through whatever flavor fundamentalism the preacher prefers."

"In the case of Hinduism, though, it actually is true. The world will sink deeper into the darkness until Shiva ends the cycle."

"By destruction."

"So that a new cycle can begin. A new Satya Yuga, a time of enlightenment and bliss. And the Shiva-Vedas will make it happen."

"How?"

He ignored the question. "The Talonor Codex proved that the Shiva-Vedas were in existence at the same time as Atlantis, around nine thousand BC. Yes?"

"That's right."

"Then they must come from an earlier *yuga*—at the latest, the Dvapara Yuga. The Hindu calendar is very old, and we know the exact date when the Kali Yuga began: 3102 BC. Specifically, January the twenty-third, in Gregorian dating. Because the words written in the Shiva-Vedas are from an earlier *yuga,* they are by definition more pure, more enlightened, than anything created in the corrupt Kali Yuga. They will form the cornerstone of the new era when it begins—when I *make* it begin."

"What, you think you're Shiva now?" said Nina, aghast.

"No, I am just carrying out his will. But to end the cycle, I must have the Shiva-Vedas. They are the key to humanity's salvation. Without the teachings of Shiva himself from a more enlightened time, the world will fall back into cor-

ruption, and everything I have achieved will be wasted. So
to get the Shiva-Vedas I must find and enter the Vault of
Shiva—and to do that, I need the Talonor Codex."

"But you've got the translations. Why do you need the
codex itself?"

"For the key, Dr. Wilde. The key the priests showed to
Talonor—the key impressed on the cover of the codex.
From the impression, I will be able to make a duplicate.
And I will use it to open the vault."

"You need more than just the key, though," she pointed
out. "The priests told Talonor that 'only those who know
the love of Shiva' can use it."

"But I do know the love of Shiva," said Khoil. "For all
my life. Shiva does not care about castes. My wife and I are
both Dalits—the 'scheduled castes,' as the government
calls them . . . or the 'untouchables,' as you probably know
them in the West. The lowest caste, oppressed and scorned
for nothing more than an accident of birth and the profes-
sions of their ancestors centuries ago." Bitterness entered
his voice. "Even now, Vanita and I still experience preju-
dice—from people whose businesses, whose lives, we could
buy and sell on a whim."

"Ah, so everything you're doing is to benefit the class
struggle, is it?" said Nina mockingly.

"In a way," Khoil replied, her sarcasm once again failing
to make it through his shield of literalism. "I believe in em-
powering the powerless, whether through free access to information—or by more direct means."

She gestured at the trio of bodyguards. "Like paying
them to do your dirty work?"

"Some problems cannot be solved by discussion. Like
Urbano Fernandez, who would have made a deal with Interpol if Madirakshi had not silenced him." The tongueless
man gurgled something, Khoil replying in Hindi. "Poor
Madirakshi. She was a loyal servant."

"Yeah, Eddie told me how loyal. She killed herself rather than be arrested."

"She was excellent at her work. Her eye was cut out by a drunk who took her for a prostitute. Vanita and I learned of her through our charitable foundation and paid for her facial reconstruction—and then we used Qexia to trace her attacker. He became the test subject for her...secret weapon, you might say."

"You're a real humanitarian," said Nina. She regarded the three men. "So you've got Bollywood Bruce Lee here," she said of Tandon, who seemed amused rather than annoyed by the insult. "What are this pair's stories?"

"Dhiren Mahajan," said Khoil, indicating the bearded giant, then gesturing to the man with the filed-down teeth, "and Nahari Singh. Nahari used to compete in illegal street fights, but not through choice—he was bonded into it through debts his family owed. He was not the biggest fighter, so his owners gave him an advantage." Singh grinned spikily at her.

"Your employee welcome package didn't include dental, then?"

"His choice. The mutilation can be useful. As you discovered." Nina rubbed irritably at her bandaged arm. "As for Dhiren, he was an enforcer for a gangster, until he became too friendly with the man's girlfriend. An ancient punishment used by the Brahmins, the highest caste, was to put a red-hot nail in the mouth of transgressors. The gangster thought it would be amusing to resurrect the tradition."

Nina looked at the bearded man in dismay. "Jesus. So the gangster, the 'owners'—I'm guessing they're not around anymore."

"They have moved on to their next cycle of existence, yes. But Dhiren and Nahari and Chapal are not simply my servants—like myself and Vanita, we are all servants of Shiva. My faith in him has brought me to where I am today. And now, I am ready to repay him by bringing humanity into a new cycle." He stepped toward the front of the drone. "So, Dr. Wilde. Now you know my intentions, I shall ask: Will you help me find the Vault of Shiva?"

Nina folded her arms across her chest. "Because of you, my friend is dead—and so are a lot of other people. Do you seriously think I'd voluntarily do anything to help you?"

"No, not really." A slight shrug. "Twelve percent was only a small chance, after all. But I had to try."

Vanita called to him. "I'm going down to the infirmary to watch the operation." She started for an exit, her two facially mutilated bodyguards following.

"I will see you at the palace," Khoil said, shifting position as he turned to watch her leave...

Moving directly in front of the drone.

Nina lunged at the machine. She grabbed for the dart gun's trigger, and pulled it. The weapon bucked in her hand with a *thump* of high-pressure gas, the steel dart exploding from the barrel—

And stopping an inch short of Khoil's chest. As fast as a blink, Tandon snapped out his hand and caught it.

Khoil flinched away from the line of fire, eyes wide behind his glasses as Tandon dropped the dart at his feet. "That—was very foolish, Dr. Wilde," he said, regaining his composure.

Vanita's reaction was more nakedly emotional. She rushed toward Nina, screaming "Get her!" to her companions. Nina tried to dodge away from them but was quickly cornered. The huge bearded man grabbed her, twisting her arms up behind her back. She tried to hack at his shins with her heels, but he wrenched harder. Her shoulder joints crackled agonizingly, ending any further thoughts of resistance.

Vanita stepped closer, holding out one hand as she spoke in Hindi. The shark-toothed man came to her. For a moment Nina feared she had ordered him to bite her again, but instead he took something from a pocket and placed it in Vanita's hand.

Click. The object was a switchblade, a glinting steel knife four inches long springing out of the handle. Vanita savagely yanked at Nina's hair, taking hold of her right ear and pressing the blade's sharp edge against it. Nina froze.

"The only reason you're not dead already is that we need you as leverage over your husband," Vanita hissed. She slid the knife across Nina's earlobe, just hard enough to cut the skin. Nina gasped in pain. "But if you do anything like that again..."

The knife jerked back sharply. Nina screamed as it sliced into her ear.

"You'll die in *pieces,*" Vanita finished, stepping back. "Chapal, come with me." She returned the bloodied knife to its owner and, shooting a final look of loathing at Nina, strode imperiously away, Tandon following.

"You crazy *bitch*!" Nina yelled after her, feeling hot blood running down her neck.

Khoil regarded her wound almost curiously, as if examining a laboratory specimen. "Nahari, tend to that," he ordered. The smaller of the two bodyguards gave Nina a mocking flash of his jagged teeth as he went to get a first-aid kit. "Dhiren, release her."

The giant let go of Nina's aching arms. She put a hand to her ear, grimacing at the sting when she touched it. The knife had gone deep enough to slash cartilage. "Jesus Christ!" she cried. "Fucking psycho!"

"I hope that will teach you not to underestimate us," said Khoil. "Do not make the mistake of thinking I am just a computer nerd." The word sounded strange in his affect-less voice. "I grew up in the slums. I fought every centimeter of the way to be where I am today. And I did whatever was necessary to achieve my goals."

Singh returned with a Band-Aid and prepared to apply it to Nina's ear, but she snatched it from him. "I'll do it," she snapped. As she fumbled with the dressing, she glowered at Khoil. "So what *are* your goals? What are you going to do once you get the Shiva-Vedas?"

He didn't answer, instead gesturing for his bodyguards to take Nina away.

10

New York City

So, that's what we're dealing with," said Eddie. "And we've got to do it by tomorrow night. Any ideas?"

The expressions of the other people in his apartment varied, but none was brimming with confidence. Mac was the first to speak. "We'll do everything we can to help, obviously," he said, "but wouldn't it be better to go after this Khoil fellow and get Nina back?"

Eddie shook his head. "He's got Zec keeping tabs on me. I'd already be on a plane to India to punch the pudgy little bastard in the face if he hadn't."

"Can't we just clobber this Zec bloke the next time he turns up?" asked Matt Trulli.

"He checks in with Khoil's people every so often. Miss a call, and..."

The faces were now all downcast. "Do you think you'll even be able to get into the vault?" asked Karima Farran, sitting with her fiancé on the couch.

Eddie indicated a six-foot length of steel ventilation ducting propped against one wall. "According to the plans Lola got for me, that's the same size as the air vents in the vault area. I should be able to fit."

Karima looked dubiously between the duct and Eddie's waist. "Are you sure?"

"We'll test it out in a minute. If I can't, I'll have to get some emergency liposuction."

"The vault's really got ducts big enough to crawl through?" Matt asked disbelievingly. "Sounds a bit *Mission: Impossible,* if you ask me. And I mean the proper original one, not the Tom Cruise malarkey. The real Jim Phelps'd never turn traitor."

Eddie smiled slightly. "You've been wanting to get that off your chest for years, haven't you?"

"Too bloody right, mate!"

Lola held up a structural blueprint. "They have to make them that big by law. When the UN was built, it was exempted from New York building codes because it's legally on international territory. But the NYC Fire Department still has to respond if there's an emergency, so when the building was refurbished a few years ago they made them bring the place up to code. One of those codes is that vaults have to have external ventilation in case someone gets locked inside...and another is that vents to underground floors have to be able to carry a minimum volume of air per minute."

"Which means," said Eddie, banging the duct with his hand, "they have to be this big. Nine inches by fourteen."

"Only," continued Lola, "they obviously knew that a vault having ducts big enough to fit a person isn't a great idea. So the ones that go into the UN's secure archives have metal plates welded inside them, so air can get through—but people can't. And the actual air vents are on the sixth-floor machine level. If you tried getting in that way, there's a seventy-foot drop, straight down."

"So the only way to get into the vault through the vents," said Radi Bashir, scratching his chin, "is to be in the room where the vault is in the first place?"

"Pretty much," said Eddie.

"And won't the guards be a little suspicious of that?"

"Well, that's something else we need to work out, innit? On top of all the other stuff—avoiding the security cameras, disabling the alarms, taking the codex from the vault, getting the bloody thing out of the building without anyone noticing..."

"I can handle the security cameras," Rad said. "That is, if Matt can get his submarine to the junction box."

"Servo'll get there just fine," said Matt, a little defensively.

"Servo?" Mac asked.

"Segmented Robot Vehicle Operations. He's like a snake—wriggling through narrow spaces underwater is what he's designed for. But we'll have to do it at high tide, which won't give us much time. If anything holds us up, he'll be left grounded when the water level drops."

"And we'll be fucked," Eddie added. "Which is why we've got to work all this stuff out now. And fast."

"Putting all the pieces together'll be a tall order," said Mac. "But if anyone can figure it out, you can."

"Thanks," Eddie said with a halfhearted grin. "But then, I've bloody got to if I want Nina back, haven't I?"

"Then we'd better come up with a plan." Mac stood, his prosthetic leg creaking as he put his weight on it. "First things first. If you can't fit through this duct, it's all over before it even begins."

"Why do you have to do it, Eddie?" Karima asked. She stood, displaying her slim body. "I could fit a lot more easily."

"I'm doing it," Eddie said firmly. "If I get caught, then so be it, but I'm not having anyone else take the fall for me. Okay, let's have a look."

He and Mac laid the duct on the floor. Lola examined one end. "Gee, Eddie. Is that really nine inches tall? It doesn't look very big."

Eddie had the same thought, the opening appearing impossibly small. He pulled off his sweater. "Okay, Matt, Rad, hold it in place. Mac, give me a hand."

As the two men gripped the duct, he lowered himself onto his stomach and extended his arms, shoulders tight beside his head as he edged forward. Elbows in, biceps... The edges of the thin sheet metal pressed against him on both sides. Could he even fit?

"You can do it," said Mac encouragingly, as if reading his mind. "Twist around a bit—left side down, right side up."

The move gave him the extra fraction of an inch he needed. He wormed into the duct. Christ, it was tight! His shoulders were the widest part of his body, so theoretically he would fit all the way in—but he was already experiencing an unpleasant sense of claustrophobia.

"Keep going," Mac told him.

Eddie grunted and kept advancing, little by little. The top of the duct rubbed against his head, forcing him to turn it sideways, adding to his discomfort. "Shit," he said, the sweat that had already formed on his fingertips causing them to slip on the smooth metal. "I can't get a grip."

"Hang on," said Matt. "I brought some things that might help."

Eddie looked ahead, his living room reduced to a rectangle surrounded by dull steel. Lola peered through the slot at him. "How you holding up, Eddie?"

"Fucking champion," he said with an unconvincing grin. Lola moved away, her face replaced by Matt's rounder features.

"Here you go, mate," said the Australian, putting something in Eddie's hand. "See if that works."

He examined the heavy object: a thick disk of dark metal, topped by a plastic casing with a switch set into it. "What is it?"

"Portable electromagnet, for underwater salvage. Self-contained; the battery's in the case, and very powerful.

Give it a try—just push the switch. Careful, though. Don't get your fingers trapped under it—it's strong enough to crush 'em."

"Thanks for the tip." Keeping his fingers clear of the metal disk, Eddie flicked the switch. The magnet instantly clamped itself to the steel with such force that the entire duct rattled. "Jesus!"

"Not very stealthy," Mac remarked drily.

"Baby steps, eh?" said Matt. "Let's see if it works first. Eddie, try pulling yourself along with it."

Eddie switched off the magnet and stretched forward as far as he could before reactivating it. Even with the disk flat on the metal, there was still a clunk of contact. "That's going to be a problem," he muttered, dragging himself forward, "and—shit!" The magnet slipped along the steel panel with a piercing screech. "And that's *definitely* going to be a problem."

Matt reappeared at the opening. "Crap. I was afraid of that. It's designed to support a perpendicular load, not parallel—it's just going to slip all the time."

Eddie switched off the magnet. "Bollocks. Thanks for trying, anyway."

"Oh, I'm not done yet, mate!" Matt retrieved the magnet, replacing it with another device. "This might work better."

"A suction cup?" said Eddie, turning it over in his hand. The flattened black rubber dome was about five inches in diameter, a U-shaped hinged metal handle attached. "Now we really are getting all Jim Phelps."

"There's a lever under the handle—you push the handle up, move the lever across, and pull the handle back down to create the vacuum. When you want to release it, just shove the lever back the other way."

Eddie tested it, air hissing from the cup as he drew back the handle. Pulling himself farther into the duct, he was relieved to find that unlike the magnet, the suction device held firm. He released it with another hiss, moved it along, then clamped it down again. Pull—

"Hrmm," said Mac, as Eddie's backside wedged against the top of the duct. "You may need to lose a few pounds there."

"Eddie got back," sang Lola, giggling, then blushed. "Sorry. It's not funny."

Karima crouched for a closer look as Eddie wriggled in an attempt to clear the obstruction. "She has a point, though. It's not so much the size of your bottom—"

"You saying I've got a fat arse?" came an echoing complaint.

"—as what you're wearing. Your clothes are catching on the edge. You won't be able to do this in jeans; you'll need something tighter."

Mac put a palm on Eddie's butt and pushed down. Eddie hauled himself farther inside. "I hope that was Karima's hand."

"Of course," said Mac, winking at her.

Now that he was fully inside, Eddie was able to advance. It was still horribly tight, but using the suction cup he reached the other end in fairly short order. Matt and Rad pulled him out. "Jesus. I'm not claustrophobic, but that might get me started." Just traversing the short distance had left him sweating. How would he manage in the vault's much longer duct?

Mac had the same thought. "Eddie, you look knackered, and that was only six feet. And when you do it for real, you'll have equipment with you. We've got to find a way to make it easier."

Eddie wiped his brow. "Okay, Matt—you've got until tomorrow to invent a shrinking ray." The joke produced a little levity in the room—which instantly vanished at the rasp of the entry buzzer. "Shit, that'll be Zec. Mac?"

Mac drew a revolver and took up position in the study as Eddie buzzed Zec into the building. "Okay," said Eddie to the others, "stay cool and I'll handle this." He was about to go to the door when he noticed a cup from which Mac had been drinking and hurriedly took it into the kitchen. The fewer people Zec knew were involved, the better.

A knock on the door. Eddie let the Bosnian in. Zec was carrying an impact-resistant plastic box the size of a brief-case, as well as a carryall. He took in the hostile faces with a dismissive eye before regarding the ducting. "This is the size of the vents in the UN?"

"Yeah," said Eddie.

He put the box down at one end of the duct, pushing it into the opening. It fit—just. "Lucky. You will need to take this with you."

"What is it?"

Zec pulled the box back out and opened it, revealing a piece of equipment that looked like the guts of a desktop scanner mounted above a transparent plastic tank some five inches deep. "Portable rapid prototyper. Fill with—"

"I've used these," Matt cut in. "There are two lasers in the scan head, and where the beams cross they turn the medium in the tank solid. They build things up layer by layer, like a three-D fax machine. Once whatever you're making's set, you just lift it out of the tank."

"So what's this one going to be making?" asked Eddie.

Zec smiled sardonically. "Your wife's hand. I will give you a memory card with her handprint tomorrow."

Matt regarded the prototyper dubiously. "What's its res-olution? The ones I've used haven't been accurate enough to copy fingerprints."

Zec took a moment to remember the answer. "Submil-limeter, whatever that means. It will be good enough."

"It'd better be," rumbled Eddie.

Matt had more technical questions. "What about the base medium—is it a photopolymer or a thermoplastic powder? How long will it take to make the handprint?"

The mercenary frowned. "Ten minutes, and the liquid is in the bag—what it is does not matter!" He faced Eddie. "All you need to know is that it will work. But once the handprint has been created, you must wait until it cools to the right heat before you use it." He opened the holdall and took out a digital thermometer. "The security scanner checks body temperature as well as handprints."

Eddie kneaded his forehead. "Great, one more thing to worry about."

Zec looked at the blueprint. "How is your plan coming?"

"It's getting there. But it'd be getting there faster if we could actually work on it. You've delivered your little toy, so fuck off and leave us to it."

Unbothered by the insult, Zec headed for the hall. "You have until tomorrow night to bring me the codex. I will be waiting."

"Yeah," Eddie said coldly. "So will I." He waited until Zec had departed, then locked the door.

Mac emerged from the study. "Bastard. I had a perfect shot at him the whole time, too—I would have put a bullet in his head if you'd given the word."

"Not just yet," said Eddie. "Can't do anything to him until Nina's safe."

"You know that he's almost certainly been told to kill you the moment you hand over this book? And they probably intend to kill Nina too?"

Eddie smiled grimly. "Course I do. That's where Plan B comes in."

11

India

A sharp rap on the door jolted Nina out of her boredom. She had been a prisoner in her suite since the previous day; meals had been brought to her, but there was always a guard in the hallway outside. She had considered escaping via the window, but it was too high for her to jump down—and she was still constantly being watched electronically, the guard entering within seconds to order her to close it. Sullenly, she sat up. "What?"

Tandon entered. "Mr. Khoil wants to see you."

She had no interest in seeing him, but decided it would at least alleviate her cabin fever. Besides, anything more she could find out about his plans might be useful. "Okay, lead on."

Tandon took her through the palace to a large, high-ceilinged room. For a moment, she wondered if she had been brought to some bizarre high-tech disco: the room was dark, lights flickering inside a tall dome-shaped framework at its center. The illumination came from dozens of large flat-screen monitors, arranged inside the frame to form an almost 360-degree wall of video.

"Come in, Dr. Wilde," Khoil called from the heart of the

display. Tandon directed her to a gap in the screens. She blinked as she entered, the view from inside the dome almost overwhelming. Each screen seemed to be showing something different—broadcasts from TV networks all over the world, webpages, complex computer-generated graphs and charts, all of them constantly changing.

Khoil stood before a slim stand resembling a lectern in the middle of it all, looking up at one particular cluster of screens. He raised a hand and made a pinching gesture with his thumb and forefinger. The information spread over several monitors shrank down to just one; a sideways sweep, and a different set of figures expanded to take its place. He took them in, then raised a hand to his ear as if holding an imaginary telephone, tapping at the air with his other index finger. On the screens, a pointer moved over a representation of a numeric keypad that had appeared over the images. Sensors in the lectern were reading his movements, Nina realized: a gestural control system. After a moment, a man spoke in Hindi over loudspeakers. Khoil issued terse instructions, then lowered his hand to end the call. The virtual keypad faded away. He checked the screens, then turned to Nina. "Welcome to my infotarium."

"Great," she said, unimpressed. "Does it get the History Channel?"

"It gets every channel. It allows me to process data in a fraction of the time it would take using conventional media. It is the most efficient way to avoid being crushed by the weight of information I deal with each day."

The constant flicker of the screens was already making Nina feel vaguely nauseous. "I think I'd prefer a newspaper."

"I should have known that as an archaeologist, you would have a preference for the archaic. But then, Vanita does not like it either. She says it gives her a headache."

"I bet you hear that a lot, huh?"

Khoil either ignored the mocking jibe or, just as likely, failed to understand it. "The future of information delivery is not why I brought you here, though." He gestured with both hands, holding them flat and moving them apart: *That's enough*. The visual cacophony disappeared, replaced by the infotarium's equivalent of a computer's desktop. He raised a hand and "tapped" in midair; an icon pulsed as if touched, text zooming to fill the display.

She recognized it immediately as a translation of the Talonor Codex—but not quite the same as the one she had read. The phraseology was subtly different, and some of the sections not yet completed by the IHA had been filled in. "Is this your own translation?"

"Yes, performed by Qexia. As I said in San Francisco, it is much more capable than the typical translation program. It learns through analysis—not just about languages, but about any subject. The more information it has, the more accurate the results."

"It obviously doesn't have all the answers, though. Otherwise why would you need me?"

"Even though Qexia produced this in a matter of hours rather than the months taken by the IHA staff, it still cannot make deductions when the database lacks sufficient information."

"Score one for experience and intuition, then," said Nina, remembering their conversation at the exhibition hall.

Annoyance briefly crossed the Indian's placid face. "However, it has told me enough for now. By analyzing the codex and cross-referencing it with all the other data accessible to Qexia, it has discovered the approximate location of the Vault of Shiva." Another midair tap, and a map swelled on the wall. "It was actually quite obvious in hindsight—any true follower of Shiva would have guessed it, but Talonor's journey helped confirm it." He pointed, a

cursor fixing on a particular location. "Mount Kailash—
the home of Lord Shiva."

"Isn't that in Tibet?"

"Yes. About seventy kilometers from the border between India and China—though since the border is disputed, it is hard to be precise."

"But definitely on the Chinese side, though," Nina
pointed out. "Could make it hard for you to go nosing
around."

"Not at all. For one thing, I have excellent connections
with the Chinese government—my company provides software and services for them. For another, the Sacred Mountain is a place of pilgrimage for Hindus. Thousands travel
there each year. It is the tallest unclimbed mountain in the
world—not even the Chinese dare interfere with the site."

"But you'd dare, right?"

Now he seemed almost offended. "Of course not. Besides, the vault is almost certainly not on the mountain itself. It took the priests a day to reach it."

"And an hour to get back."

"A paradox that Qexia noted. It may be that a river connected the two locations, and they were able to return
downstream in a fraction of the time needed to get up it."

Nina almost pointed out that Talonor had traveled
away from the river to visit the Hindu temple, but decided
that giving him potentially helpful information was a bad
idea. Instead, she shifted the subject. "I still don't see how
opening the Vault of Shiva will bring about the end of the
world. So you make an amazing archaeological find,
tablets that may have been written by Shiva himself—then
what? That on its own won't bring about the apocalypse."

"The apocalypse is coming, no matter what, Dr. Wilde."
Khoil faced her, reflections on his glasses turning his eyes
into disks as blank as his expression. "Humanity is sinking
into a new dark age of violence and depravity. Barbarism

will reign. Within the next fifty years, modern society will be destroyed."

Nina cocked her head. "You're not the first person to make a prediction of imminent Armageddon. The Book of Revelation, Nostradamus, all that 2012 Mayan calendar nonsense . . . and every one of them was wrong."

"Not this time. It is inevitable." He waved a hand, more screens lighting up around them. Images appeared—deforestation, factories belching pollution, rioters, burning buildings—as well as chart after chart in which the lines shot alarmingly either up . . . or down. "Qexia makes logical predictions based on available data. Every prediction produces the same result—the end of civilization as we know it. The only variable is the time line."

"Nice little PowerPoint demonstration," Nina said sarcastically. "But applying math to a prediction of doom doesn't mean it'll happen. People have been doing that since Thomas Malthus in the eighteenth century, and we're still here."

"But you cannot deny that society is becoming more degenerate as we descend deeper into the Kali Yuga. It is written in the Mahabharata: 'Sin will increase and prosper, while virtue will fade and cease to flourish.' See for yourself." Another gesture, and the depressing display was replaced by columns of text. "These are the most common search terms entered into Qexia. Billions of people have access to the greatest source of knowledge in history, and what are they looking for?" He jabbed at the screens, words flashing an angry red under his virtual touch. "Sex! Pornography! Trivial news about worthless celebrities! Images of violence and destruction! Society's innermost desires laid bare. Moral corruption is all around us. Is this worth saving?"

"Okay, so it's not perfect, but . . ."

A small smile creased Khoil's smooth cheeks. "Shall we see *your* innermost desires, Dr. Wilde?" A stylized keyboard was superimposed over the screens; he "typed" in the air, the keys blinking as he entered a string of text.

Nina was unnerved to see her name among the words, more so when a new list appeared. "Wait, how did you get—"

"Qexia remembers everything. Who used it, and when, and why. And then it analyzes that new data, and adds it to everything else it has learned. It can even tell with a high degree of probability whether you or your husband are using it." More commands, and the list split into three columns: one headed by Nina's name, one by Eddie's, and the last labeled INDETERMINATE. He highlighted one of the items in Eddie's list. "For example, I find it unlikely that you would have an interest in this particular subject."

Nina scowled, even as she blushed at the discovery that her husband apparently had a kink of which she was unaware. "Oh, I'm going to have a talk with him about *that*."

"You are hardly innocent yourself, Dr. Wilde. Shall we see?" The cursor hovered over her list.

"Uh—no, okay, point taken!" Khoil smugly dismissed the display. "So what are you planning on doing with all this information? Blackmail everybody who's ever used the Internet?"

"No. I am going to bring about the end of the Kali Yuga." He said it with the same flat, robotic matter-of-factness that characterized the rest of his speech. "The collapse of present civilization is inevitable, but because it is part of the cycle of existence, restoration—a new Satya Yuga, a new dawn of virtue—is also inevitable. My computer models have told me that the sooner the Kali Yuga ends, the shorter the period of chaos before the Satya Yuga begins. As I said, it could take fifty years for the collapse to happen naturally, fifty years of decadence and decay, meaning the recovery would begin from a lower point. It could take a century for the new era to begin—a century of pain and suffering. But if the collapse were to happen *now* ... it would take only ten years."

"That's still ten years of chaos."

"Better ten than a hundred." He stepped closer to her. "I am not a passive man, Dr. Wilde. I rose from the slums by seeing opportunities and taking them, changing the world around me to my advantage. This will be the ultimate opportunity, and I must take it, for the good of all humanity. I will end the Kali Yuga—but I will also guide the beginning of the Satya Yuga."

"The downfall of civilization as a business opportunity, huh?"

"More a guiding hand. I have been assembling resources worldwide—people with vital skills, stockpiles of food and shelter, secure data archives in remote locations like Mongolia and Greenland, a satellite communications infrastructure that will be unaffected by wars on the ground. They will all be put to use to help those in need following the collapse."

Nina narrowed her eyes. "With strings attached, I'm guessing."

"The world must learn that Shiva is the one true lord of creation. Which is why I hired Urbano Fernandez. Some of the items he obtained for me were for their protection; they are irreplaceable cultural treasures that would surely be stolen or destroyed during the chaos."

"And they'll just happen to be in your private collection for 'safekeeping' while all this is going on, right?"

"But," he went on, ignoring her, "the others will provide me with leverage in places where the word of Shiva might not be heard."

"Places like Saudi Arabia," she realized. "If there's a global collapse, nobody'll be paying for their oil—and they don't have a hell of a lot of other resources. So then you tell them, 'If you want help, if you want the Black Stone back, I want something in return.'"

"Correct. Money may not be much use after the collapse, but influence will be. Having power over the Saudis gives me influence over Islam, power over the Italians gives me influence over Roman Catholicism, and so on. I will use it to spread the word of Shiva—the true, uncorrupted word that waits inside the vault."

"Sounds kinda far-fetched, if you ask me," Nina scoffed. "You won't turn over centuries of belief and tradition with blackmail."

"People will do anything when they are hungry and desperate. When one god has failed them and another offers them hope, will they take it? I think so."

Nina slowly circled him, Tandon shadowing her. "So how are you planning on bringing all this about? I don't see how a search engine can be a harbinger of the apocalypse."

"Then you are shortsighted, Dr. Wilde. Qexia will play a vital part."

She could tell that he was itching to impress her with his cleverness; the question was, how much would his ego let slip? She injected a disbelieving, faintly mocking note into her voice. "You're going to end the world with search results? How?"

He raised his hands, the virtual keyboard appearing on the screens. Some commands, and the walls lit up with numerous pages from news sites around the globe. "People choose sources of information not because they trust them to be impartial, but because they reflect their own view of the world. Their biases—their passions, if you like." He regarded the screens. "All these pages are about a terrorist bombing in Mumbai two weeks ago. As you can see, it was covered by dozens of news agencies in different countries, each of which had its own interpretation of events."

"That's hardly news, if you'll excuse the pun."

More commands. "When people want information about a subject, they turn to a search engine. Like Qexia.

Now, these are the results a Hindu living in India would see when he searched for information about the bombing."

A "cloud" of results appeared, the ones Qexia deemed most relevant dominating the center, others smaller on the periphery. Nina examined the central cluster; they blamed Pakistani-backed Islamic militants for the attack. "Okay, but apart from looking prettier, I don't see how that's any different from what you'd get on Google."

"Then see what the same search would give to a Muslim in Pakistan." He typed again. The search cloud reloaded... with considerably different results.

"These... these are all accusing the Indian government of lying," Nina saw. "Blaming the Pakistanis for something they weren't involved in." The larger implications struck her. "This is stirring up tensions between India and Pakistan."

Khoil nodded. "As I told you, Qexia *learns* about its users. As they provide it with more information, it builds up a better picture of their beliefs. It was designed to target advertising more precisely... but it has other uses."

"You're fixing the search results," said Nina accusingly. "You're lying to them."

"Not at all. It gives them what they *expect* to find— feeding their biases. Inflaming their passions. All sources of information throughout history have filtered their results to favor a particular point of view. I am doing the same, for the most noble of reasons."

"*Noble?*" Nina snapped. "You think bringing down modern society and causing God knows how many millions of deaths is noble?"

"If it is for a greater purpose, then yes."

"And how were you planning on doing this?" She waved a hand at the screens. "Inflaming passions, starting a war, yeah... but between who?" As soon as she spoke, she realized that Khoil might have already answered the question: He had chosen the subject of his demonstration without hesitation, as if it had already been on his mind. India and Pakistan were nuclear-armed enemies, on the edge of open conflict for decades. Had his urge to show off his technology, his intellectual superiority, tipped his hand?

However, he proved unwilling to elaborate. "You will find out soon. As will the rest of the world. But that is not why I brought you to me. Come this way." Khoil exited the dome, Tandon pushing her after him.

He rounded the framework supporting the screens and led her to one side of the room. A desk held several pieces of high-tech equipment, but Nina's attention was caught by something obsolete. A glass display case contained a small computer of a type she didn't recognize, but from its styling—and time-scuffed condition—it appeared to be of 1980s vintage.

Khoil noticed her looking at it. "My first computer," he said. "A Spectrum Plus. Everything I have achieved with Qexia began with that." Something approaching warmth entered his voice. "As a boy, I made money for my family by repairing and selling broken devices we found in the dump—radios, tape players, and so on. I could not believe that somebody had thrown away a computer! The only thing wrong with it was the power supply, and once I repaired it we were going to sell it ... but I decided to experiment with it first. I wrote some simple programs—and, as the saying goes, I caught the bug."

"Your humble beginnings," Nina said dismissively. Under other circumstances a rags-to-riches story might have been interesting, but she was in no mood to indulge Khoil's nostalgia.

His tone chilled once more. "Indeed. Now come here." Tandon shoved her to the desk. "Hold out your right arm."

Suspiciously, Nina regarded the machine Khoil was adjusting. It resembled a lathe, only where she would have expected to find a cutting tool, there was a highly polished prism. "What is it?"

"A laser scanner. Your palm print is needed to remove the Talonor Codex from the United Nations' vault." He indicated the machine beside it: a rapid prototyper, identical to the one Zec had delivered to Eddie. "Using the pattern from the scanner, this will create an exact duplicate of your hand—one good enough to fool the security system."

Nina shook her head and folded her arms tightly. "No way are you getting my palm print."

"One way or another, your hand will be sent to New York. It is up to you whether it is a copy...or the original."

Tandon's expression suggested he would be more than happy to make it the latter. Reluctantly, Nina held out her arm. Khoil positioned it over the scanner, then tapped a control. The prism began to spin, so rapidly that it became a ghostly blur. A bright blue laser light shone from the body of the scanner, the needle-thin beam spread into a flickering grid by the prism. The pattern moved smoothly over the length of Nina's hand. A bleep from the machine, and the light vanished, the prism stopping with a click.

Khoil checked a reading, appearing satisfied. "Your palm print has been recorded. Now we have everything we need."

Nina pulled her hand away. "Except the codex. And without that, you've got nothing."

"That," said Khoil, "is entirely up to your husband."

12

New York City

Eddie waited in a corner of the spacious marble lobby of the Delacourt hotel, watching the doors to 44th Street. He could see a small but excited crowd through the glass, hotel staff keeping back anyone who had no legitimate business in the building.

Almost eight PM. The tide would reach its highest point at eight fourteen, and he still needed Lola's go-ahead before the operation could begin. Matt would have to work fast.

Someone pushed through the throng outside and was briefly quizzed by a doorman before coming in: Zec, dressed in a heavy overcoat and seeming irritated at having his entry challenged. He spotted Eddie and sat next to him. "What's going on?" he asked, indicating the bustle outside.

"Paparazzi," said Eddie disinterestedly. "Some celebrity's in the hotel." He gave the Bosnian a sour look. "You got the thing?"

Zec handed him a small memory card. "Your wife's handprint. Put it in the prototyper, and the machine will do the rest. Just remember to wait until it cools to body temperature before putting it on the scanner." His eyes narrowed. "I was also told to remind you what will happen to your wife if you do not bring me the codex."

"I'm not fucking deaf," Eddie growled, aware the statement might not be entirely truthful. "You already told me."

"Just doing my job."

"Your wife and son know about your job?" Zec was unprepared for the question, and looked sharply at him. "Think your wife'd approve of you threatening to kill mine? Kid proud of Daddy the murderer?"

"Shut up," Zec snapped. "The only people I have killed are legitimate mission targets. Civilian casualties were not my fault."

"Well, that makes it all better, dunnit?" Eddie regarded him sourly. "No way Hugo would have worked with you if you'd told him that. But who needs morals when you've got money, right?" The accusation appeared to sting the Bosnian, which gave Eddie a moment of gratification. "Now, I want to talk to Nina."

"I thought you might." Zec made a call. "Mr. Khoil? Chase wants to speak to his wife." He listened to the reply, then handed the phone to Eddie.

"Mr. Chase," said Khoil. "I hope you are ready to bring me the codex. Otherwise, you know what will hap—"

"Yeah, yeah, spare me the fucking threats," Eddie snapped. "I already had them from your errand boy. Where's Nina?"

"She is here with me."

A pause, a hollow echo down the line, then Nina spoke. "Eddie? Are you okay?"

"I'm fine—what about you?"

For a moment, it seemed that she hadn't heard him. "Eddie? Are you there—oh, thank God. Yeah, I'm okay. Look, Eddie, you can't go through with this. I know part of what the Khoils are planning. They—"

"Enough," said Khoil. The faint echoing effect disappeared. "Mr. Chase, it is time to bring me the codex. Do so, and your wife will be returned to you unharmed." With that, the line fell silent.

Eddie returned the phone to Zec, using all his willpower not to say out loud the thought dominating his mind: Khoil was lying. Nina wasn't with him, the delay of the satellite connection proved she was still in India. The moment Khoil—who from the instant response on his side of the call clearly *was* in the States, eager to take personal delivery of the Talonor Codex—got what he wanted, she would be killed.

And so would the man who obtained the codex for him, Eddie knew. But all he could do for now was play his part—and hope that Plan B worked.

His phone trilled. "Lola?"

"Everything's ready," said Lola. "You remember the locker numbers?"

"Burned into my mind."

"Okay. Good luck." She rang off.

Eddie stood, picking up a large black leather briefcase with gleaming steel trim. "That was the go-signal," he told Zec. "I'll meet you back here when I'm done."

"With the codex."

"Obviously with the fucking codex. You just be ready with Nina." He headed for the doors, glancing back at Zec ...then past him, to a couch. Dressed in a suit, reading a newspaper, Mac briefly looked up at him. At his feet was another black briefcase.

Eddie stepped outside, feeling the bite of the December cold as he pushed through the crowd and walked to the end of 44th Street. The United Nations complex rose on the other side of First Avenue, a towering grid of lights against the dark sky.

He raised his phone again. "Matt? It's Eddie. I'm ready."

"Roger that, mate," said the Australian. "We're in the pipe, five by five."

* * *

On the far side of the UN, a boat bobbed in the East River. Radi Bashir shivered in his thick coat as he gazed nervously at the glowing glass slab of the Secretariat Building. He didn't know what the rules were regarding boating off Manhattan, but he was sure they were breaking them by dropping anchor in the busy waterway. Any official attention they attracted would undoubtedly be magnified when it was realized that all three of the boat's occupants were foreign nationals . . . and two of them were Arabs.

Karima popped up through the hatch to the lower deck. "Eddie just called. He's going in." She ducked back. With a last look around for any boats that might belong to the NYPD's Harbor Unit, Rad climbed down after her.

Matt Trulli had set up shop in the small cabin, two laptop computers and a complex remote-control unit crammed onto a little table and secured with duct tape. A porthole was open, cold air coming through it; below it was a large spool of fiber-optic cable, the slender but strong glass thread running out through the window. The spool was connected to one of the laptops—and the other end of the line to the Remotely Operated Vehicle currently picking its way through a water pipe beneath the river's western bank.

"All right, you little beaut," Matt muttered, using two joysticks to guide the ROV. "Go on in there . . ." On the laptop's screen, a view from one of the robot's cameras revealed a fat, plastic-sheathed cable disappearing into the darkness of the circular channel. The spool slowly turned, the robot's fiber-optic control cable feeding out as it moved forward.

The ground under Manhattan was crisscrossed by myriad networks of underground conduits, from subway tunnels to steam pipes to the city's telecommunications backbone. This particular system, originally constructed in the early twentieth century to provide the city's fire hydrants with a supply of water straight from the river, had been out of use for almost a quarter of a century, superseded by more powerful pumping systems—until an enterprising telecom company realized it was the perfect way to spread the hundreds of miles of fiber-optic lines needed to meet the city's ever-growing demand for broadband without having to dig up half the streets in Manhattan.

The cables had been installed entirely by robots, designed to crawl through the narrow, flooded confines. Matt's machine was following their tracks . . . but considerably more quickly. Servo was a yard-long, vaguely snakelike construct, made from three tubular sections linked by universal joints: a flexible torpedo able to bend and twist through narrow underwater spaces. The rearmost segment housed the propeller and steering vanes, the middle one the battery pack, while the front section contained cameras, lights, and a folded manipulator arm.

Matt glanced at the other laptop, which displayed a graphic of the pipeline system overlaid on a plan of the United Nations. A blinking cursor showed Servo's position, not far from the outline of the Secretariat Building. "What's the time?" he asked.

"Eight oh four," Karima told him.

"Christ, we've only got ten minutes to high tide. Pick up the pace, Servo!" he told the screen as he thumbed the throttle wheel on one joystick. The fiber-optic spool turned faster.

* * *

Eddie reached the IHA offices. "Working late, Lola?" he said in what he hoped was a casual tone. There were still a few staff members around even this late; the IHA was full of people who could lose all track of time poring over some piece of ancient junk, his own wife one of the worst offenders. He couldn't go to the vault until his friends completed their work, so this was the least suspicious place to wait.

"Yes, just finishing some paperwork," Lola replied; then she lowered her voice. "I used Nina's security code to give you access to the lockers. Just use your own ID when you get down there—it's all in the system. As far as the guards will know, Nina's given you authorization to open them."

"They won't check and find that she's not here?"

"But she *is* here," said Lola with exaggerated innocence as she tapped her keyboard. "The computer says she's had one of the conference rooms booked all day. And computers are never wrong, right?"

Eddie grinned. "Thanks, Lola." Still carrying the heavy case, he went into Nina's office.

He checked his watch. Eight ten. *Come on, Matt!*

* * *

Karima watched the map intently as the cursor crept across it, painfully slowly. Servo was now beneath the Secretariat Building, but the old pipeline system branched and turned as it progressed inland, the ROV needing to follow a convoluted route to its destination.

She looked at the view on the other laptop. The pipe divided ahead, one leg continuing straight on while the other made a ninety-degree turn. "Which way?" Matt asked.

"Left," she told him. "About twenty meters ahead there's another junction. Turn right, and up."

The pipe beyond the next intersection ascended at a forty-five-degree angle. "Go left at the top," said Rad. "Then it's a straight line to the junction box."

"Time?" asked Matt as he piloted the robot toward the final turn.

"Eight twelve," said Karima.

"Two minutes to high tide...Christ." Another turn of the throttle.

The robot reached the top of the shaft. Alarmingly, it

was instantly clear that the new pipeline was not completely full of water—a shimmering line sliced across its
top.

The surface. The tide was at its highest. And it might not
be high enough.

Matt shoved the throttle to full. On the screen, the con-
duit rushed past like something from a video game. "How
far?"

"Twenty meters," said Rad, staring at the map. "Fifteen..."

"Watch out!" Karima cried as something flashed into
view ahead. An unidentifiable hunk of flotsam carried
there by tidal currents blocked the way—

Servo couldn't stop in time. The image spun crazily as
the robot hit the obstacle...

And stopped.

"Shit. Shit!" Matt gasped. The view swayed dizzily as
Servo reeled from side to side, but couldn't pull free. He
worked the joysticks, trying to make the robot squirm past
the obstruction.

The water's surface churned as backwash from the propeller created ripples—but even through the distortion
Karima saw it was lower than before. "Matt! The water's
dropping!"

Eight fifteen. The tide was inexorably retreating.

Matt frantically jerked the controls. "Come on, Servo,
you can do it! Come on!"

Still at full power. But still not moving.

"Come *on*!" Another twist, the camera rasping against
the wall—

The view suddenly tumbled, the ROV corkscrewing
down the pipe as it finally kicked free. Matt struggled to re-
gain control. "How far, how far?"

"Ten meters," said Rad.

The water level was still falling. The camera breached
the surface, rivulets streaming down the lens.

Another few seconds, and the robot submarine would run aground...

"Almost there!" Rad cried. "Three meters, two—"

The pipe widened out. The ROV had reached an access shaft, a rusting ladder rising upward. Matt reversed the propeller. Servo skidded to a stop on the bottom of the pipe, kicking up a bow wave.

"Bloody hell," the Australian said, blowing out a long breath. "That was way too close."

Karima examined the screen, seeing nothing but the pipeline disappearing into the distance. "Where's the junction box?"

"Above, in the shaft." He switched to a second set of controls to operate the ROV's manipulator arm. It had a camera of its own mounted on its "wrist"; the view changed to an even more fish-eyed angle as the arm unfolded. The bottom of the image was dominated by a pointed probe: a cutter. "Let's have a dekko..."

The camera tilted upward, an LED spotlight flicking on to illuminate the shaft. The small lens made it hard to judge scale, the ladder seeming to have been made for giants, but the manhole cover at the top was probably less than three yards above. Far nearer was their objective—a fiber-optic junction box fixed to the shaft's side. The main cable trunk ran through it, but another thick line emerged from its top and ran upward, connecting the UN's underground data center to the rest of the digital world.

"That's it," said Rad, relieved. He indicated a lock on the box's front panel. "Can you cut through that?"

"No worries," Matt told him, guiding the arm closer. He flicked a switch; in seconds, the cutter's tip glowed red hot. Carefully tweaking the controls, he touched the tool to the panel and moved it in a circle around the lock. The junction box's casing was anodized aluminum, watertight and protected against corrosion, but the sheet metal was thin. Molten droplets fell into the water as the cutter sliced through it.

In less than a minute, the entire lock dropped out of the panel. Matt switched off the cutter and retracted it, a robotic claw swinging up to take its place. It took hold of the edge of the burned hole and tugged until the panel opened. "Okay," he said. "Now what?"

Rad examined a schematic. "My source said that the diagnostic port is...this one." He indicated one of several sockets on the printout. Matt moved the arm to give them a better look at its real-life counterpart. "Second row, the bottom one."

Matt pulled the arm back, tipping it down to look at Servo's equipment bay. Inside was a length of fiber-optic cable, plug connectors on each end. "It'll take me a few minutes to hook up the data link through Servo. You sure this program of yours'll work?"

Rad dismissed the map from the second laptop's screen, starting up another application. An unappealingly functional program titled *Levenex FODN Diagnostic 3.2a* appeared. "He says there's a back door that'll get us into the UN system. I've got the instructions—once we're in, I can find the digital feeds for the vault's cameras."

"This contact of yours," Karima said dubiously, "he *is* reliable, isn't he?"

Rad smiled. "Well, I obviously can't reveal my sources, but I trust him." A beat, the smile turning down a notch. "More or less."

"I see...Still, I'll call Eddie and tell him we're in position." She took out her phone.

* * *

Eddie hadn't sat down the whole time he was waiting, instead pacing around Nina's office until his phone rang. "Okay. I'm moving," he told Karima, then hung up. He collected the case and walked out.

Lola mouthed *Good luck* as he passed. He nodded, then went to the elevators. Steeling himself, he pushed the lowest button and began his descent to the third basement level.

To his relief, his journey was uninterrupted, nobody else boarding the lift. At the bottom the doors opened, and he stepped out. He made his leisurely way to the secure storage area, wanting to give Rad as much time as possible to hack into the system.

But he couldn't wait long. Every passing second was another slice off Zec's deadline.

He arrived at the security station. "Evening, Lou. Henri."

"Workin' late, Eddie?" Jablonsky asked. Vernio looked up from the Nintendo DS he was using as a boredom-buster and nodded in greeting.

"Yeah. Nina's engrossed in some ancient wotsit or other. She asked me to check some files for her. It's a glamorous job, being the special assistant to the director, eh?"

Jablonsky smiled, gesturing to the computer. "What do you need?"

Eddie inserted his ID and gave him the appropriate locker numbers. Vernio checked them on the screen. Tension rose up the Englishman's spine. If Lola's use of Nina's security code had been discovered...

He couldn't see the screen directly, but a faint wash of green over the Haitian's face was enough to tell him that he had been approved. "Huh," said Jablonsky. "Lola just put some files in those lockers."

"You know how it goes," said Eddie, shrugging. "These scientist types: 'I've finished with those, send them downstairs,' then half an hour later it's, 'Oh, I need to check that thing again, can you go and get it?' Still, at least I only need to take notes instead of faffing about signing 'em out of the vault."

"Small mercies, huh?" Jablonsky let him through the gate and started down the central aisle. "This way."

Eddie glanced toward the vault door as they turned off into one of the side stacks, navigating the maze until they reached the first locker on Eddie's list. Jablonsky used a key attached to an extending chain on his belt to open it. One of the items inside was a large box file, held closed with an elastic band.

The guard moved to retrieve it, but Eddie stepped forward, putting down the briefcase. "It's okay, mate. I'll get it." He reached into the locker for the file—and while the other man's view was obstructed, he surreptitiously jammed a rolled-up piece of cardboard into the rectangular slot in the lock plate.

The box file was heavy and awkward, an object clunking about inside. "Okay," he said, backing up. Jablonsky closed the door. It clicked. Eddie's heart froze for a moment—if he couldn't get back into the locker without a security key, it would seriously complicate things . . .

A thin line of cardboard was barely visible in the gap between the door and the frame, the bolt pressed against it. It had worked—just.

Covering his relief, he picked up the briefcase and followed Jablonsky to the next locker. No need to jam this one, as its contents were only a decoy, a collection of documents plucked from Nina's office at random. This time, he allowed the security guard to collect them for him. The locker closed, they headed for the reading area, Eddie glancing up at the cameras along the route. The other guard would be watching him—but so would his friends.

He hoped Rad was as good as he claimed.

"Here you go, Eddie," said Jablonsky. The reading area, a series of booths with high sides for privacy while reading classified material, was fortunately empty. "Sit where you like. When you're finished, just wave—one of us'll come get you." He indicated a camera, positioned so that while it couldn't see anything being read, any occupants of the booths were still visible.

"Cheers." Eddie went to the booth farthest from the main entrance and sat, putting down the briefcase and the box file and spreading the papers across the desktop. He made a show of finding some specific page until Jablonsky was out of sight, then opened the file.

Inside were two items: a three-liter plastic container of a thick transparent liquid, and an earpiece, taped to the top of the box. He removed the latter, tapping it twice as a signal before pushing it into his right ear.

"Eddie, are you there?" Karima. Her voice was distorted, his underground location making the signal crackle. "If you can hear me, give me a microphone check." He hummed a snatch of the *Mission: Impossible* theme. "Very funny. I've got him," she added for Rad and Matt's benefit.

"Is everything set?" he whispered.

"Rad's still working on the cameras."

"How much longer will he need?"

Karima passed Rad her headset. "Eddie? I need another few minutes to Photoshop the last couple of cameras—but I also need to record the footage of you that I'm going to use to make a loop. Two minutes should be plenty."

"Anything special I should do?"

"Move around a little so it's obvious they're not watching a freeze-frame, but make sure you're in exactly the same position at the start and the end. You remember that movie *Speed*?"

"Yeah, great film. I thought the sequel was a bit pants, though. What about it?"

"The bad guy blew up the bus because the loop didn't match exactly."

"I thought it blew up 'cause it crashed into a plane."

"Either way, it blew up! So you've got to get it right. Keep an eye on your watch, and be back in the same position when the two minutes are up. Ready?"

"Yep."

"Okay, three, two, one . . . start."

Eddie took up a neutral pose, pretending to peruse the documents. The two minutes that followed seemed to crawl by. A maddening itch started in the small of his back, but he resisted the urge to scratch it, knowing that any distinctive movements might be remembered when the footage was replayed on a continuous loop on the security monitors.

The second hand on his watch ticked around, passing the minute mark once . . . twice. "Okay, got it," Karima reported.

Eddie relaxed. "Great," he said, scratching his back.

"Don't move too much, though—you need to be in the same position when Rad starts the loop."

"How long will that be?"

"Just give him a minute . . ."

* * *

It took more than the promised minute, but not by much. Aboard the boat, Rad had been working furiously on the second laptop, taking the hijacked digital video footage recorded on the hard drive and using his arsenal of professional video-editing software to create a "mask" that would erase the timecode from the corner of each frame. This way, the correct time could be superimposed over the two-minute loop when the recording was sent to the monitors at the security station.

"Okay, I'm ready," he finally said. He switched to another program, the feeds from several of the security cameras arranged in a grid. The archives were empty, nothing moving except the constantly changing timecodes. Because the images were stationary, a single still frame with the original timecode masked out would serve to cover what Eddie was about to do. "Get back into position and I'll give you a countdown. Karima will talk you through."

On the camera covering the reading area, Eddie moved back into his neutral position. "He's ready," said Karima.

"What're the guards doing?" Matt asked, peering at the other video feeds.

"They're both at the security station," said Rad. "Okay, Eddie. Three, two, one...*now.*"

He hit a key. The images flickered as the live footage from the security cameras was replaced by Rad's recordings. "Timecodes are okay," he said, anxiously checking each screen.

Karima was more concerned with the guards. If they had noticed the brief glitch...

They hadn't. Both men remained seated, one still playing with his DS. "Eddie, it's working. *Go!*"

* * *

Eddie opened the briefcase. Inside was the case containing the rapid prototyper. He took it out and used a strap to fasten the container of liquid—the prototyper's silicone-based medium—to its handle, then put the briefcase back under the desk and quietly carried both case and bottle into the stacks.

He retraced his route to the sabotaged locker and tried the door. It rattled, the bolt catching the edge of the lock plate. "Shit," he whispered, pulling harder. If he couldn't get in—

The cardboard wedge shifted, the bolt squeaking free. He froze. The locker was open, but if the guards had heard the sound... 'Karima! The guards—are they moving?"

"No," came the reply. He released a relieved breath, then turned his attention to the locker's contents. Another box file was inside; he opened it, taking out a small but powerful LED flashlight on an elastic strap, a screwdriver with interchangeable heads, a pair of wrist straps, the suction cup, a heat gun—a clone of the device attached to

Matt's ROV—and a small squeezable plastic bottle. Lining them up on the floor, he began to remove his clothes.

Through the earpiece he heard Matt humming "The Stripper"—Rad's computer was displaying the live signals from the cameras as well as the faked ones going to the guards' monitors. "Tell Matt to pack that in," he muttered. The tune stopped.

He dropped his clothing to the floor...revealing a skintight polyurethane bodysuit. The super-slick garment had been designed for swimmers, reducing drag as they passed through the water to such an extent that they had been banned from professional competitions. But slickness—and tightness, the suit as constricting as a Victorian corset—were exactly what Eddie needed. Around his waist was a belt, also pulled tight.

He stuffed his clothes into the locker, then carefully shut the door and donned the wrist straps, clipping the heat gun, the screwdriver, and the suction cup to them. He then put the flashlight's strap around his head and reached up to push the case and the silicone container on top of the lockers, followed by the plastic bottle.

Now the hard part began. Eddie jumped to grab the top of the lockers, feet against the doors. He was not wearing his usual boots, but close-fitting black climbing shoes, with rubber soles for maximum grip. As quietly as possible, he pulled himself up.

The space between the dusty surface and the suspended ceiling was barely more than a foot, but Eddie knew it would soon feel positively expansive. As the plans Lola procured had promised, there was a ventilation grille a few feet away. Pushing his belongings ahead of him, he crawled to it.

A minute's work with the screwdriver, and the vent cover was freed at one end. He turned his attention to the other, only unfastening the screws halfway so that he could tilt the grille down on its makeshift hinge.

Shuffling to the end of the newly created ramp, he fastened the case to the back of his belt with another strap, then took the small bottle and squirted its contents over the front of his bodysuit. It was a lubricant; he had actually bought it from a sex shop. Looking into the darkness of the duct, however, he doubted he would get much pleasure from it.

"Okay, I'm going in," he said, holding the suction cup. "Tell me if the guards move."

"I will, Eddie," said Karima. "Good luck."

"Thanks." He switched on the flashlight, pressed the suction cup against the metal floor, and pulled himself inside.

It was worse than he had imagined. The short section of duct at the apartment had been clean; this was filthy, a grimy layer of God-knew-what having been drawn in by the ventilation system several floors above. But he continued, advancing with each hiss of the cup. The case and plastic container ground complainingly over the grille as he hauled them along behind him like a train.

Even with the benefit of the bodysuit, the duct was horribly cramped. He tipped his head to shine the light down the shaft. He had to cover over fifty feet before reaching the vault—where his first obstacle waited.

Karima's voice crackled in his ear, the metal duct making radio reception even worse. "You okay, Eddie?"

"Yeah," he grunted. He was sweating, the situation not helped by the tight synthetic suit.

"Good. The guards are still at the desk."

"Okay." His movements had already become a routine. Release the suction cup, stretch and plant it against the metal six inches farther ahead, apply suction, pull himself forward, repeat. The extra weight he was dragging made it more draining. His own body, pressed against the duct on all sides, was almost blocking the flow of air. The vent was getting stuffy, stifling—and it would soon become a lot hotter.

He fixed his attention entirely on advancing, trying not to think about the metal pressing in on him. Another six inches, and another. He looked ahead. The flashlight caught something in the distance.

He squinted, blinking away more sweat. The first obstacle: the metal baffle plates welded into the duct about thirty-five feet away. He would have to use the cutter to remove them.

Six more inches. Another six. His shoulders ached, but he had to endure the pain—the duct was too narrow for him to shift his weight. His back itched furiously, sweat building up inside the bodysuit.

Keep moving. Pull. Pull. Another foot covered—

The duct floor flexed under his weight. A flat metallic *clonk* echoed through the vent. He froze.

"Eddie!" Karima's voice was anxious. "What was that?"

"Are the guards moving?" he whispered.

"Yes! One of them just stood up!"

* * *

"Eddie?" called Jablonsky. The noise sounded like something being dropped. He looked at the monitors. Eddie was still in the booth, apparently not having heard anything. The noise wasn't him, then. So what was it?

"Maybe a locker popped open," Vernio suggested. It had happened before.

"I'll take a look." Jablonsky set off down the aisle.

* * *

Rad switched the laptop's video grid to show the untampered feeds from all the cameras so he could track the guard. "Eddie!" Karima said. "He's moving, he's coming toward—"

The boat suddenly lurched as waves slapped the hull. A shaft of dazzling light shone through the open porthole. "You on the boat!" boomed an amplified voice from outside. "This is the NYPD Harbor Unit. Come out on the deck, right now!"

13

Eddie heard a faint clacking somewhere below: the guard's footsteps.

Getting closer.

What had happened to Karima? She had cut off mid-sentence. "Karima!" he whispered. "Can you hear me? Karima!"

• • •

The beam of light shifted as the NYPD boat closed in. "I say again," the cop barked through his bullhorn, "this is the police! Show yourselves!"

Rad looked at Karima. "What do we do? If they board us—"

"Forget that!" cried Matt. The spool of fiber-optic line was unwinding in fits and starts. "Their boat's snagged the line! If it breaks, we'll lose the link—and the cameras'll come back on!" He spun the drum to pay out more line. The fiber-optic thread was strong and flexible—but ultimately it was nothing more than glass, and would snap if overstressed. "Try to stall 'em until I can get this loose!"

Karima and Rad shared nervous looks, then Karima

opened the hatch, taking off her headset before slowly climbing to the deck. A dazzling light shone in her face. Through the glare she made out a larger blue-and-white boat alongside their vessel. "Come on out where we can see you, miss," ordered the cop.

"Is there a problem?" she called as Rad emerged behind her. Glancing back through the hatch, she saw Matt still desperately turning the spool.

"Yeah, you could say that. Weighing anchor in the middle of the East River ain't a smart move." On the police boat's deck, two officers moved to board the smaller craft. The light played over the two Jordanians. "Now, would I be right in thinking that you're not American citizens?"

* * *

The footsteps got closer. Eddie forced himself to remain statue-still, trying to suppress even his breathing.

Click-click-click...click...click. The guard had stopped—almost directly below him.

* * *

The first cop jumped aboard, making the boat sway. He regarded Karima and Rad with evident suspicion, then looked across at the dark crystal tower of the Secretariat Building. Even without speaking, his thought processes were clear: Arabs...skyscraper...*terrorists.* One hand moved to the butt of his holstered gun. "You better have a damn good reason for being out here."

* * *

Jablonsky put his hands on his hips, looking around. None of the lockers was open. Maybe the noise had been a gust of wind through the ventilation system, or something heavy being moved on the floor above.

He was about to return to his post—then decided that

since he was up, he might as well do a round of the archives.

He started toward the reading area.

* * *

"All right, okay, I'm coming!" came a voice from below-deck. Matt clambered through the hatch, glaring at the cop. "What's going on? You almost screwed everything up!"

The second cop came aboard behind his partner. "Screwed what up, sir? You mind telling us who you are?"

"Matt Trulli," said Matt, fumbling in a pocket.

"Hey!" warned the first cop, his gun now out of its holster. "Slowly."

Matt grimaced. "Whoa! Just getting my ID, okay? I work for the United Nations." He gestured toward the tower as he produced his UN identity card. "Oceanic Survey Organization. These are my assistants."

"This ain't the ocean," the gun-happy cop pointed out.

"It's a tidal waterway, so it counts for what we're doing."

The second cop appeared satisfied by his ID. "And what would that be?" he asked, returning the card.

"Pollution survey. We're trying to track how far upriver oceanborne pollutants are being carried by tidal currents. And you nearly lost a hundred grand's worth of equipment when your boat snagged my control line!"

The cop peered over the side. "What equipment?"

"I've got an ROV collecting samples from the riverbed. It's using a fiber-optic line—I had to unwind it before you snapped it."

"Why are you working this late at night?" the first cop asked, still suspicious.

"Because we're looking at the tides. And it's, well, high tide."

He narrowed his eyes. "There's a high tide during the day, too."

"Yeah, and a lot more river traffic! Just having you guys go by almost finished us; imagine what it'd be like with everyone else chugging past."

The second cop crouched to look into the cabin. Whatever he was expecting to see—stacks of explosives, bags of drugs—it didn't match the reality of the computer equipment on the table. He straightened. "How much longer will you be out here?"

"Depends how long it takes me to get all my samples. An hour, probably less."

"Huh." The cop stared at him for a long moment, then turned to return to his own vessel, ushering his partner with him. "We'll be back in forty-five minutes. It'd be best if you're done by then."

"We know who you are," the first cop added menacingly, sliding his gun back into its holster as he reboarded the patrol boat. With a burble from its diesel engine, the police vessel swung away, heading downriver.

The trio quickly returned to the cabin, Karima retrieving the headset. "Eddie!"

* * *

Eddie heard the guard walk away in the direction of the booths—which he would find empty.

A buzz in one ear. "Eddie? Are you there?"

"What happened?" he whispered.

"A police boat. They've gone, but they'll be back."

"That doesn't matter right now. Tell me what the guards are doing."

* * *

Jablonsky reached the reading area—and stopped in surprise. Papers and files were spread out on the desk where he had left Eddie, but the man himself was not there.

"Eddie?" No reply. He paced up and down the aisles, seeing no sign of anyone. Frowning, he returned to the security desk. "Where is he?" he asked.

Vernio looked up from his DS. "What?"

"Eddie. Where'd he go?"

"He's in the reading area. Look." The Haitian pointed at the monitors.

Eddie was indeed back in his booth. "Huh," said Jablonsky. "I musta just missed him." He returned to his seat, deciding that the visitor must have gotten up to stretch his legs.

* * *

At that moment, Eddie would have given almost anything to be *able* to stretch his legs. He couldn't hear any more footsteps, but didn't dare move until he got an all-clear. "Karima? What's happening?"

"He just got back to the desk," she said, interference still breaking up her words.

"About fucking time." Slowly, extremely carefully, Eddie moved forward again. There was a faint *thump* as his weight shifted, but the sound was not loud enough to carry. He gripped the suction cup and resumed his advance, more deliberately than before.

The remaining distance crawled by, inch by sweat-dripping inch. Ten feet to go. He could see the baffles clearly now. Six feet. Three. Two. Just a little farther ...

The suction cup tapped against one of the metal plates. "Thank Christ," he gasped, mouth bone-dry. He unfastened the cutter from his wrist. "Okay, I'm about to start cutting. Ask Matt how long it'll take."

"He wants to know how thick the metal is," Karima replied after a moment.

"Not very. A millimeter, maybe. The plates are eight inches long."

"Okay. Matt thinks four or five minutes to remove each plate."

"How long before the river police come back?"

"About thirty minutes."

Eddie chewed his lower lip. Adding the time it would take him to traverse the last length of duct inside the vault itself would leave only fifteen minutes for him to do everything he needed—and Zec had told him the rapid prototyper would need about eight minutes to carry out its job. Tight timing. Maybe too tight.

But he had no choice. "Okay, I'm switching on the cutter." Its tip quickly became red hot.

The heat was concentrated in a small area, but he could already feel it. The tool was designed to be used underwater, the liquid medium acting as a natural radiator. Here, trapped in the duct's confines, the hot air had nowhere to go.

He touched the cutter to the plate where it was welded to the duct's ceiling. The metal started to soften. He had to be precise with his cutting. If he left any protruding metal, he could slice himself wide open as he crawled past it.

The work was painfully slow, progress measured in millimeters. But a gap gradually opened up along the top of the plate. A minute passed, and it extended about halfway along. Matt's estimate seemed accurate. He kept working.

* * *

Jablonsky was, not for the first time, envying his companion's electronic time-killer. He checked the monitors again. The archive's aisles were empty, the images seeming almost like still photos; only the timecodes assured him that they were live. The only sign of life was in the reading area. Whatever Eddie was doing for Dr. Wilde, it was obviously engrossing—he had barely moved since returning to his seat.

He considered making another patrol...but resisted.

He still had three more hours on duty—might as well spread out the "excitement." In twenty minutes, maybe.

* * *

After another minute, the plate had been entirely separated from the ceiling. Eddie switched to the bottom. More care was needed here; if he accidentally cut through the duct floor, molten metal could drop onto the suspended ceiling below and start a fire.

The need for greater accuracy slowed him down. More than three minutes passed before the plate finally came loose. He caught it with his thumb and forefinger before it fell. "Ow, ow, shit," he hissed, carefully laying the hot piece of steel flat before blowing on his fingers. A quick check of the duct; there were some sharp-looking edges, but nothing capable of giving him more than a superficial cut.

He started on the other plate. With the cutter at full temperature it took slightly less time, but by the end he felt as though he was working inside an oven. He lowered the second piece of metal, then checked his watch. The obstacle had cost him over ten minutes, and he still had to reach the vent.

He switched off the cutter. "I'm going through."

"Okay." Karima sounded more tense than before. "We've got less than twenty minutes before the police come back. If they make us leave, we'll have to cut the camera feeds. You've got to be out of there by then."

"No pressure, then..." He fastened the cutter back onto his arm, careful to keep the still-hot tip clear of his skin, and raised the suction cup. The routine of movement began again, six inches at a time. He passed over the cuts, feeling the metal tugging at his bodysuit—then something gave. "Shit."

"What's wrong?"

"Got a cut." He moved forward again, trying to push

himself upward. Nothing seemed to snag this time. "Hope it's just the suit and not me. I don't want to leave a nipple in here." He had hoped to raise a laugh from the other end of the line, but Karima was too worried.

He was now above the vault itself. Directly ahead was his next obstacle. Blocking the duct was a rack of ventilator fans, blowing air down into the vault. "Okay, I'm at the fans. Let's have a look..."

He tilted his head to direct the flashlight beam over the machinery—and didn't like what he saw. "Shit. The screws holding the grille in place go right into the frame—I can't get at them. I'll have to cut them out." He took the cutter from his wrist again. The rack's frame reached to the duct's top, bolted to the ceiling above. If he cut the vertical supports, he might be able to slide the entire unit out of his way into the section of ducting on the other side of the vent...

He reached around the fans and cut one of the supports farthest from him first. That corner of the rack dropped slightly, rattling. One down. He repeated the task on the other side—

The whole far end of the assembly lurched, the edge of the grille dropping two inches from the opening in the duct. Shit! The fan system was heavier than it looked. He saw that the separate power cords to each fan joined into one thicker cable that disappeared through a hole in the duct roof. A plan formed: Cut through the third support, then keep a firm hold on the cable as he severed the last strut to stop the entire thing from crashing down on the vault's weight-sensitive floor.

He started cutting the first of the nearer supports. Through the grille, he could make out the vault's interior, dimly lit by emergency lights: another safety feature to help anyone who got locked inside. At least he wouldn't have to work entirely by the glow of his little head-mounted light—

The cutter severed the third strut—and the entire fan assembly, grille and all, plunged as the final overstressed support was torn from the ceiling.

Eddie's free hand lashed out, clamping around the cable as it shot past. The weight slammed his elbow painfully against the edge of the opening. The power line slithered through his sweat-soaked grip. He tossed the cutter across to the other side of the hole and grabbed the cable with his other hand—

Knocking the suction cup over the edge.

If it hit the floor, the alarm would go off...

He heard a *thump* of impact—

The faint sound was not followed by the scream of sirens. Instead, Eddie heard a rapid fluttering like the beating of a moth's wings. Grimacing at the pain in his arm, he squirmed forward and looked down. The assembly hung an inch above the floor. The suction cup had landed on one of the fans, jammed against the frame as the whirling blades beat against it.

"What was that noise?" Karima asked, alarmed.

"My fan club," he rasped, pulling the cable back up. "Did those guys hear it?"

"It doesn't look like it." The vault's thick walls had muffled the sound.

He hauled up the rack until it was swaying two feet off the floor, then knotted the cable into a butterfly loop to hold it there. "How much time?"

"Thirteen minutes—but Eddie, they could come back before then."

"Yeah, I needed to hear that, Karima. Okay, I'm going to climb down."

Forcing the cable out of his way, Eddie dragged himself forward. The opening beneath him made movement easier, but he didn't drop through it—yet. Instead, he pulled himself over the gap, still towing his cargo, then unfastened the strap from his belt, leaving it hanging over the edge, and carefully lowered his legs into the vault.

The fans swung on their makeshift tether, the flapping sound still coming from the suction cup. The pedestal desk containing the security terminal was about two feet to one side. Eddie swung down to land on it with a *thud*.

He was in!

Leaning down, he recovered the suction cup . . . and realized he was screwed.

The fan blades had slashed a ragged tear in the synthetic rubber. He tested it on the desktop, but knew even before he pulled the lever that it was useless. A pathetic puff of air came through the rip. It couldn't create a vacuum.

Which meant he had no way to get back through the duct.

"Buggeration," he whispered. He would have to find another way out, and soon.

First things first. He stood and pulled the strap, slowly tugging the case over the edge. It dropped—he caught it, gripping the second strap and dragging the plastic container after it. Both bulky items retrieved, he put them on the desk and opened the case.

The rapid prototyper was inside. He lifted it out, closed the case, and set the machine on top of it, pouring the glutinous liquid into the tank. As soon as it was full he switched on the machine, darkly cursing as it ran through a self-test mode, the laser head whining along its tracks. Thirty seconds, wasted. Finally it was ready.

He inserted the memory card and pushed the START button.

Two beams flickered across the tank, the liquid hardening where they crossed. The laser head slowly moved along the machine's length. A ghostly shape took on form beneath it. A hand, wraith-like and insubstantial.

And two-dimensional. The prototyper built up objects layer by layer, the lasers gradually focusing higher as they moved back and forth. Each layer was less than a millimeter thick, so making something substantial enough to trick the handprint scanner would take time.

Time that was running out.

Eddie looked around the vault. The simplest way out would be to set off the alarm by dropping something on the floor; the guards would open the door to investigate. But they were armed, and he wasn't, and even if he got past them he didn't fancy his chances of escaping the building. A man in a skintight bodysuit carrying a large book made of gold would be hard to miss.

What else could he do? He glanced at the hole in the ceiling. No way out there without the suction cup.

But there was something else he could use...

* * *

While Rad and Karima kept watch on the monitors, Matt went up on deck. He regarded the UN building for a moment, hoping Eddie would get his arse in gear, then looked downriver. At this time of night, water traffic was minimal, the lights of other vessels standing out clearly even from a distance.

He recognized the pattern of one of them.

The Harbor Unit boat.

It was more than a mile away, and in no hurry to reach them. But it was definitely coming back upriver. He jumped back into the cabin. "We've got a problem!"

"We're not the only ones," said Rad, jabbing a finger at the laptop.

On the screen, one of the guards had just stood.

* * *

"Gonna do the rounds," said Jablonsky. "Don't let Mario distract you from the monitors, huh?"

Vernio waved a dismissive hand. "Nothing's happening—he's hardly moved."

Jablonsky glanced back at the screens. Eddie was still at the desk. He turned in the direction of the reading area... then changed his mind, deciding to check the other side of the archives first. He could look in on the Englishman at the end of his patrol.

Which wouldn't take long.

14

The object in the prototyper's tank was now almost finished—and somewhat disturbing. Eddie could easily recognize it as Nina's right hand, a small childhood scar visible at the base of her first finger . . . but it had no color, a translucent, boneless mass like some primitive deep-sea creature.

The fingers were complete, loops and whorls discernible in the lifeless flesh. The laser head whirred back and forth over the thickest part of the hand, the ball of the thumb, as it added the final layers. Eight minutes had gone, and it still wasn't finished. Karima had warned him that one of the guards was patrolling, but there was no point worrying—there was absolutely nothing he could do about it.

The scanner whined back to its rest position—and stopped. The prototyper bleeped three times. Done.

Eddie gingerly touched its end product. The "hand" was soft, rubbery, almost but not quite like flesh. It was also hot. He dipped the digital thermometer into the liquid. More than a hundred degrees Fahrenheit. He kept it in place, watching the display. The figure dropped by a tenth of a degree, then another.

He carefully lifted the hand out of the tank. It flopped grotesquely as it emerged from the thick liquid. He used a wipe to clean off the excess goo, then checked the temperature again: 99.1 degrees. Almost down to human body temperature. He didn't know how far above or below the norm the temperature sensor in the handprint scanner would accept, but doubted it was more than a few tenths of a degree.

He typed in Nina's security code. One, eight, six, zero, nine, two, four, six, zero, nine. The panel lit up: CODE ACCEPTED. Now the system was waiting to confirm her identity biometrically.

Ninety-eight point eight degrees. Almost normal. He laid the hand palm-down on the panel. The line of light moved beneath it. He glanced around at the locker, waiting for the LED to turn from red to green.

It didn't.

The monitor flashed up a message, polite but chilling: UNABLE TO CONFIRM. PLEASE RESCAN.

It hadn't worked. The system had recognized the fake...

No, Eddie realized, forcing himself to be calm. If it had detected trickery, it would have raised the alarm. It just hadn't quite matched the silicone palm print to the one in its memory.

Ninety-eight point four. Below normal body temperature. And it would only keep falling.

What was wrong? He lifted the hand from the scanner, flashlight beam darting over it as he searched for any flaws—

There! Between the first and second fingers, bisecting the scar. A hairline split in the silicone. The two halves of the scar had slipped apart by a tiny amount... but enough for the computer to find something odd about the easily identifiable feature. He put the hand back on the scanner, nudging the gelatinous nonflesh into what he hoped was perfect alignment.

The scanning beam moved again. Eddie looked around—

A single point of green appeared among the grid of red lights. "Yes!" he said, pumping a fist.

"Eddie, did it work?" Karima's voice crackled in his ear.

"Yeah, it's open. What's going on outside?"

"That guard's still on the far side of the archives, but he's circling—and the police are on their way back to us!"

"I'll have to get a shift on, then." He moved to the very edge of the desk, balancing on his toes—then let himself topple forward, one arm outstretched to arrest his fall on the lockers.

He reached out with his other hand and opened the large door. The case containing the codex was inside. He slid it out—then, swinging the heavy container as a counterweight, shoved himself back upright. For one horrible moment he wavered, rubber-shod toes clawing at the edge, before arching his back and standing tall.

Eddie opened the case. A golden light filled the vault: his flashlight beam reflecting off the orichalcum cover of the Talonor Codex.

He had it.

Now...he had to get away with it.

* * *

Jablonsky had completed his rounds of one side of the labyrinth. Humming to himself, he started toward the vault to begin his circuit of the other.

* * *

Matt hurried back up to the deck. The police boat was about half a mile away—heading straight for him.

* * *

The desk was clear, almost all Eddie's equipment shoved into the overhead vent. Aside from the case containing the codex, the only thing left was the screwdriver.

He held it between his teeth as he hauled the hanging ventilator back up until it was at shoulder height. Supporting the weight of one end on his collarbone, he took the screwdriver in his free hand ... and stabbed it into a fan.

The blades instantly jammed. The motor protested, whining angrily. He pushed the insulated handle down harder. With an electrical crack, the motor burned out.

He yanked out the screwdriver and did the same to another fan. This time, the motor sparked, an acrid burning smell hitting his nostrils as smoke coiled out of it.

• • •

Jablonsky crossed the central aisle in front of the vault door and was heading for the reading area when his walkie-talkie squawked. "Hey, Lou," said his partner. "The computer's showing something wrong in the vault."

He went back to the curved steel door, looking down the main aisle to the security desk. "Has the alarm gone off?"

"No, but there's some problem with the ventilation system. I'll open it up so you can check."

Jablonsky inserted his card and waited while Vernio went through the procedure to open the door. After a minute, the heavy door hummed open.

He caught the sharp tang of smoke in the air as he entered. A crackle from above; he looked up at the grille to see a blue spark flicker behind it. "Yeah, something's shorted out," he reported into his radio. "Better call it in."

Leaving the vault door open to disperse the smoke, he headed back to the main desk as Vernio picked up the phone to summon an engineer.

• • •

Watching the laptop screen, Karima saw that the guard had his back to the vault—and the other was looking away as he made a phone call. "Eddie, *now*!"

* * *

The locker swung open. Inside was the case containing the Talonor Codex—and Eddie Chase, squeezed into the space even more tightly than he had been in the duct.

He had used the cutter, retrieved from the vent, to sabotage the lock mechanism inside the door. Now he hurriedly unfolded himself, using the handles of the lockers above to climb out. Standing with one foot on the edge of the locker's floor, he recovered the case and jumped across to the central desk.

The guard was still walking away from him. He stretched out one leg to nudge the locker shut, then drew back—and made a flying leap through the open vault door.

He cleared the pressure-sensitive floor by less than the length of a toe. Pain shot through his ankle at the awkward landing, but he held in a grunt and flung himself sideways behind the nearest bank of storage lockers.

One rubber sole squeaked on the floor—

Jablonsky looked around at the sound.

Eddie heard his footsteps stop. He froze, pressed against the cabinets.

The steps resumed . . . coming back.

"What's wrong?" Vernio called.

"Thought I heard something." Jablonsky was almost at the vault. Eddie braced himself—he was going to have to fight his way out after all . . .

One of the damaged fans sparked again. Jablonsky stopped. Eddie could see his shadow. One more step and he would be found—

The guard turned away, apparently thinking the sound was just another spark. Eddie waited until he was clear, then quietly tiptoed back to the locker where he had stashed his clothes.

* * *

The spotlight beam stabbed through the porthole. "Time's up!" the cop said through the loudhailer. "Get moving."

Matt ran up on deck. "We're stowing our gear! Give us a minute."

"Okay, you got your minute—but if you aren't moving by the end of it, you're coming with us."

"We're moving, we're moving!" Matt leapt back into the cabin. The live feeds showed Eddie hurrying back to the reading area, the codex under one arm, a bundle of clothes in the other.

"Eddie!" Karima cried. "We're out of time!"

* * *

Eddie reached the booths. He had dumped the codex's case in the locker; now he flung open the briefcase and dropped the gleaming artifact inside before pulling on his trousers over the filthy bodysuit.

* * *

"Maintenance is on the way," said Vernio, putting down the phone.

"I'll go get Eddie." Jablonsky headed for the reading area.

* * *

Eddie fumbled with his sweater. No time to clean the muck off his hands—

* * *

"Come on, move it!" growled the cop.

Matt ran back on deck and took the controls. "We're

going! Jesus Christ, mate!" He started the engine, the diesels clattering. "The UN'll be narked about this!"

He pushed the button to winch up the anchor, then opened the throttle. The boat moved off, turning downstream.

In the cabin, the fiber-optic spool spun faster and faster as the line was drawn out. It caught against the porthole's brass frame—

And snapped.

* * *

Vernio looked up sharply as the monitors flickered. Was the electrical problem spreading?

His eyes went to the visitor—

* * *

"Yo, Eddie."

"Yeah?" said Eddie, dropping into the chair just before Jablonsky entered the reading area.

"Afraid I'm going to have to ask you to leave," the guard said apologetically. "There's an electrical problem, and we gotta clear the room while it's being repaired. Safety rules."

"That's okay, I'm finished anyway." He gathered the papers and put them into the files. "Health and safety, eh? Surprised they don't make you wear a hard hat and a Day-Glo jacket."

Jablonsky grinned. "Seems it's getting that way, sometimes. You need a hand?"

"Nah, I've got it." Eddie stacked everything so he could carry it with one arm, pretending that the now-empty box file was still heavy, and picked up the briefcase. "Okay, let's go."

* * *

Karima came on deck, Rad following. She looked back at the police boat. "That was close."

"Did Eddie make it?" Matt asked.

"He's on his way out."

"Thank Christ," said Matt, relieved. "Only problem now is: How the hell am I going to explain to the Oceanic Survey Organization that their hundred-thousand-dollar ROV is stuck in the UN's basement?"

* * *

Jablonsky led Eddie back to the first locker and opened it. "There you go."

"Thanks." He put the box file inside, surreptitiously plucking the piece of cardboard from the lock. "Okay, all done."

He stood back as Jablonsky closed the locker, waiting for him to escort him out of the archives. But the guard hesitated.

"What's up?" Eddie said, as casually as he could.

"You got something on your hand."

He brought it up—and saw a black smear across the heel of his palm, dirt from inside the duct. "Huh," he said, wiping it on his thigh. "Must have smudged something." A smile, hopefully not looking as forced as it felt. "Nina'll kill me if I've made a mess of some hundred-year-old document."

After a moment, the smile was returned. "I won't say anything," Jablonsky joked. "Okay, I'll see you out."

Eddie returned to the security station and signed out, then walked down the corridor. As soon as he was out of sight, he increased his pace toward the elevators.

* * *

Back in the archive, Jablonsky returned to the vault. He looked up at the grille to see if the faulty ventilator was still sparking. It had stopped . . . but something wasn't right. It took a moment for him to realize what: The grille wasn't straight, its slats not parallel to the vent's outer edges, as if it had been lifted through the hole and turned slightly to balance on its corners. What the hell?

He was about to climb on the desk to inspect it close up when he spotted something else: a dirty mark, right on the desk's edge. It looked like part of a footprint...

Horrible realization hit him. He jumped up on the desk and reached for the overhead vent. "Henri! I think—"

The grille dropped at his touch. Jablonsky pulled back in shock as the ventilation unit plunged downward, jolting to a stop when its knotted power cable snapped tight. The entire duct shook, more objects dropping out of the open vent. An empty plastic container, some kind of suction cup...

Someone had been in the vault. And there was only one suspect.

"Holy shit!" he yelled. "Sound the alarm! Stop Chase from leaving the building!"

* * *

Eddie was in the lobby. Briefcase in hand, he headed for the exit. The security guards on duty had their usual expressions of bored politeness; at this time of night the building was quiet. Only a few more yards...

Someone's walkie-talkie crackled, a frantic voice gabbling on the other end. A moment later, an alarm bell sounded.

Eddie was already moving. He shoulder-barged the door open before the security locks could slam into place and emerged on United Nations Plaza, sprinting for First Avenue. Shouts rose behind him as guards rushed out of the Secretariat Building in pursuit.

The entrances to United Nations Plaza were controlled by traffic barriers—and tall security gates. One was open, a car having just gone though. He ran for it as it closed. Another alarm sounded in the gatehouse. The men inside jumped to their feet.

Eddie hurdled the traffic barrier—and practically dived through the outer gate as it clanged shut just behind him. Stumbling, he crossed First Avenue, cars hooting as he weaved between them and ran like hell for 44th Street.

A look back. The UN guards were stuck behind their own barrier, waving furiously for someone in the gatehouse to reopen it. He reached the far sidewalk and darted around the corner, ahead seeing—

The crowd. It was much bigger than before, the ranks of the paparazzi swollen by a legion of young women. Online rumors had spread that the object of their affection was in the hotel—and was neither alone nor with his girlfriend.

Eddie also saw an NYPD car parked across the street, a cop leaning against it keeping an eye on events, but he ignored her and pushed through the crowd to the doors. The doorman recognized him from earlier, and let him inside.

Zec was where he had left him—and a brief glance confirmed that Mac was too, standing as he saw Eddie. The Scotsman made his way to the doors, crossing in front of his friend—and passing him something while Zec's view was momentarily blocked. Eddie slipped the object into his pocket and sat beside the mercenary as Mac left the hotel.

"Do you have it?" Zec asked.

Eddie opened the case. The Talonor Codex gleamed inside. With a slightly disbelieving look, Zec raised the cover to confirm that it was genuine. Scribed metal sheets were revealed within.

"What?" said Eddie. "Don't look so fucking shocked, I told you I'd get it. Now..." He closed the case and lifted it on to his knees—then pulled Mac's revolver from his pocket. "A trade's a trade. You get this; I get Nina. Sound fair?"

Zec didn't appear surprised that Eddie had acquired a gun. "She is with Mr. Khoil in his plane."

"And where's his plane?"

"A private airport, upstate."

"Then take me to it. We need to get moving—I attracted some attention at the UN. The quicker I'm out of here, the better."

"Give me the case," said Zec. Eddie stared at him coldly. "You still have the gun. But I take the case." After a moment, Eddie passed it to him. "Good. Now, let's go."

They both stood. Eddie pocketed the gun and started toward the exit, Zec following—just as a man and a woman emerged from an elevator across the lobby. Seeing them through the glass doors, the crowd outside responded with excited cries and camera flashes.

Grant Thorn was the man—and Macy Sharif was his companion, both of them dressed to party...with a slightly disheveled look that suggested they had just come from a private event of their own. Another man hurriedly stood and joined them; a bodyguard, muscles bulging beneath his dark suit. He opened a door for the couple, holding up a hand to wave back Eddie and Zec. "Let 'em through, let 'em through, please." Annoyed, Zec tried to push past, but Eddie stopped in front of him.

The star and the student stepped out onto the street to be greeted by strobes, shrieks, and shouted questions from paparazzi and fans alike. "Grant, Grant!" one photographer called. "Who's the babe?"

"Where's Jessica?" another demanded.

"Which one?" asked the snapper next to him.

"Any of 'em!" He fired his camera in the couple's faces. Grant blinked, and Macy flinched back. "She know about this, huh?"

"Grant, over here!" someone else yelled. "It's me, Sally! I was at the premiere of *Nitrous,* remember? You said you liked my hair!" Hands were thrust over the shoulders of the front row, more cameraphones flashing. The paparazzi exchanged irritated looks at having their pitch invaded by amateurs and tried to shove them back, arousing shrill complaints from the crowd.

"Come on, let 'em through!" the bodyguard growled. The hotel staff moved to part the crowd so they could reach the limo that had just arrived.

"Fuck this for a game of soldiers," said Eddie impatiently. He went through the door and barged into the throng, elbowing a photographer out of his way. The man staggered and knocked over a young woman, who shrieked.

Her friends pushed back. The crowd became a scrum, arms and legs flailing. Eddie forced his way between them, Zec right behind. The heavy briefcase bashed against shins and thighs.

Grant and Macy reached the limo, the bodyguard and doormen pushing people back so its door could be opened. A ripple surged through the crowd, another fan tripping with a scream. A photographer stumbled over her to the pavement, glass cracking in his lens.

Eddie stopped, path blocked. Zec pushed up behind him—and a man fell against the Bosnian, almost knocking him over. The briefcase jolted in his hand as something bashed against it and dropped to the ground. He looked down sharply, but the handle was still firmly in his grasp as the man struggled to recover his own fallen case. Zec raised an arm to swat him away.

"Hey, hey!" yelled a woman before he could make the swing. "NYPD—everyone, move back!"

Eddie squeezed past the policewoman as she shouted more orders, reaching the edge of the crowd. Zec emerged behind him, angrily tugging the case free of the crush. "Jesus," Eddie said as the limo pulled away. "Who'd be fucking famous if you have to put up with that all the time?"

"Who was that?" Zec said.

"Grant Thorn." He got a blank look in return. "The film star?"

Zec shook his head. "I don't watch movies. No realism anymore."

"You're a fun guy, aren't you? Okay, I hope you've got a car. I'm not paying for a bloody cab all the way upstate."

15

The drive took more than an hour, Zec at the wheel with Eddie beside him, gun in hand. The briefcase sat on the backseat, untouched by either man during the journey.

They reached a private airfield, where a security guard waved them through the gate. A jet waited on the runway, armed men standing nearby. Eddie steeled himself as Zec stopped beside the plane. He might be shot the moment the Bosnian turned over the briefcase...

"Get out," said Zec. Eddie stepped into the cold wind blowing across the runway. The jet's hatch was open; a figure appeared at the top of the steps. Pramesh Khoil.

The guns of the men around the car were all now aimed at Eddie. Shrugging, he pocketed the revolver and advanced as Zec retrieved the case. "All right, Khoil," he called, "where's Nina?"

The Indian ignored him. "Do you have it?" he shouted to Zec. The mercenary nodded, holding up the briefcase. "Bring it to me."

Eddie reached the steps. "Hey! I asked you a question. Is Nina in there?"

Zec pushed past him. Khoil backed up to let him into

the aircraft, then looked contemptuously down at Eddie. "No, Mr. Chase, she is not. She is still in India, and now no longer necessary. Like you." He gestured to his men. They advanced on the Englishman.

"Just a sec," Eddie said, covering a surge of cold fear with cockiness. Khoil, who had been about to retreat into the cabin, paused. "You might want to check your merchandise."

Khoil whipped around to face Zec, expression accusing. "It's in the case," the mercenary protested. "I looked before we left New York. It never left my sight."

"Open it now," Khoil ordered. "Open it!"

Zec set the briefcase down and flicked the catches. Khoil shoved him aside and yanked it open. He stared at the contents for a long moment... then ran down the stairs. "Where is it?" he almost screeched.

"No idea," Eddie replied, truthfully. "A mate of mine's got it, and I told him to put it somewhere I didn't know about. Just to be safe." His expression hardened. "So. Where's Nina?"

The shocked Zec emerged from the cabin, holding the case's contents: several dumbbell weights fastened together with duct tape. "I—I don't understand," he told Khoil. "The codex was inside! How did he do it?"

"Doesn't really matter now, does it?" said Eddie. "But I thought you'd try something like this, and as soon as I heard the satellite delay when I was talking to Nina I knew I was right. So I wanted some insurance." He leaned closer to Khoil. "The deal still stands. I get my wife back, and you get your book. But fuck with me, and it'll be destroyed. Understand?"

Khoil's lips were tight. "Come inside." He stalked back up the steps, almost barging Zec out of the way. Eddie followed, relieved to have survived his triple cross.

The question now was: How desperately did Khoil want the Talonor Codex?

He entered the cabin, an armed guard following. Inside, another Indian man standing between him and Khoil gave him an unpleasant smile, exposing jagged teeth. "Is the codex intact?" the billionaire demanded. "Have you damaged it?"

"Not yet," Eddie said. "I told you, I don't give a shit about your book or what you want it for. All I want is Nina. If I get her back unharmed, you'll get it the same way. Sound fair?"

"Yes," Khoil hissed.

"Great. Now I want to talk to her."

Khoil went to one of the luxurious seats. Eddie expected him to pick up a phone, but instead he pushed a button, and a flat-screen monitor smoothly emerged from the chair's arm. The blank black eye of a webcam was set into its bezel. A menu appeared; Khoil tapped an option, and an animated CONNECTING... icon popped up.

After several seconds, the bird-like face of Vanita Khoil appeared. "Well?" she said. "Do you have it?"

"There has been a...complication," Khoil said. "Get Dr. Wilde."

"What? Why do we still need her? We should have—"

"*Get her!*"

Vanita's eyes narrowed in clear anger at his outburst, but she looked off camera and issued an order in Hindi. After a short wait, someone was pushed into frame behind her.

"Ay up, love," said Eddie. "So how's India?"

"Eddie!" Nina cried. "What's going on?"

"Well, I got the codex—"

"You did *what*?" she gasped. "I *told* you not to give it to them—they're going to kill us once they get it!"

"Yeah, I know that—that's why I *didn't* give it to them, the bunch of backstabbing twats. Once you're safe, then I'll turn it over."

"You will not," she said firmly. "Whatever these two are planning, it's not—"

"Bite your tongue!" snapped Vanita. "Pramesh, why is Chase still alive?"

"He exchanged the real codex for a dummy, without Zec even noticing." The Bosnian lowered his head, humiliated. "One of his friends has hidden it. If we do not let Dr. Wilde go, he has threatened to destroy it."

"*What?*" the outraged Nina yelped in the background.

"Qexia will be able to identify all his friends," said Vanita, ignoring the interruption. "We can track them down—"

"There isn't time," Khoil cut in. "We can't risk losing the codex, not now. Make arrangements to have her sent back to America."

Vanita looked silently into the camera for several seconds before replying. "No."

Khoil was taken aback by her blunt refusal. "But if they destroy the codex—"

"They won't." She leaned closer to the camera. "Chase. Give up the codex, now, or your wife will suffer."

"Do anything to her and you'll never get it," Eddie countered. The normally unemotional Khoil had been unable to conceal his genuine fear that the codex might be lost. As Eddie hoped, he was desperate to get his hands on it.

But Vanita was more willing to gamble. She gave a sharp order to Tandon, who grabbed Nina.

"Hey!" Eddie shouted. "I'll have the fucking thing melted down into Home Shopping Network jewelry if you do anything to her. You think I'm kidding?"

"Do you think *I* am?" Vanita replied. "Chapal!"

Tandon took something from a pocket. Before Nina could react his hand whipped up—and pulled a plastic bag tightly over her head. She struggled, trying to claw it from her face, but it was too thick to tear. He tugged harder, the bag tightening around her throat.

"Let her go!" Eddie shouted, lunging at Khoil. The shark-toothed man darted forward and slammed him against the curved fuselage. He fumbled for the revolver, but the guard pressed his gun's muzzle hard against his cheek.

On the screen, Nina jabbed at Tandon with her elbows. But the martial artist was too quick, twisting out of the way of her blows.

"Give us the codex," said Vanita. "Or she dies."

"Fuck off!" Eddie snarled. "If I give it to you, you'll kill her anyway!"

Her lips curled at the insult. "But first, she will suffer. Over and over."

Nina was now grasping uselessly at the plastic drawn tight over her mouth, face distorted and indistinct as her breath misted up the bag. Eddie watched helplessly. The only way to help her was to surrender the codex—but that would condemn them both to death. Certainly if he was dealing with Vanita.

Which meant he had to deal with Khoil, find something the dispassionate, logical half of the partnership would respond to . . .

Nina's muffled choking sounds became weaker, more desperate. Vanita's gaze was cold, intense, waiting for him to break—

"All right!" he yelled. "I'll give you the codex!"

A thin smile of triumph spread across Vanita's face. "Chapal," she said, waving a dismissive hand. Tandon released his hold. Nina staggered away from him, pulling frantically at the bag. It finally came free and she gasped for air.

The gun was withdrawn. "On one condition," Eddie added.

Vanita scowled, about to order the suffocation to resume, but Eddie had already turned to Khoil. "We've both got something the other one wants and isn't willing to lose, but neither of us trusts the other not to fuck about, right?"

"Crudely put," said Khoil, "but correct."

"Okay, so here's my new offer. A straight swap. I bring the codex, you bring Nina, and we make an exchange. Somewhere public with lots of people around. Soon as we're done, that's it—we go our separate ways. No tricks, no double crosses. How does that sound?"

"Unacceptable," Vanita said from the screen, but Khoil spoke over her: "Good—in principle. Where do you suggest?"

"I don't know yet. But..." He decided to make at least the appearance of a concession in the hope of pacifying Vanita. "We'll do it on your turf. I'll come to India, and we'll agree on a place once I'm there."

Khoil mulled it over. "That is...acceptable," he said, with a glance at the image of his wife, who was clearly displeased in the extreme.

"In Bangalore," she insisted. "The exchange will take place here in Bangalore."

"So long as I pick the spot," Eddie agreed reluctantly, sensing she was itching for an excuse to torture Nina again.

It seemed to work; Vanita said nothing. Khoil turned to Eddie. "You will fly back with me?"

Eddie half laughed. "I don't fucking think so, mate. I'll sort out my own flight. And I won't be taking the codex in my carry-on luggage, you can be sure of that. But," he went on, knowing what Khoil was about to say, "you'll get to see it before I hand it over, so long as I see Nina at the same time. We both get what we want, and everyone's happy. Do we have a deal?"

"We have a deal."

"Good. Nina, are you okay?"

"Oh, super fine," she croaked, rubbing her neck. "Eddie, don't give it to them."

"Sorry, love, but I've got to. I know you're going to be really pissed off about it, but you can rant and rave at me once you're safe, okay? I'll see you soon."

Nina was about to say something else, but Vanita angrily terminated the video link. Khoil looked at the armed guard. "Escort Mr. Chase off my plane."

"What, don't I even get a hot towel? All right, I'm going," said Eddie as he was prodded with the gun. "Oh, one last thing." He jerked a thumb at Zec. "Tell laughing boy here to give me his car keys. I'm not walking all the way back to fucking Manhattan."

Zec wasn't happy, but he handed them over under Khoil's stern gaze. "How am I supposed to get back?"

"That is not my concern," the Indian told him icily. "After your failure tonight, I will have to reconsider your continued employment."

"Don't worry, mate," Eddie said, jingling the keys. "I'm sure someone with your talents'll be able to find other work. I mean, New York always needs street sweepers." With that, he stepped out into the night.

* * *

"Eddie!" Lola cried as Eddie entered the room. "Are you all right?"

"I'm fine," he said, seeing all the concerned faces anxiously awaiting news. They were in Matt's Brooklyn apartment, the Australian joined not only by Karima, Rad, and Lola, but also the members of Plan B: Grant and Macy, drawing a crowd with their "tryst" to provide the necessary confusion; Amy Martin, on duty as an NYPD officer, to distract Zec at the crucial moment . . . and Mac, who had actually carried out the switch.

On a table was the now-empty briefcase, lid open to reveal the trick mechanism that made it possible. The high-power electromagnets provided by Matt, unsuited for their originally intended purpose, had found another application. The metal plate attaching the handle to the case had been unscrewed...as had that of the identical briefcase containing the weights. Only the magnets inside each case kept them firmly attached—until a radio-control circuit built by Matt was triggered by Mac as he "accidentally" fell against Zec and banged the cases together in the scrum outside the hotel. The electromagnets inside the case containing the codex shut off, causing it to drop away. A moment later the magnets in Mac's decoy case did the same—then reactivated once Mac's hand was clear, snapping the dummy case back on to the handle Zec was gripping.

The entire exchange took under half a second, before Zec could recover from the collision. When Matt first suggested the idea, Eddie was extremely doubtful that it could work, but after dozens of practice runs they had made successful switches two times out of three.

Mac stood. "Thank God. What happened? Where's Nina?"

"She wasn't there, just like I thought. But she's safe, more or less...for now. Khoil agreed to another exchange. I'm going to India to make the swap."

"Do you really think he'll play fair?" Macy asked, concerned.

"Not even for a second. Which is why I'm not going to either. But at least this time I'll have more control over the situation."

Mac raised an eyebrow. "Interesting how you think making the exchange on Khoil's own turf counts as having more control."

"Well, that's why I was hoping you'd give me some backup."

"If you need any more help from me, mate," offered Matt, "just ask."

"The same goes for us," said Karima. Rad nodded in

agreement. Lola, Macy, and Grant also piped up with offers of support.

Eddie shook his head. "Zec saw you. He's not in Khoil's good books right now, but that doesn't mean he won't have told him who was involved. If Khoil decides to keep him on and he recognized you, we'd be screwed."

"He might still recognize Mr. McCrimmon from the hotel," Amy pointed out.

"He only saw him for a moment, so we'll have to chance it. But everyone else, he knows. So it's just me and Mac."

"Thanks for that, Eddie," Mac said with a wry smile.

Objections rose from all quarters, but Eddie cut them off. "You've all been absolutely bloody fantastic," he said. "If I ever go in for a life of crime, I want you lot to be founding members of Eddie's Eleven."

"I'm not hearing this," said Amy, pretending to put her fingers in her ears.

Eddie smiled, then became serious. "But like Mac said, we're going to be on Khoil's home turf. It'll be a lot more dangerous. And I can't ask you to take any more chances for me—hell, I won't let you. Me and Mac are professionals, we've trained for this stuff. You haven't. Sorry, but that's the way it is."

Disappointment filled the room. "I just hope you're right, man," said Grant. "But good luck anyway. I want you and Nina at the premiere of my next movie!"

"Who'll be your date?" Eddie asked mischievously, looking at Macy.

Grant grimaced. "Yeah, I've...kinda got to talk to Jessica. I didn't have a chance to tell her beforehand. Don't want her to hear about all this first on TMZ, huh?"

"Too late for that," said Macy. "I've already had five calls from friends wanting to know if I'm really dating you. Word gets around fast these days!" She eyed him hopefully. "You know, since it's already out in the open, maybe we could try something for real?" Grant looked like an animal trapped in headlights.

"Matt, you've got a shower, right?" said Eddie. "I think Macy needs a cold one." That got a laugh from everybody except Macy. "All of you, thanks so much for everything. I really appreciate it—and I know Nina will too once she stops being mad at me for stealing her bloody book." He looked at Mac. "Is it safe?" Mac nodded. "Good. We'll have to get it to India—Lola, I'll need one last little thing off you, some UN paperwork."

"Whatever you want," she said.

"Great. But we'll have to get going—we've got a lot more planning to do, and not much time to do it." He frowned. "And I've just realized—if *Indiana Jones and the Temple of Doom* isn't a reliable source of information, then I know sod-all about India..."

16
India

"So," said Mac, leaning against Eddie's seat, "how much have you learned about India?"

Eddie held up the guidebook he had bought at JFK before their flight to Delhi departed. "Well, I found out that Delhi and New Delhi are the same place, that Bangalore's called the Silicon Valley of India even though it's not in a valley, and that if I ever want to look at a bunch of temples, I can stick a pin anywhere on a map and find some. Apart from that, though...not really helpful. I've got no idea where would be a good place for the swap."

"You don't have any useful contacts in India?"

"Only Saheli, and she's out of the country. There's this guy from Interpol I met recently, Kit, but I don't know if he'd be up for helping with something like this—he seemed a bit by-the-book. What about you? You went there in the SAS, didn't you?"

"Yes, but that was almost thirty years ago. And I was acting as an adviser to the National Security Guard for the Queen's state visit, not being a tourist."

"Then unless we can get someone local on our side, we'll have to wing it."

"Never really ideal in a hostage situation."

"Yeah, I know." Eddie closed the book. "Mac...I really appreciate you doing this for me."

The Scot smiled. "What are friends for? Besides, I know you'd do the same for me. Although"—his eyes twinkled— "I can't imagine what I might possibly be doing that would need that kind of help. You and Nina do have a knack for getting into extreme situations."

"Tell me about it," Eddie said ruefully. "I've been shot at more in the past four years than in the bloody Regiment! But," he went on, resolute, "I'm going to get Nina *out* of this situation."

"We both are," said Mac firmly. He held out his hand; Eddie grasped it. "Fight to the end."

"Fight to the end," Eddie repeated. They exchanged a look of comradeship, and more, then released their grip as the airliner's seat belt lights came on. The plane was descending.

"See you on the ground." Mac headed to his seat. The two men were sitting separately for a very simple reason: security. Eddie suspected that news of his theft of the Talonor Codex would have spread beyond New York. Waiting for him—and anyone accompanying him—when the plane landed could well be the Indian police.

Or, worse, Khoil's people.

Either way, he would know soon enough.

* * *

He found out before even reaching the terminal.

The airliner stopped just short of its gate at Indira Gandhi International, where the captain announced that due to a security issue, passengers should remain seated until given the all-clear. Mac looked back at Eddie in concern, getting a resigned nod in return. The plane then advanced to the jetway. A trio of armed police officers boarded, their leader speaking to one of the flight attendants before they marched down the aisle. "Edward Chase?" the officer in charge asked.

Eddie smiled politely. "My mates call me Eddie."

"Come with us, please."

He concealed his worry beneath a mock-casual shrug as he stood and was handcuffed before being led from the aircraft. Never mind finding a location to make the exchange; there might not even *be* an exchange.

He had to convince his interrogators of his reasons for stealing the codex. If he could persuade them that letting him carry out the exchange not only would save Nina's life but could also both recover the codex and lead to the arrest of the man who had ordered its theft, maybe he had a chance of release...

That chance vanished as he was brought through a keypad-locked door into the terminal's security area. Waiting outside one of the rooms was a man he had seen on Khoil's plane—the one with the filed teeth.

The leading officer glanced around to make sure nobody was watching, then accepted a wad of banknotes that was quickly spirited into a pocket. "Oi, what's this?" Eddie said loudly, knowing full well what it was: Khoil had cops on his payroll. If he made enough of a scene, he might attract attention from someone honest—but the corridor was lined with interrogation rooms, not busy offices. Noisy protests would be expected, and ignored.

"Take him with Mr. Singh," said the officer, nodding toward a side passage that led to an exit. The two other cops grabbed Eddie's arms as Singh gave him another unpleasantly pointed smile.

"Get the fuck off me!" Eddie shouted. He tried to break away, but with his wrists cuffed his actions were limited—

and the two cops were prepared for trouble, one driving a fierce jab into his kidneys. They started to hustle him down the passage—

"Stop!" someone shouted, voice commanding. "What's going on here?"

Eddie looked around—and to his surprise saw Ankit Jindal striding toward him, a senior uniformed officer right behind. The cops froze, unsure what to do—and Singh immediately took off at a run, barging through the exit.

"These twats were about to hand me over for some private questioning," Eddie growled.

Kit reached him and looked down the corridor, but Singh was gone. "Who was that?"

"One of Khoil's lot."

The senior officer glowered at his subordinates, giving them a tongue-lashing in Hindi before holding out his hand to the leader. Reluctantly, the man gave him the banknotes. The officer made a disgusted sound as the three cops filed away. "I will deal with them," he told Kit. "What about this man?"

"He's an Interpol matter," said Kit. "I'll handle him. Do you have a room available?"

The officer indicated a nearby door, then followed the shamed men down the corridor. Eddie watched them go. "What'll happen to them?"

Kit sighed. "A slap on the wrist, probably. Bribery is very common in India—everyone from clerks to politicians has their hand out. We're starting to make progress, but when you have a billion people who have lived with that system all their lives, it takes time for things to change." He opened the door and ushered Eddie into an interview room.

"So what're you doing here?" Eddie asked. He sat, Kit facing him across a small table.

"Interpol put a red notice—an arrest order—on you. It was too late to stop you flying from New York, so I decided to meet you when you arrived. And it seems I was just in time. What on earth is going on, Eddie?"

Eddie recounted what had happened since he left the Interpol officer in France. "So I'm bloody glad you turned up when you did," he concluded. "Khoil—or his wife, just as likely—probably thought they could torture the codex's location out of me. I'd have made it really fucking hard for them, but I'm still happy I didn't need to."

Kit leaned back thoughtfully. "I've been looking into the Khoils. Some very interesting things have turned up."

"What kinds of things?"

"A lot of financial activity. They've been buying up land and properties in odd locations and putting enormous amounts of money into the aid organization they run. It's all legal, but there seems to be an organized plan behind it all. What that plan is, though, I don't know."

"But it's made you suspicious."

Kit smiled slightly. "My radar is beeping. There's nothing connecting the Khoils directly to the thefts carried out by Fernandez's gang, but we obtained Fernandez's bank records, and over the past several months various sums of money went in soon after equally large sums went out of the Khoils' businesses. Minus the percentage you would expect a money launderer to take, of course."

"Isn't that enough to act on?"

"No, it's only circumstantial. There's no paper trail. But I think you were right about their involvement. The difficulty will be proving it. We still haven't got anything useful from the dead woman in Lyon, only your word that she was working for the Khoils."

"Have you questioned them yet?"

"I didn't want to tip my hand. Eddie, you have to understand that the Khoils are extremely powerful. I may be a member of Interpol, but we work in conjunction with local law enforcement. No Indian cop would be willing to risk his career by taking action against them unless he's absolutely certain of his case—and even then, it wouldn't take much to buy him off, as you just saw."

"So," said Eddie, "where does that leave us? You going to have me shipped back to New York?"

"Perhaps." Kit regarded him silently for a moment... then produced a key and unlocked the handcuffs. "But not just yet. I really do think that there's a case against the Khoils—and that if I help you, we'll not only be able to rescue Nina, but catch them in the act. Kidnapping across international borders is Interpol's responsibility, and since Nina was taken from the United States the trial would take place there. Pramesh and Vanita would find it a lot harder to buy their way out of trouble in New York."

Eddie pulled off the cuffs. "You'll help me, then?"

"Yes. It will be a risk professionally—but I think the chance is worth taking." He smiled. "So what do you have in mind?"

* * *

Even on this December day, it was still over seventy degrees out. Eddie wound down the window of Kit's non-air-conditioned car, but the pollution from the congested highway immediately encouraged him to put it back up. "Is traffic always this bad?"

"Almost," said Kit as they crawled toward central Delhi. "But it's worse than usual right now because of the preparations for the G20 summit. Several main roads have been closed."

"Politicians always have to inconvenience everybody else, don't they?"

It took close to forty minutes to traverse the last mile

of their journey, accompanied the entire way by a chorus of blaring horns and screeching brakes. As Kit had warned, closed streets forced them into a lengthy diversion before they reached the Orchard hotel, a mile from the central government district of Vijay Chowk. Someone was waiting for them in the lobby—but not, to Eddie's relief, another of Khoil's henchmen. "What kept you?" asked Mac.

Eddie grinned and shook his hand. "Little problem at customs. How'd you get here so fast?"

"I took the Metro. Less than a pound to get from the airport right into the center of Delhi. I wish the Tube in London was that cheap." He regarded Kit. "And I thought you didn't have any friends in India."

Eddie made the introductions. "Kit's been checking out the Khoils," he went on. "And he thinks he's got something."

"Nothing definite," Kit said apologetically. "But enough to catch my interest regarding the art thefts. All I need is proof."

"We'll get some for you," said Eddie. "Proof of kidnapping, too. And we've got the perfect bait. At least, I hope we have. Mac?"

"Let's find out." He went to the reception desk. "Do you have a package for me? The name's McCrimmon, Jim McCrimmon."

The receptionist tapped at her computer. "Yes, we do. I'll bring it for you." She went into a back room, returning with a large and heavy cardboard box.

"What is it?" Kit asked.

"What I'm wanted for," Eddie told him. As well as shipping labels for an overnight courier company, the box also bore a United Nations customs waiver and numerous DO NOT X-RAY stickers arranged by Lola, allowing it to be transported without the usual checks—a trick Eddie had used before to get items that would otherwise raise a lot of questions into other countries. "That codex thing—and also my new Wildey."

Kit gave him a questioning look. "Your what?"

"A gun. A *big* gun. Thought it might be handy."

Mac shook his head. "You haven't bought another of those ridiculous things, have you?"

Eddie snorted. "It's a good gun, and anyone who makes jokes about me compensating for something can fuck right off. We've got other things to think about—like how we're going to rescue Nina."

They retreated to a quiet corner of the hotel bar. "Can't you get them to make the exchange in Delhi rather than Bangalore?" asked Kit, after Eddie explained the situation. "I can arrange backup more easily."

"Khoil demanded it," said Eddie. "Or rather, his wife did. Probably shouldn't have said yes, but we're stuck with it now."

"It does give him the home advantage," noted Mac. "Wherever we choose for the actual handover, he'll be able to have his people in place beforehand."

"I wasn't planning on giving him much advance warning. Ring him up, tell him to meet us at such and such a place in an hour. We can keep an eye on anyone who turns up." He looked at Kit. "But we've got to pick a place first. Do you know Bangalore?"

Kit nodded. "I go there quite often. There are a lot of new millionaires in Bangalore from all the technology companies. Several of them have tried to build up art collections...without caring where the art came from."

"Do you know any local police?" Mac asked.

"Some, but they may not be willing to act against the Khoils without very solid evidence. But I can ask for help, at least."

"Great," said Eddie. "What about a place to make the exchange? Somewhere very public, preferably with security around."

Kit thought for a moment, then smiled broadly. "Do you like cricket?"

17

Bangalore

"I *don't* like cricket," Eddie muttered as he entered the grandstand.

"That's because you lack taste and class," Mac joked, coming through the gate behind him.

"I don't know why you like it. I mean, you're Scottish. It's not exactly your national sport."

"Scotland has a fine cricket team."

"Yeah, and when was the last time they won anything?"

Mac made a faintly irritated sound. "It's about the sportsmanship, not the winning."

"Bet you don't say that when England lose, do you? And it's the most boring sport imaginable. Give me footie or Formula One any day."

"I don't think you'll find this boring," Kit said, catching up to them with a heavy bag—a flash of his ID had allowed it to be brought into Bangalore's M. Chinnaswamy Stadium without being searched. "Indian matches aren't like yours."

Mac raised an eyebrow as he took in the scene. "You're not joking."

If British cricket events were staid and reserved, this was

more like a carnival that happened to have a cricket match going on in the middle of it. Music blasted from loudspeakers, the crowd singing along, clapping and even pounding out beats on makeshift drums. Flags and banners waved, and in front of the grandstand was a display that would have left any blazer-wearing member of the Marylebone Cricket Club choking on his gin and tonic as a trio of cheerleaders danced and gyrated.

Eddie grinned. "Okay, Kit, you're right—this is already a hundred times better than any other cricket match I've ever seen."

Mac huffed, then continued along the grandstand toward his seat while Eddie and Kit descended the steps to find theirs. They had chosen their positions carefully; Eddie was in the front row with a couple of empty seats around him where Khoil—and Nina—could sit when they arrived, with Kit a couple of rows behind so he could observe events, and if necessary make a rapid exit with the codex. Mac was farther away, equipped with binoculars to give Eddie advance warning of potential trouble.

Eddie sat, watching the people filing into the grandstand around him. Most were male, displaying a mixture of ages and clothing styles; none seemed remotely interested in the balding Caucasian in the front row, the cheerleaders dominating their attention.

He glanced back at Kit, who responded with a small nod. Farther off, he saw Mac in his seat, more men taking their places around him. So far, so good. He took out his phone and attached a Bluetooth headset to one ear, then entered a number. "Okay, Mac. Give me a check."

"I see you," said Mac, "and I see Kit. No sign of Nina or this Khoil fellow."

"Well, it's not time for the exchange yet. Anyone look suspicious?"

"Not that I can see. Just a lot of very excited cricket fans."

"Now, *that's* suspicious."

"You just don't appreciate the subtleties of the game. Kit, on the other hand—"

"Yeah, I had to put up with you both wibbling on about it the entire bloody flight down here. Maybe you should adopt him."

"Does that mean I can finally get rid of you? I only have time for one surrogate son."

Eddie laughed, then took another look around. Still no sign of Nina or Khoil. "Keep your eyes open, Dad. Let's see what happens."

With great fanfare, the match began. Eddie feigned interest while keeping watch. The first innings ended, marked by music and another butt-shaking dance from the cheerleaders. Second innings, third. Then: "Eddie," said Mac over the headset. "To your left."

Eddie turned to see Khoil coming down the steps. No Nina. He checked if anyone else was approaching from the other side, and saw the man who had choked Nina with the plastic bag. Kit gave Eddie a concerned look, but an almost imperceptible shake of the head told him to stay put and maintain a watching brief.

Khoil sat to Eddie's left, the man in black on his right. "Mr. Chase," said the billionaire.

"Mr. Khoil," Eddie replied. "Can't help noticing you've forgotten something."

"As have you," said Khoil, leaning to look under Eddie's seat and finding nothing. "Where is the codex?"

"Where's Nina?"

"In my car."

"Then get her in here. You can afford the tickets."

"Do you have the codex?"

"You'll get it when I get Nina. That was the deal. Now bring her in."

Khoil made a brief phone call, then leaned back and watched the action on the pitch. "Sport has never been of much interest to me," he said, almost conversationally, "but my father was a great fan of cricket, so it has a certain nostalgic appeal. But even it"—he indicated the cheerleaders—"has become debased. A sign of these corrupt times."

"They can get rid of the cricket and just leave the dancing girls, far as I'm concerned," said Eddie, more concerned with whether or not the other man was armed. He couldn't see the telltale bulge of a gun under his close-fitting clothing, but that didn't mean he lacked a weapon.

Khoil shook his head patronizingly. "Yes, I thought you might think so. You are predictably lowbrow, a symbol of this age."

"You don't know me, mate."

"I know you better than you can imagine. Your Qexia search results tell me a lot; I have seen them. So has your wife. She was not pleased."

Eddie winced inwardly. "That settles it. We're switching back to Google."

Mac's voice in his ear competed with the noise of the crowd as the batsman scored a four. "Eddie, Nina's here. One man with her, your left."

He looked. The guy with the filed teeth was escorting her down to the front row. She seemed unharmed, but was disheveled and anxious. Even when she reached him, the look of relief couldn't mask her worry. "Are you okay?" he asked.

"More or less," she replied.

He saw a dressing covering the bottom of her right ear. "What happened?"

"Vanita almost gave me the van Gogh treatment."

Eddie rounded on Khoil. "You fucking—"

"Enough," Khoil said coldly. "I have brought your wife, as agreed. Now bring me the codex."

Eddie bit back an angry remark and was about to signal to Kit when Nina spoke. "Eddie, you can't give it to him. Even for me."

"I'd swap the bloody Crown Jewels for you," he replied—but he was surprised by the degree of insistence in her voice. She was concerned about much more than her own safety. "Why's it so important he doesn't get it?"

"Because he thinks it'll help him start the Hindu version of the apocalypse."

Eddie raised his eyebrows. "Okay, that's important. How?"

"I don't know. But that's what he told me, and I don't see him rushing to issue any denials."

"The end of the Kali Yuga is inevitable, Dr. Wilde," said Khoil. "As I explained, it will be better for it to happen sooner rather than later. For the good of all humanity."

"You see?" Nina said scathingly. "He's another nut with too much money and delusions of godhood. Am I a magnet for these people, or something?"

Eddie regarded the Indian dubiously. "Can he do anything like that? I mean, the guy owns a search engine, not a nuclear bomb factory. What's he going to do, put up a link saying 'Click here to play global thermonuclear war'?"

Khoil smiled faintly. "If you do not believe I pose a threat, then you have no reason not to hand over the codex." His expression hardened. "I have brought your wife. Give it to me. Now."

Eddie cast the briefest of sidelong glances at Tandon to make sure he was within striking distance before responding. "You know what? I think I'm going to listen to my wife."

"It would be very unwise to go back on our deal."

"What're you going to do about it?" He indicated the cheering crowd behind them. "It's not like you can just kill us in front of all these people."

"All these people," said Khoil, a sudden rising smugness turning his plump face almost toad-like, "are *my* people. They work for me."

"Bullshit," said Eddie. "I only told you where to meet an hour and a half ago."

"My company is a major sponsor." He indicated a billboard emblazoned with the Qexia logo. "Which gives me a certain amount of influence here, and after I received your call I announced a surprise treat for three hundred of my most cricket-loving employees—a trip to today's exhibition match. Any member of the public who had already paid for one of the seats in this block was told there had been a booking error and given a complimentary upgrade and free entry to another match of their choosing. As you said"—a small, cold smile—"I can afford the tickets."

Eddie and Nina exchanged worried looks. "Mac," said Eddie, trying to pick the Scot out through the waving banners as another run was scored, "trouble."

"Colonel McCrimmon will not be able to help you." Eddie whirled on Khoil in shock at his use of the name. "Yes, I know who he is—and where he is sitting. He cannot interfere. Qexia provided a list of your friends, and it was a simple matter to cross-check with Indian immigration files—my company wrote the software, so we planted back doors in the code—to see if any of them had recently arrived in the country."

"Mac!" Eddie shouted. Through the earpiece he heard the grunts of a scuffle.

"Some of my larger employees are making sure he does not leave his seat," said Khoil. "And as for your friend Mr. Jindal from Interpol..."

Eddie jumped up and twisted to give Kit the signal to run. Kit stood—and immediately slumped back into his seat as the huge bearded figure of Mahajan, directly behind him, smashed a fist down on his neck like a hammer. A crack as a ball was hit for a four, and the stadium erupted in cheers, drowning out his cry of pain.

Adrenaline surged through Eddie's body. Two immediate threats: the man in black and the guy with the teeth, who had just grabbed Nina from behind. But they would have no choice but to back down if their boss was in danger.

He whipped out his gun, shoving the Wildey's long barrel into Khoil's face—

But Tandon was faster, one hand jabbing with blinding speed. His knuckles hit Eddie on the side of his neck—and the Englishman dropped as if his bones had turned to jelly, collapsing at Khoil's feet. He tried to move, but all he could do was twitch, nerves blazing where Tandon's attack had struck a pressure point and induced instant paralysis. The gun clunked to the concrete. He heard Nina scream his name, but couldn't even turn his head to look.

Khoil's expression was far from its usual state of bland neutrality, though; it was now one of wide-eyed fright. He staggered back, almost falling over his seat. The spectators behind him hurriedly helped their boss back upright.

"What're you doing?" Nina screamed at them. "Help us!"

No one did. "Get—get them out of here," said Khoil, shakily straightening his glasses. "Quickly!" As Tandon recovered Eddie's gun, Mahajan arrived, bearing Kit's bag. Greed replacing shock, Khoil looked at it. "Is the codex inside?" Mahajan nodded. "Excellent." He followed Singh and the shrieking and struggling Nina up the steps. Mahajan gave the bag to Tandon, then effortlessly picked up Eddie in a fireman's lift and strode after them.

The eyes of everyone in the grandstand remained firmly fixed on the game.

* * *

Mac had been shoved back down by the two big men in the neighboring seats when he tried to respond to Eddie's urgent call. He managed to strike one a painful blow to the chest with his elbow—only for the other to press a sharp knife against his abdomen.

He could do nothing but watch helplessly as Eddie was knocked down, then hoisted like a sack of potatoes. What had happened to Kit, he had no idea—his view of the Interpol officer's seat was blocked by one of his hulking captors.

"Bastards!" he snarled, struggling to break free, only to feel the knife tip pierce his skin. Blood swelled on his shirt.

Khoil, his servants, and his prisoners were now all out of sight. He had to get after them—but first he needed to deal with his captors...

Another crack from the pitch as a ball was hit clean over the boundary for a six. The crowd's reaction was even wilder than the previous shot—frenzied roars and cheers filled the stadium as thousands of excited fans leapt to their feet.

Jostling Mac's attackers.

The knife was knocked away, just for a second—

Mac wrenched himself from their grip. He whipped up his elbow again, smashing it into one man's nose with an explosive snap of crushed cartilage and a burst of blood.

The knifeman struck at him as he twisted and kicked—

The blade stabbed deep into his left leg below the knee with a dull thud. Expecting a shriek of pain, the knifeman froze in confusion—and took a savage chop of the Scotsman's hand to his throat. Tongue bulging from his gaping mouth, he let out a strangled shriek of his own as Mac yanked the knife out of the prosthesis and stabbed it down through the Indian's hand, pinning it to his thigh.

Mac jumped up, punching the broken-nosed man out of the way as he pushed past. People in nearby seats responded in shock at the sudden flurry of violence, but he ignored them, looking for his friends. He spotted Kit slumped in his seat, but Eddie and Nina were gone.

He hurried to Kit, who was groggily stirring, one hand clutching his aching neck. "Kit! Are you all right?"

"Someone hit me from behind," Kit gasped. He felt beneath his seat—and realized the case was gone. "What happened?" he demanded, rounding on the man next to him. "I had a bag—where is it?"

"I saw nothing, I was watching the game," the man mumbled, avoiding his gaze.

"What? How could you not—"

"They're all Khoil's people," said Mac. "He told Eddie he bought three hundred tickets for his employees. Two of the larger ones were sitting beside me."

"What happened to them?"

"They're still there. I doubt they'll be getting up for some time."

Kit saw that Eddie's seat, and those around it, were empty. "Eddie and Nina! Where are they?"

Mac's face was grim. "He's got them—and I don't know if Eddie was alive or dead. Where would he be taking them?"

Kit shakily got to his feet. "He's got an estate to the east of the city."

"Then we've got to follow them. Come on."

"And do what? I told you I wouldn't be able to get much support from the local police without proof, and none of these fools will testify against Khoil." He waved an angry hand at the crowd. "And the Khoils have a lot of security. *Armed* security."

"We'll worry about that when we get there." Mac started up the steps, limping on his artificial leg where it had been loosened during the struggle. Cricking his neck, Kit followed.

* * *

By the time Eddie could move again, he and Nina were on their way to Khoil's estate. They were in the back of a Range Rover, Mahajan driving and Tandon covering them with Eddie's own gun. Khoil was in an identical 4×4 ahead, chauffeured by Singh. Nina helped her husband sit upright. "Are you okay?"

"No, I feel fucking terrible." He squinted at Tandon. "What the hell did you do to me?"

"I hit one of your *snayu marma* pressure points, paralyzing the nerves," said Tandon. "I could have killed you, but Mr. Khoil wants to do that somewhere more private."

"So we've got something to look forward to, eh?" He eyed the gun, wondering if he could move fast enough to grab it.

Tandon smiled thinly and drew the Wildey back a little, clearly knowing what Eddie was thinking. "I wouldn't try it. It will take about twenty minutes before you're fully recovered. And by then we'll be at the palace."

From the painful stiffness in his muscles, Eddie realized the man was right. He slumped back, leaning against Nina for support. "Palace? Your boss thinks he's a king, does he?"

"I think it's more like Vanita fancies herself as a queen," said Nina.

The gun jabbed toward her. "Do not speak against the Khoils," Tandon said, scowling. "They are great people."

"Oh, yeah, they're lovely from what I've seen of 'em," said Eddie.

The little convoy eventually turned off the road, passing through a guarded gate in a high wall. Beyond, a lengthy drive ran parallel to the runway. The two Range Rovers stopped at the far end. The Khoils' private jet was still parked on the tarmac; Nina saw that the odd little aircraft she had spotted earlier was being loaded, wings folded, into a shipping container, a forklift standing by to lift it onto a truck.

Vanita Khoil waited for them, accompanied by a pair of armed guards. She glared at Nina and Eddie as they were taken from the second 4×4, before rounding on her husband. "Do you have the codex?"

"Yes, I do," he replied, signaling to another man nearby. "Take the codex to the infotarium. I want the impression

of the key scanned and fed into the prototyper immediately." Singh gave the man the bag, and he boarded a golf
cart and drove away toward the palace.

"Then why are they still alive?" Vanita demanded impatiently.

"I could hardly kill them in full view of the crowd. Even
my employees might have found that too much to keep to
themselves. Besides, I had a better idea." He whispered to
her; Vanita's face lit up with a malevolent smile.

"That may be the best idea of your life," she purred,
clicking her fingers. Mahajan shoved Nina and Eddie forward, Tandon keeping them covered with the Wildey. "I'd
like you to invite you to dinner." She looked to the nearby
tiger compound, smile widening. "With three very special
friends of mine..."

18

Kit stopped the car on the shoulder. "That's it.
Mac looked through his binoculars at the security
barrier a hundred yards down the road. "Two men outside,
another one in the hut. All armed." He lowered the binoculars. "I thought India had strict gun-control laws?"

"It does. But it's possible to get a license under special
circumstances—such as protecting one of the country's
most prominent businessmen."

"And I imagine said businessman's money helped him
get it." He surveyed the long wall surrounding Khoil's
property. "How big is this place?"

"Over three square kilometers. They have their own
airstrip—even a wildlife preserve. Their own little private
world."

"Too private. They can do anything they want to Eddie
and Nina, and nobody would know." Mac turned his attention back to the gate. "Could you use your police cre-
dentials to get us in?"

Kit shook his head. "They'd demand a warrant, and getting one will be very difficult, especially at short notice.
The local magistrates are like the local police—it would

take a great deal of persuasion for any of them to risk their careers by acting against people as powerful as the Khoils."

"So what can we do? We have to get them out of there."

"Unless we can find a way in without being seen, which I don't think we could until dark, there's nothing we can do unless they get some kind of signal to us. Then I could claim probable cause for entry and demand police backup, but without something definite..."

"Sod it!" Mac banged a fist down on his thigh in frustration. There was nothing he could do to help his friends.

* * *

At gunpoint, Nina and Eddie were marched through an underground passage to one of the observation bunkers. "Who the hell owns *tigers*?" Eddie said in disbelief after Nina explained the sanctuary's purpose. "I thought they were computer nerds, not the Indian Siegfried and fucking Roy!"

"Did the SAS teach you anything about dealing with wild animals?" Nina asked hopefully.

"Yeah—stay away from them!"

"I was hoping for something more specific. And speaking of staying away, why the hell did you come to India? I told you not to give them the codex!"

Eddie shook his head in disbelief. "You're still going on about that? I know you're bloody mad for old junk, but you can't seriously think that I'd put some book above your life!"

"It's not just 'some book,' Eddie," said Nina, exasperated despite the danger. "It's a vital part of whatever the Khoils are planning. They want to start a war, some kind of global catastrophe, I don't know what—but before they can, they need the codex so they can find the Vault of Shiva and take the Shiva-Vedas."

"What do they need them for? If they've got the power

to start a war, then I don't see how some ten-thousand-year-old stone tablet's going to make a difference."

"It's eleven thousand years, at least—"

"Yeah, because getting the dates right is really important just now."

"*And,*" she went on, irritated by his sarcasm, "Pramesh thinks that without them, the plan won't work. He's trying to bring the world into the next stage of the Hindu cycle of existence, or some warped version of it, at least—but if he doesn't have the Vedas, Shiva's own pure teachings, he's convinced that everything will fall back into chaos and corruption."

"So," Eddie said as they approached the end of the passage, "the Khoils want to start World War Three...for the good of humanity?"

"Pretty much."

"Christ." He shook his head again. "We know how to pick 'em, don't we?"

They entered the bunker, one of the guards pointing at the elevator platform. Eddie quickly surveyed the surroundings as they stepped onto it. The bunker was octagonal, with a rectangular extension opposite the entrance to accommodate the elevator. Raised metal walkways led up to the windows, which looked out slightly above ground level. A desk was home to a computer and a telephone, a map of the tiger sanctuary and its tunnels on the wall beside it. He took in as much information from the map as he could before a guard operated a control, and the platform rose with a hydraulic whine.

They emerged into sunlight, surrounded by a cage. Nina recognized the clearing where she had watched a tiger be tranquilized a few days earlier. "There are cameras all over the place," she warned, pointing out a stout metal pole nearby. A black sphere at its top turned to observe their arrival. "They're watching us."

"Indeed we are, Dr. Wilde," said a voice, startling them.

Khoil. But not in person; his tone was tinny, coming through a small loudspeaker on the triangular aerial drone. It descended into the clearing, camera pointed at them.

"I wouldn't miss this for the world," Vanita added.

Khoil spoke again. "You may have noticed a new addition to my *vimana*."

"Yeah, I see it," said Nina. Where the dart gun had been before, a larger and more deadly weapon was now mounted beneath the compact aircraft's body: Eddie's Wildey. She glowered at her husband. "You *would* have to buy another of those stupid things..."

"As you saw with the dart gun, I am a good shot. But Vanita only wants me to use the gun as a last resort. Her tigers prefer live prey." The cage lowered into the ground, leaving them standing in the open. The drone pivoted as if gesturing into the surrounding trees. "The nearest tiger is forty meters in that direction. Move toward it." The gun swung back.

They reluctantly stepped off the platform. "What do we do?" Nina whispered, looking around fearfully.

"First thing, don't get eaten," Eddie replied, trying to mask his own worry. Without a weapon, they had almost no chance of surviving a tiger attack. "Second, bring down that drone and get my gun. Did he say it had a dart gun on it before?"

"Yes."

"Then he's in for a fucking surprise if he fires it. Okay, stay close and follow my lead." They entered the trees, the drone descending under the overhanging branches to follow them.

Eddie peered into the vegetation. Forty meters; about 130 feet. If the predator was hunting, they wouldn't see it until it was almost upon them. With a light breeze blowing through the foliage, the visual confusion of the undergrowth and the dappled sunlight cutting into the shadows made it almost impossible to pick out movement.

He looked back at the drone. It was about ten feet behind, slightly above head height. He needed something heavy enough to knock it off balance...

A chunk of broken branch on the ground, moldering among the decomposing leaves. He pretended to stumble, scooping it up as he caught his fall. "Stop," he whispered. "Get ready to run."

"Which way?"

"Any way that isn't at the tiger!" Eddie half turned toward the drone, concealing the hunk of wood behind his body. Nina looked nervously into the trees for any telltale flashes of orange.

The drone came to a hover eight feet away. "Keep moving," ordered Khoil.

"Think I'd rather stay here," said Eddie. "Anyway, how do you even know where the tigers are?"

"The tigers are all tagged with a GPS—"

Eddie suddenly hurled the piece of wood at the drone, knocking the little aircraft back. *"Run!"*

He grabbed Nina's hand, and they turned and charged through the undergrowth, swatting low branches aside. The drone recovered and almost angrily spun to follow. The firing mechanism attached to the gun's trigger pulled back—

The Wildey fired with a colossal boom, the bullet narrowly missing Nina to blast a fist-sized chunk of bark out of a tree—but the effect of the gun's recoil on the drone itself was nearly as damaging. It was thrown backward, spinning wildly into another tree trunk. If its rotor blades had not been shrouded inside impact-resistant plastic, its flight would have ended there; as it was, it bounced off and wobbled drunkenly back into a hover.

"If you're talking, you're not reacting," Eddie said by way of terse explanation as he and Nina crashed through the bushes. Any animals nearby would certainly be able to hear them, but he hoped the tiger had reacted like the birds that had burst in fright from the trees and fled from the sound of the shot.

"Where are we going?" Nina panted.

"Outer wall—I saw where we were on that map. There might be a way out."

They emerged from the trees. Ahead was a twenty-foot gray concrete wall: the preserve's boundary. About sixty feet distant Nina saw a ladder attached to the wall—but its lower section had been raised like that of a fire escape, the lowest rung almost twelve feet up. "Eddie, over there."

"If I give you a leg up, you can pull it down—"

A rifle cracked above them, the bullet kicking up a small explosion of earth at their feet. Two men with guns ran along the top of the wall, a third aiming another shot. Nina and Eddie bolted as a second round slammed into the dirt.

More gunfire spat from the wall as they ran. "Back into the trees!" Eddie yelled.

"That's where the tiger is," Nina protested.

"Tigers don't have guns!" He vaulted a fallen log back into the shadows, Nina just behind. The firing stopped. Eddie slowed, getting his bearings—and hunting for any nearby movement. The immediate area seemed tiger-free. "Okay, so the wall's out—we need to get to another one of those bunkers. Next one was, er...this way."

He pointed in what seemed to Nina to be a completely random direction. "You sure?"

"Sure-ish." He set off. Nina looked around nervously in case anything striped and clawed was watching from the bushes, then scurried after him.

"What do we do when we get to the bunker?" she asked in a near-whisper. "We can't lower the elevator from out-side."

"If we nobble that drone and get my gun back, I can shoot out a window. There was a phone in that first bunker—if the others're the same, we can call Mac or Kit. We just have to steer clear of Hobbes and his mates."

A faint whine caught Nina's attention. She looked up into the trees, but saw nothing. It had to be close, though; Khoil had boasted that the drone's rotors were inaudible past six meters. "I can hear the plane."

Eddie stopped. "Where?"

"Up there somewhere." She pointed.

"I can't hear it." He stared intently into the foliage, seeing nothing.

The noise grew louder. "It's definitely there," Nina hissed. "There, there!"

"Wait, I hear it—" Eddie began, only to stop as the drone dropped down through a gap in the branches and hovered ten feet away. It turned slightly, pointing the gun at him...

But it didn't fire.

"What's it waiting for?" he wondered out loud.

Nina tugged frantically at his arm. He turned his head—and saw a bush, no more than fifteen feet away, lazily lean over with a faint crackle of bending branches as something pressed against it.

Something large.

"Uh...tiger," Nina whispered. "There's a goddamn *tiger* behind that bush!"

Eddie was already looking elsewhere. "That tree," he said, nudging her. Off to one side was a broad saman tree, its thick trunk forking a few feet above the ground, providing a step. "Move to it, slowly."

He put himself between Nina and the predator, then they sidled toward the tree. The bush became still. "I can see it," Nina whispered, voice tremulous. A shape had taken on form among the slashes of sunlight and shadow, crouching low behind the bent branches. Black lines over white and orange converged around a pair of intense yellow eyes, watching them unblinkingly. She remembered that tigers were lone hunters, silent stalkers that observed their prey carefully before springing into a sudden, deadly strike...as this one was doing. Fear squeezed at her chest. "Oh, shit, Eddie, I can *see* it."

"Me too." Only five more feet to the tree—but the tiger could cover the gap in a single leap. It slowly raised its head, then lowered it almost to the ground. Judging the distance.

Preparing its attack.

"Go behind the tree so it can't get straight to you," he told her. "Then start climbing."

"What about you?"

"I'll be up there like a fucking rocket, don't you worry!" They reached the saman. Nina ducked below a branch and circled it. "Okay, get ready..."

The tiger slowly drew back on its powerful legs, ready to leap. It clearly knew that its prey had seen it...and was utterly unconcerned, thinking they posed no threat—and had no chance of escape.

"Climb!" Eddie whispered.

Nina pulled herself up, kicking off the forked trunk as she scrambled higher. Eyes fixed on the tiger, Eddie grabbed the overhanging branch and started to climb.

The animal drew back its lips to reveal a pair of three-inch-long fangs. It pounced—

And skidded to a stop, its head snapping around. The drone had moved closer for a better view—and the tiger heard the whine of its engines. A sound associated with pain, capture. It reared back and roared. The drone hurriedly retreated, but by then Eddie and Nina were both more than ten feet up the tree and desperately climbing higher.

Eddie saw the tiger glare at them. "Can tigers climb trees?"

The answer came a moment later as it jumped onto the fork and scrabbled after Nina, claws ripping into the bark.

"Fuck off, Tigger!" Eddie yelled, kicking at it. He hurriedly pulled back his leg as the tiger swatted at him, slashing a chunk from his boot's sole. It growled and clambered across to the other side of the fork after him.

The bough Nina was climbing shook as the animal jumped off it. A smaller branch she was using as a handhold snapped; she swung, clutching at the broken stub with a stifled shriek. Half hanging off the swaying limb as it bent under her weight, she saw the branch of another tree not far away. She moved farther along the bough, reaching out. "Eddie! Over here! The tiger'll be too heavy to get across!"

"So will I!" Eddie shouted back. He weighed almost seventy pounds more than her, and if the tiger followed him the branch would break under the combined strain.

"You've got to, it's gonna catch you!" She edged closer to the new branch. The drone moved in like an eager voyeur.

Eddie looked down. Nina was right—the tiger was making frighteningly fast progress, claws ripping into the trunk just behind him. He clamped both hands around a branch above and pulled himself up as the tiger swiped again, barely missing his feet. Dangling, he swung along the bough like a monkey—then let go.

Nina got a firm hold on the other tree and hauled herself across just as the branch she had left thrashed violently, Eddie landing on it in an explosion of loose leaves. The drone was caught in the swirling cloud of green and brown, its soft whine abruptly becoming a harsh buzz as leaves were sucked into its rotors and hacked to shreds. The aircraft lurched, briefly losing lift before recovering.

The sight gave Nina an idea, but she was in no position to act upon it. Instead she kept moving along her branch. Behind her, Eddie clung sloth-like to the other branch's underside.

The tiger shifted position, preparing to jump at him.

"Come on!" Nina shouted as she reached the trunk. Eddie pulled himself along, stripping more leaves where his thighs were wrapped around the branch.

The tiger leapt—

Eddie opened his legs, swung down—and used the momentum to throw himself at the other tree, grabbing Nina's branch with one hand.

The tiger landed on the spot where he had been, the bough thrashing again—this time with a sharp crack of wood as it partially split away from the trunk. Suddenly fearful, the animal gripped the branch tightly as it tipped downward, ending up swaying almost fifteen feet above the ground.

Eddie dropped to a lower fork as Nina descended. The tiger was trying to crawl backward along the branch, afraid of the fall, but its sheer size restricted its movements. "It's stuck!" he cried, jumping down to the ground. "Leg it!"

Nina landed beside him—and pulled him behind the tree as the drone fired a second shot. Again it was thrown back by the recoil, but this time Khoil was prepared, and recovered more quickly.

By then, Nina and Eddie were running again. The ground became wet, their feet kicking up splashes as they skirted a marshy area near the central lake. "That way to the bunker," said Eddie, pointing.

Nina looked back. The tiger was not pursuing them, either still stuck in the tree or frightened away by the gunshot—but the drone was swooping after them like a tiny jet fighter. "How many shots in your gun?"

"Five left."

Perhaps there was something to be said for the Wildey after all; a normal gun would have had more ammo and less recoil. "I've got an idea how to bring down the drone, but we'll have to split up."

"That's about the worst thing we could do."

"If we don't, we'll get shot!" The Wildey boomed again, the Magnum bullet blasting a hole right through the trunk of a small tree just ahead of Eddie, splinters making him flinch. "Split up!" Nina shouted.

"I'm not leaving you on your own!"

"I won't be far—just get it to follow you under a low branch!"

Eddie realized what her plan was. She peeled away; he kept going, looking back at the drone to make sure it was still following him. Fronds whipped at his face as he jumped through a clump of bushes.

The drone rose to clear them. Another thunderous gun-shot seared past his head and slammed into the soggy ground. He had lost sight of Nina, but could hear her crunching through the undergrowth on a parallel course.

Another large saman tree bowed down ahead, branches drooping. "Nina!" he shouted, hoping she would take it as a signal. The drone was still coming, a carbon-fiber wasp with a lethal sting. *Three* lethal stings, only four of the seven bullets fired. It descended to clear the outermost foliage, fixing Eddie in its sights—

Nina leapt up and grabbed the overhanging branch, pulling it down onto the machine.

This time, more than mere leaves were sucked into the rotors. Branches crunched into the ducts, the whirling blades slashing against them—and jamming.

The drone spun out of control as one of its three rotor pods failed entirely with a horrible chain-saw rasp. The Wildey fired again, but the bullet flew harmlessly into the surrounding vegetation. Nina released the branch and dived at the gyrating aircraft, slamming it to the ground. She pulled the firing lever out from the Wildey's trigger guard a moment before it clicked.

Eddie ran to her and lifted the drone to release his gun, then looked into the camera. "See you soon," he promised the observers with a menacing smile before cracking the Wildey's butt against the lens.

"How many bullets are left?" Nina asked.

He checked. "Two."

"Will that be enough?"

"If it's not, we'll be tiger crap by tomorrow. Now, where's that bunker?" They set off at a jog and soon reemerged into sunlight, finding the lake to their left. Tall reeds rose from the water, giving them some concealment. "Okay, this way," said Eddie, leading her along the bank. He hopped over a mud hole. "Watch out for that."

"Watch out for *that*!" Nina said in alarm. Eddie spun, seeing another tiger emerge from the lake and splash through the reeds toward them. He aimed the Wildey at it—then lowered the barrel slightly and fired. The combination of the gunshot and the explosion of mud and spray in front of the animal's face prompted it to turn tail into the trees.

"You didn't shoot it?" said Nina, surprised.

"Enough people want us dead already without adding the World Wildlife Fund to the list," he said, keeping the gun raised until he was sure the animal had gone. Nina jumped the hole, and they continued along the bank. "Should be off to the right somewhere."

"Yeah—there's a path." Nina bent low under a branch and followed the faint trail through the trees before holding up a hand. "I can see the bunker—and a camera pole." There was no way to reach the low concrete structure without being spotted.

"We'll have to move fast," Eddie said, hefting the Wildey. "You ready?"

She looked back to make sure the tiger was not returning, then nodded. "Let's do it."

They ran into the clearing. The camera turned to face them. "They've seen us!" Nina cried.

Eddie moved to the window beside the raised elevator platform and fired his last bullet at point-blank range. The window was toughened, but it couldn't withstand the power of a Magnum round, shattering into a million crystalline fragments. He looked through. Nobody was in the bunker. Like the first one, it had a computer station at a desk—and a phone.

The opening was too small for him to fit through. He helped Nina slide inside; a chunk of glass still caught in the frame ripped the hip of her trousers, leaving a smudge of blood on the broken window. She grimaced, but wriggled through and hurried to the elevator controls. The metal platform descended into the ground.

Eddie hopped off it. "What's that noise?" he said, looking along the underground passage. An odd echoing sound reached him.

"Goats," Nina told him. "They must keep the tiger chow down here. Someone ought to tell the Humane Society."

He went to the phone. "Okay, let's see," he said, starting to enter Mac's number. "Just hope—" A tone warbled in his ear. "For fuck's sake!" he snapped, banging down the receiver. "It's an internal system."

"Get an outside line," Nina hurriedly suggested. "Nine, push nine!"

He tried again, but with no better result. If the phone was connected to the outside world, there was no indication of how to reach it. "Bollocks! We'll just have to make a run for it." He glanced at the cut on her hip. "You okay?"

"It just stings. I'll be fine." They ran down the passage.

Behind them, a shadow passed over the broken window, something sniffing at the smeared blood.

The third tiger. The male, largest and deadliest of the three.

Nina and Eddie rounded a bend in the passageway to find a pen behind a gated metal fence. A dozen miserable-looking goats reacted in alarm to the new arrivals. Eddie was about to run past when Nina pulled him back. "Someone's coming!" The ringing clamor of running footsteps echoed down the concrete tunnel.

The only place they could retreat was back into the tiger preserve. Instead, Eddie turned to the pen—and bashed open the gate's bolt with his Wildey, waving his arms wildly. The goats panicked, leaping and bumping against one another before making a break for freedom. He held out his arms to force the animals toward the approaching footsteps. One got past him, but the others swerved away and charged down the corridor.

"Now what?" Nina asked.

"Go with 'em!" Eddie ran after the fleeing herd. Nina was about to follow when the lone goat tore back past her, little hooves clicking on the concrete floor. She jumped out of its way, then started in pursuit.

Eddie kept pace with the frightened animals, urging them onward faster and faster down the narrow tunnel. Another bend ahead, the footsteps louder—

Two of the Khoils' security guards rounded the corner—and were knocked down by the stampede. One man took a pair of sharp horns to the stomach, screaming as blood jetted out. The other threw up his hands to protect his face as other goats scrabbled over him.

Eddie kicked the wounded—but still armed—guard in the head, silencing his screams. But the other man also had his weapon, sitting up and spotting Nina in front of him. He raised his gun—

The Wildey cracked against his temple. He collapsed.

Eddie shoved the empty Wildey into his jacket, then collected the two men's guns, Heckler & Koch USPs. "Nina, take this," he said, holding out the first guard's weapon.

She accepted the USP, checking the passage ahead. The goats had disappeared around another corner. "Looks clear."

"There's bound to be more of 'em, so stay behind me."

They cautiously moved down the corridor. A shadow

loomed from beyond another corner—Eddie raised his gun and peered around.

The shadow was only a goat, standing in another bleak concrete chamber at an intersection, a storage area with crates and sacks of animal feed stacked high in recesses to each side. Other goats milled about, unwilling to go any farther.

Beyond them was an open metal door—and a flight of stairs leading up. It was where Eddie and Nina had been brought into the tiger preserve, the passage to the first bunker off to one side.

Waving Nina back, he rounded the corner, gun aimed at the stairs. Some of the goats backed away from him—then stopped.

Was someone hiding in the doorway? Was that what was scaring them?"

Eddie moved past the stacks of supplies, quickly checking that nobody was lurking behind them before crouching for a better view up the stairs. No one in sight. "I think it's clear."

Nina warily rounded the corner—then froze at a faint squeak of wood from the farthest stack of crates. "Eddie!"

He looked around—but at her, not the sound. "What?"

Singh leapt from atop the crates and slammed him to the ground.

The goats scattered, one of them almost knocking Nina over as it barreled past. By the time she recovered and brought up her gun, Eddie and Singh were grappling on the floor, too intertwined for her to shoot without risking hitting her husband.

The Dalit was on top of Eddie, hand clenched around his gun arm. Eddie twisted his wrist and fired. The USP's muzzle flame scorched the back of Singh's neck, but the bullet missed him, cracking off the wall. Singh yelled, then lunged with rage-driven strength—and bit Eddie's forearm.

"Jesus *Christ*!" Eddie roared as the sharpened teeth

sank into his flesh. The pain was so intense that he couldn't keep hold of the gun. It clanked across the floor. Singh grabbed for it, but couldn't reach without releasing his animalistic hold on Eddie's arm. He opened his mouth, blood running down his chin as he groped for the USP once more.

Nina kicked it away just before his fingers closed on the butt. She jumped back as the clawing hand snatched at her legs. "Eddie, what do I do?"

"Fucking *shoot him*!"

"I'll hit you!"

Eddie struggled, managing to land a punch against Singh's side. In response, the wiry maniac jerked up a knee at his groin. Eddie did his best to twist away, but was still caught a painful enough blow to make him flinch involuntarily—giving Singh an opening. He drove his fist and forearm down into a hammer blow on Eddie's face, cracking his skull against the unyielding concrete floor.

Eddie's vision jarred, unnatural colors silently exploding over Singh's face as the blood-dripping grin widened and dropped toward his throat. He willed Nina to jam her gun against the other man's head and pull the trigger—but she was no longer there.

He felt Singh's breath on his neck, the razor teeth about to tear into his throat.

S ingh suddenly felt breath on *his* neck.

He looked around—and the tiger that had followed the scent of blood and the bleating of frightened animals into the bunker ripped its mighty fangs deep into the throat of its unsuspecting prey before he could even scream. The huge predator dragged the flailing Indian across the floor, slashing at his abdomen with its claws.

Nina had run back in pure reflexive fear when she saw the tiger. Heart slamming like a pneumatic drill, she pulled the bloodied Eddie away from the carnage. "Come on, we gotta move."

"You're not kidding!" he said, seeing the tiger tear out Singh's throat. The fearful symmetry of its face was marred by a gush of bright red blood. "Where's my gun?"

"Here." She retrieved his USP.

He was about to fire it to scare away the tiger when someone shouted in Hindi from the stairs. "Cover your ears," he said, pulling Nina away from the exit, past the tiger and its quivering meal. The yellow eyes stared coldly at them with the promise that they would be next, but it didn't move to attack.

Nina put her hands to her head as Eddie raised the gun. He aimed—not at the tiger, but at the floor behind it. The first booming gunshot sent stinging chips of concrete at its rear legs. It dropped Singh's body, whirling to face them with a snarl of fury.

Eddie fired again, and again, each shot blasting little craters out of the floor at the tiger's feet. Overcome by the noise and the painful insect bites of shrapnel, it turned and fled.

Up the stairs.

The shouts above quickly turned to screams. "Okay, sounds like they're busy," said Eddie. "If anyone gets between you and the door, shoot 'em!"

They hurried up the stairs. Someone fired a shot, only for a voice as enraged as the tiger to yell at them: Vanita. More screams, then a loud crash.

Eddie reached the top to see that the tiger had pounced on one of the guards, knocking over a table. Other people were fleeing through the main doors and up the stairs to the observation level. A guard cowering behind a workbench saw him and whipped up his gun, but a single shot from the USP sent him tumbling with a bloody hole in his forehead.

Nina spotted Vanita halfway up the stairs, screeching orders for someone to get a tranquilizer gun. Her husband was higher up, watching the chaos with an unbelieving expression—which changed to fear as he saw Nina point her gun toward him. She didn't know if she could have pulled the trigger, but the threat was enough; he turned and ran out of sight to the upper floor.

"Nina!" Eddie pointed to the doors. "Go!" He took down another armed guard before they both burst out into the open, blinking in the bright sunlight. "Where now?"

"We can drive out of here," said Nina. She ran to a nearby golf cart.

"In *that*?"

"There's a garage under the palace—we can get something faster." She climbed into the driver's seat, Eddie jumping aboard behind her and pointing his gun back at the doors—although another scream from the building suggested that the tiger was still everyone's biggest concern.

Nina stamped the accelerator to the floor. The golf cart lurched away, electric motors whining as it powered up to its top speed of twenty miles an hour. "It's not exactly a Ferrari, is it?" Eddie complained.

"It's better than running. Just." She guided the cart down the road to the palace. Even at its less-than-scorching pace, it still covered the distance in just over a minute. The ramp to the garage was off to one side—but she swerved away from it, heading for one of the doors into the huge house itself.

"Where are we going?" Eddie demanded.

"The codex—we need to find it."

"Oh, for fuck's sake!"

"I know where it is," she insisted, stopping and jumping from the cart. With a noise of frustration, Eddie ran ahead, kicking open the door and darting through with his gun raised.

The hallway was clear. They hurried inside. "Where're we going?"

"The infotarium."

"The *what*?"

"Khoil's name, not mine." They reached the high-tech room, where Nina held back again as Eddie burst in, confirming that nobody was inside before nodding for her to enter.

The lights were low, the sphere of screens displaying stylized clouds. Nina ran to the desk where her hand had been scanned, seeing the codex in its open case. She slammed it shut and picked it up. "Okay, got it."

She turned to leave, but Eddie's attention was caught by another piece of equipment beside the laser scanner. A rapid prototyper...with something in the tank. He snatched it out, finding that unlike the silicone liquid he had used in New York, the medium this time was extremely fine grains of plastic. "This looks familiar."

Nina grabbed it from him. "It's from the codex's cover—the key! He's made a copy of the key!" One side of the thick and surprisingly heavy circular object bore the faces of the five Hindu goddesses, their husband Shiva at the center. She opened the codex case and slotted it into the impression in the orichalcum cover before snapping the lid shut again. "We've got to delete the pattern so he can't make another—"

"No, we don't," Eddie countered at the sound of pounding feet outside. "What we *do* need is to get out of here before we get killed!"

The footsteps came closer. Eddie brought up his pistol—

A man bearing an MP5 submachine gun rushed into the room—and took two shots to his chest. Eddie ran to him, pocketing the USP and picking up the MP5, then glanced at the display cabinet containing Khoil's first computer. "A Spectrum, eh?" He smashed the glass with the gun's stock, making Nina jump, then did the same to the little computer inside it.

"What was that for?" she gasped, startled by the petty vandalism.

He grinned. "I was a Commodore 64 kid. Now where's this garage?"

They ran from the infotarium, Nina directing them to the elevator. Another guard charged around a corner ahead—and took a burst from the MP5 across his chest. Shouts echoed behind them; more people were coming.

A short side passage led to the elevator. Nina pushed the call button, but Eddie booted open the door beside it and waved for her to go down the stairs. She took them two at a time, the heavy case banging against her legs, and emerged in the basement.

Eddie arrived a second later, eyes widening in admiration as he took in the gleaming cars. "Wow. This lot's nearly as good as Kari Frost's collection."

Nina was in no mood for comparisons between maniacal billionaires past and present. "All I care about is: Does he have anything *fast*?"

"Oh, yeah." He indicated a two-tone slate and charcoal-gray hunk of sculpted, purposeful curves—the Bugatti Veyron. "Fastest production car ever built. "

"We don't need the Guinness World Records, just start it!"

A glass-fronted cabinet near the elevator contained numerous keys, each with the fob displaying the manufacturer's logo. Eddie searched for the distinctive EB of Bugatti, then smashed the glass with the MP5 and snatched out the keys. He tossed them to Nina. "Your turn to drive."

"Me? But—"

"Unless you want to shoot."

"I'll drive," said Nina quickly, running to the Veyron. She threw the gun and case inside and lowered herself into the low-slung, luxurious interior as Eddie rounded the supercar, the MP5 raised.

A chime as the elevator arrived—

Eddie fired before the doors had even fully opened, a guard thrashing backward into the confined cabin. He glimpsed Tandon and released another burst, but the Indian squeezed himself flat against the side wall. For a moment Eddie considered running across to finish him off, but then the Veyron started with a growl from its massive sixteen-cylinder engine. He swung into the car. "Go!"

Smoke belched from the screaming tires as Nina pressed the accelerator. "What the hell's with this gear stick?" she cried, trying unsuccessfully to shift into second gear.

"It's a sequential—push it forward to change up!" Eddie leaned out of the door, seeing Tandon running for cover behind the McLaren. He fired another burst—just as Nina figured out the gears and upshifted. The car leapt forward, throwing off his aim. The McLaren's windshield shattered as Tandon dived behind it. Eddie cursed and pulled himself inside the Veyron, lowering his window as the supercar shot toward the ramp.

Nina kept accelerating, the engine note thunderous in the underground space. There was a horrible crunch as the Bugatti's front air dam scraped the foot of the ramp, then they powered toward the square of daylight ahead—

One of the Range Rovers skidded to a halt at the entrance, broadside on to block their escape.

Nina fought her instinct to brake, instead jamming the accelerator all the way down and bracing herself...

The Veyron reached the top of the ramp—and went airborne. It smashed into the Range Rover at window height, slicing off the 4×4's roof in an explosion of glass. The driver ducked just quickly enough to avoid decapitation, the supercar's underside clearing his head by an inch as it arced over him and smashed back down to earth.

Air bags fired, punching Eddie and Nina back into their seats. Dazed, Nina tried to straighten out, and found that the Bugatti wouldn't be breaking any more speed records: The suspension was wrecked, one of the rear wheels loose and bashing against the bodywork. Despite the damage, she still managed to wrestle the car toward the gate.

Eddie sat up, raising his gun—and seeing a potential target. Mahajan and another man were driving a golf cart toward the palace, the Khoils on the rear seats. He fired at them. Khoil and Vanita flung themselves out of the cart as bullets caught the guard and sent him flailing to the ground. Mahajan ducked and swerved the little vehicle to put it between the gunman and his employers.

Nina headed for the long drive—only to see a second Range Rover brake to block it. With its low clearance and damaged suspension, the Veyron had no chance of negoti-

ating the grass shoulders to get around it. She instead made
a hard turn, bringing the supercar onto the runway.

Eddie glanced back at the golf cart. Vanita had snatched
up the fallen guard's MP5 and was pointing it at the Veyron. "Down!" he shouted as she opened fire. Bullets puck-
ered the Bugatti's bodywork, but none reached the cabin;
the Veyron's engine was mounted behind the seats, the
huge block taking the clanging impacts. There was a loud
hiss and a gush of steam as one of the radiators was punctured, adding to the wounded car's woes.

Nina skidded past the parked jet and the now-closed
container holding the smaller aircraft, aiming along the
length of the runway and slamming up through the gears.
The Veyron had all-wheel drive; even with one of them
crunching against the wheel arch the response was still
frightening. In the mirror, the golf cart was suddenly reduced to a dot as the car blasted through the sixty-mile-
per-hour mark in barely four seconds, thundering on
toward a hundred. "Jesus!" she yelped.

"Bloody hell," said Eddie, pushing himself upright. "I'm
jealous that you're driving now!"

She was not as thrilled with the experience. The collapsed suspension was making the steering wheel judder
like a jackhammer, even holding the car in a straight line
becoming harder with each passing moment. Dashboard
warning lights started flashing—the radiator was not all
that had been damaged. The speedometer passed one hundred...then dropped back down. "I think this thing'll
need more than an oil change at its next service," she
warned.

Eddie looked back. The steam had been replaced by
greasy smoke, swirling in the Veyron's slipstream. The second Range Rover was now in pursuit.

Ahead, even with the Veyron slowing, they were rapidly
running out of runway. Beyond the poles of the landing
lights at its far end, Nina could see the estate's boundary

wall. She brought the car into a sweeping, shuddering turn onto an access lane leading to the main drive. Only a short distance to the main gate, and freedom—if they could get through it.

If they could get *to* it. The engine rasped alarmingly, the stench of burning oil filling the cabin. Even with her foot to the floor, their speed was still falling. Sixty miles an hour, fifty. Nina straightened out as they reached the road, seeing the gate ahead. Guards ran to block their path.

Armed guards.

"Go through them!" Eddie shouted. "Crash the gate!"

"There's no power!" Nina protested. Forty miles an hour and still slowing, even as she dropped through the gears in a desperate attempt to maintain speed. The vibration from the wrecked wheel was getting worse, the Veyron's back end starting to weave. "We're not gonna make it!" Thirty...

A huge metallic bang shook the car as the broken wheel finally sheared off its axle, tearing off the Veyron's back quarter panel and bouncing down the drive. The already low-slung supercar's ground clearance was reduced to zero as the unsupported body hit the road like an anchor. Grinding over the asphalt, it screeched to a stop.

The guards ran toward them, guns raised—

And whirled at the sound of another vehicle behind them.

The barrier shattered as Kit crashed his car through it. One of the men was hit by a length of broken wood and bowled off his feet to smash through the guard hut's window. The other two leapt out of the car's path, bringing their guns to bear—

Kit spun the steering wheel and yanked on the hand brake. The car fishtailed, its rear end swinging around and swatting away one of the guards with a *thump* of flesh against steel.

The remaining man dived aside in the nick of time, rolling and bringing up his gun—

Mac kicked open the passenger door. It hit the crouching guard just as he fired, knocking the gun downward. A semicircle of red sprayed over the tarmac as the bullet hit the luckless man's kneecap. He fell on his back, dropping the gun as he screamed and clutched the wound.

Mac tossed the fallen weapon out of his reach, then waved to the occupants of the crippled Veyron. "Well, come on! We haven't got all day!"

20

Kit lowered his cell phone, his normally sunny face somewhat clouded. "That...did not go well. But it could have been worse."

"What did your bosses say?" Nina asked. "Are they going to arrest the Khoils? Or at least investigate them?"

"Unfortunately, no. Not without more proof."

"But we've got proof," said Eddie, indicating the Talonor Codex. The golden book sat on a desk in Kit's small but modern Delhi apartment, the Interpol officer having arranged a flight from Bangalore back to the capital on a government transport aircraft. "They had that thing in their bloody house. That's got to be enough for Interpol to take action, surely?"

"It's your word against theirs. *I* know you recovered it from them, but that isn't firm evidence. If Khoil had left a single fingerprint on it, that would be enough, but you said yourself that he never actually touched it. And"—Kit sighed—"the Khoils have already been busy. They have lots of friends in high places—and they seem to have spoken to all of them in the last few hours. Politicians, lawyers, judges ... We need absolutely irrefutable evidence before we can take any action."

"So there's nothing they can be charged with?" Nina said in disbelief. "What about the simple fact that I'm sitting right here in India? I was goddamn *kidnapped*!"

"I looked into that. But unfortunately, the immigration agency has a record of you arriving—alone—at Bangalore airport three days ago."

"That's impossible! They brought me straight to their own airfield."

"That's not what the computer says, I'm afraid."

"And guess whose company wrote the software on that computer?" said Eddie rhetorically.

Mac made a grumbling sound. "It seems we have a stalemate. There's not a great deal they can do to us without arousing suspicion against themselves, but we've got nothing on them either."

"I have one piece of good news, though," Kit told Eddie. "The Interpol red notice issued on you has been rescinded. I've told my superiors that the Talonor Codex has been recovered—and that you helped. I strongly implied the whole thing was some sort of sting operation. You'll still have to be questioned back in New York, but for now you're off the arrest list."

Eddie wasn't especially overjoyed. "Fucking marvelous. We've got the codex back, but it doesn't matter, 'cause they've got what they needed from it." He tapped the plastic replica of the key beside the golden book. "They've probably made another copy already."

"I told you we should have deleted the pattern," Nina said.

"So the Khoils will be able to find the Vault of Shiva?" Kit asked.

"Unless we find it first," said Nina.

Eddie frowned. "Not much chance of that, is there? We don't know where it is."

"Nor does Khoil. He had a translation of the codex, and made some deductions from it, but hadn't pinned down an actual location."

"What deductions?" asked Mac.

Nina thought back to Khoil's boastful claims at the palace. "He said it was somewhere near Mount Kailash— Shiva's home."

"The Sacred Mountain," said Kit, nodding. "The logical place."

"Have you been there?"

"No, unfortunately." He smiled. "My work doesn't give me a lot of time for pilgrimages. Perhaps someday."

"Do you have an atlas?"

Kit found a book and opened it to a map of the northern half of the Indian subcontinent, the contours of the Himalayas in grays and purples above the greens and browns of the rest of India. Tibetan China was above it at the top right of the page, Nepal sandwiched between the two much larger countries. "Here," he said, pointing at a spot above Nepal's northwestern corner, near the disputed Indo-Chinese border. "These two lakes are Manasarovar and Raksas Tal—both holy places. Drinking the water of Manasarovar is meant to cleanse you of all your sins for a hundred lifetimes."

"Might be worth me having a swig," said Eddie.

Mac cocked his head. "Just the one?"

"Mount Kailash is north of them," Kit continued. "Lord Shiva supposedly meditates at the summit."

"Waiting to end the world, according to Khoil," said Nina.

"And begin it again," he reminded her.

"Maybe so, but for all its faults, I'd kinda like to keep the one we have now."

"Exactly what did Khoil tell you about this plan of his?" Mac asked.

"Not enough," she said, sighing. "Although I think he

may have given away more than he intended when he was showing off how he's rigged the Qexia search engine. He used India and Pakistan as an example of two countries that would only need the right spark to go to war—maybe that's already part of what the Khoils are planning."

Mac nodded. "Both countries have nuclear weapons. If they started throwing them about, things would escalate beyond just the two of them very quickly."

"But what would the Khoils gain from that?" asked Kit.

"Global collapse," said Nina. "Pramesh wants to force the world into the next stage of the cycle of existence—end the Kali Yuga, and start a new Satya Yuga. A new golden age," she added for the benefit of the two puzzled British men.

"That's rather arrogant of him," said Kit thoughtfully. "The Kali Yuga is supposed to last more than four hundred thousand years, and Shiva is the one who will end it. Not a man."

She smiled darkly. "Arrogance is about his only personality trait, unless you count nerdiness. But he said he has to have the Vedas from the Vault of Shiva for his plan to work. Without Shiva's teachings to inspire them, people will just stay in the gutter."

"So what if he doesn't get these Vedas?" Eddie asked.

"I don't know. If he believes in them that much, maybe he won't carry out his plan at all."

"Well, then. We get them before he does. Problem solved!"

"Easier said than done. We don't know where the vault is." Nina looked at the map more closely, brow furrowing as she trawled through her memory of everything she had learned from the Talonor Codex. Some clue was tantalizingly close to revealing itself, but without access to the translation she couldn't pin it down. "And...I'm not entirely sure that the Khoils do, either. Something isn't right. Do you remember what I was telling you about Talonor—when you realized that what he was writing was a tactical report?"

"Some of it. What about it?"

She tapped a finger on the map. "Something about Talonor's journey. He visited a temple where he met the Hindu priests—who showed him the key to the vault of Shiva." She lifted the replica, tilting it so light picked out the reliefs of Shiva and the five goddesses. "He said the vault was one day away from the temple. Or rather, one day to get there, and one hour to get back."

"How's that possible?" Mac wondered.

"Khoil thought they might have come back by river," said Nina. The Himalayas were riddled with blue lines running down from glaciers, so that didn't narrow the possibilities. "But Talonor said he went away from the river to reach the temple. And then..." She snapped her fingers. "From there, he carried on northeast until he discovered the Golden Peak."

"The Golden Peak?" asked Kit.

"The site of an Atlantean settlement."

He was surprised. "There was an Atlantean settlement in Tibet? I've never heard that."

Nina realized she'd made a gaffe. "Oh...yeah. It's something we kept out of the public record for security reasons, because it contained the..." She trailed off and glared at her husband, who was making a show of holding his head in his hands. "Knock it off, Eddie. Uh, things I can't tell you about. Sorry." She gave Kit an apologetic shrug.

"I understand," he said. "Every organization has its secrets—I should know!"

"How does that help us, then?" Eddie asked. He indicated an area above and to the left of Mount Kailash. "This is where the Golden Peak is, more or less."

"To the north*west* of the sacred mountain," Nina
pointed out. "Talonor said he continued north*east*."

"There couldn't have been a translation error?" suggested Mac.

"No, not for something that basic. That means the Vault
of Shiva can't be at Mount Kailash." She checked the map's
scale. "The Golden Peak is almost a hundred miles north-
west of there. Talonor was the greatest explorer of his
time—he couldn't possibly have made such a huge naviga-
tional error. But Khoil doesn't know that. He's working
from all the information Qexia has trawled from the Internet—but nothing about the Golden Peak has ever been
publicly released." A triumphant smile. "Guess computers
can't do all the work for you after all."

"So if it's not there, where is it?" Eddie moved his finger
diagonally over the map. "If he went northeast to reach the
Golden Peak, the vault's got to be somewhere southwest of
it."

"Yeah . . . but the codex specifically said that he met the
priests at a temple on a holy mountain. Kit, are there any
other—"

"Kedarnath," Kit cut in, his expression suggesting he
was chastising himself for not having thought of it earlier.
"Kedarnath, of course! Here." He indicated a particular
peak on the Indian side of the disputed border. "Lord Shiva
lived on Mount Kailash, yes—but he had a second home
on Mount Kedarnath."

"So he had a holiday cottage?" said Eddie. "I'd pick
somewhere a bit nearer the sea myself. But then, I'm not a
god."

Nina grinned. "You just think you are. So what's the
story of Kedarnath?"

"There are three, actually," said Kit. "The great Hindu
texts have many different ways of telling the same stories.
One of them is that two of Shiva's followers, Nar and
Narayan, performed great penance before a lingam of

Shiva—a symbol of the god," he clarified for Eddie and Mac. "Shiva was pleased and granted them a boon—a wish. They asked if he could make a home closer to his followers than Mount Kailash, and he agreed. In another, five brothers followed Shiva there to beg forgiveness for having killed their cousins in a war. He gave it, and told them he would live there to watch over them."

"And the third version?"

"Shiva's wife, Parvati, thought Mount Kailash was too far from India—she wanted to be nearer the people she loved. So she asked Shiva for another home that was closer to them."

Eddie laughed. "That sounds familiar. The bloke has to move house because his wife wants to be somewhere she thinks is nicer."

"Are you telling me you *liked* living in Blissville?" said Nina, of their move out of Queens back into her native Manhattan five months earlier.

"It was a lot cheaper, I'll give it that."

She huffed, then turned back to Kit. "What else can you tell me about Kedarnath?"

"Not much. I've never been there. But there is a temple there—one of the oldest and holiest in India. It's dedicated to Shiva."

"How old?" Eddie asked.

"I don't know, but very."

"Old enough to have been there when Talonor visited," Nina said thoughtfully. "Everything fits: Talonor thinking that Shiva, with his trident, was the same god as Poseidon; the temple being southwest of the Golden Peak; the entire site being considered a sacred mountain, the home of a god." Her expression brightened. "And Khoil's looking in the wrong place. He's started from a false premise—that the sacred mountain mentioned in the codex is Mount Kailash. And since he doesn't know about the Golden Peak, he's got no way of realizing that!"

"So the vault is somewhere on Mount Kedarnath?" Kit asked.

"Seems like it."

"Then I can't see how it hasn't been found already. Kedarnath is not like Mount Kailash—lots of people have climbed it. And the temple is a major tourist attraction, as well as a site of pilgrimage."

"It could be hidden. In a cave, through a crevice— however many tourists have been there, I doubt they've crawled over every square inch of the entire peak."

"It doesn't help us find it either, though," Eddie said.

"I know. If I had the translation...wait a minute. I'm a dumb-ass." She looked at Kit's laptop. "I can *get* the translation. Can I use your phone?"

* * *

One call to Lola in New York later, and—after Nina assured the relieved PA that she and Eddie were okay— the IHA's translation of the Talonor Codex sat in Kit's inbox.

"So computers do have their uses, then?" joked Eddie.

"For some things, yeah," Nina admitted as she scrolled through the text. "I don't know why I've suddenly gotten this reputation as a Luddite, though. I've used computers to help me my entire career. It's when you rely on them to *think* for you that you have a problem—as Khoil hopefully won't find out until it's way, way too late." She remembered something and gave her husband a scathing look. "Speaking of problems...we need to have a little discussion about your Internet surfing habits."

"Eh?"

"Khoil knows what you've been looking at. *Everything.* Qexia has a record. He showed me."

"Oh, *that.* Yeah, he mentioned it. And next time I see

him, I'm going to kick his arse so hard that he'll shit out of his mouth."

Mac tried to hide a smile. "Something you want to share, Eddie?"

He put his hands on Nina's shoulders and grinned. "Only with my wife."

"*I* don't want to share...*that*," Nina protested.

"I bet you'd like it once you tried it."

"I don't want to try it! We shouldn't need..." She blushed. "Props."

He kissed the top of her head. "Such a prude."

"Shut up. Oh, here it is." She highlighted part of the text. "Talonor describes the part of the mountain where the priests said the Vault of Shiva is hidden. 'A ridge, higher above us, many stadia distant across hard but passable terrain. It was marked by a notch like that in the edge of a damaged blade.' Everything in military terms again," she remarked to Eddie.

"Can we use that to work out the vault's location?" Kit asked.

"We should be able to, since we know where the temple is. Do you have Google Earth or something on your laptop?"

He did; a few minutes later, the screen showed a virtual view of Kedarnath mountain from the village of the same name. Off to the northeast, there was indeed a ridge with what could be described as a notch cut into it, though the relatively low resolution meant it could just as easily be a glitch of the rendering system.

"The ridge is, let's see...about three and a half miles from the village," said Nina. "The vault's supposedly somewhere up there."

Eddie brought the camera higher, pulling back for an aerial view. "It says the village is at about eleven thousand feet, but the ridge is..." He moved the cursor across the screen. "Christ, it's almost twenty thousand feet high in places."

"Steep climb," noted Mac. "You'd have to take it slowly, or risk getting altitude sickness."

"That'd explain why the priests needed a full day to get to the vault, I guess," said Nina. "But they wouldn't have had anything close to modern mountaineering gear, so there must be a way that's passable by foot. Could they have gone through the notch?"

"Depends how big it is." Eddie indicated the angular graphic on the screen. "That doesn't tell us anything. Could be fifty yards deep, or five hundred. We'd need to see it for real."

"What are the chances of that?" Nina asked Kit. "You said that Eddie's no longer Public Enemy Number One—are we free to travel?"

"You really want to go to Kedarnath?" he asked. "Is that a good idea?"

"Whatever the Khoils are planning, it seemed to be on a deadline, otherwise they wouldn't have been in such a desperate rush to get hold of the codex. And they both seem pretty smart—they might not be archaeologists, but they'll figure out that Mount Kailash isn't the right place sooner rather than later. And when they do, they'll start looking for other possibilities. Since they're both devout followers of Shiva, I'd guess they know about Mount Kedarnath and his pied-à-terre."

"You want to go climbing the Himalayas?" Eddie asked. "In *December*? It'll be a bit bloody nippy."

"Pramesh seemed completely sincere about needing these ancient texts, the Shiva-Vedas. If we can find the Vault of Shiva and get the Vedas first, that'll be a big spanner in his works—not to mention an archaeological find to match anything we've seen so far."

Mac tapped his foot on the floor, the prosthetic leg

making a dull creak of metal and plastic. "I'm afraid you'll have to count me out, then. Much as I love freezing my arse off on mountainsides, I'm not really up to the task anymore. I have a slight deficiency in the limb department."

Nina smiled at him. "Mac, you've already done way more than I can ever thank you for."

"I might still be able to do something useful, though. Peter Alderley is coming to India as part of the British delegation for the G20 summit. The Khoils might be pulling every string they can in the Indian government, but I highly doubt they'll have any influence at MI6. I'll talk to him and see if he can find out anything."

"Oh, great," Eddie groaned. "My favorite person."

"We should meet him," Nina said, teasing. "You can apologize in person for dropping his invitation down a drain."

"Tchah!"

Mac smiled. "I'm sure Peter will enjoy that. But whatever Eddie may think of him, he takes his work very seriously—and threats to global security are very much part of MI6's remit. Especially with twenty world leaders in the same place at the same time."

"Do you think that's their plan?" said Nina. "Attack the G20? Then manipulate the media to place the blame on different countries?"

"It'd be a pretty good way to kick off a war," Eddie said.

"But how would they do it?" asked Kit. "You've seen the security—entire sections of the city are closed off. Nobody would be able to get close enough."

Nina gave him a grim look. "If that's what the Khoils are planning, they'll find a way. No, scratch that—they'll already have *found* a way. They've been working on it for months, ever since they started stealing the cultural treasures. All they need are the Shiva-Vedas, and they'll have all their pieces in place. So Eddie's right—we have to get to the Vault of Shiva first."

"Just the two of us, then?" said Eddie. "Since I know I've got absolutely no chance of talking you out of this."

"Just the *three* of us," Kit said, to everyone's surprise. "If you're going, I'm going with you."

"You've done a lot for us too, Kit," said Nina. "You don't have to do anything else."

"Oh, but I do. First, does either of you speak Hindi?" Nina and Eddie shook their heads. "You might not get very far without someone who can. Second, until Eddie is fully cleared, I will probably have to take personal responsibility for his actions—and I will have a hard time doing that if he is three hundred kilometers away up a mountain!"

"Will your bosses be okay with that?" Nina asked. "I doubt if searching for the lost vaults of gods is in your job description."

"But my job is about more than tracking down lost art," Kit reminded her. "It also covers the theft of valuable antiquities. And the writings of Lord Shiva himself must surely qualify."

Mac lightheartedly raised a finger. "They haven't technically been stolen yet."

Kit laughed. "Then consider it crime prevention! But you will need my help, and I am happy to give it."

"Have you got any climbing experience?" Eddie asked.

He nodded. "And I can get the clothing and equipment we will need."

"I think we have a team, then," said Nina. "Kit, thank you."

He smiled, then picked up his phone. "I have a long call to make to Lyon." He entered a number, then went into the next room to hold the conversation in private.

Eddie looked at the image of Mount Kedarnath on the laptop. "You really think it's there?"

"Yes, I do—and we could be the first people in thousands of years to find it. But we have to get there before the Khoils."

Mac leaned forward in his chair. "It won't be easy, Nina. The conditions in those mountains at this time of year will be awful. Eddie may have had survival training, but even so, one wrong step could kill all of you."

Eddie snorted. "Your pep talks were a lot better back in the Regiment."

"I'm getting more careful with age. You might want to consider trying it. Both of you." He gave them a meaningful look, then stood. "Speaking of which, age affects the body as well as the mind, so if you'll excuse me..." He headed for the bathroom.

"Cheeky old git," said Eddie, with a fond look after his former commanding officer. "I'm always careful. Ish." He noticed how Nina was looking at him. "What? Don't tell me you agree with him."

"Of course I do, Eddie. We almost got killed at the Khoils' estate. Several times."

"Par for the bloody course with us, isn't it? And being chased up a tree by a tiger'll make a great story to tell at a pub sometime."

"And what about the story when you almost got your throat ripped out by a psychopath because you didn't hear him coming? Will that be on the list too?"

"Yeah, okay, that wasn't so good. But I still came out on top."

"Only by sheer luck." She took his hands in hers. "Eddie, I'm just worried that if you carry on like you always have, and deliberately ignore the fact that it's affected your hearing—"

"I'm not bloody deaf, all right?" he snapped. "That Pennywise-toothed little bastard got lucky, that's all."

"Or you were unlucky," said Nina quietly. "And you

only have to be unlucky once to..." She couldn't speak the terrible thought.

He squeezed her hands and gave her a reassuring smile. "Well, at least it should be nice and quiet up in the mountains, right?"

21

So much for quiet," said Nina as she stepped off the bus ...into a noisy crowd.

From what she had read, she had expected the Himalayan village of Gaurikund to be nothing more than a small pit stop on the way up to Kedarnath. But even with a covering of snow and a chill winter wind, the narrow streets of colorful, tight-packed, and high-stacked buildings were bustling with activity.

"They're pilgrims," said Kit. "Kedarnath is closed in winter because of the weather—so the priests from the temple all move down to Gaurikund."

"They close the whole *village*?" Eddie asked incredulously, hauling a large rucksack out of the bus. "Guess we're not checking into a hotel once we're up there, then."

"I'm afraid not. And we have to walk from here—this is as far as the road goes. It's another fourteen kilometers to Kedarnath."

Eddie looked up the valley. Though shrouded in gray clouds, the looming dark mass of Mount Kedarnath was still discernible, its highest peak over three miles above. "Nice weather for it."

Nina was more interested in the people. They were of all ages, dressed in everything from utilitarian cold-weather clothing to layers of brightly colored traditional Indian apparel to simple orange robes that seemed highly unsuited to the cold conditions. "They're all here to pay homage to Shiva?"

"Not all of them," Kit replied. "Gaurikund is a holy site for other gods as well. There is a hot spring where Shiva first told Parvati that he loved her—people come to bathe in it. It's also where their son Ganesha was born."

"He's the one with an elephant's head, right?" said Eddie. Kit nodded.

"I'm impressed," said Nina. "How did you know that?"

"It was in *The Simpsons*."

"Ah." She sighed and shook her head. "The source of all modern knowledge."

"But did Bart and Homer explain why he has an elephant's head?" Kit asked Eddie with a smile, getting a negative response. "Parvati was bathing in the spring, and Ganesha was standing guard. Shiva arrived unexpectedly— he had been away for a long time, and didn't recognize Ganesha as his son. Ganesha tried to stop him from seeing Parvati, so Shiva cut off his head."

"Whoa," said Eddie. "That's a bit harsh."

"Parvati thought so too! She demanded that Shiva bring him back to life. But Shiva couldn't find the head, so he took the head from an elephant and used that instead. That is one of the stories. As usual, there are many others."

Eddie was puzzled. "If there's so many different versions of every story, how do you decide which one to believe?"

"You believe the one that you most believe in," said Kit with an amused shrug. "It must sound strange to Westerners, but it has worked for us for thousands of years."

"It's the version the Khoils believe that worries me," said Nina. She looked up at the brooding mountain. "How do we get to Kedarnath?"

"There's a path up the valley. I'll ask someone how to get there." Kit stepped into the crowd, asked a man a question in Hindi—and got a look of utter disbelief in return. A second attempt earned him first a laugh, then an expression of concern, most likely for his sanity.

"Okay," said Nina, pursing her lips. "Maybe it's a harder journey than we thought."

The sound of a scuffle made her turn. The pilgrims parted, backing away from an elderly man with a wild, almost dreadlocked mane of gray hair and a long beard, wearing nothing but an orange robe. He was dancing, sandaled feet skipping through the snow, and waving a gnarled stick at anyone who got too close.

"Bloody hell," said Eddie. "He must be freezing!"

"He's a yogi," Nina realized. "A holy man. They give away all their possessions and travel through India in search of enlightenment."

"Maybe, but if I were him, I'd search for it somewhere warmer."

The yogi continued his crazy little dance, the onlookers seeming caught between respect for him and annoyance at his antics. He laughed for no particular reason into a man's face, then spotted Nina and Eddie. He tipped his head with a look of curious recognition and strode over to them.

"Er...hello," said Nina, drawing back. Though she didn't want to be uncharitable, the yogi would definitely benefit from a wash in the hot spring.

He fixed her with an intense gaze, foolish capering replaced by seriousness. "I know who you are, and why you are here," he said, his accent thick. "Nina Wilde."

Nina was shocked. "How—how do you know my name?"

"From here, I can watch the entire world," he intoned.

"Is that a Hindu saying?"

"No." A crazy smile split his face, and he jabbed his stick at a dish on a nearby building. "It just means we have satellite TV! Ha ha!" He danced a brief jig, kicking up slush. "I saw you in Egypt, in the Sphinx. 'What kept you?' Very funny!" He laughed again—then before Nina could react he squeezed her breasts.

"Oi!" Eddie shouted, shoving him back. "Fuck off, Yoda!" He raised a fist.

Kit hurried over. "Eddie, no!" he cried, interposing himself between the giggling yogi and the aggrieved Englishman. "He's a Pashupati Yogi."

"I don't care if he's Yogi fucking Bear!" Eddie growled. "He just grabbed my wife's tits—that gets you a smack in the mouth whoever you are."

"Eddie, it's okay," said Nina, cheeks flushing. "No harm done, and . . . well, he's obviously a little, uh . . ." She tried to think of a nonoffensive term. "Eccentric."

The yogi cackled. "No, no. Rich people are eccentric. I am *mad*!"

"He's not mad," Kit said impatiently. "The Pashupatis are a sect of Shiva worshippers—sometimes called the Order of Lunatics. Some of them pretend to be mad to drive away people who want to associate with a holy man for their own personal gain." He turned to the old man. "Go on, be on your way."

"No, wait," said Nina. "He said he knows who we are—"

" 'Cause he saw you on TV," Eddie cut in.

"—*and why we're here.*" She addressed the yogi. "Why are we here?"

"You seek the Vault of Shiva, of course."

The trio exchanged concerned looks. "How do you know that?" Nina asked.

"Why else would you be here? You are the famous Nina Wilde, you search for ancient legends and reveal them to the world. The other legends of this mountain, the pool of Parvati, the Shivalingam, they are all known. So you are looking for the one that is not."

"Nobody knows the legend of the Vault of Shiva," said Kit. "Dr. Wilde only discovered it recently."

The yogi was affronted. "*I* know it! So does everyone who lives here." He dropped his voice to a mock whisper. "But they will not tell anyone, because it is their great secret."

"So why're you telling us?" asked Eddie.

"Because I am mad!" He whooped before becoming serious once more. "But you will not find it, Dr. Wilde."

"You seem pretty certain of that," she said.

"The Vault of Shiva is not real; it does not exist. Sometimes, a legend is just a legend. You should go home."

"That's not really an option. We have to find the vault. Before someone else does."

He eyed her quizzically. "Someone in particular?"

"We can't talk about it. I'm sorry."

His gaze revealed a thoughtful intelligence as he considered her words...then the crazy mask returned. "Everyone has their secrets! Ha! So sad. Nobody with a secret can ever reach the end of the path to enlightenment."

"The only path we're bothered about is the one to Kedarnath," said Eddie, annoyed. "You know where it is?"

"Of course I do! I was born in these mountains, I was married in..." He trailed off, briefly lost in some memory, then faced Nina. "You are going up to Kedarnath, though there is nothing to find?"

"Yes, we are."

"Even in this weather?" He waved his stick at the cloud-shrouded mountain.

"Yes."

He shook his head, muttering something in Hindi. "Very well," he continued. "I will show you the way."

"I think we can manage, mate," Eddie said.

Nina's refusal was more gentle. "That's very generous, but we'll be fine. Thank you."

"No, no, I insist," said the yogi. "You need a guide—

there are many big falls. And I will find you a warm place to sleep at Kedarnath."

"I thought there wasn't anyone there?" said Kit.

"There is not, but I will still find you a place! Come, come. The path is this way." He pointed up the street.

"If you come with us," said Nina, "you'll be walking eight and a half miles up a mountain in the snow—why would you do that for us?"

He replied as if the answer was perfectly obvious. "Because it is the right thing to do! You need help, I am here to help. What other reason could there be? Now come, this way."

"Are we really going to let him come?" Eddie asked Nina.

"Can we stop him? I mean, if he wants to follow us to Kedarnath, there isn't much we can do about it."

"If he gets hypothermia, I'm not carrying him back down the bloody mountain," he grumbled.

"Well," said Nina, "looks like we have a guide, whether we want one or not." She picked up her pack. "Oh, you didn't tell us your name, Mr. ...."

"Girilal Mitra," the old man said, bowing. "Very pleased to be at your service. Now, I hope you have good shoes—it's a long walk!" Dancing again, he pushed through the crowd. The trio hesitated, then followed.

Nina noticed that while the pilgrims were startled by the old man's behavior, others whom she assumed to be locals reacted with little more than weary disdain, or even ignored him entirely, as if well used to his antics. "So...how long have you been on the path to enlightenment?"

"Some paths, you cannot know how long they are until you reach the end," said Girilal.

"Very profound, but that's not what I asked."

"I know. But here is one path I know well." The stick pointed at an arched gate, painted brick red, at the foot of a steep flight of steps leading up between the buildings. "The way to Kedarnath. Are you sure you want to go?"

"Yes," Nina said firmly. "I'm sure."

"I thought so. Well!" He clapped his hands. "Let us begin!"

* * *

Eight and a half miles: Nina had traversed similar distances across rough terrain with relative ease in the past. The difference here was that barely a yard of the trek was on the flat. Before they were a mile from Gaurikund her legs were aching from the constant, punishing climb up the steep snow-covered path. Kit was faring better, but not by much, and even Eddie, laden with the largest pack, was starting to show signs of strain.

The ascent didn't appear to bother Girilal, however. He hummed a tune as he strolled, and even occasionally skipped, along. A shrill wind whistled down the slope, flapping the hem of his grubby robe.

"I can't believe you're not cold," said Nina. Even with the exertion of the walk, she was glad of her thick hooded jacket and weatherproof trousers. "Do you use some mind-over-matter meditation technique?"

"Oh, nothing like that," he said cheerily. "I *am* cold. I just don't show it!"

Eddie grunted disapprovingly. "Deliberately risking frostbite is pretty fucking stupid, mate. Why do it? Getting rid of your worldly goods is one thing, but does Shiva say you've got to torture yourself?"

"How I serve my penance is my choice," Girilal replied, for the first time since they had met him revealing a hint of negative emotion—not so much anger as sorrow.

"Penance for what?" Nina asked.

"For my sins, of course. I cannot reach enlightenment until Lord Shiva has forgiven me for everything bad I have done."

"The Catholic way's easier," said Eddie. "Quick confession, couple of Hail Marys, and you're sorted."

"Like you've ever been to confession," joked Nina. "You'd be in there for hours! The priests would have to work in shifts."

"Don't make me add clipping my wife around the ear to my list."

Girilal resumed his humming, leading the way. The trees became sparser as they ascended, the unobstructed wind picking up. Along the way they passed a few tiny settlements, handfuls of huts huddled together—all without roofs. Nina at first thought they were derelict, until Girilal explained that the merchants inhabiting the little hamlets moved down the mountain during the winter; when Kedarnath was closed to pilgrims and tourists, they had no customers. The roofs were removed to prevent them from collapsing under the weight of snow.

The clouds closed in, the valley disappearing into a gray haze. Kit read a Hindi sign as they stopped to rest. "Four kilometers to go."

"We've only walked six miles?" said Nina in breathless disbelief. "It feels like sixty!"

Once recovered, they carried on up the slope, which became steeper and rockier. By now, they were above the tree line, the only vegetation small bushes poking out from the snow. The dampness of the surrounding clouds intensified the cold still further. Nina tried to offer Girilal a blanket, but he refused, resolutely picking out the path ahead of them.

Another marker post, and another. Although the mountainside was getting no steeper, the climb became harder as the air thinned. Their rest stops increased in length and frequency. The last marker: half a mile to go. They kept ascending. Then...

"Look at that!" said Nina, awed. They emerged from the fog—and for the first time since arriving in the northern

Indian state of Uttarakhand, she was able to see the true majesty of the Himalayas.

Lower down, the mountains had been little more than ominous shadows, concealed in the murky clouds. But now she could see them clearly, lit by the stark winter sun. The sawtoothed main peak of Mount Kedarnath itself dominated the view, its lower, secondary summit off to the west, but even with the valley's sides obscuring the surrounding landscape she could take in other snow-covered mountains rising beyond. She had been in the Himalayas before, but circumstances had not been conducive to sightseeing. This time, she was truly able to appreciate their scale.

Eddie was not so impressed. "Yeah, it looks pretty amazing," he said, "but you won't like it so much when you try to climb the bugger." He pointed to the northeast. The ridge they had seen on Kit's laptop was revealed for real, more jagged and imposing than its computer-generated counterpart. "We've got to get up that."

"There's the notch," said Kit. There was indeed a V-shaped gap in the natural barrier, but even its lowest point was considerably higher than their current location.

Girilal turned his face from the falling sun to regard the ridge. "You think the Vault of Shiva is over there?"

"That's right," said Nina.

"That is a very dangerous part of the mountain. Many who have gone there have never come back. Are you sure you want to follow them?"

"Yes, I'm sure."

"I could live without it," Eddie muttered.

"I cannot stop you, of course. But I wanted to warn you. Well, I tried! Now, come, come. The village is just ahead."

After a short distance, they crested a rise to reach flatter ground. The track ahead was lined with a long string of small huts leading to the village proper; like those in the hamlets down the mountain, their roofs had been removed. The buildings at the path's end were more solid works of brick and stone, squeezed tightly into the narrow valley floor. The absolute stillness of the scene was eerie, the village in hibernation, waiting for life to return in the spring.

"The pilgrims stay here," said Girilal, waving his stick at the skeletal huts. "The tourists have more money; they stay in the hotels."

"Are you taking us to a hotel?" Nina asked.

"Oh, no! They are private property—that would be breaking and entering, and your policeman would have to arrest me!" He directed a laugh at Kit. "No, I know somewhere better."

At the end of the line of huts was a small bridge over a narrow gorge. They crossed it and entered Kedarnath proper. A central street wound up the slope, the houses' doors barricaded by sandbags to keep out snow and meltwater, locks wrapped in cloth to protect them from the cold. At the far end was the village's tallest building, a broad stone hall with a high square tower.

"Is that the temple?" Nina asked Girilal.

"Yes—one of the twelve *jyotirlingas*, the holiest Hindu shrines, where Lord Shiva himself appeared. That is where I am taking you."

Kit looked at him sharply. "You're going to open the temple?"

"I am a humble servant of Shiva; I have been there many times. It is the best place for those in need of shelter to stay the night. And," he added, grinning, "I know where the priests hide the key."

Kit didn't seem happy, but raised no further objections as they approached the temple. The building was impressive: it had a squat, sturdy appearance, being built from large stone blocks to withstand the elements, yet the blunt functionality was balanced by detailed carved figures set into alcoves around the colorful entrance. An imposing statue of a bull stood guard outside.

Girilal led them through a gate, but rather than going to

the temple's entrance he crossed to the building's corner
and brushed snow off a small pile of bricks, muttering to
himself as he looked beneath each in turn. Finally, he triumphantly held up a large brass key. "I told you!" he said,
skipping to the door and unwrapping the cloth from the
heavy padlock before opening it. "Come inside, come!" He
kicked off his sandals, then picked them up and stepped
over the sandbags.

Kit placed his hands together and lowered his head
toward the temple, then unfastened and removed his boots
before entering. Eddie looked at Nina with a shrug before
following suit. She did the same, hopping on one foot as
she fumbled with the laces, and went inside.

The interior was dark; with the village closed for winter,
there was no electricity. Eddie was about to delve into his
backpack for a flashlight when a soft glow illuminated the
entrance hall as Girilal lit a lamp. Figures emerged from the
darkness: statues. Behind them, mythic scenes were painted
on the walls. "Please, accept the hospitality of Lord Shiva,"
said the old man.

"Thank you," said Nina. She looked more closely at the
statues. "These are beautiful. Who are they?"

"The Pandava brothers," said Girilal. "The heroes of
the Mahabharata. They came here seeking Shiva before
they died. They were serving penance for killing their
cousins in battle, and because of that Shiva did not want to
bless them, so he took the form of a bull to hide from them.
But they found him, and he tried to get away by sinking
into the ground. The brothers caught the bull by its hump
just before it disappeared, and the hump turned to stone
and became the Shivalingam. The temple was built around
it." He faced the next room, hands together in prayer.

Nina couldn't help noticing that his crazy-man act had
all but disappeared. "What will you do now you're here?"

"I will pay my respects to Shiva, of course, and ask him
to protect you on the rest of your journey."

"Can you ask him to stick up a sign pointing to his vault as well?" Eddie said. Kit gave him a somewhat irritated look. .

"Eddie, we're in a sacred Hindu temple," Nina chided him. "Behave yourself."

Girilal laughed. "It is all right, Dr. Wilde. Shiva has a sense of humor—some say Ganesha was created from his laughter! Now please, make yourselves warm. I will be back soon." He went into the darkened hall.

Eddie took a combined paraffin heater and stove from his pack and set it up. "This'll be cozy," he said as he lit it. "Better than kipping in a tent, though."

"What's the plan?" Nina asked.

"It'll be night soon, so best bet's to start off at first light tomorrow and head for that ridge. We should be able to get over it before it gets dark again—if we can find a way up."

"A *safe* way," added Kit. "After what Girilal said, I'm wondering if we should have brought more climbing gear."

"We've got enough," said Eddie, nudging his pack. Metal clinked inside it. "Long as we don't have to scale any sheer cliffs, we'll be fine—if the weather holds."

"Do you think it will?" said Nina.

"Place like this, it can completely change in five minutes. Only way to know is to keep an eye on the conditions, and if it gets dodgy be ready for it." He looked at the others' packs. "Okay, so who's got the nosh?"

Provisions were retrieved, and sleeping bags unrolled and laid out around the heater. Kit started preparing the food. Nina looked into the adjoining hall. "Girilal?" she called. "Do you want anything to eat?" No reply. "I'd better see if he's all right," she said, concerned that the long, cold trek might have finally taken its toll.

The next, larger room was dark except for a faint orange glow, the temple windowless as further protection against the weather. Padding closer, she saw that the light was a candle, behind a curtain. Girilal's voice reached her, speaking quietly in Hindi. She parted the curtain and entered the small chamber beyond. "Girilal? Are you okay?"

The old man was sitting cross-legged on the stone floor before a small altar, the flickering candle beside him lighting the turquoise walls. He looked around, startled. "No, you should not be in here!" he said, scrambling to his feet.

"I'm sorry!" said Nina, backing out. "I just wanted to make sure you were all right."

He composed himself and lowered his head. "No, I should apologize. I should have told you what I was doing, and asked you not to disturb me. It is my fault."

Despite wanting to respect his privacy as he prayed, Nina couldn't help but look at the altar. "Is that..."

"The Shivalingam, yes." While lingams were usually cylindrical, this was instead a small three-sided pyramid of polished black stone, red stripes painted across it. "For those who have reached enlightenment, Lord Shiva will manifest himself as a pillar of cosmic light and bless them."

"Have you...?"

"No." He shook his head with sad resignation. "I am not worthy. I have too much to seek forgiveness for." He picked up the candle and gently but firmly ushered Nina out of the chamber. "Now," he said, his voice becoming more positive, "you said something about food?"

22

Even inside the temple, cocooned in her sleeping bag and wearing several layers of clothing, Nina still woke up shivering. Eddie was already awake, heating water on the stove. "Morning, sunshine."

"Morning," she said blearily. "What time is it?"

"About twenty to seven. Sun'll be up soon. We'll need to get moving once it is. Got a lot of walking ahead."

"Can't wait." She sat up, seeing that the outer door was ajar, letting in a slit of predawn light. "Where are Kit and Girilal?"

"Kit's gone for a piss. Dunno where the old guy is; he went out about twenty minutes ago. Maybe he's taking a dump."

Nina groaned. "I could have lived without you putting that image in my head, Eddie." She unzipped the sleeping bag. "What's on the menu?"

"Coffee first, then breakfast. Lots of high-calorie stuff—we're going to need it. Cereal, porridge, that kind of thing."

"Mmm. Delicious," she said, unenthused.

"Hey, you wanted to come here. I had another look at

the map now we've seen the terrain firsthand, by the way. Think I've worked out a route. Girilal thinks it'll be safe."

"How well does he know the area?"

Eddie smiled conspiratorially. "Better than he lets on. Sneaky old sod. I don't think this is the first time he's been up here in the winter."

Nina indicated the next hall. "He must come to worship at the Shivalingam. Poor guy. Whatever it is he's doing penance for, I don't think he believes he'll ever be forgiven for it."

"Well, maybe he'll get a better crack at things in the next life." He looked up as Kit reentered the temple.

"Morning, Kit," Nina said. "Is Girilal outside?"

He briskly rubbed his cold fingers. "Yes. He said he wanted to watch the sun rise."

"He must be freezing!"

"He must be *mad*," Eddie amended. "Kind of ironic, since that's what he was already pretending to be."

Nina shook her head. "He's just looking for forgiveness, and I don't see how he's going to find it, because he can't forgive *himself*. I feel really sorry for him."

"No need for that, Dr. Wilde," said Girilal cheerfully, skipping over the sandbags into the temple. Nina blushed at having been overheard. "But I feel sorry for you. You will not find the Vault of Shiva, because it is not there. Please, make this old man happy and go back to Gaurikund. Do not risk your lives for a legend."

"That's sort of what we do," Eddie said with a wry smile.

"And you say *I* am mad!"

Nina smiled. "Thank you for caring, Girilal, but I'm afraid we're long past that point."

"Well, I can at least wish you well and see you on your way."

"After breakfast," she said. "Care to join us?"

He laughed. "Of course! I am mad, not stupid!"

. . .

By the time they left the temple the sun was up, though the sky was mottled with cloud. Girilal shook their hands. "Please, come back down the mountain with me," he said hopefully. "It will snow later, I can tell."

"We'll be fine," Nina assured him, her breath steaming in the cold air. "Thank you for all your help."

He bowed his head in modesty. "I am only doing what should be done. But I have asked Lord Shiva to watch over you, and I hope he will be generous."

"I hope so too," said Kit, peering up apprehensively at the ridge.

"Then have a safe—and uneventful, ha!—journey. Perhaps we shall meet again if you return."

"*When* we return, you mean," Eddie said.

"*When* you return, of course! Dr. Wilde, Mr. Chase, Mr. Jindal... be safe."

"You too," said Nina. "Will you be okay getting back to Gaurikund?"

Girilal grinned. "I shall sing, and I shall dance, and I will be back there as quickly as if I had flown like a bird!" He did a little jig in the snow.

Eddie held up a hand. "Listen, mate—we know you're not really mad. So you don't need to keep up the act."

Girilal pursed his lips. "I didn't even realize what I was doing. Perhaps I have been doing it for so long, it has become natural."

"Perhaps you've been doing it too long," said Nina pointedly.

"Perhaps. In that case, I shall walk in a very normal way back to Gaurikund. Good-bye. And good luck."

"Thank you," she said. "And I hope you find what you're looking for."

"So do I," the old man said, waving as he set off back down the long path.

Eddie turned to gaze up at their own destination. "Okay, that gap in the ridge is about three miles from here, and over a mile higher up. We've got a long bloody climb. Let's get started."

Nina detected a new tone in his voice. "That was very military, Eddie. Were you like that in the SAS?"

"If I was doing things like in the SAS, we wouldn't still be standing here—we would have been *running* up the mountain with full gear and weapons before the sun was even up."

"Speaking of weapons," said Nina, regarding him suspiciously, "did you bring..."

"Course I did." He unzipped his coat to reveal the Wildey tucked in its holster.

She put a hand to her head. "Oh, God. *Why?*"

"Hey, you never know—we might run into a yeti."

"Yeah, that's just the headline I want: 'Legendary Himalayan creature discovered—and has its head blown off by demented Englishman!'"

"Better than 'World's most famous nonfictional archaeologist eaten by snow monster'—innit?" He started uphill. "Well, come on. The Vault of Shiva's not going to find itself. And, oi! What do you mean, *demented*?"

Nina and Kit followed him, sharing a smile.

* * *

The ascent began relatively easily, but before long parts of the slope became steep enough for them to need to use telescoping aluminum climbing poles and even their hands to scrabble up it. The grass hidden beneath the snow gave way to nothing but earth and rock.

They kept climbing, Eddie scouting out the best route. Even with his experience, they had to double back a few times when the way ahead became too steep to ascend without climbing gear, something he wanted to avoid for as long as possible. But there was a route to the foot of the ridge, however convoluted and draining.

Rest breaks became more frequent the higher they got. "God, this is killing me," Nina gasped as she flopped down on a boulder. She pulled off one glove and rubbed her temple.

Eddie was with her in a moment. "Got a headache?"

"A bit. It's not serious," she assured him. "I just need to get my breath back."

"You took some altitude sickness medicine this morning, right?"

"Yeah, I did. Really, I'm okay. What about you, Kit?"

The policeman was taking deep, slow breaths. "I'm fine. I think. This is the most exhausting case I have ever been on."

"Art theft doesn't usually take you up the Himalayas, I suppose," said Eddie, surveying the area. The landscape below was hidden by mist, but he could see clouds visibly rising, strong winds pushing them up the mountainside. He looked higher. The patches of cloud had grown thicker and darker, and the air was noticeably more hazy than when they had left Kedarnath. "Girilal was right. I think we're going to get snowed on."

Nina regarded the clouds unhappily. "Nice Christmas cardy snow, or horrific flesh-stripping blizzardy snow?"

"Three guesses. How's your head?"

"Better. A bit."

"Give it another minute, then." He patted her shoulder.

As she waited for her headache to subside, Nina's attention turned to the ground around them. Even under the snow, it had a distinctly stepped appearance, as if long terraces had been dug into the slope. "Have you noticed this? It almost looks like it was once cultivated."

"Up here?" Eddie said skeptically. "There isn't even grass this high up."

"There have been warmer periods in the past—there

used to be vegetation in the Antarctic, remember. Maybe the priests at Kedarnath in Talonor's time grew things up here. Or maybe there were people who lived closer to the Vault of Shiva—they'd need to get their food from somewhere."

He shook his head. "Could just be a fluke of layers of rock or something."

"Yeah, I know. And if it were used for cultivation, it would have been a long time ago—there's a lot of erosion. It's still an interesting possibility, though."

"Depends on your idea of interesting."

"Quiet, you."

Once Nina's headache faded, they set off again. The ridge loomed over them, a colossal wall of stone. From this distance, the "notch" was revealed as a deep pass in its own right. Eddie checked it with binoculars. "There's a way up to it. Pretty steep, and there'll be a lot of zigzagging, but I think we can do it without having to rope up."

"Can we reach it before it starts snowing?" Kit asked.

He looked at the sky. The clouds had thickened still further. "Probably not. It might not be too bad, though. Not much wind at the moment."

"Let's hope it stays that way," said Nina.

They picked their way up the steepening route to the pass. About half a mile short, they stopped to eat. It was now past midday; only five hours before sunset. Rested and nourished, the trio pressed on until they reached the bottom of the path.

The sun was lost behind cloud, the temperature falling. Nina realized the clouds themselves were closing in. Kedarnath's peaks were already obscured, and the upper parts of the ridge disappeared into the leaden gray. As she watched, a lone snowflake drifted past. It seemed to be a fluke... then another appeared. And another.

"Shit," muttered Eddie as the fall began in earnest. He tried to pick out the switchback path above him. "We've got about another three hundred feet to climb, and there's nowhere to put up a shelter if it gets bad. We'll either have to go back down and wait it out, or get to the top no matter what the weather does."

"Can we make it all the way up?" asked Nina.

"Dunno." He studied the clouds. "If the wind doesn't pick up we should be able to, but..." A shrug. "Depends how keen you are to see what's up there."

"There is kind of a time factor," Nina reminded him. "If the Khoils figure out the Kedarnath connection, they'll be on their way here too—and probably by helicopter."

"Bad weather'll affect a chopper just as much as us. If we can't get up there, neither can they."

"But as soon as it clears, they'll be able to fly straight there." She looked at the winding path above. "If you think it's too great a risk, then...we'll wait it out until the weather improves," she said reluctantly. "But if you think we *can* make it, we should try. For all we know, the Vault of Shiva might be right on the other side of that ridge. It might be *in* that ridge."

"Great, dump all the life-and-death decisions on your husband..." Eddie stared up at the pass once more. "Okay, we'll try it. You all right with that, Kit?"

"If you think we can make it, I will trust you." He smiled. "You seem to know what you're doing."

"Christ, I wish that was true all the time! Okay, let's go. Be careful."

Eddie took the lead, probing the rock beneath the snow with his aluminum pole. Fat snowflakes whirled around them, eddies of wind gusting them up the ridge into the climbers' faces.

The path narrowed as they moved higher, the steep slope transitioning to actual cliff. Midafternoon, but beneath the overhanging clouds it felt more like evening. The landscape below disappeared into a dismal sea of gray as more snow fell. The pass above was only vaguely visible through a disorienting swirl of snowflakes.

They continued the ascent. Before long the climbing poles became useless, everyone needing both hands to keep a firm grip on the rock. At the end of another leg of the zigzag path, Eddie stopped and squinted up through the falling snow. "Not far to go, but if it gets any narrower we might have to get out some spikes and rope up. It'll slow us down, but it'll be safer." He shifted his gaze to the main mass of Kedarnath—and his expression changed. "Wait, fuck that! We need to get to the top, right now!"

Nina looked. "Why? What's happening?" A dark cloud bank had moved across the peak, angling upward from the mountain's side like a Nazi salute.

"A storm's coming! That cloud—it's called a flag cloud, and when it's tilted up like that it means the wind's blowing really fast."

"How fast is really fast?" Kit asked nervously.

"Seventy, eighty miles an hour—it's a fucking *blizzard,* and it's coming right at us! Move it!" He started up the path.

"I'm movin', I'm movin'!" cried Nina, sidestepping along the narrow ledge as fast as she dared. Kit was right behind her. The wind picked up, its shrill whistle chilling in more ways than one.

The approaching storm seemed as tangible as the rock face, a black wall closing in to crush them. Eddie reached the last leg of the path, the entrance to the pass at its top. He stretched his legs wide to clear a broad gap in the ledge—and felt stones shift underfoot, adrenaline kicking at his heart as he fought to keep his balance. He rasped his boot against the rock until it found solidity, then hopped over, warning the others to be careful.

Nina reached the final section, seeing the pass—and also the storm lunging down like an attacking bear. Panting, the freezing air searing her lungs, she moved to the gap. The wind was roaring now, tearing at her clothes. Kit clung to the rock wall a few steps behind her.

Eddie waited on the far side, hand out. She steeled herself, jumped—and cleared it. "Kit, come on!" she called.

He leapt—

The storm hit.

It was almost a physical blow, the wind slamming against them. Visibility was reduced to inches in a second. Eddie clutched Nina's hand; she reached back with her other to grab Kit's sleeve, pulling as hard as she could as he clawed for a handhold. The weight of his backpack made him wobble, one foot slipping—then he found support. She tried to yell for him to follow, but couldn't even hear her own voice over the fury of the storm. All she could do was tug the Indian in the same direction Eddie was pulling her, and hope none of them fell and dragged the others over the edge . . .

Perversely, the last few feet were the hardest, the steep, snow-slicked slope offering no handholds. Eddie kicked his toes hard into the frozen scree, dragging Nina after him. His outstretched hand, already numbing, touched something solid.

The wall of the pass. They had made it—

And were no better off. The split in the ridge was barely eight feet wide at its foot—and it acted as a channel for the storm. The vicious windchill made the temperature plummet. Within moments, the group's backs were coated in snow and ice, their clothing flapping like flags in a hurricane.

"Keep moving!" Eddie gasped. If they stayed in the natural wind tunnel, they would freeze to death in minutes—there was no chance of erecting a tent in time, even if it could withstand the storm. One arm over his face, he reached back with the other to pull Nina along. Kit held on to her backpack, stumbling in their wake.

Now Eddie understood why this part of the mountain

had such a fearsome reputation. The pass was an obvious shortcut—but if the weather changed suddenly, it could become a death trap.

How long was the pass? He lowered his arm, the cold biting at his eyes. Nothing visible except wind-driven snow streaming past.

He squeezed Nina's hand, hoping to feel her do the same in return, but got no response. Another look ahead as he staggered on. Still nothing visible but the disorienting hyperspace tunnel of rushing snowflakes. He could feel ice forming on his eyelashes, freezing them together.

He used his elbow to find the wall. There might be some nook, a fallen boulder, a tiny cave that could provide just enough shelter for them all to huddle inside until the storm passed. But he felt nothing except solid rock...

The wind suddenly changed, blowing at him not from behind, but from the side. A tornado of snowflakes whipped around him. Forcing his ice-crusted eyes open, he looked around. The rock walls seemed no different from the rest of the pass.

Why had the wind shifted? Something was diverting it— maybe even blocking it. Shelter. But he still couldn't see anything—

He looked up—and found it.

About seven feet above in the eastern cliff was a fissure, a horizontal slash in the rock. Roughly five feet high, and deep enough that nothing but shadow was visible within. If they could all squeeze inside...

He turned, taking the icy blast directly into his face as he shouted to Nina and Kit. "Cave...up there! Nina, climb up!"

She pushed her hood against his. Even that close, he could barely hear her over the wind. "Can't feel...hands."

"It's our only chance! Come on!" He shoved her to the wall. "Kit, help her up!"

The two men took hold of Nina and lifted her. "Reach

up!" Eddie shouted. "Get into the hole!" She stiffly raised her hands, groping numbly for the gap. Finding it. Eddie and Kit pushed her higher, and she all but fell inside. Realizing that the wind had dropped, she crawled deeper into the fissure.

"You next!" Eddie told Kit. The Indian said something, but it was lost in the wind. Eddie bent to give him a leg up, taking hold of Kit's boot with his freezing fingers. Legs flailing, Kit wormed into the tight opening.

Eddie jumped up after him, but the edge of the little cave was slick with ice. His hands, useless lumps of meat, couldn't get a grip. The storm was sapping his strength by the second—if he didn't get into shelter very soon, he never would...

Kit reappeared in the cave mouth. He knelt and held out his hands. Eddie reached up. Kit grabbed his wrists and pulled. With the last of his strength, Eddie scrambled up the wall, boots rasping on the rock.

He slumped into the fissure, almost knocking Kit over as he landed on him. The cave was deeper than he had thought; they moved into the darkness, flurries of snow still clawing at them in a last-ditch attempt to stop their escape before the ferocious wind finally dropped.

"Thanks," Eddie gasped, getting a weak grunt of affirmation in return. He saw Nina in the shadows ahead and dragged himself to her. "Help me...with the heater."

She pulled off his backpack and opened it. A minute later, the paraffin heater was lit. They piled their packs up behind them to block the wind. Eddie massaged Nina's hands through her gloves as the trio hunched tightly around the heater. "Don't try to warm up too fast," he warned. "Get the circulation back first."

"Will we have frostbite?" she asked, worried.

"I don't think we'll have to saw off any fingers, but no point taking chances. Can you feel anything?"

"Yeah. Pins and needles."

"Believe it or not, that's good. How about you, Kit?"

Kit flexed his fingers. "Feeling better. And I *think* all my toes are still attached..."

"Great. Let's see where we are, then." He fumbled in his pack for a flashlight.

Nina blinked in annoyance as she was momentarily dazzled, then followed the beam as it slid over the rocks around them, moving deeper and deeper. "How far back does it go?" The passage twisted out of sight about thirty feet away.

"Dunno. Think we've found a good place to sit out the storm, though."

She looked at the cave floor, which was coated with grit and small stones. "Looks alluvial. It must carry meltwater during the spring thaw."

"I didn't know you were a geologist," said Kit.

"It's useful stuff for archaeologists—helps us figure out how deep things might be buried." She took the flashlight from Eddie and scanned the walls. "Where does the water come from, though? It must open out somewhere."

She made as if to crawl down the passage to investigate, but Eddie pulled her back. "Oi! Get properly warmed up first. Might as well have something to eat while we're at it."

"Well, if we must..." They smiled at each other, then Eddie poked through the packs for supplies.

After half an hour, they were more or less recovered and ready to move. Nina had already taken the lead. "It carries on around this corner," she reported, shining the light ahead.

"How far?" Kit asked.

"I don't know—I still can't see the end. But it gets wider." She continued on.

"Jesus, slow down," Eddie complained. "It's not like we've found the Vault of Shiva..." He trailed off.

"Do you think...," said Kit, eyes widening.

"With her luck, I wouldn't be bloody surprised. Come on!" He shuffled down the confined passage after his wife, Kit behind him.

They caught up with Nina. The tunnel was indeed getting wider—and higher. "I can see daylight," she said. A faint gray cast over the rock walls was discernible ahead.

Eddie tugged down his hood. "There's no wind." That wasn't entirely true—he could feel a breeze on his cold-reddened cheeks—but it was nothing compared with the gale blowing at the other end of the tunnel.

There was another bend to traverse, but the gloomy daylight was now clearly visible beyond it. "It opens out," Nina said, Eddie and Kit flanking her as they rounded the corner.

And stopped, frozen in surprise.

"Well, bloody hell," said Eddie as he took in the incredible sight. "I think we found it."

23

The cave emerged at one end of a narrow canyon sliced into the ridge. Snow was falling, but wafting gently down, not blasted by the blizzard. The top of the rift high above them acted as a windbreak, diverting the storm's fury over it. All that was visible of the sky was a ragged line of gray.

But the onlookers had lost all interest in the weather.

The almost sheer sides of the valley had been carved into tiers decorated by ornate sculptures and columns and niches, dozens of arched entrances into chambers within the mountain between them. The elaborate architecture was unmistakably Hindu, gods in many forms gazing out from the walls, but it appeared incredibly ancient. The erosive effect of time had taken its toll, most of the carvings weathered and missing sections, and great chunks of the tiers themselves had collapsed, smashing the floors beneath them and littering the valley floor with broken rubble.

"My God," said Nina, walking out into the falling snow. The valley's far end was obscured by haze and shadow, but she could see enough to be awed by the sheer scale of their discovery. She counted seven tiers on each side, rising about seventy feet up the rocky walls. "It must be thousands of years old. Over *eleven* thousand, if it's the same place Talonor mentioned."

Kit was equally amazed. "How can it never have been found? We're only a few kilometers from one of the holiest sites in India—*someone* must have seen it!"

"Nothing to see from up there," Eddie realized, pointing skyward. "We're on the north side of the ridge, so it'll never get any direct sunlight." He peered at the topmost tier. "The cliffs overhang it at the top. You probably won't know there's anything down here even if you're looking right over the edge."

"The Vault of Shiva must be here, somewhere," said Nina, awe changing to excitement. "How long is the valley, do you think?"

"Only one way to find out," he said, gesturing along the canyon's length. "Go and see."

They started down the valley. The wind howled mournfully high above them. As they advanced, new features emerged from the gloom: lines strung across the canyon connecting the different levels. At first they were just single ropes, drooping under the weight of snow, but then more complex crossings appeared—ones with lines to support both feet and hands, and even actual rope bridges, swaying in the breeze high above.

Eddie regarded one dubiously. "No way *that's* been here for eleven thousand years. Rope bridges don't last long if someone's not maintaining them."

"You think someone's been here more recently?" Kit asked.

"Looks like it." Nina went to one of the arched openings, examining the carvings beside it before shining the flashlight inside. "Most of these inscriptions are in Vedic Sanskrit... but there are others in Classical Sanskrit, which didn't come into use until some time around four hundred BC."

She entered the chamber, finding it piled high with the trash of centuries. The ground-level rooms would flood during the spring thaw, so anything left in them was apparently considered worthless by the valley's inhabitants. Much of what she saw in the beam had rotted beyond recognition, but she caught a glint of metal and carefully extracted it from the garbage. "And look at this."

"A sword?" said Eddie.

"A scimitar, or what's left of one." She examined the corroded hilt. "And there's text on it—it looks Arabic. Parts of India were conquered by Muslims from the thirteenth century onward, so this has to date from at least then."

"I didn't think they came this far into the Himalayas," said Kit.

"It might have been an expedition, looking for a trade route to China—or even searching for the Vault of Shiva. Who knows? But they obviously got this far." She returned the sword to its place, and they continued up the canyon.

More ropes crossed the valley overhead, and Eddie also spotted other lines hanging down between levels and across gaps where the stonework had broken away. Even as the place fell into ruin, it was clear that somebody had still been living there. But nothing they saw could provide a clear idea of when it had finally been abandoned.

That line of thought soon left their minds, though. The valley's far end loomed through the murk, a near-vertical wall of dark rock three hundred feet high. A huge stone staircase had once risen to the height of the uppermost tiers, but the structure had now almost completely collapsed into a vast pile of rubble. The only way up to the jutting stub remaining at the very top was by navigating the intact sections of ledges along the valley's sides, crisscrossing back and forth on the ropes and bridges to reach places where one could climb up to the next level. A three-dimensional maze, where one slip would result in a fatal plunge back to the start.

But what waited at the finish suggested that the journey would be worth the risks. "It's Shiva," Nina gasped.

At the top of the ruined staircase was a broad ledge... and standing at its back, beneath the overhanging rock face, was an enormous statue of the Hindu god. Two-legged, but four-armed, the colossal figure was poised as if dancing. The sculpture, hewn from the rock face, stood sixty feet tall, towering over the bizarre settlement below. Its head was cocked at a steep angle, lips curved into a teasing half smile that suggested it knew a secret... and was challenging onlookers to discover it.

Kit bowed his head in respect to the giant. "I would say we've found what we were looking for."

Nina hurriedly took off her backpack and groped inside it. "Where's the damn thing gone...here!" She retrieved the replica of the key and held it up. "Look! It's the same face, the same expression. This really is the key to the Vault of Shiva! We've *got* to get up there."

Eddie surveyed the crumbled tiers. "Do you really want to risk climbing across on those ropes?"

"There might be another way up, something we can't see from the ground." She pointed at the ruins of the stairway. "See, we can get up to the second level on that, then we can get at least one floor higher if we use the carvings to climb up to that gap in the next ledge."

"And what if the whole lot comes down as soon as we put any weight on it?"

"We'll just have to hope Shiva was listening to Girilal when he asked him to look out for us."

"If Shiva really was watching out for us, he would have made it a nicer day." Eddie took in the dark gray sky above the canyon, snow-bearing clouds still scudding overhead. "And we've got less than an hour before it gets dark."

"I'm not going to just sit here," Nina said impatiently.

"Let's at least see how far we can get, okay? We'll come back down before it gets dark and set up camp."

"All right, Christ!" They headed for the base of the stairway. "Stick the rucksacks in that room there so we don't have to lug them with us."

Nina put the replica key in the inside pocket of her coat; then, the packs stowed, they started to ascend the rubble. It only took a few minutes to pick their way to the ledge on the second level. The carvings Nina had pointed out were an elaborate latticework with images like bulls and elephants worked into the design. "It won't be an insult to the big man up there if we use these as footholds, will it?" Eddie asked Kit.

Kit smiled inside his fur-lined hood. "We're here for a reason that will honor him, so I don't think Lord Shiva will mind."

"Great. I like having God on my side. *Any* god." He brushed snow off the carvings and started to climb. "They're all solid," he called back down from the next level.

Nina came next, breathing heavily with the exertion. Eddie helped her up, then did the same for Kit. "Okay, so now where?" she said. The gap in the ledge through which they had climbed was too wide to jump, but it looked possible to climb across using the wall carvings to reach some dangling ropes farther along.

Eddie tested the carvings, then picked his way carefully across the gap. The stone face of a cow crunched alarmingly when he stood on it; he hurriedly found an alternative foothold and completed the crossing. Avoiding the weak spot, Nina and Kit followed. By the time they were both on the other side, Eddie had tested the ropes to see if they would hold his weight.

"Are they okay?" Nina asked.

"Too okay, if you ask me," he replied.

"You think someone has been here recently?" said Kit.

"Yeah. In the last few years, definitely."

"Then somebody knows about this place," Nina said. "Girilal! That'd explain why he was trying so hard to persuade us not to come up here. He was worried we'd find it."

"He had the perfect cover," Kit mused. "He could watch everybody who came to Kedarnath or Gaurikund, and nobody would give a second thought to a yogi in either place."

"But he didn't do anything to stop us, did he?" said Eddie as he shimmied up the hanging ropes. "He could've killed us in our sleep if he'd wanted."

"Maybe...maybe he was *warning* us," Nina suggested, not liking the idea as soon as she said it.

Eddie looked down at her. "About what?"

"I don't know. I mean, we were in enough physical danger finding this place, but..." She tried to dismiss the thought, and climbed up after Eddie.

Another room carved out of the cliff awaited her on the next tier, stone figures framing the arched entrance. As Kit climbed up, she shone her flashlight inside. It was considerably deeper than the ground-level chamber. Bundles of wood were stacked haphazardly near the doorway...but farther back, the beam found something more regular.

Wooden boxes.

She advanced inside, bark fragments crunching under her boots. The boxes were old, the rough wood discolored and moldering, but the utilitarian construction was unmistakably the product of the industrial era. And as she got closer, she picked out words stenciled on them.

The language was English.

"Nina? You coming?" Eddie asked from the entrance.

"Eddie, look at this." She crouched beside one of the boxes, reading part of the text. ".577/450 MARTINI-HENRY. Any idea what it means?"

"It's ammo," he told her. "Point five seven seven caliber

with a four-fifty-cal round. The Martini-Henry was a really old rifle."

"How old? And who used it?"

"The British Empire. Don't know exactly when— Victorian times, I suppose."

She straightened. "Which means the colonial-era Brits found this place too. They definitely would have made a record of it . . . if they'd ever returned."

"You're saying whoever lived here killed anyone who found it?"

"Looks that way." They returned to the ledge, where Kit was waiting.

"So who were they? And when did they leave?"

A faint sound reached them over the wind's constant wail: an echoing whisper.

Growing louder.

More voices joined the sinister chorus, the mutterings coming from all around them. Metal scraped and clinked against stone.

"I don't think they did," Nina whispered.

Men emerged from the dark openings below them across the valley. Through the falling snow, the only details she could make out were that they all wore robes of dark blue and their heads were shaven.

Eddie looked down through the gap in the ledge. "Shit. There's more of them underneath us."

"Who are they?" Kit asked nervously.

"Guardians," guessed Nina. "They protect the Vault of Shiva. And I think they've been doing it for a very long time."

"Maybe we can talk to them." Kit called down to the shadowy figures in Hindi. His words didn't appear to have any effect, more men coming out of the chambers.

"What did you say?" Nina asked.

"I told them I'm a police officer, and that we mean them no harm."

"I don't think they believed you!" Eddie cried. *"Down!"*

He pushed Nina to the floor. Something flashed across the narrow valley and clanged off the stonework just above them before spinning away. Kit ducked as another object scythed at him. It hit the wall with a ringing screech and landed in the snow beside Eddie. A flat hoop of gleaming steel about nine inches across, a *chakram,* inscribed with Sanskrit text—and with a razor-sharp outer edge, as Eddie discovered when he tried to pick it up.

"Ow! Fuck this Xena bullshit," he growled as another *chakram* slashed overhead. He took out his gun. Their attackers clearly recognized the weapon, warning shouts prompting them to move into cover. He heard movement on the tier below and aimed the Wildey down through the gap. A robed figure darted out of sight.

"What do we do?" said Nina, anxiously watching the entrances on the far wall. Faces stared back at her from the shadows. Hiding in the nearby chamber was not an option: it had no other exits, an inescapable trap.

"If I take a couple down, it should put the others off." Eddie pointed the gun at one of the archways, the faces instantly vanishing into darkness. "Just need a good shot..."

"Eddie!" Nina warned, seeing a man climbing through another gap in the ledge about forty feet away. Eddie whipped the gun around—as something heavy struck his hand with tremendous force and a savage bolt of pain surged up his arm.

The Wildey was jarred from his grip, clanging off the edge of the tier and tumbling down to the ground. "Buggeration and fuckery!" Eddie spat, clutching his hand.

The object that had hit him lay nearby. It was a dumbbell-shaped piece of metal almost a foot long, the bulbous sections formed from four thick, curved arms. A *vajra,* another ancient Indian weapon, which could be held and used as a club—or hurled at a target.

The climber saw that he had disarmed his opponent—and reached over his shoulder to draw a sword from a sheath across his back.

"Uh, I think we should go," said Nina, pulling urgently at Eddie's sleeve.

"Go *where*?"

"There's only one place we can—up!" She started to scale the carved wall to the fifth level, Kit doing the same.

Eddie looked across the valley. The robed men emerged from cover and began to climb the walls. The man who had thrown the *vajra* ran along the ledge toward him, sword raised.

He snatched up the Indian weapon and hurled it at the running man. The *vajra* hit him hard in the face with a dull clang. He collapsed, face bloodied.

Eddie was about to run to the fallen figure and get his sword when a fusillade of missiles from the other side of the canyon deterred him. He ducked to avoid another *chakram* and several fist-sized stones, then scrambled up the wall.

Nina was already hurrying along the next tier. "Eddie, this way!" she shouted, reaching one of the rope bridges. Its widely spaced planks were coated with snow, icicles hanging from them.

"Are you bloody mad?" he gasped as Kit helped him up.

"There isn't a way up from here!" This section of ledge was truncated by a gap far too wide to jump, and any carvings they could have used to shimmy across had also been scoured away by whatever had fallen from above.

"Shit!" He looked down. The guardians had the home advantage, knowing the fastest routes up through the different levels, and were quickly gaining. Across the valley, though, he spotted an intact stairway connecting the level opposite to the sixth tier. If they could find a way to the top level, they might be able to get across to the giant statue of Shiva . . . "Nina! That key—will it get us into the vault?"

"What?" she asked, surprised. "I don't know. Why?"

He pointed up at the enormous figure, frozen in its dance. "If we can get inside, we might be able to shut them out."

"But they'll have a key too!"

"Maybe we can jam the door. Go on, get across!"

She hesitantly took hold of one of the bridge's guide ropes. "I don't think this is safe..."

"If they can use it, so can we!" More stones hurtled across the gap, smacking against the wall. Eddie threw one back. It hit a climbing man; he screamed and fell to the ledge below. "Go!"

Nina put one foot on the first plank. It creaked, but held. Both hands clutching the ropes, she took another step, and another. Icicles cracked and fell away as she moved across.

"You go next," Eddie told Kit, picking up another stone. The guardians seemed reluctant to attack Nina, concentrating their missiles on the two men. Maybe they were worried about damaging the bridge. He ducked another lump of rock, then looked back down. Some of the guardians were only two tiers below, running along the ledge to reach more ropes where they could continue their ascent.

Nina was more than halfway across, taking the bridge step by frightening step. The planks were not regularly spaced, requiring her to look down to be sure of finding a foothold—which gave her a horrible swaying view of the ground fifty feet below. But she pressed on. Only fifteen feet to go...

Movement through the wafting snow. Guardians were scaling the ropes to the fourth tier, only one level below.

She quickened her pace, gasping "Shit, shit, *shit*!" in time with each step. Two planks left, one, *there*! She looked back, seeing the progress of the guardians on the other side of the valley—and to her horror finding that they were not

only more numerous, but closer. "Eddie!" she yelled, jabbing a hand at the robed men rapidly picking their way up
the wall. "They're right behind you!"

"Go!" Eddie ordered Kit, waiting for him to traverse a
couple of planks before following. The bridge juddered violently with the extra weight, more ice breaking free and
exploding into shards on the hard ground below. "Nina,
get up to the top!"

She was about to protest when the first guardian
reached the ledge on the other side—and sent a *chakram*
spinning at her like a lethal Frisbee. She shrieked and
ducked, the disk whistling overhead to clang off the wall.
She hopped up and hurried toward the stairs, jumping over
the dogtoothed gaps in the stone.

Kit picked his way across the bridge, Eddie right behind
him. A plank cracked alarmingly as the Indian stepped on
it. He gasped, transferring his weight to the support ropes.

The bridge wobbled. Eddie clutched the ropes as one
foot slipped off a plank, the wood painfully scraping the
back of his calf. Kit looked back in alarm. "Keep going!"
Eddie told him, levering himself back up.

He waited for Kit to reach the second to last plank, then
started after him. The bridge's guitar-string vibration eased
as they got closer to the end—

A plank snapped under his weight.

Eddie dropped before catching himself on the ropes, legs
flailing helplessly in empty space. The bridge lurched violently, a whipcrack ripple running along its length—jolting
his left hand from the ice-crusted rope.

Kit stopped on the final plank, looked back—then
turned around. "No, keep going!" Eddie shouted, but the
Interpol agent was already returning.

* * *

Nina reached the stairs, a series of stone blocks jutting a
foot out from the wall, and was about to climb them when

she saw Eddie dangling from the bridge. She was on the verge of running back to help when she caught movement in her peripheral vision.

Above her. A man hung from one of the ropes between the uppermost tiers, legs wrapped over it as he pulled himself along. More guardians were starting across on other lines.

If any reached the top level before her, the explorers were doomed.

She ran up to the sixth tier, her eyes searching frantically for the next flight of steps.

* * *

Kit reached Eddie. He wound one of the support ropes around his arm, stretching out his other hand. The Englishman strained to lift himself up, his right fist clenching the quivering rope.

The bridge swayed. Another crack from under Kit's feet. The plank was breaking—

Eddie lunged—and caught Kit's hand.

The Indian pulled him up, the board moaning and splintering. Eddie brought up his foot and found support—not on the wood, but on one of the ropes supporting the planks. "Okay, get across, go!" he shouted. Kit turned to complete his crossing.

Eddie looked for Nina. She was almost at the stairs to the top level—

What the hell? He saw a man seemingly hanging in midair, before realizing he was traversing a rope to the top tier.

And would reach the ledge in front of Nina.

Kit reached the far side and stopped to wait for him. "No, go and help Nina!" Eddie shouted as he continued across the bridge. "They're gonna catch her!" Kit saw the men on the ropes, then ran for the stairs.

* * *

Nina arrived on the highest tier. The top of the broken stairway leading to the statue was beyond its far end. She would have to jump the gap to reach it, but it looked an achievable distance.

If she could get there. The man on the rope was making alarming progress. She started to run. He was only ten feet from the ledge, effortlessly pulling himself closer. She ran faster, feet slithering in the snow. He would be at the ledge in moments. She had to get past him—

His hands reached the stone.

The guardian swung himself on to the ledge, revealing a sheathed sword across his back. Nina was still a few yards short. She tried to swerve past him before he could get to his feet—but he drew his sword and swung it to block her path.

She skidded to a stop. Another robed man had crossed the valley behind her. Trapped—

There was an arched entrance to another chamber just a few feet back. She darted inside. Some of the rooms went deeper into the mountain than others—maybe they were linked, by passages she could use to escape . . .

Not this one. She could see the back wall. Another storage area, objects piled at random.

The guardian was a deadly silhouette framed in the arched doorway.

* * *

Kit pounded along the sixth level, following Nina's tracks. He passed a taut rope, one of the guardians halfway across. A glance down told him that Eddie had made it over the bridge—

Something dropped from the broken tier above.

It was a statue, pushed by a man on the next level. It blew apart like a bomb as it hit the ledge in front of him. Kit tried to hurdle it, but his foot clipped the heavy stone core and he tripped. He landed hard, sliding on the snow...

And going over the edge.

• • •

Running down the fifth tier, Eddie heard someone scream behind him. He looked back and saw Kit fall from the ledge above, plunging toward the ground—

He slammed to a stop as his leg caught in a bunch of tangled ropes, leaving him painfully hanging upside down forty feet in the air. More guardians were crossing the bridge.

Eddie hesitated, then ran back. "Kit! I'm coming!"

• • •

Nina retreated into the small room. The items within seemed to be the former property of previous adventurers unlucky enough to encounter the lost valley's defenders. Mildewed clothing, rotten leather bags, wood and metal boxes, but nothing helpful.

The guardian entered the chamber. He didn't seem angry, or triumphant—the only aura he gave off was that he was simply doing his job. He raised his sword.

An old rifle among the detritus. Nina snatched it up, spun, pulled the trigger—

A dry metal click. The gun was empty, and even if it had been loaded the barrel was scabbed with rust.

But it had still shocked the guardian into freezing, the corroded muzzle just inches from his throat. A relieved smile turned sardonic as his hand tightened around the sword's hilt—

Nina jabbed the rifle at his neck with all her strength. The man's eyes bulged in pain as he reeled back, choking. She whipped the gun around and swung it at his head. The vintage weapon's wooden stock shattered with a very satisfying crack, pitching her erstwhile attacker into the piled garbage.

She raced back out. The guardian who had pushed the statue over the edge saw her and shouted commands to his comrades.

No sign of Eddie or Kit. Nina ran for the end of the tier. The top of the ruined stairway was across the gap. At the back of the ledge, she saw large stone doors between the statue's feet, circular markings upon them. A lock?

She had a key.

The guardian was in pursuit. She pushed harder, angling at the tier's corner to narrow the gap as much as possible. If she misjudged it, she would die.

Jump—

The valley floor rolled past seventy feet below . . .

Nina caught the very bottom step with her leading foot and threw herself forward. Her boot slipped on the snow. She fell, her cry abruptly cut off as she hit the unforgiving stone.

She slid down the ancient stairway, feet sweeping a miniature avalanche over the edge—

She clawed at the steps, finding snow, stone beneath— and a crack where a slab had been dislodged in the collapse. Nina stabbed her fingers into it. Her death-slide stopped, legs hanging over the void. She found a hold with her other hand and pulled herself up.

The guardian was still running along the uppermost tier. He would make his own jump in seconds. Nina staggered up to the deep, broad ledge and headed for the doors. There was a circular indentation at the center of the carvings.

The same size as the replica key.

She pulled it from her coat. Behind her came a *thump* as the guardian cleared the gap and landed on the stairs, bounding up them after her.

* * *

Eddie reached Kit and grabbed the ropes. "Hang on!"

"I'm hanging!" Kit shouted back. "Eddie, they're almost across the bridge!"

The first of the guardians was only a few steps short of the ledge. Looking up, he spotted Nina running for the statue—with a robed man chasing her. "Shit!" He pulled harder—

One of the ropes, weakened by age and weather, snapped. Kit screamed, but jerked to a stop once more after falling only a foot, other lines entangling his ankle.

The first guardian was off the bridge, drawing a savage-looking knife. The man behind him had a sword. More men ran down the stairs toward the two intruders. The only possible escape route was down the ropes to the tier below—but Eddie couldn't do that until Kit was free. He kept lifting. "Grab the ledge!" he said. Kit bent at the waist, struggling to reach the icy stone. "Come on, you've almost got it!"

The other man's fingers closed around a carved outcropping. Eddie let go of the ropes and grabbed his wrist, pulling him onto the ledge. He was safe.

But Kit didn't even have time to say thanks. The first guardian reached them, lunging with his dagger—

Eddie jerked sideways, the blade slashing his padded sleeve. He whipped up one arm to knock the man's hand away from him—and slammed his other fist into his face. The robed man fell on his back with a starburst of bright blood around his mouth.

Kit freed his leg, raising his own fists as he faced the group running in from the other direction. "What do we do?"

"Climb down the rope," said Eddie.

"We'll never make it in time!"

"Not if you keep yakking—go on! I'll hold 'em off." He

snatched up the downed man's knife as Kit took hold of the rope and hopped over the edge, quickly shimmying down—

And scrambling back up again, even faster. "Eddie, there's a man with a sword underneath me!"

Eddie held up the dagger—and another guardian mirrored his move, only with a blade about three times longer. More men approached from behind. "Well...arse."

* * *

Nina reached the doors. What she had thought to be carvings were actually separate objects set into the stone: five large wheels arranged in a circle around the "keyhole," smaller wheels set around their edges with dozens of words in Sanskrit written upon each one. What it meant, she had no time to wonder—all she could do was jam the replica key into the lock and hope something happened.

Nothing did.

The key was a perfect fit, but there were no pins or levers or other mechanisms inside the hole. The horrified realization hit her that the key was symbolic, not physical—the wheels had to be aligned with the faces of Shiva and the five goddesses in a particular way. It was a *combination* lock.

And she didn't know the combination.

Key in hand, she spun to find the guardian right behind her, his sword raised. She screamed—

The blow didn't come. Instead, he held the blade to her throat and dragged her back to the top of the steps. She saw that Eddie and Kit had been captured as well, a dozen men surrounding them.

Her captor was apparently the leader, bellowing a command in Hindi. The others responded by seizing their prisoners and forcing them to the edge of the ledge. Eddie struggled, but a guardian smashed the hilt of a knife against his head.

Nina was thrust forward, wobbling on the brink. Eddie and Kit were shoved into similar precarious positions.

One push would hurl them to their deaths.

She heard her captor take in a breath to shout the order that would kill them.

24

S top!"
  The command didn't come from the man behind Nina. It boomed up from the valley floor, echoing off the stone walls. She looked through the snow—and saw a single figure at the foot of the ruined stairway, dressed in simple orange robes.

Girilal.

The leader hesitated, not delivering the fatal push... but not pulling her back to safety either. He shouted down to the old man in Hindi, sounding angry—yet also somehow respectful. Girilal replied in kind, his voice commanding without a hint of chattering faux-lunacy.

Whatever he was saying, it worked. With a frustrated grunt, the leader stepped back, hauling Nina with him. Keeping his sword to her neck, he waved for the others to pull Eddie and Kit away from the edge.

To her shock, his next words were in English. "Come with me," he growled.

• • •

The prisoners were taken to one of the chambers cut into the mountainside. It was much deeper than the others Nina had seen, a passage leading from the archway into a large room with a sheet of animal skin hanging across the entrance to keep out the elements. Fires burned in alcoves carved in the walls, the smoke carried away through cracks above.

She counted at least twenty of the guardians. All were men, ranging from middle age to their teens. They wore the same dark blue robes and their heads were shaved, monklike. But they were clearly not passive seekers after spiritual perfection. They were warriors, defending the valley to the death.

Another two men brought in Girilal, their attitudes a mix of contempt and deference. The yogi smiled at Nina, then began talking to the leader, his animation in stark contrast with the younger man's stoic disapproval.

"He knew about this lot all along," Eddie muttered. "And he didn't bloody warn us."

"He did, though," said Nina. "He tried everything he could to put us off. But he couldn't tell us about these people without confirming that the Vault of Shiva actually existed...which was exactly what he was trying to avoid."

"But who are they?" Kit asked. "And what's his connection to them?"

Girilal glanced across. "I will answer your questions soon. But first I have to persuade them not to kill you, so please be patient!"

"I think we can give him a little more time," said Nina, nervously regarding the hostile faces surrounding them.

The two men conversed for several minutes before the leader, still clearly displeased by Girilal's interference, stood before the trio. He was around thirty, tall, with a wiry muscularity. "I am Shankarpa," he said. "You say you are here to protect the Vault of Shiva?" His English was halting, rusty.

"Yes," Nina replied. "I'm Nina Wilde, the director of the United Nations' International Heritage Agency." Shankarpa's expression was one of incomprehension until Girilal provided an explanation in Hindi. "My job is to find important historical sites so they can be shown to the world—and protected from thieves."

"*We* protect the vault from thieves," he told her firmly.

"Yeah, we noticed," said Eddie. "You're a bit more active than your average rentacops, though."

Nina shushed him. "We're not the only people looking for the vault. Another group wants to steal the Shiva-Vedas. They've already killed to find out where they are, and they'll kill you too if you try to stop them."

The mention of the Vedas raised a commotion. "How do you know of the Shiva-Vedas?" Shankarpa demanded.

"From a man called Talonor. He visited Kedarnath thousands of years ago—the priests told him about the vault, and showed him the key." She indicated the replica among their confiscated possessions.

He picked it up, holding the faces of the gods to the firelight. "Where did you find this?" The question was accusing, as if it had been taken from him personally.

Nina decided to simplify the explanation. "Talonor pressed the key into a sheet of gold—this is a copy made from it."

"A copy?" He tapped the dense plastic. "It is not the real key?"

"No, it—wait, *you* don't have the real key?"

"It was lost long ago," he said, glowering.

"Hold on," said Eddie. "You mean you're guarding the Vault of Shiva...but you can't get into it yourselves?" He laughed sarcastically. "How do you even know there's anything in it?"

"Nobody can enter the vault without the key," Shankarpa said angrily. "The doors have been closed for more than a thousand years—and no outsiders have ever lived to reach them. Until today."

"But now you have the replica, can you open it?" asked Nina.

Now his dark expression had a hint of shame. "That secret...is lost too."

"Well, that's one way to keep the place safe," Eddie said mockingly. "But if the bad guys find it, they'll just blow the doors open."

"We *will* protect the vault," Shankarpa insisted. "We have watched over it since Lord Shiva placed his sacred possessions here."

"How can you have been here all this time?" asked Kit. "There are no plants to eat, no animals."

"No women," Eddie added. "You'd have to be pretty bloody dedicated to spend your lives up here."

"They are," said Girilal, leaning on his stick. "The guardians come from the villages around the mountain—it is our great secret." Shankarpa said something in Hindi, a clear order for him to shut up, but the old man shook his head. "Not everybody knows, only a trusted few. We— *they* watch the children of their village for those worthy of the honor of protecting the Vault of Shiva. If they are willing, they are trained by the other guardians, and spend the rest of their lives here."

"You said *we*," Eddie noted. "You're one of them?"

"I was. No more."

"Why not?" asked Nina.

"I made a mistake. I thought I was doing the right thing, but..." He sighed, shaking his head sadly. "I hurt someone I loved, took away the thing that was most important to her. I have tried to seek forgiveness, but do not think I can ever find it. So I wander between Kedarnath and Gaurikund as a mad old man, ignored...or insulted."

"Your own penance," Nina realized. "But for what?"

Girilal turned to Shankarpa, putting a hand on his

shoulder. "For him, Dr. Wilde. Shankarpa's real name is Janardan. Janardan Mitra. He is my son."

* * *

Night fell outside, the rumble of the storm fading. In the underground chamber, Girilal had persuaded Shankarpa that the three visitors should be allowed to live.

For the moment. The guardians' constant looks of suspicion as they ate told them they were still only one barked order away from death.

"Where do they get the food?" Nina asked Girilal. "We saw some ground on the way up that looked as if it might once have been cultivated, but it can't have been used for hundreds of years."

"The villages provide it," the yogi explained. "A few times each year, some of the guardians come to Kedarnath, dressed as pilgrims, to collect it."

"It's not exactly a feast," said Eddie, looking at the meager bowls of vegetables and rice. "What do you do if you run out of food and the weather's too bad to get down the mountain?"

"Lord Shiva gives us the strength we need to survive," rumbled Shankarpa.

"Maybe, but I'd take a can of beans over faith any day."

"Eddie," Nina warned. The last thing they needed was to antagonize their captors. "Girilal, you said you hurt someone you loved. I'm guessing you meant Shankarpa's mother."

He nodded. "It was my own fault. I thought it was right to tell my wife about the vault, and that she could be trusted to keep the secret. She could—she is a better person than me. But my mistake..." He looked at Shankarpa. "My mistake was also telling our son. Our only child. He was young, he was headstrong, and he thought a lifetime of serving Lord Shiva as a warrior would be better than living in a poor village."

"And it is," said Shankarpa firmly. His English had already become less stiff, the mere act of speaking it unlocking old memories. "Would you rather I carried tourists up the mountain on my back for a few rupees?"

"There is no shame in serving others," his father told him, before addressing Nina again. "He had made up his mind. When he was old enough, I agreed that he could join the guardians. He gave up everything to serve Shiva, and I was happy for him. But there was someone who was not."

"His mother," said Nina.

Girilal lowered his head. "Yes. I did not discuss it with her until the decision was already made. I thought she would feel like me, that she would be honored to have Janardan chosen for such a great task. I was wrong."

"She was losing her son."

"Yes. And she hated me for it. I took away what was most precious to her, without even thinking. After that, she . . . she did not want to speak to me again. She left me." He looked up; Nina saw that his eyes were glistening with tears. "I hurt her more than I could have imagined. That is why I became what I am—I gave everything I owned to her. But it was not enough. Nothing I could give her could ever replace her child. I sought forgiveness . . . but I will never get it. I do not deserve it."

Shankarpa was unmoved. "She never understood what it means to serve Shiva. She was weak."

"Do not speak of her like that!" Girilal snapped. The other guardians reacted with surprise at the challenge to their leader, and even Shankarpa was taken aback by the anger in the old man's voice. The yogi took a breath, then continued more quietly. "I am sorry. I did not mean to shout. You made your decision, as I made mine. The difference is . . . you did not regret it."

"No, I did not." His dark eyes flicked across to Nina, Eddie, and Kit. "What do we do with you, hmm? My father thinks you can be trusted. But why should I?"

"Protecting secrets is part of what we do," said Nina. "We stopped a catastrophe that would have killed billions of people, and kept it a secret to prevent global panic."

"And this guy Khoil and his wife," added Eddie, "they've got a catastrophe of their own in mind, and they're dead set on getting hold of what's behind that statue up there before they kick it off."

"If the Khoils can't get the Shiva-Vedas, they might not go ahead with whatever they're planning."

"If it is Shiva's will," said Shankarpa, "who are we to stop it?"

"But it isn't Shiva's will," Nina replied. "It's the *Khoils'* will—and they're very definitely not gods. They don't want to destroy the world so it can be reborn. They just want money and power for themselves. I doubt Shiva would approve."

He nodded slowly. "If you are telling the truth about these people, what can we do to stop them?"

"Nothing," said Eddie. "If they find this place, first thing they'll do will be airlift in mercenaries. Lots of 'em. With lots of guns."

Shankarpa sat back, mulling their words over before speaking in Hindi to his companions. The discussion went on for some time, varying degrees of disagreement emerging.

"What're they saying?" Nina asked Kit.

"They're deciding whether they can trust us, and, if we're telling the truth about the Khoils, what they can do to stop them." He listened to the conversation for a few moments, unsettled. "They are also still arguing about whether or not they should kill us. Some of them have very strong feelings about it."

Nina noticed the man she had hit with the rifle glaring at her, an ugly purple bruise on his throat. "Yeah, I figured that. Good thing we didn't actually kill any of them."

Girilal leaned closer, lowering his voice. "I think he will let you live."

"How can you be sure?"

"He is my son. I have to believe that he will do what is right."

Eddie watched the debate. None of the factions appeared particularly pro-mercy. "Just hope you were a better dad than you give yourself credit for..."

It was several minutes before Shankarpa reached a decision, shouting down the more vocal objectors. "If we let you live," he said to Nina, "what will you do for us in return?"

"The first thing will be to tell the Indian government and the United Nations about this place. It will still be a secret," she pressed on, seeing he already had very strong reservations. "We won't go public. But if the UN knows about the vault, we can protect it."

Shankarpa didn't seem convinced. "And what else?"

"If you'll let us, we can try to open the vault." She indicated the replica key.

He laughed in disbelief. "You want the guardians of the Vault of Shiva to help you open its door?"

"All the Khoils want are the Shiva-Vedas. We can take them someplace secure. If they're not here—and they know that—they'll have no reason to come. Whatever other treasures are in the vault will be safe."

"And why should you be trusted with the sacred words of Lord Shiva over this man Khoil?"

"Because the Khoils want to use them to gain power. But I want to show them to the entire world," she said defiantly. "Everyone will be able to read the teachings of Shiva. Isn't that what he would want?"

"She is telling the truth," Girilal added. "She is very famous for this. Even in Kedarnath!"

"I can help you," Nina insisted. "If you let me."

Shankarpa remained deep in thought for a long mo-

ment. "I will...let you try to open the vault," he finally
said. "Tomorrow, when it is light."

"And what if we can't get in?" Eddie asked.

A thin smile. "Then you will die."

He nudged Nina. "No pressure on you then, love."

"Gee, thanks."

"If others come, we will protect the vault, as we always
have," said Shankarpa. "And we will have more than just
our swords." Eddie's Wildey was among the group's belongings, the guardians knowing enough about firearms to
have removed the magazine and ejected the chambered
round.

"You'll need more than just one gun," Nina said.

"Perhaps we *have* more. But if you open the vault, we
may not need them." He issued an order. Several men
stood and surrounded the prisoners. "They will take you to
a room where you can sleep." He smiled coldly. "Enjoy
your stay."

• • •

In contrast with the previous day, the slash of morning sky
above the valley walls was a deep, empty blue. Sunlight
turned the snow above almost to gold. But the warm glow
didn't reach into the depths of the narrow canyon; even the
giant statue of Shiva, standing beneath the overhang, was
shrouded in eternal shadow.

Accompanied by Shankarpa and Girilal, and escorted by
about half of the guardians, Nina, Eddie, and Kit made the
laborious ascent to the broad ledge at Shiva's feet. Nina
had the replica key with her, as well as some of her archaeology tools, but she had no idea how much use the latter
would be. She suspected the lock was not one that could be
picked.

Even in the shade, enough diffuse light came down from
above for her to get a good look at the door. The lock was
far more complex than she had realized. A circular hole at

ANDY McDERMOTT

334

its center for the key, five large wheels arranged around it in a pattern resembling a flower—and around their circumferences were smaller ones, twenty in all, the "parent" wheels sharing one with each of their neighbors where they touched.

But the complexity didn't end there. Each small wheel was divided into three pieces: two eye-shaped sections aligned with the rim of the bigger disk, and a third like the central pinch of an hourglass between them to fill in the rest of the circle. The edge of each "eye" had ten words in Vedic Sanskrit carved into it, the ends of the hourglass another five. Thirty words per disk, twenty disks...six hundred words in all.

Somehow, they had to be arranged in the right combination. What that combination might be, Nina had absolutely no idea.

She reached up to one of the large disks, and, after getting a silent nod from Shankarpa, turned it. Metal and stone grated behind the surface, some kind of undulating runner system lifting it—and the smaller disks it carried—outward as it rotated, just enough to clear the neighboring wheels before dropping back down into the next position. By turning the smaller disks through 180 degrees and then rotating the big wheels, each eye section could be swapped between them and moved to any part of the lock. It was an extremely complicated, but also incredibly clever, piece of ancient engineering.

"I think I see what you have to do," she announced.

"Glad you do," said Eddie, bewildered. "I haven't got a clue. All this Professor Layton crap does my head in."

"It's not that complicated, really." She inserted the key into the central hole with the carvings of the Hindu gods facing outward. "See? Five goddesses, five small wheels, and five big ones. Presumably, you have to position all the wheels correctly to open the lock. It's just a matter of figuring out the right combination of these words."

"Oh, that all? Doddle."

"How many combinations are there?" Kit asked.

"Let's see. Six hundred words, so the factorial of six hundred."

Shankarpa stepped closer, examining the mechanism in a new light. "What does that mean?"

"The factorial? It's the number of possible combinations of a number of items. If you had four, the factorial would be four times three times two times one—twenty-four. Five would be five times four times three, and so on—one hundred and twenty."

Eddie's brow crinkled as he tried—and immediately failed—to extend the sequence to the puzzle. "So six hundred times five ninety-nine times five ninety-eight . . . Christ, I can't even do the first one without my head hurting."

Nina's mental arithmetic skills were considerably better. "Six hundred times five hundred and ninety-nine is three hundred and fifty-nine thousand four hundred. Multiply that by five hundred and ninety-eight and you get, uh . . ." She frowned herself as the numbers very rapidly grew beyond even her ability to handle them in her head. "Hold on, let me write this down."

She took a notebook and pen from her pack. But it didn't take long for her to admit defeat. "Okay. Let me put it this way. If you said a trillion—"

"There's a *trillion* combinations?" Eddie interrupted. "Bloody hell!"

"I'm not finished. If you said a trillion, trillion, trillion, *trillion,* and kept on saying trillion over a hundred times more, *that's* how many variations there are. If you tried one combination every second for the five billion years before the sun explodes and destroys the planet, you couldn't even do one percent of them."

"That's a bit of an overkill way to open the doors."

She smiled a little. "If something's too much overkill even for you, it must be bad."

"We don't have five billion years to spare, though. There must be a quicker way."

"You're right. Whoever built it wouldn't have made a lock so complex that even the people protecting it wouldn't be able to figure it out." She looked at Shankarpa. "Have you ever tried to open it?"

"A few have tried," he said, "but without the key, the secret has been lost."

Her gaze slowly circled the pattern of interlocking wheels, then went to the center. She examined the keyhole. "So the key is the key."

"Duh," said Eddie.

"If you'll pardon the pun. But it can't be a coincidence that the faces of the goddesses on the key line up with the wheels. They're a clue. Maybe you don't need to have the entire thing in an exact configuration—just match each goddess to one particular word. What do the words say?"

Girilal ran his finger around one of the small wheels, reading the ancient text. "Many different things. 'Moon, waterfall, sadness, dog, traveling, invincible, stranger, yellow...'"

"They're completely random," said Kit. "Maybe they have to be arranged into a sentence?"

"I don't think Shiva would have designed his vault's lock around a game of Mad Libs. It's something simpler than that, to do with the goddesses..." It struck Nina that she had yet to ask the obvious question. "Who *are* the goddesses?"

Shankarpa pointed them out. "Parvati; Uma; Durga; Kali; Shakti."

"Shiva's wives. And if you had to describe each of them in a single word," Nina went on, excitement rising as the solution came to her, "are those words on any of the wheels?"

"Durga is the *invincible* warrior-mother," said Girilal.

Shankarpa almost shoved his father aside as he darted

closer to examine the wheels. "The words! We have to find the right words!"

"Talonor didn't get it quite right," Nina realized. "What he wrote in the codex was a misinterpretation, a mistranslation—it's not the 'love of Shiva' you need to know to open the vault. It's the 'loves,' or 'lovers'—the wives of Shiva! If you don't know their stories, you'll never find the right combination." She hurriedly turned her notebook to a new page. "We need to know the words—all of them."

"Six hundred words?" Eddie said. "That'll take a while."

"You got an appointment?" She took her pen and started writing as Girilal began to recite the words.

* * *

"Rat."

"Rat," Nina repeated, writing it down.

"Hmm...dust."

"Dust." After thirty minutes, her list was a little more than half complete. The tedium of the task had overcome the initial thrill, most of the guardians sitting contemplatively at the statue's feet waiting for her and Girilal to finish. Kit was hunched up in his thick coat, half asleep, while Eddie paced impatiently around the ledge. Even Shankarpa, watching his father work, showed signs of boredom.

"Smiling."

"Smiling."

"Ah...now, let me think," said Girilal, finger pausing over one particular word. "Some sort of bird. It could be 'buzzard,' or it could be..."

"Helicopter," said Eddie.

Nina glanced at him. "I don't think that's *quite* right, Eddie."

"No, I mean I can hear a helicopter. Listen."

She strained to hear as Shankarpa called for silence. A

faint thudding became audible, the unmistakable chop of rotor blades. "And I thought you were worried about your hearing," she whispered to Eddie.

"It's high frequencies that're knackered. Low ones aren't a problem. Yet. And choppers aren't exactly quiet."

"Is it Khoil?" asked Kit, standing.

Nina anxiously stared at the ragged banner of blue above the canyon. There was an outside chance that the helicopter's arrival at the hidden valley was just a coincidence . . . but she wouldn't have wasted even a single dollar betting on it.

The noise drew closer, echoing from the valley walls. The whine of engines rose beneath the pounding blades. A shadow flicked across the sunlit summit of one of the cliffs as the helicopter passed overhead, and was gone. The engine shrill faded.

Nina exchanged a look of relief with Eddie . . .

The sound's pitch changed. The helicopter was coming back.

"Get into cover!" said Eddie, waving the guardians into the shadows. The approaching rotor noise was louder, the aircraft descending.

The shadow reappeared on the cliff, moving more slowly. The helicopter was above them. A fine spray of snow whipped down from the overhanging rock, caught in the downwash.

Eddie watched as the crystalline fall moved from one side of the ledge to the other. "It's circling," he said. "They're trying to get a better look into the valley." He advanced a few steps, looking up past the overhang. "I can see it—they're coming around! Everyone get back!"

He retreated as the helicopter's lazy orbit brought it over the far end of the valley. It was civilian, painted red and white with a rather bulbous fuselage that reminded him of a fat, short-billed bird in flight. He didn't know the type, which meant it had entered service after he left the SAS;

aircraft recognition was a standard part of military training.

One thing was clear, though. It belonged to the Khoils. The Qexia logo was emblazoned on its side.

The chopper drifted across the canyon. Eddie glimpsed a face behind the side window, sunlight glinting off a camera lens. It disappeared from view behind the cliff above, blowing down another swirling sheet of snow, then the engines increased power and it flew off to the south.

Nina ran to the top of the stairway, but it was already out of sight. "Did they see the statue?"

"Even if they didn't, they still got pictures," Eddie said grimly. "Couple of minutes in Photoshop and they'll be able to brighten things up enough to spot it. And soon as they do..."

"They'll be back. In force." Nina hurried to the door. "We don't have much time," she told Shankarpa. "We've got to figure this out, fast."

Girilal resumed his work with more urgency, Nina hurriedly scribbling down each new word. The remainder took only twenty minutes to translate. "Okay," she said, flicking back through the pages, "we've got five goddesses, and six hundred possible words to describe them. Let's narrow it down."

It was a tortuous process. Shankarpa told the other men what they needed to do, but everybody had slightly different views of the goddesses. There were multiple words that could apply to each of them; Kali, for instance, fit the descriptions of *black, death, terrifying, salvation, rage,* and *uncontrollable,* and the other four Hindu figures had similarly varied lists.

Nina wrote each set on a separate page, tearing them from the notebook and lining them up in front of the door. "Well, it's a start," she said. "Eddie, how long do you think we have before that helicopter comes back?"

"Depends where it's going, and if Khoil's all set up to go or if he needs to put a team together."

"If he's flying from Delhi," Kit said, "it would take about an hour. And that would be the logical place for him to assemble his men."

"Then we need to start trying the lock," said Nina. "Okay, so each goddess has several words that *could* be used to describe her. But what are the *best* words? When you think of Kali, say, what's the first word that comes to mind?"

"Death," said Eddie immediately.

"You're just saying that because of *Indiana Jones and the Temple of Doom*."

"No, he is right," Shankarpa said. "Kali is the goddess of death, the destroyer of evil."

"The destroyer of *ego*," Girilal corrected. "She is like the mother who sees when her children have bad in them—and drives it out. If you face Kali and you are not pure, if you fear her because you know you have done something that deserves punishment...she will destroy you."

"Glad my mum wasn't that strict," Eddie said.

"So, the word representing Kali is *death*," said Nina. "Okay, we have to get the segment with the word *death* on it around to the wheel next to Kali, and then line it up with her. Let's see..."

She turned the appropriate large wheel, bringing the smaller disk to the position where it was shared with an adjoining wheel. A half turn of the little disk switched the eye section onto the new carrier; two turns counterclockwise brought it to a third large wheel, and a final counterclockwise move placed it next to the key. Nina rotated the small wheel to align the word with the goddess. There was a moment of almost comical silence as the onlookers all held their breath, but nothing happened.

"I suppose it was too much to hope that we'd hear a big click," she said. "What are the other words?"

Several minutes of debate produced—more or less—a consensus. Parvati was represented by the word *love*. While Uma prompted some argument over whether she, Parvati, or Shakti best fit the term, she was eventually agreed to embody *motherhood*. Shakti herself was attributed with *femininity*—though as Girilal pointed out with a smile, the word could also be interpreted as *sexuality*. Finally, Durga, the fearless warrior, was *invincible*.

With Kali's part of the combination already in place, the task now was to bring the other pieces to where they belonged. Nina took a step back, puzzling out the sequence of turns needed to bring everything into the right place. There was a certain Rubik's Cube quality to the task: without careful planning, moving one word into position at the center could carry another away.

But she was sure she could do it.

* * *

Snow was rubbed into the chosen words to mark them, so all Nina had to do was switch them from wheel to wheel to bring them into the correct positions, then rotate the smaller disks to line up the precise word with each goddess. In an odd way, she realized as she worked, she was almost enjoying herself. Shankarpa and the other guardians didn't seem any better disposed to her, and there was the looming threat that helicopters laden with armed men could thunder overhead at any moment, but the immediate challenge was a purely intellectual one.

After five minutes, one more turn brought the last wheel into alignment. "Okay, almost done!" she said. Now that all five were in position, she could turn them to line up the individual words. Kali was already paired with the word *death,* and one by one she turned the others. Shakti, Uma, Durga . . . and finally Parvati.

Another breathless silence . . .

And again, nothing happened.

"Buggeration and fuckery," she muttered.

Eddie gave her a surprised look, then drew back to check the rest of the door, aware that the guardians were now watching him more mistrustfully than ever. "There's not a handle we're supposed to turn?"

"This is all there is," said Shankarpa.

"Try another combination," Kit suggested, urgency entering his voice as he nervously regarded the men surrounding them. "Shakti might be *motherhood,* not Uma."

"I don't think it'll make any difference," said Nina. They had overlooked something. But what?

Shankarpa interrupted her thoughts, pushing her back from the door. "You have failed."

"Wait a minute, mate," Eddie said, moving toward him—only to have several sharp blades raised to his neck. "She's good at this stuff, but even she doesn't always get it first time. I once nearly fell into a pit full of spikes 'cause she couldn't tell her left from her right."

"Way to make me look competent to the impatient guys with swords, Eddie," Nina muttered.

Other guardians threatened Kit with their weapons. At Shankarpa's command, they forced the three visitors toward the edge of the ledge. Girilal protested, but his son angrily dismissed him.

"If you kill us, you'll be fucked when Khoil's people turn up," growled Eddie.

"We will deal with them as we will deal with you," Shankarpa promised. "Shiva will protect us."

"Shiva," Nina whispered. That was the clue! Something about Shiva had been literally staring her in the face the whole time she worked on the lock. "It's *Shiva*! I know how to open the door!"

Shankarpa's condescension was clear. "And perhaps you also know how to fly off this ledge. It is the only thing that will save you now."

"No, no, look!" She pointed at the statue towering over them. "*Look* at Shiva! Look at his head!"

The certainty in her voice made him hesitate. Holding up a hand to signal the others to stop, he glanced at the colossal stone figure. "What about it?"

"Don't you see?" Nina said desperately. "It's tilted to one side!"

"So?"

"So the key's in the wrong position! I put it in with Shiva's head aligned vertically because... because that's what you automatically do. But you're meant to line it up with the statue." She demonstrated, turning an imaginary object in her hands. "The words are in the right order, but the wrong places. If you turn the key so Shiva's head matches the statue, then all the goddesses move around by one position. *That's* what we have to line them up with!"

Shankarpa looked between her and the statue. "Do you really believe this? Or are you just trying to save your life?"

"Well, both! But I do think I'm right—I *know* I'm right. If I'm wrong, then you can throw us off the ledge."

Eddie raised a finger. "Nina, love? Remember how now we're married, we're supposed to make big decisions together?"

"I would also like to distance myself from that remark," Kit said hurriedly.

"I'm *right*," she insisted. "Shankarpa, at least let me try. You might have to wait five minutes longer to kill us—but on the other hand, five minutes from now you could be walking into the Vault of Shiva!"

"You should let her," added Girilal. "It is the right thing to do."

Shankarpa shot his father an irritated glare, but acquiesced. "Do not fail," he told Nina curtly.

"Yeah, really," Eddie added as the guardians, swords still raised, escorted them back to the door.

"I won't," Nina assured him. She removed the replica

key from the central hole, then reinserted it...rotated by one-fifth of a turn. She looked up at the statue. Shiva's blank stone eyes gazed back at her, the faint smile on the tilted head encouraging her to continue.

Turning the wheels to match the new positions of the goddesses was now a purely mechanical task, taking just a few minutes. She rotated each smaller disk to what she thought—prayed—was the correct alignment. Love, motherhood, invincibility, femininity...

Death.

The last word was in place. Silence...

Click.

Something moved behind the wheels, a restraint finally released after countless centuries. More clicking, louder, then the rattling clank of chains—

With a swirl of escaping dust, the doors swung inward.

The guardians let out exclamations of awe, some dropping to their knees to offer thanks to Shiva. Shankarpa was wide-eyed with surprise. Fully opened, the doors stopped with a crunch of stone.

"So, my son," said Girilal quietly, "are you going to apologize to Dr. Wilde?"

His eyes narrowed. "We will see what is inside first— what we are sworn to protect." He hesitated before reluctantly saying, "Come with me, Dr. Wilde."

Awestruck, Nina followed him into the darkness of the Vault of Shiva.

25

The space behind the doors was huge, on a scale to match the statue guarding it. The echo of Nina's and Shankarpa's footsteps as they moved through the entrance quickly disappeared, lost in a vast cavern.

There was something inside the doors. As Nina's vision adjusted to the darkness, it revealed what she at first took to be two stone blocks, about five feet high and three feet apart, before realizing they were merely the ends of larger constructs. Together, they formed the two halves of a steeply sloping ramp that rose a good thirty feet at the far end, dropping almost to floor level before rising back up; the comparison that leapt instantly to her mind was a ski jump.

There was no snow inside the chamber, though. So what was it for?

An answer came as she and Shankarpa moved farther into the cave, the others following. Something was perched at the top of the ramp, slender parts extending out to each side like wings...

Not *like* wings. They *were* wings.

"It's a glider!" Nina cried, completely forgetting the

threat of the guardians as she ran for a better look. "Khoil told me about the stories in the ancient Indian epics where the gods had flying machines. I thought they were just legends—but they were true!"

"The *vimanas*," said Girilal. He laughed. "My father told me those stories when I was a boy—and I told them to my own son. Do you remember?"

"I remember," said Shankarpa, amazed.

Nina started to climb the ramp, eager to see the craft at the top. "What Talonor said in the codex all makes sense now. This is why it took the priests one day to get up here, and only an hour to get back—they flew! They released the glider, it slid down the ramp, then hit the ski jump at the end and flew out down the valley." She examined the stone slide; it was smoothly polished, with a small lip at the outer edge to guide a runner on the glider itself.

Eddie looked back through the doors, seeing the cliff at the far end of the canyon. "They'd have to pull up pretty sharpish when they took off. Cock things up, and you'd smack into that wall."

Nina shone her flashlight at the glider. It had an organic appearance, the wings formed from gracefully curved wooden spars. The wood itself was dark and glossy, given some kind of treatment to strengthen and preserve it. Between the spars, the fabric of the wings was still stretched taut. It appeared to be a fine, lightweight silk, covered in dust and yellowed with age.

"This is incredible!" she said as Shankarpa ascended the other ramp. "The ancient Hindus had actual, working flying machines before the Greeks even came up with the *myth* of Daedalus. And it took until the sixteenth century before Leonardo designed anything similar." The glider's undercarriage was made from the same wood, a trapezoidal frame with ski-like metal runners attached. These weren't as corroded as she would have expected; the cavern was dry as well as cold. The craft seemed designed to carry at least two people, lying prone on a slatted platform beneath the wing.

Girilal grinned up at her. "Well, it is often said that we Indians invented everything."

"Who says that?" Eddie asked.

"We Indians," Kit told him.

Nina directed her light along the ancient aircraft's fuselage. At the end of the slender wooden body was a fan-shaped tail. There was something affixed beneath it, a long black cylinder protruding out past the end of the glider's frame. At first she was puzzled as to what it might be... before a cord hanging from its end gave her a clue: a fuse. "Here's something else you might have invented before anyone else," she said. "Rockets."

"You're kidding!" said Eddie. "I thought the Chinese invented them."

"I think they'll be very annoyed when they find out someone beat them to it. They came up with gunpowder around the ninth century, but our friends here were using it thousands of years earlier. It must be how they got up enough speed to launch."

Below, Girilal walked around the base of the ramp. "Look here," he called.

Nina aimed the flashlight down to find him prodding his stick at a stack of more black tubes. "Careful, don't poke them! They've been here for who knows how long—they might be unstable."

Eddie had a different opinion. "More likely they won't work at all. Depends how they made the gunpowder—if they didn't corn it properly, the different ingredients'll probably have separated by now." He caught his wife's surprised expression. "I did explosives training in the SAS—it's handy to know this stuff if you're going to blow things up."

"Well, either way, let's not put any naked flames near them." She descended the ramp. By now, her eyes had become more accustomed to the low light. "Oh, wow. This isn't the only glider—the place is more like a hangar." To one side were several more *vimana*s. Other mysterious objects lurked in the darkness. "This flashlight isn't going to cut it," she said. "We need something bigger."

"This might do," proclaimed Girilal. The old yogi had wandered a little farther into the cavern, and was standing by a metal brazier on a stone pedestal. Nina illuminated it—and discovered that a narrow groove had been cut into the floor behind it, leading deeper into the chamber. She followed it with the light until it split, and tracked one of the arms until it divided again, eventually reaching another brazier some distance away. There was a liquid at the bottom of the channel, but from Girilal's excitement she knew it wasn't water.

She went to him. "It's oil," she said, stirring away the covering of dust with a fingertip and sniffing it. "A lighting system. Start one fire, and it spreads through the whole cave to light the other braziers."

"I thought we didn't want to start any fires," said Eddie, looking at the pile of rockets.

"We'll be safe as long as nobody knocks this thing over. Let me get my stuff."

She retrieved her pack from outside, finding a box of waterproof survival matches. "Shall we take a look?" she asked Shankarpa.

"Light it," he ordered.

She struck the match and touched it to the line of oil. It took a moment to ignite, but when it did the results made everyone flinch back. A line of fire raced away down the groove, splitting again and again at each branch as it spread through the cavern. Something hissed and fizzed inside each brazier in turn as the fire reached it—small packets of gunpowder catching light, the heat spreading to the tinder and coal above them. Flames began to rise.

The great chamber filled with a flickering amber light.

Objects gradually took on form, incredible treasures; golden statues of gods and men and animals; elaborate carved friezes decorated with jewels and precious metals; beautifully painted frescoes and gorgeous embroidered silks showing scenes from the lives of Shiva and his wives. Among the artworks were strange machines, as mystifying in the glow from the braziers as they had been as shadows. A giant wheel with dozens of leather pouches hanging from its rim; a great wooden framework, hundreds of glinting metal arrowheads protruding from it; a massive stone roller studded with long, thick iron bars. Not far from the ramp was what resembled a miniature palace, cupolas picked out in gold. Connected to a circular ring around its top was an enormous fabric bag, which stretched away, deflated and flaccid, almost to the vault's side wall.

"Bloody hell," said Eddie. "Shiva's got a big garage."

"This is amazing," Nina whispered. "What *are* all these things?" She went to the little palace. It had a gate in one wall; she gingerly pushed it open to reveal another brazier inside, as well as several straight-bladed swords in a rack on one wall. "It's like a dollhouse."

"*Mayayantras,*" said Girilal. "Magic machines. The Vedas and the epic texts tell of them being used in battles."

Shankarpa was more specific. "This is a *sarvatobhadra,*" he said, going to the great wheel. It was supported on each side by wooden beams. He held up a pouch, which had something heavy, about the size of a human head, inside. The leather had been cut into a shape strongly resembling a slingshot. "It throws stones, hundreds at a time."

"Everyone must get stoned!" Eddie cried nasally and tunelessly. All eyes turned to him. "You know, Bob Dylan? Okay, you probably *don't* know. Forget it."

"How did they get them in here?" asked Kit. "None of them would fit through that cave into the valley."

"They must have been assembled in here," said Nina.

"They're exhibits—just as much Shiva's treasures as any of these statues." She joined Shankarpa. "These things are all mentioned in the epics?"

"Yes, and in the carvings in the valley," he said. He pointed to the grid of arrowheads. "That is a *sara-yantra*—it fires a hundred arrows at once. An *udghatima*—the stone roller—to break down castle walls."

Nina looked more closely at the ancient war machines. Stone and metal weights were suspended from chains running through pulleys to their axles. She had seen—and almost been the victim of—similar simple but effective gravity-powered mechanisms before; they were still primed even after the endless centuries. "Impressive. Just don't touch them—they might go off." She indicated the "dollhouse." "What about this?"

Father and son exchanged looks. "A flying palace," said Shankarpa.

"From what was written in the Ramayana, I thought it would be a lot bigger." Girilal sounded almost disappointed.

Eddie and Kit, meanwhile, had been examining the interior. "You know what this is?" said the Yorkshireman. "A hot-air balloon." He rapped the brazier. "Here's your fire, and you've got the bottom of the balloon up there."

Nina regarded the great mound of fabric in wonder. "It's incredible. First the Chinese lose gunpowder to India, and now the French have to give up balloons. There'll be some very angry historians once word about this place gets out."

"*If* it gets out," said Shankarpa, a warning tone returning to his voice. "All these are just toys compared with the power of the words of Lord Shiva. We must find the Shiva-Vedas—and then I shall decide what to do with you."

"Where would they be?" asked Kit.

"In the deepest part of the vault," Nina suggested. "Come on."

She led the way into the cavern, following the flickering

trail of oil. They passed numerous other siege machines—some resembling ballistas and catapults, others battering rams shaped to look like elephants and goats, as well as more examples of those near the ramp—before approaching the rear wall.

It was immediately obvious where the Shiva-Vedas were kept. A figure guarded a narrow passageway cut into the rock, a statue twenty feet tall.

"You know what?" said Eddie. "Looks like Spielberg was right all along."

Shankarpa was awed by the sight. "Kali...," he whispered.

The jet-black goddess was almost something from a nightmare, mouth twisted in fury. Her eyes and protruding tongue were painted blood red, her naked body adorned with a garland around her neck—not of flowers, but of human skulls. But the most prominent feature was her arms: all ten of them. Most of them clutched weapons, deadly blades shining in the firelight—several swords, a trident, the double-ended club of a huge *vajra,* even the disk of a *chakram.* One foot was firmly planted on the floor beside a small opening at the end of the passage, the other suspended threateningly above it as if ready to stamp on anyone trying to pass beneath.

The guardians responded to the sight with great reverence, even fear. Worshipping one Hindu god, such as Shiva, did not preclude also worshipping others, and as both Shiva's wife and one of the most powerful deities in the pantheon Kali demanded respect.

Even Eddie felt a little intimidated. "I see why she's the goddess of death. Ten arms to kill you with? She's not messing around."

"No, no," said Girilal, almost amused. "There is much more to Kali than death. Do you see? Two of her hands are empty."

Nina saw that instead of holding weapons, the thumbs and fingers formed symbols. "What do they mean?"

"That one," he said, pointing with his stick, "is a sign that she will protect you. She may be fierce, but she is also a loving mother—and a mother will do anything to protect her children. The other means 'do not be afraid'—you have nothing to fear if you trust her."

Kit moved forward, gazing up at the towering figure. "So Lord Shiva left Kali to guard his vault?"

"Who else but Kali would he trust to destroy all intruders?" Shankarpa said firmly.

Nina directed her flashlight at the statue for a better look. "The question is...will she destroy *everyone* who tries to get the Shiva-Vedas? Do you know how to reach them?"

"That knowledge was also lost a long time ago."

"Swell. So we'll have to figure this out too." She brought the light down to examine one of the statue's weapons, but Kit blocked the beam. "Excuse me, Kit—I need to see."

"Oh, sorry." He moved away...

Into the passage.

"Kit, wait!" Nina shouted as she suddenly realized the danger—but too late.

The statue came to life.

The eight arms bearing weapons all moved at once as ancient mechanisms inside the statue ground into action, slashing down into the narrow tunnel. One of the swords stabbed at Kit. He jumped back in shock—

Not quickly enough. The giant blade's tip hacked deep into his shin with a spurt of blood.

He screamed and fell, clutching the wound. Kali's arms screeched back to their original positions and juddered to a stop.

Eddie was the first to risk advancing, pulling Kit out of the passage. "Let me see," he said, carefully easing up Kit's blood-soaked trouser leg to find that he had been cut to the bone, a chunk of his calf muscle peeled back like dog-gnawed meat. "Shit, that's deep. Nina, is the first-aid kit in your gear?"

She retrieved it, Eddie putting on a pair of disposable vinyl gloves and starting to clean the wound. "This'll hurt," he warned Kit. "Sorry, but there's no anesthetic. I'll go as easy as I can."

Nina held the injured man's hand. "Just try to stay calm."

"That is...easier said than done," Kit gasped through his teeth. "My parents always warned me that if I behaved badly, Kali would punish me. But I never imagined it would actually happen!"

"You haven't behaved badly. It would have happened to whoever went into the passage." She looked up at the statue, its red eyes staring menacingly back at her. A booby trap, a last line of defense for the treasures at the heart of the vault. But there had to be a way past it—the priests who had shown the Shiva-Vedas to Talonor obviously knew it...

"Okay, I'm going to stitch it up," Eddie reported. "How're you feeling?"

"Like the goddess just chopped off my foot," Kit rasped.

"You'll be okay. Just try to breathe slowly." He pushed the needle through the flesh, and Kit's entire body tensed.

Girilal and Shankarpa moved past to stare in awe at the statue. The old yogi hesitantly extended his stick into the passage, pushing the tip down on the first stone slab of its floor. Kali burst into movement again, the long sword arcing down. The blade chopped through the wood as both men jumped away, then returned to its original position.

"And this was a very good stick," Girilal said sadly, holding up the truncated end of his staff.

Even while trying to comfort Kit, Nina couldn't help turning her mind to the trap. "Anyone walking down the passage triggers it. And even if you could climb to the end without touching the floor, you still have to drop down to go through the opening at the end. And when you do..." She indicated the giant stone foot poised above the gap. "You get stomped."

"Just like Shiva," said Girilal, thoughtful.

"What do you mean?"

"There was a demon called Raktabija," he told her, "who seemed impossible to kill in battle because every time he was cut, when his blood touched the ground another copy of him leapt up. Only Kali was strong enough to destroy him—she drank all the blood from Raktabija's body, then ate his clones! But she became drunk with victory and danced across the battlefield, crushing the dead under her feet. To stop her, Shiva pretended to be one of the corpses, and when Kali realized she had stepped on her husband, she was ashamed and became calm again."

"Did she kill him?" Nina asked.

"No, she stopped just before she crushed him."

Eddie finished stitching Kit's injury. "Doesn't help us get past, though."

"There has to be a way through," Nina said. She saw a spear beside another siege engine. "Shankarpa, try that. Maybe there's a pattern to the way the arms move, a safe route."

Shankarpa pushed the spear's tip against the slab. The arms swung into action once more, blades flashing through the air. Nina's hope that a route through the gauntlet might be revealed was rapidly dashed; the stabbing, hacking, and crushing blows covered the passage's entire width.

"So much for that," she said as Shankarpa withdrew the shortened spear.

The leader of the guardians frowned. "But you are right—there must be a way. I will see if anyone remembers anything from our carvings." He turned to the other robed men.

Nina could tell from the tone of their responses that they were unlikely to be saying anything useful. She moved back to Kit as Eddie applied bandages. "Are you okay?"

"This has not been my most fun day," he said in a strained voice.

"Just hang in there. We've come this far, we've found the Vault of Shiva—we'll get you home safely. Somehow." She looked at Girilal. "Is there anything in the stories of Kali that might get us past?"

He shook his head. "I am sorry, but I cannot think what."

Her gaze moved back to the statue—and the two hands that had not moved during the attack. "The symbols she's making: 'I will protect you' and 'Do not fear.' Do not fear, I will protect you . . . from what?"

"From her," suggested Eddie. "She's the big threat."

"Kali is not a threat to those who trust her," Girilal insisted.

"So how does she protect you if she's the one attacking you in the first place?" asked Nina. "Unless . . . if you *believe* she won't harm you, you have nothing to fear?"

Eddie indicated Kit's leg. "I don't think a positive mental attitude'll stop you from getting shish-kebabed."

"I'm not so sure. Girilal, can you look after Kit?"

"Wait, what're you thinking?" Eddie demanded as the yogi took her place.

She picked up the spear. "I've got a theory—I want to test it."

"Couldn't you just write a thesis, or whatever you PhDs do?"

Ignoring him, Nina went to the passage, stopping just short of its entrance. There was a splash of blood where Kit had been stabbed. Raising the spear, she held its broken end a few inches past the splatter. "Okay, let's see what happens . . ."

She pushed the spear down—and held it there.

Another fearsome crash of ancient machinery, eight arms sweeping down—

And stopping short. There was a loud bang as something inside the statue arrested its movement.

Nina kept the spear held down. The arms retreated.

Shankarpa ran over. "What did you do?"

"I believed that Kali would protect me," Nina replied. "And she did. Stand back, let me show you."

She pushed the spear down again. The sword lunged— and this time she jerked the wood away. The blade continued to the limit of its travel, hacking another piece off the wooden shaft.

"If you're afraid, that's what you do when Kali attacks you," she explained. "You jump back—and get hit anyway. But if you're not afraid, if you stand your ground . . ." She lowered the spear once more, keeping it pressed firmly to the stone. Another bang echoed through the passage as the sword stopped abruptly before impact. "If you stay in place, there's something in the machinery that keeps it from hitting you. The symbols in her other two hands are the clue for how to get through. It's like the key—you have to know the *meaning* of the stories about Shiva and the goddesses to get inside."

Eddie waved an arm at the array of lethal weapons. "You want to take a stroll through that lot to see if you're right?"

"Well, uh . . . not particularly. But if it's the only way we can get through, then someone's got to do it."

"It's not bloody going to be you, that's for sure." He stepped up to the passage. "I'll do it."

"What?" Nina cried. "Oh, no you won't! If you're not going to let me go, I'm sure as hell not going to let you. One of these guys can do it." She jabbed a thumb at the guardians.

Shankarpa was not pleased by the suggestion. "You want us to risk our lives to test your . . . theory?"

"You want to find the Shiva-Vedas as much as we do."

"*Our* lives do not depend on it."

"They might if the Khoils turn up." Between the excitement of opening the vault and the danger posed by the statue, she had forgotten there was another threat hanging over them. "Dammit! They could be on their way already. We *have* to get inside!" She faced Shankarpa. "Look, I'm sure that if you're not afraid and just walk down the passage, you won't get hit and you'll be able to get to the inner chamber. But we're running out of time to do it."

"Then we'll have to stop pissing about and get on with it, won't we?" Eddie said . . . as he stepped into the narrow tunnel.

"Eddie, no!" Nina screamed, but the blades were already descending—

The longest sword jerked to a stop with its tip barely an inch from his groin.

"Gah!" he yelped as it withdrew, feeling certain parts of his body doing some withdrawal of their own. "I'm bloody glad that stopped when it did."

"Are you out of your *mind*?" Nina shouted. "You could have been killed!"

"Or worse! Look, someone's got to go down here—and actually doing it's better than arguing about it. Okay, next step." Suppressing a shudder, he advanced down the passage.

The long sword remained stationary as the other blades shot forward, a scimitar swooshing across at neck height only to stop as if hitting an invisible wall. The weapons retracted. Another step. This time nothing happened. Not all the slabs were connected to the trap. Warily, he moved on.

The *vajra* dropped like a wrecking ball, stopping so close to his head the displaced air ruffled his hair. Next was another sword, almost cleaving diagonally across his chest. Four arms had made their attack: halfway.

Another step—

The *chakram* sliced at him—and its circular edge bit through his sleeve into his arm.

Nina gasped, about to run to help him. "No!" he growled through the pain. "Stay back! It's stopped!" The arm holding the *chakram* had been stopped by the mechanism restricting its movement—but Eddie had been just far enough out of position for it to catch him.

He leaned away, grunting as the metal pulled clear of his flesh. The *chakram* clunked back to its original position, a thin line of blood glistening on it. He peeled back the torn fabric of his sleeve to examine the injury. He had been much luckier than Kit; the cut would only need one or two stitches.

But that would have to wait. Forcing back his fear, Eddie slowly walked the rest of the way down the passage. Three more weapons struck at him—and each stopped just before impact. Kali was indeed protecting him.

But there was still one more obstacle. "Okay, now what?" he called as he reached the raised foot. The gap beneath it was a little higher than the duct he had crawled through at the United Nations; he would fit, but it would be a tight squeeze.

"Any ideas?" Nina asked the men around her.

"He must be like Shiva on the battlefield," said Girilal. "He must pretend to be dead and shame Kali into ending her rampage."

Considering the legend, it seemed to fit, but she still wasn't keen on the idea—and neither was Eddie when she relayed it to him. "I won't be *pretending* to be dead if you're wrong. Can't I just wedge it with something?"

"I'm sure whoever built it thought of that," she said. The floor beneath the foot was a mosaic of smaller tiles; she guessed that they were intended to give way if too much pressure was put on them, pressing any props into the ground as the foot descended. "But I think Girilal's right. You have to slide under it and play dead—if you try to get out while it's coming down, it'll drop and finish you off. The whole trap is about trusting Kali *not* to kill you, however scary it looks."

"I'm not scared," he said, starting to wriggle under the statue. "I just don't want my obituary to say that I died by being squashed by a giant foot like something out of Monty bloody Python. It'd be embarrassing."

Despite her tension, the joke made Nina smile. "Your obituary isn't going to be written for a long, long time, Eddie. Nobody would dare."

"Well, let's hope you're right." He was now fully beneath the foot—

A tile gave slightly, his weight tripping another trigger. With a nerve-scraping grinding, the foot started to descend.

His instinctual response was to get clear—but he suppressed it, summoning every ounce of self-control to hold still as the foot pressed down on him. He tried to stay calm as the pressure increased, controlling his breathing—but the weight began to force the air from his lungs. "Shit!" he tried to say, but the word was choked short in his throat.

The rasp of stone continued, flesh and bone not slowing the statue's relentless descent in the slightest. Pain coursed through Eddie's rib cage as it was squashed against the floor. He struggled to writhe free—but was pinned in place.

Kali was going to crush him!

He turned his head to give Nina a last anguished look, seeing her staring back at him in horror, realizing too late that she had been wrong—

The noise stopped.

The pressure suddenly eased, the foot rising slowly back to its original position. Gasping, he drew in several long breaths of cold, dusty air before crawling through the hole. "I'm in," he croaked.

"Thank God," Nina said. "Are you okay?"

"I feel like toothpaste, but I'll be all right."

ANDY McDERMOTT

"What can you see?"

He glanced around; the new chamber was almost completely dark. "Nowt—a torch'd be handy. Roll one down to me."

Nina drew back her arm as if throwing a bowling ball and sent her flashlight skittering down the passage. Eddie caught it and switched it on. The new room was small, the walls engraved with images of Shiva, the paint on the ancient carvings still surprisingly colorful, and line upon line of Vedic Sanskrit. But the object that caught his attention was against one wall.

It was an ornate chest, standing upon gilded legs shaped like an elephant's and decorated with pearls and small gemstones. Like the walls, it was painted: Shiva, seated in the lotus position, gazed serenely back at him.

"Can you see anything?" Nina called.

"Yeah, there's a fancy box, and..." He panned the light around. Part of the statue's mechanism was revealed: several large cogs. "I need something to jam up the works. A stone, or a metal bar, something like that."

A quick search by Shankarpa's men produced a thick iron rod from one of the siege machines. It was tossed down the passage with a clang. Eddie jammed it between the teeth of the cogs, then experimentally put his weight on the floor beneath the foot. There was another clang as the bar was slammed between the cogs when they tried to turn, but it held firm. After a few moments, the mechanism reset.

He leaned under the foot and waved. "Okay. Who wants a look?"

Shankarpa was first, cautiously advancing down the passage. The statue's arms jerked, but again the metal rod held everything in check. Nina followed.

"Check it out," said Eddie as they crawled through the entrance. He illuminated the chest. "You think Shiva's diary's inside?"

Shankarpa was too overawed to respond to Eddie's lack

of respect. He went to the chest, hands hovering just above the lid as if afraid to touch it, then looked back at Nina. For the first time, he seemed unsure of himself. "What should I do?"

"Open it," Nina told him. "If the Shiva-Vedas are inside, we need to know—so we can decide how to protect them."

He nodded, about to raise the lid—but again couldn't bring himself to touch the box. "I . . . I can't do it," he said. "I do not know if I am worthy—"

"Oh, give it 'ere," Eddie snapped, flipping the chest open.

Shankarpa flinched back, and Nina glared at her husband. "Eddie!"

"What? You said we needed to get a move on. Now, what's inside?" He held up the flashlight.

At first glance, the contents seemed almost unworthy of the effort and danger endured to find them. The interior was like a rack, metal dividers separating and supporting a row of stone tablets, each the size of a large hardback book, about half an inch thick. There were perhaps forty in all.

But Nina knew that they represented an incredible archaeological find, the ancient wonders in the cavern outside nothing more than baubles compared with the intellectual treasure in the box. While she didn't personally believe they had been written by an actual god, the tablets were an account of a civilization every bit as ancient as that of the Atlanteans—and one of the foundations of a religion that, unlike that of the long-lost race, was still alive and well today.

Delicately, she lifted out a tablet, finding text inscribed on both sides: Vedic Sanskrit, a language with which she had only a passing familiarity. She turned one face toward Shankarpa. "Can you read it?"

Awe returned to his face. "Yes. Yes! It...it is the word of Lord Shiva—about the great cycle of existence!"

Nina carefully returned the tablet to its place. Shankarpa eagerly gestured for her to remove another, but she shook her head. "We need to decide what to do with them. Pramesh and Vanita Khoil know where the lost valley is—so they'll be coming. No matter what happens, we have to keep them from getting hold of the Vedas. Is there anywhere else you could hide them?"

"There are some caves to the northeast. But I don't know how safe they would be—they are not deep. If a storm hit..."

She put a hand on his arm; Shankarpa reacted to the touch with surprise. "Look, I know you still don't exactly trust me, and I can understand that. But if you let me, I can take the Vedas somewhere completely safe—the Khoils won't be able to steal them. It's what I do, it's the IHA's mission: to find ancient treasures, and to protect them for the benefit of all humanity. Your father believes in me. Will you?"

Shankarpa looked between her and the chest, frowning...then coming to a decision. "You think we will not be able to stop these people?"

"They'll come in force," Eddie told him. "And they'll kill every man here if you get in their way. There's how many of you, twenty-odd? The Khoils'll probably bring that many—and they'll all have machine guns."

"Please," said Nina. "The IHA can protect the Vedas. You and the other guardians might be able to slow down the Khoils...but you won't be able to stop them."

The Indian made a little noise of self-disgust. "All right. I will let you take them to a safe place. But I will come with you."

"First, let's start thinking about how we're going to get them out of here." She closed the lid. "Eddie, can you help him move it?"

"Great." He sighed. "Halfway up a mountain, cut up by a killer statue, and squashed by a giant foot, and I still have to cart boxes around for you."

Nina sheepishly regarded his torn sleeve. "Oh. Right. I forgot. Sorry."

"It's okay. 'Cause it's you, I'll do it as a favor. Although I might want you to do something in return when we get back home." He grinned lecherously. "Maybe involving props."

"*God,* Eddie! Of all the times to be thinking about... *that.*"

"What are you talking about?" demanded the impatient Shankarpa.

"Absolutely nothing," Nina told him as she took the flashlight. "Okay. Now, both of you, lift it up. Make sure you support it from underneath."

They obeyed, Shankarpa taking hold of the chest before giving Nina an outraged look. "Wait, you do not give me orders! I am the leader here!"

"This is what happens once you let a woman into your men-only club," Eddie said. "Next thing, it'll be frilly bedclothes and putting the toilet seat down."

"Just move the thing," Nina snapped as she crawled back out. Eddie and Shankarpa carefully raised the chest and maneuvered it to the passage. There was just enough room for it to fit beneath the giant stone foot, though the elephant legs scraped the floor as it was eased through.

Once both men were clear, they brought it into the cavern proper. Shankarpa gave an order to two of his men, who reverently carried the chest toward the doors. "They will take it down to the ground," he told Nina.

She indicated the other items around them. "What about everything else?"

"We will close the vault. Now that we know how to open the lock, I will decide what to do later. For now, we leave."

Eddie crouched beside Kit. "How's the leg? Think you can walk on it?"

"I don't think I'll be able to get back down the ridge," he admitted. "But there's a cell phone mast at Gaurikund—when you get into phone range, you can call Interpol and get them to send a helicopter."

"We'll be able to take the Vedas as well," said Nina. "If we contact the Indian government, they can arrange security."

"Sounds good to me," said Eddie. He motioned to Girilal to help him lift Kit.

The Interpol agent gasped in pain, but managed a strained "I'm okay" as they supported him. Everyone followed the men carrying the chest. "I'll give you my superior's number. He'll be able to—"

Eddie stopped suddenly. "Wait!"

"What is it?" asked Nina.

The echoing thud of rotor blades answered her question. Not one set: several.

The Khoils had found them.

Keep hold of Kit!" Eddie ordered Girilal as he ran for the doors. The other guardians were already sprinting for the entrance to investigate.

Nina went after them. "What do we do? It'll take ages to get the chest out of the valley!"

"I don't think we'll even get the chance—no, get back!" he shouted at the men ahead of him.

Too late. The noise of the blades got louder, pounding subsonic *thump*s that they could feel as much as hear—but it was another, more deadly sound that made Eddie throw Nina into the cover of one of the ancient war machines. A machine gun opened fire, tracer rounds searing through the open doors. Gouts of blood burst from the guardians' bodies as the gunner sent a stream of death into the vault.

Shankarpa flung himself back as bullets cracked into the stone floor. He scrambled to join Nina and Eddie behind the solid, spiky roller of the *udghatima*. "The chest! Where is it?"

"There!" Nina pointed. The two men carrying it had put it down beside the ramp before going to the doors.

A freezing wind blasted into the cavern as the helicopter

descended. Eddie looked out from behind the roller. The chopper was a Chinook; a large, twin-rotor transport aircraft designed to lift heavy cargoes—or large numbers of troops. The rear ramp, facing them, was fully lowered, the gunner lying on his belly and letting rip with a bipod-mounted M249 machine gun. Behind him were at least a dozen more men, dressed in black combat gear and body armor, carrying MP5Ks.

The surviving guardians tried to run for cover, but the gunner cut them down. One man attempted to leap from the top of the broken stairway to the uppermost ledge. A burst of machine-gun fire and his legs exploded into bloody chunks of meat, sending him tumbling screaming to the ground.

The firing stopped. The Chinook's engines increased power, and it climbed out of sight. Beyond it, Eddie saw the red-and-white helicopter that had overflown the valley earlier—and a third aircraft, a compact black-and-silver MD 500. That particular model was based on the US Army's MH-6 Little Bird gunship—and its users were taking advantage of its military heritage. One of the cockpit's doors was open, the barrel of another M249 aiming down into the valley.

He ducked back. "Christ, they've got three choppers out there! No idea how many guys in them, but it looked like a lot."

"We've got to get the Vedas somewhere safe," said Nina, glancing out at the chest. Shielded by the stone ramp, it had escaped damage during the onslaught, but now seemed terrifyingly fragile.

"We'll never be able to get it outside—not without getting shot to shit." He took another look around the *udghatima*. "We should—shit!"

Ropes dropped in front of the ledge. The Chinook was hovering above the overhang. At any moment, troops would rappel down. The MD 500 was also hanging above the valley, ready to provide covering fire.

"They're coming," Eddie told Shankarpa. The ropes wavered, snake-like, as the mercenaries began their descent. With his Wildey, he could have picked them off before they reached the ledge, but the only weapons to hand were knives and swords.

Unless—

He looked at the giant stone roller shielding them. "Nina, you said these things were ready to go—how do you set them off?"

"How should I know? You're the death machine expert!" They hurriedly examined the machine. Once a lever was pulled to release a chock, a heavy weight on a chain would drop—and turn a sprocket to spin the roller.

But the wall-smasher would be no use against their attackers. It could crawl along on small wheels—but it wasn't pointing toward the entrance, and there seemed no way to steer it.

"This one's no good," said Nina, "but we could use one of the others to hold them off. If we can get to them before—"

"We can't," said Eddie. "We're out of time." The first of the black-clad troopers came into sight, slithering effortlessly down the rope and swinging onto the ledge. He raised his weapon and ran to the side of the entrance.

Eddie recognized him. Zec.

More mercenaries landed. Zec leaned around the door to check the interior, signaling another two men to cover him and his partner as they entered.

"What can we do?" Nina whispered.

Shankarpa drew his sword from his back. "We fight them."

"You'd be dead before you got within twenty feet," said Eddie. But they were fast running out of options as the mercs advanced. The only direction they could go without being seen was back into the vault's depths—and the chances of their evading discovery shrank with every extra man who touched down.

No choice. "I don't like to say it, but all we can do is hide."

"But they'll get the chest," Nina protested.

"I don't see how we can stop 'em—not without getting killed. Come on. You too," he added to Shankarpa, who seemed on the verge of rushing out in a kamikaze attack. "Move it."

He directed Nina and Shankarpa toward the vault's rear, keeping the giant roller between them and the mercenaries as they investigated the bodies, hunting for survivors. The trio passed the miniature palace, skirting the fabric of the deflated balloon and angling back around to where Eddie hoped Kit and Girilal were still waiting. The hard part would be getting to them unseen; the braziers were burning hotter and brighter than ever, and there were still dashes of flame in the oil channels.

He peered through the wooden framework of a war machine. The Chinook had moved off, taking the ropes with it. That meant for the moment that no more mercenaries would be entering the chamber. The knowledge was far from reassuring; they were still outnumbered more than two to one by armed men.

The mercs divided into three-man teams, spreading out to search the cavernous space. Eddie spotted Girilal cautiously peering out from behind an elephant statue. He guessed that Kit was with him; the old yogi didn't seem the type to abandon an injured man.

"Okay, we've got to reach Kit and Girilal and find somewhere to hide," he whispered. "Maybe under one of those machines."

"How do we reach them?" Nina asked. They would have to cross the open space around one of the oil channels—in direct line of sight of the entrance.

"We'll have to time it right." The nearest group of mercenaries had reached the *udghatima*, shining flashlight beams at the great roller. "If they go behind it..."

"I will make them," said Shankarpa. Before Eddie could stop him, the Indian had picked up and thrown a small piece of gold jewelry. It clonked off something near the *udghatima*. The beams flashed around to find the source of the noise.

"For fuck's sake!" Eddie hissed, angry. "Now they know there's still someone alive!" Two of the men in the team moved out of sight to investigate, but the third was holding position, shining his light suspiciously around him. "Okay, we'll have to risk it. Get ready. Soon as he turns away..."

He ducked as the beam swept around, scanning the path into the vault before turning back to the roller. "Go!" He pushed Nina out first, then followed Shankarpa across the aisle—

The beam whipped back, catching them before they were even halfway across.

"Shit!" Eddie dived behind the elephant statue as a shout and the chatter of automatic fire reached him simultaneously. Bullets pitted the stone behind him. More shouts from other directions, the rapid tramp of running footsteps as other mercenaries closed in.

Kit was there with Girilal. He tried to push himself upright, but gasped in pain as his leg gave way. He would have to be carried—making him and his helpers easy targets.

Nina looked around the other end of the statue, seeing more men running through the cavern. "Eddie, they're coming!"

They were trapped; the approaching mercenaries had clear lines of fire on each side. Eddie searched desperately for a weapon, but there was nothing he could reach without exposing himself to gunfire.

No way out. The nearest group of mercs was seconds away, preparing to whip around the statue and blast everyone they found there—

"Zec!" Eddie shouted, startling his companions. "Zec, it's Eddie Chase! Can you hear me?"

No reply for a moment, only the pounding boots closing in—then a Balkan-accented command of "Hold your fire!" as three men burst around the corner, weapons raised, fingers tight on the triggers...

But no shots.

Another team of mercenaries appeared at the other end of the statue, boxing in the five survivors. Laser sights flicked on, green dots settling on heads and hearts. More footsteps, this time marching. Zec appeared, regarding Eddie curiously. "Chase. This is a surprise."

"For me too," Eddie replied, raising his hands. "I thought Khoil was going to fire you."

"He almost did. But for this operation, he needed a man with experience who could assemble a fighting force quickly."

"Well, even though he was wrong about you being a good bloke, Hugo seemed to think you knew what you were doing, so I suppose that makes sense."

"Hugo?" whispered Nina, confused. "What is this, Mercenaries Reunited?"

He shushed her. "So where's Slumdog Billionaire and his wife?"

The comment amused Zec. "They are in one of the helicopters. I think they will also be surprised to see you." He ordered the other mercenaries to continue searching the vault, then gestured for the prisoners to pick up Kit and take him to the entrance.

"What are you doing?" Nina quietly demanded as the armed men ushered them along. "He's the asshole who kidnapped me—why are you being all buddy-buddy with him?"

"'Cause if I hadn't been, we'd all be dead," Eddie replied. "Keeping him talking was the only way to keep us alive."

Her face brightened. "You've got a plan, right? Tell me you've got a plan."

"Er...only if you count 'see if something good happens before we get shot.'"

"Riiiight...," she said, hope fading as quickly as it had risen. "I was after something a bit more, y'know, specific."

They reached the ramp, Nina glancing at the chest containing the Shiva-Vedas. The mercenaries obviously had no idea of its significance, but Khoil would be unlikely to overlook it. Was there any way they could hide it from him?

Zec brought them to the end of the ramp, where they lowered Kit so he could sit with his back against it. His men held them at gunpoint for several minutes while the other mercenaries continued their sweep of the cavern. Eventually they returned, reporting that there was nobody else alive. The Bosnian relayed this over his radio headset. "The Khoils are on their way," he told Nina and Eddie. Outside, the red-and-white helicopter flew up the valley.

"I can't wait," Nina said sourly. The bodies of the guardians were scattered nearby, rivulets of blood congealing on the floor, and even though she was trying not to look at them, just the awareness of the bullet-torn corpses was making her feel sick.

Eddie was looking at them, though; more specifically, at their weapons. Most of the fallen swords were too far away, but there was a long-bladed dagger that had ended up only a few feet from the stone ramp. With a distraction, he might be able to reach it and stab one of the mercenaries, giving him a chance to grab a gun...

He noticed Girilal watching him, the yogi following his gaze to the dagger. The realization that the holy man knew what he was planning was somehow unsettling. He turned away, keeping the knife in the edge of his vision.

More snow blew through the doors. A figure was lowered into view: Tandon. Unlike the mercenaries, he was not rappelling but being winched down in a harness. Zec signaled to two of his men, who hurried out and pulled him onto the ledge. They unfastened the harness, which quickly rose out of sight as the winch line was wound back in. A short time later it returned, now bearing the giant bearded form of Mahajan. The two bodyguards took up positions awaiting the arrival of a third person.

Pramesh Khoil.

His two servants quickly freed him from the harness. He brushed himself down, then entered the vault. His triumphant march broke step when he saw who was waiting inside. "Dr. Wilde," he said, the flat voice not quite concealing his surprise. "And Mr. Chase. The recurring bugs in my otherwise flawless program."

"I told you knowledge and experience are more useful than any computer," Nina replied. "You're too late—the Shiva-Vedas are already gone. The IHA airlifted them out of here."

A smug smile crossed the plump face. "I think not. Until now, the weather conditions were too severe—and the only helicopters that have entered the airspace are mine. Where are they?" He received no answer. "No matter. We will find them." He took in the vastness of the vault, eyes widening. "It is here, it really exists..."

"Sounds like you had some doubts," said Nina.

"The failure to find anything at Mount Kailash was becoming a concern, yes."

"So what brought you here?"

Another smile. "Ironically, you did. Or more accurately, Mr. Jindal did," Khoil continued, indicating the startled Kit, "and his cell phone. My people learned that you had left Delhi, and that made me wonder: Where had you gone? So I had my telecom company track his phone through the cellular network, and discovered he had gone to Gaurikund. The only possible reason for you to go there was if you believed you had located the vault. Once I put *that* new information into Qexia, everything made sense. I feel slightly foolish for not having thought of the connection to Mount Kedarnath sooner."

"Garbage in, garbage out," said Nina scathingly. "You were acting on bad data. That's what happens when you rely on technology."

"Yet it was technology that allowed me to find you. And the vault." The wind rose again, and he turned to see Vanita being winched down, Tandon and Mahajan helping her onto the ledge.

"Great, she's here. Now the party can start," Eddie muttered.

Khoil was about to say something in defense of his wife when he noticed Girilal, who had been standing behind Shankarpa, for the first time. "A Pashupati?" he said, intrigued.

"Girilal Mitra, at your service!" said the old man, his voice shifting conspicuously back to the manic singsong. He danced around his son to meet Khoil. Zec and some of the mercenaries aimed their guns at him, but Khoil waved them down. "So you are Mr. Khoil, the computer man."

"I am, yes."

"Ha!" Girilal leaned on his stick, staring disapprovingly at the billionaire. "You are a very bad person."

To Nina's surprise, Khoil seemed stung by the allegation. "No! I am a loyal servant of Lord Shiva, like you. I am doing his will."

"And is this his will?" asked Girilal, waving a hand at the bodies. "Why would one of his loyal servants kill his other loyal servants, hmm?"

"A true servant of Shiva would know that death is of no consequence," proclaimed Vanita loudly, striding into the chamber with Mahajan and Tandon. She was wrapped in layers of cold-weather clothing, and seemed decidedly annoyed to be there, not even giving the wonders of the vault a second glance. "Especially when it will help end the Kali Yuga. Now, where are the Vedas?" She gave Nina an icy look. "I assume she knows."

"They are here somewhere, my beloved," Khoil assured her.

"Somewhere is not good enough. Find them, now!"

Khoil turned back to Girilal. "I have no quarrel with a holy man. Do you know where to find the Vedas? If you tell me, I will let you go free."

"And what about my friends?" Girilal countered. "Will they go free too?"

"I am afraid that will not be possible."

"Ha!" snorted Girilal, banging down his stick. "You are a bad man. Very bad." He waved a dismissive hand. "Shiva wants nothing to do with you. And neither do I." Ignoring their guns, he shuffled past the mercenaries and sat huffily on the ramp, facing away from Khoil.

Zec glanced questioningly at his employer, but Khoil, seeming genuinely startled by the yogi's rejection, shook his head. "Search the vault. Find the Vedas."

"What do they look like?" Zec asked.

"According to the text from Atlantis, they are stone tablets with text in Vedic Sanskrit. They will probably be in a container for protection, a box or chest."

Zec and all but two of the mercenaries spread out to begin their search. "You'll never find them," said Nina as Vanita began to pace impatiently, her husband looking up in fascination at the *vimana*. "It's a big cave, and they could be absolutely anywh—"

"Found them," called Zec from beside the ramp.

"God *damn* it!"

Zec and another man brought the chest to the Khoils and opened it. "These are them, yes?" he asked.

Khoil, hands shaking in excitement, carefully lifted out one of the tablets and examined the ancient text. "Yes," he breathed. "The Shiva-Vedas! The words of Lord Shiva himself." He looked at Vanita, the light of the zealot in his eyes. "We have them! We will wipe away the corruption of the Kali Yuga. A new age—and we will create it." He delicately replaced the tablet in the rack, then closed the lid. "Chapal, Dhiren! Prepare it for transport."

The two bodyguards came to him as the mercenaries returned. Mahajan carried a backpack, from which he took a roll of strong plastic netting and a bundle of harness straps. He and Tandon wrapped up the chest so it could be winched away.

"Now, what about them?" Vanita asked impatiently, indicating the prisoners. "I think they have lived far too long."

"I agree," said Khoil.

"Good! Then kill them!" She glared at Zec. "Now!"

Zec nodded, about to issue a command—

Shankarpa dived at Khoil with a scream of rage.

Zec swept up his MP5K, catching the guardian a savage blow across his face and knocking him down by the foot of the ramp. Another mercenary kicked Shankarpa in the chest and aimed his gun at his head—

Girilal snatched up the dagger and stabbed it to the hilt into the merc's throat.

The other mercenaries whipped around to face the unexpected threat as the trooper fell, a spray of red spurting out from the wound. Zec fired at the old man. The burst of bullets hit Girilal in the chest and stomach, slamming him to the floor.

And in the moment of confusion, Eddie moved—

He grabbed the gun hand of the nearest man and twisted it around, clenching his trigger finger. The shots hit another mercenary at point-blank range, not even his body armor enough to stop them from ripping into his chest. He spun and collided with another pair of men, bowling them over.

Eddie slammed an uppercut into the first man's jaw, hearing teeth snap under the impact, then tried to wrench the MP5K from his grasp. Even through the nerve-searing pain, the blood-spitting merc managed to resist, crunching an elbow into Eddie's sternum and knocking him backward. He tripped over Kit's injured leg, making the Indian cry out, and fell heavily to the floor.

The other gunmen brought their weapons to bear, fingers tight on triggers, but Zec thrust his own gun into Eddie's face before they could fire, shoving a boot on his chest. "Don't move," he growled.

All eyes were on the two men.

Except Nina's.

The sudden chaos had opened up an escape route, however briefly. She took it, throwing herself over the bottom of the ramp into the channel between its two halves. Some of the gunmen whirled at the movement, but she was already in the cover of the rising walls as they fired. Stone chips bombarded her like hailstones as she ran.

"Kill her, kill her!" Vanita screeched. The mercs rushed to the ramp and unleashed more bullets down the narrow passage, but Nina was clear, sprinting into the depths of the Vault of Shiva.

27

Get her!" Zec ordered. Two of his men ran after the fleeing American.

Vanita turned to Khoil. "Bring the helicopter back, now."

"The chest isn't ready," he said. Mahajan and Tandon had broken off from their preparations to protect their master and mistress when the shooting started.

"I'm not talking about the chest. *I* want to get out of here!"

"She won't get away," said Zec.

"I don't care. Once I'm aboard, *then* we'll collect the chest." She strode toward the doors, imperiously waving for her bodyguards to follow.

They looked at Khoil for instructions, caught between conflicting commands. "Chapal, go with her," he said, exasperation creeping into his voice. "Dhiren, go after Dr. Wilde. Zec, finish securing the Vedas and take them to the ledge." Mahajan grunted and lumbered after Nina's pursuers. Tandon followed Vanita, while Zec gestured for two of his men to continue preparing the chest.

The remaining mercenaries surrounded the prisoners.

Girilal clutched weakly at the bullet wounds. Blood soaked his torn robes. Shankarpa, groggy from the blow to his head, pushed himself up—and saw him. He cried out in Hindi, trying to reach the dying man, but two of the mercenaries kicked him back down.

"He's his *dad*!" Eddie protested. Khoil's face remained dispassionate, but Zec relented, a silent nod prompting the mercs to back away. He released Eddie from under his foot, keeping his gun trained on him.

Shankarpa crawled to the yogi, horrified. "Father!" he gasped, putting a hand on Girilal's chest in a futile attempt to stop the bleeding.

Girilal moaned softly at the touch. "Janardan?" he whispered. Blood bubbled in his mouth.

Shankarpa gripped his hand. "I am here, Father. I'm here!"

"Oh, Janardan...what have I done? I have taken a life. How...how will I explain myself to Shiva?"

"Lord Shiva is a warrior," said Shankarpa, in desperate insistence. "He has fought many battles, he has killed demons and evil men. It is not a sin to fight to protect—" His voice caught. "To protect those you love."

Girilal's eyes closed, a tear running down one cheek. "You must...find your mother. Tell her...I am sorry, I am so sorry. Ask her if she can...forgive me. Please. Please, my son...say you will do this for me."

Shankarpa's eyes welled with tears of his own. "I will, Father. I will. I promise."

"Thank..." He convulsed, a soft cough speckling his chin with blood. "Janardan, oh...my son..." A strangled moan escaped him, his whole body shuddering...

Then he was still.

Eddie felt a tightness in his throat as he watched the devastated Shankarpa slowly release his hold on his father's hand. Anger spiking through sorrow, he looked at Khoil and Zec. The Indian was still unmoved by the sight, but Zec appeared troubled, almost guilty.

Beyond them, Vanita had been fastened into the harness, ready to be winched to the helicopter. The chest was secure in its own straps, the two mercenaries carrying it to the ledge. "Pramesh!" she shouted over the rotor noise. "What are you waiting for? Kill them!"

Khoil nodded to Zec. "Do as she says."

"Ready weapons!" Zec barked. The mercenaries snapped into action, MP5Ks locking on to Eddie, Shankarpa, and Kit. "Aim—"

Another shout—from the depths of the vault. *"Bob Dylan!"*

The strange war cry was followed by a loud bang, then a series of thudding clanks, getting faster and faster—

Eddie realized what it meant. He grabbed Shankarpa's arm. "Down!"

They dropped, Eddie covering Kit with his body and pressing against the side of the ramp—as a fusillade of stones rained around them.

* * *

Nina had used the vault's contents as cover to block her pursuers' aim as she ran. But she knew she couldn't evade them forever—she had to take offensive action.

At the moment the thought formed, she found herself beside the great wheel of a *sarvato-bhadra*—a stone-thrower.

Like the other ancient war machines, it was still primed for action.

She yanked the lever to release the mechanism, yelling *"Bob Dylan!"* as a warning to Eddie. The large weight descended, its chain rattling and screeching. The wheel picked up speed startlingly quickly, the leather slings attached to its rim whipped outward by centrifugal force.

Something else also moved outward as the machine

spun faster, a metal block protruding from a slot running from the wheel's center to its rim. A trigger: Another block was mounted on the support frame. As the wheel reached its full speed, they clanged together—

Releasing the slings.

The wheel was mounted on the axle a few degrees off vertical. As it turned, it swayed from side to side—hurling the stones across the cavern in a deadly bombardment. They flew over the ramp, barely missing the *vimana* at its summit...and smashed down at the entrance.

* * *

Zec threw Khoil aside as a head-sized chunk of rock arced down and shattered where he had been standing.

Others were less lucky. One mercenary was hit in the face with a sharp crack of splintering bone. Another took a blow to the chest, his bulletproof body armor no defense against the force of the rock that punched razor-sharp fragments of broken ribs into his heart. The other men scrambled for cover.

Vanita screamed for the winch operator to raise her as more stones bounced off the floor and flew out onto the ledge. Tandon flung himself out of the way as pieces hurtled past them. One of the mercenaries who had brought out the chest was struck on his knee, the joint bending backward with a horrible snap and pitching him over the edge. The helicopter, an Indian-built Dhruv, ascended, yanking Vanita off the ledge.

The chest sat near the edge, stones skimming past it.

Shankarpa pointed back into the vault. "Go!" he shouted to Eddie as he leapt up and sprinted for the doors.

Eddie pulled Kit upright, vaulting into the gap between the ramp's sides and dragging the Interpol agent after him. "We've got to find Nina!" he said as he hauled him down the narrow channel. Ahead, he saw the stack of black rockets, the first burning brazier beyond. Nobody was chasing them—yet. But the confusion wouldn't last long. With nobody to reload it, the *sarvato-bhadra* was limited to a single salvo.

• • •

Nina abandoned the war machine—the stones had passed harmlessly over the three men pursuing her. She fled deeper into the vault.

• • •

Shankarpa raced for the open doors. A mercenary fired at him, but he was already through. He saw the chest at the top of the broken steps but could do nothing about it. Instead, he ran past it as fast as he could.

Jumping—

Cold air whistled in his ears as he sailed over the gap, seventy feet of nothingness beneath him . . .

His foot reached the very edge of the topmost tier. He was moving too fast to stop, slamming against the wall and tumbling to the snow-covered floor. He forced himself back up and ran again, heading for one of the arched openings.

A roar of engines echoed through the valley—the MD 500, swooping down—

He dived through the entrance as bullets tore into the ancient carvings behind him. The shooting stopped, but the rotor noise remained constant. The gunship was waiting for him to reappear, the gunner assuming the chamber had only one way out.

He was wrong. Shankarpa headed into the darkness, the image of his father's face filling him with a furious demand for vengeance.

The guardians of the Vault of Shiva would carry out their duty. To the last man.

* * *

The clatter of stones died away. Khoil cautiously looked
out from behind the statue where Zec had thrown him,
straightening his glasses. The three prisoners had disappeared—but the chest was still in sight outside. The empty
harness reappeared, flapping in the rotor downwash as the
Dhruv returned.

"I—I think it would be best if I went to the helicopter
next," he told Zec. "But have the chest sent up immediately after."

"As you wish," said Zec, concealing his contempt for
his employer's near-panic. "When it's aboard, shall I evacuate the rest of the men?"

"Yes." Khoil hurried to the doors.

The Bosnian followed him. "What about Wilde and
Chase?"

The names made Khoil flare with anger. "Find them and
kill them!" He calmed, rationality regaining control. "If
they are still alive by the time the Vedas are aboard the helicopter, we will evacuate—and use rockets to collapse the
entrance." They reached the chest, and Tandon. "Go inside," he ordered his bodyguard. "I would like you to kill
Dr. Wilde and Mr. Chase."

Tandon smiled and bowed. "It will be my honor."

"We leave in five minutes. Go!"

Tandon ran into the vault. Zec signaled for his men inside to join the hunt. As they scattered, he began to strap
Khoil into the harness.

* * *

Eddie supported Kit as they hurried through the vault, but
the Interpol agent gasped in pain with every step. "I can't
keep going," he said, teeth gritted. "Leave me, find Nina."

"I can't just dump you," Eddie replied. "If we—"

"You have to! I'm slowing you down. Look, in there." He waved a hand at the balloon's palatial gondola. "Hide me inside."

"If someone finds you, you won't stand a chance on your own."

Kit forced a smile. "I can take care of myself. Come on, quick!"

Reluctantly, Eddie guided him into the palace. The Indian took one of the swords from the rack before slumping in a corner. "Now go, go."

"I'll try to decoy them away from you," Eddie promised. He moved back outside, hearing sounds above the constant rumble of the helicopters.

Footsteps—close by. He scurried away from the balloon, moving into cover behind a statue. Peering around it, he saw four mercenaries advancing on his position. He had to draw them away from Kit; despite the policeman's brave words, a sword was no match for a gun.

He looked deeper into the cave, the flickering glow of the braziers revealing a shadowy pathway between the vault's piled treasures. It was narrow, but the other end would, he thought from exploring the great space earlier, join up with one of the broader aisles.

The mercs were getting closer to the balloon. Eddie picked up a bejeweled *vajra* and ran for the passage, tossing the ceremonial weapon. The loud clang caught the mercenaries' attention, as he'd hoped—and they ran after him.

But only three of them. The fourth hesitated, then moved cautiously toward the gondola, MP5K raised.

Eddie swore under his breath but kept running, rounding a corner before his pursuers had a chance to shoot. But he heard gunfire anyway—from deeper in the cavern.

Mahajan and the other mercenaries had found Nina.

* * *

Nina shrieked as bullets shattered a wooden carving just behind her, splinters landing in her hair. She leapt behind a large statue of a cow. The great stone animal shielded her, the gunfire stopping—but she only had a few seconds' respite before the men had her back in their sights.

The giant spiny roller of an *udghatima* lay ahead, her only possible escape routes to either side of it. The one behind the machine was narrower, hemmed in by elaborately carved friezes of dark wood, while the wider route ran alongside an even larger statue, this one of a bull, kneeling on all four legs to form a bovine wall. She raced down the latter path, searching for a way out at the far end—

There wasn't one. The two paths converged beyond the *udghatima,* blocked in by more ornate friezes. She could climb them, but the mercenaries would catch up before she reached the top. An easy target.

Panic rising, she whirled and looked back down the narrower path. No exits or hiding places there either. But there was a large lever protruding from the *udghatima,* holding its mechanism in check for untold centuries...

Mahajan reached the corner first. A malevolent smile crossed his scarred lips as he advanced down the narrow path toward her. The two mercs ran around in front of the *udghatima* to cut her off.

She was trapped.

Unless...

Nina seized the lever and strained to move it. It creaked, long-frozen gears scraping against each other—then coming free with a jolt. The weight dropped, chain lashing in its wake.

The roller turned.

And the entire machine lurched, the small wheels set into its base driving it forward. Mahajan brought up an arm to protect his eyes as a spray of grit and dust flew off the thick metal bars jutting from the stone.

The mercenaries froze, just for a moment, the unexpected motion of the bus-sized siege engine catching them off guard. It was a moment too long. An iron bar smashed down on one man's arm, breaking his wrist with a horrific crack. The other screamed, trying to back away—but was trapped between the *udghatima* and the bull statue. The gap closed—

The screaming stopped, replaced by several wet *thump*s. A crimson splatter encircled the spinning roller. The *udghatima* continued to rumble onward until it struck the statue, the pounding iron bars tearing away chunks of stone.

One of the bull's great horns broke off and fell, demolishing part of the frieze. Nina saw the dancing light from one of the oil channels through the mangled hole in the carvings.

Jagged wood clawing at her coat, she squeezed through the gap. Behind her, Mahajan snarled and ran after her, tearing at the broken frieze with his hands to widen the opening.

* * *

Clutching the sword, Kit heard someone approaching. The light from a nearby brazier cast a glow through the ornate gondola's entrance: a shadow flicked past. The footsteps moved away...

Then slowed. Stopped.

Returned.

The shadow reappeared. Kit held his breath, forcing himself upright on his good leg. The mercenary's curiosity had been piqued—the little parody of a palace would make a good hiding place.

An MP5K poked through the opening. The compact weapon had a second grip beneath its muzzle, the merc's black-gloved left hand holding it tightly. The gun swept the interior, the mercenary about to step inside to complete the search—

Kit stabbed the sword into the back of his hand.

The blade's tip ripped through skin and muscle between the bones. The merc yelled—as Kit twisted it through ninety degrees. The sword forced the bones apart with a crack before popping free in a spurt of blood. The mercenary's howl became an agonized screech.

But he was far from immobilized, lunging into the gondola with the MP5K still held in his other hand. Kit swung the sword again in a desperate attempt to swat it away before he fired.

Ancient and modern weapons collided as the mercenary pulled the trigger. The first bullet scorched a line across Kit's chest, the rest of the burst of fire punching holes in the walls before the final flash of muzzle flame ignited the wood and oil-soaked cloth in the central brazier.

Kit lunged at him. The gun flew across the gondola as both men crashed into a corner. The mercenary snatched out his combat knife, drawing back his arm to plunge it into Kit's chest—

Kit struck first. The sword pierced the merc's body armor and sank deep into his stomach. With a gurgling wail, he staggered and fell . . .

On top of Kit, knocking him down. The explosion of agony through the nerves of the Indian's wounded leg was so great that he almost passed out.

The fire in the brazier flared as little packets of gunpowder among the kindling ignited, angry flames surging. Hot air swirled into the open mouth of the balloon, the fabric rustling . . .

* * *

Eddie threw himself between two large metal statues of Hindu gods, bullets clanging behind him. He had taken a wrong turn, finding himself in a dead end among the war machines and ancient treasures; it only took a few seconds to double back, but that was all the time his three pursuers needed to catch sight of him. Now they were homing in as relentlessly as foxhounds.

He burst out from the far end of the confined space, hopping over the faint licks of flame in an oil channel. A brazier was aflame to one side, the warm light revealing another *udghatima*—and beyond it a siege machine, a twin of one nearer the entrance, that could be the answer to his prayers.

If he could reach it. And if it still worked.

He sprinted for the wooden grid. Behind, the men charged through the narrow passage.

He passed the brazier, the huge stone roller . . .

A shout of "There!" behind him—

Eddie dived, slithering across the stone floor as an MP5K crackled—and yanking a lever on the machine.

It was a *sara-yantra*—an arrow-firer.

A rapid-fire series of *thwack*s rippled through the framework as the firing mechanisms for a hundred arrows were triggered. The missiles hissed down the aisle, a horizontal storm of spiked death that bounced off metal, cracked against stone—and thunked deep into human flesh. The gunfire stopped, replaced by choked screams.

Eddie got up. Not all the ancient weapon's arrows had fired, but he was still more than happy with the end result. Three twitching bodies were sprawled on the floor, so many arrows poking up from them that they looked like porcupines. "Bunch of pricks," he muttered, running to them and scooping up one of their guns.

Now that he was armed, he could find Nina and Kit. But there were still the other mercenaries to worry about, and if he called out to her he would give away his position. Instead, he went back toward the entrance.

◆ ◆ ◆

Nina rushed through the shadows. She had meant to go back to reach Eddie, but was unable to find a route through the tightly packed treasures. All she could do was follow the side wall, heading for the back of the cavern.

And Mahajan was behind her, closing with every giant step.

* * *

Two mercenaries ran out in front of Eddie as he approached the entrance—and took bursts of bullets to their heads, the Englishman aiming above their body armor. He saw the ramp ahead, the open doors beyond it...and Khoil rising from the ledge as he was winched away.

Eddie dropped behind the incline and shot back as a mercenary outside opened fire. Zec sprinted for cover, but the other merc was caught in the open. With a more distant target, Eddie was forced to aim for the center of mass rather than trying to score a lethal head shot, but the impact of the bullets was enough even against armor. The mercenary staggered, slipped on the snow—and fell over the edge. His echoing scream ended abruptly a couple of seconds later.

Eddie ran for the doors. He had spotted the chest, ready to be winched into the chopper. Nina would be mad, but shooting it to bits or flinging it over the edge would be one way to spoil Khoil's plans—

A heel slammed into his back.

Tandon had been lurking behind the ramp, and made a flying leap from its raised end as Eddie ran past. If Eddie hadn't been moving away from the punishing blow, it might have broken his spine. As it was, the impact was still hard enough to knock him down.

He rolled, bringing up the gun—only for Tandon to kick it out of his hand. Cobra-fast, the Indian struck again, his boot scraping Eddie's cheek as the Englishman jerked out of the way.

He grabbed Tandon's ankle, trying to twist it around and trip him, but Tandon threw himself into a somersault, wrenching his foot from Eddie's grasp. He landed perfectly, spinning as the Englishman clumsily got up.

Zec aimed his MP5K at Eddie—but Tandon blocked his line of fire as he lunged, striking at a pressure point on his opponent's chest. Only Eddie's reflexes—and the thick padding of his coat—saved him from the paralyzing punch, which hit a couple of inches off target but still felt like someone taking a hammer to his rib cage. He groaned, reeling.

Tandon spun again to deliver a high kick at Eddie's head. This time, his foot made solid contact. Eddie spat out blood as the other man's heel crunched against his jaw. Dazed, he staggered through the doors. Zec tracked him, but held his fire: His boss's bodyguard wanted his fun.

Another kick, this time plowing into Eddie's stomach. He whooped for breath, almost collapsing—as Tandon struck once more, knuckles stabbing at his throat. Eddie brought up an arm just in time to block the blow, but it was still searingly painful.

A windstorm whirled around him as he stumbled toward the steps, the Dhruv moving into position above to winch up the chest. Any thoughts of sabotage were now forgotten as Eddie raised his fists. Tandon was fast, but if he caught him at just the right moment he could use the brute force of a punch to crush his nose, blinding him with pain, and toss him over the edge. He would still have Zec to worry about, but one problem at a time...

Tandon's hand flashed at Eddie's eyes. He swept up his bruised arm again to deflect the blow, then twisted with all his strength to smash his fist into the other man's face—

The Indian's palm snapped up, stopping the punch an inch short.

Before Eddie could react, another savage kick caught

him in the midsection. Winded, he lurched backward, wobbling at the top of the broken stairway...

With a cruel smile, Tandon darted at him to deliver a final strike. It wasn't a kick, or a punch—insultingly, it was nothing more than a poke to Eddie's chest.

But it was enough to push him down the stairs.

With a yell, Eddie bounced down the stone steps—and flew off the end into the void below.

28

The tiers along the valley sides flashed past as Eddie fell, one, two—

A white line rushed at him. He desperately grasped at his only chance of survival—and jolted to an agonizing stop as he caught one of the ropes stretched across the valley.

The line shook, batting him like a cat toy as he clung with one aching arm—and saw Tandon looking over the edge of the steps above, the expectant satisfaction on his face replaced in quick succession by disbelief, then anger. The Indian shouted to Zec.

He was a sitting duck. He had to reach the valley's side before Zec shot him—

A crack—and he fell again.

The rope had broken!

Only at one end. He was swinging like Tarzan—straight at a cliff face.

Eddie braced himself, but knew he had no chance of surviving the impact. The wind whistled in his ears as he followed his inexorable arc toward the wall. He would hit under the fourth tier, smacking against the carved rock.

But it wasn't rock. An archway loomed, darkness beyond—

The rope caught on the edge of the fourth tier as he whipped beneath it—flicking him upward through the doorway. He sailed across the room, bouncing off the ceiling before falling again...to land with a huge *thump* amid an explosion of something soft.

He choked, grains filling his nostrils and mouth. For a moment the fear of suffocation overcame any other thoughts and he thrashed wildly, coughing and spitting—to find that he had landed on a pile of rice sacks, the supplies secretly provided to the guardians by the villagers around Mount Kedarnath, the impact bursting them.

"Saved by Uncle Ben," he groaned as he achingly stood, rice cascading from him like dried snow, and staggered to the entrance. He would have to climb all the way back to the vault to help Nina and Kit—

Only the fact that he was looking up at the ledge as he emerged kept him alive. Several mercenaries were lined up across the top of the stairway—aiming down at him. Muzzle flashes bloomed like deadly sunflowers. He jumped back from the hailstorm of stone fragments that erupted around the archway.

Shit! He was pinned down, no other way out of the room—and now the MD 500 joined the assault. There was no way he could reach the vault without being cut to pieces...

More shots—but from a new kind of gun. The onslaught stopped, and he heard a scream. A sharp clang of lead against thin aluminum, and the MD 500 hurriedly ascended.

Not a new kind of gun, he realized. A very old one.

The Martini-Henry. The weapons the guardians had taken from the unfortunate British explorers in the nineteenth century were not all rusting relics. Some had been well cared for.

The surviving .577/450-caliber ammo was easily powerful enough to penetrate a helicopter's fuselage. The MD
500 might be acting as a gunship, but it was still a civilian
aircraft, lacking any kind of armor. One good shot could
kill the pilot, sever a hydraulic line, rupture a fuel tank. Retreating was the smart move.

But that still left the Chinook, an ex-military helicopter
with armor where it was needed...

Another scream. Eddie risked a glance outside to see a
mercenary tumble down the steps and plummet to the valley floor. The others had switched their aim to the new
threat—but now they were at a disadvantage. With its
short barrel, the MP5K—designed for compactness and
easy concealment—had a limited effective range and comparatively low power. The Martini-Henrys, on the other
hand, had proved their range, precision, and fearsome
punch in battles throughout the British Empire. He
couldn't see the guardians, but their gunshots told him they
were in positions on both sides of the valley above, a good
fifty yards from the vault's entrance—almost twice the accurate range of the mercenaries' weapons.

Zec had apparently come to the same realization. He
shouted an order, and the mercs pulled back. The MD 500
opened up with its M249, trying to force the guardians to
retreat into the caves.

Eddie steeled himself, then ran out onto the ledge,
searching for a way back up the tiers.

* * *

Nina reached the back of the vault. The statue of Kali
glared down at her in the firelight, blood-red tongue extended mockingly.

Mahajan was right behind her. After what had happened to the two mercenaries, she knew there was no way
she would be able to trick him into range of another siege
engine. Instead she ran down the narrow passage to the

room that had contained the Shiva-Vedas. The goddess's weapons jerked impotently as she tripped the triggers beneath the paving slabs.

She dropped and squirmed under the giant stone foot. Mahajan was already in the passage. There was no light in the chamber—she had to rely entirely on memory to find what she was after...

The iron rod jamming the machinery.

She pulled it—and it caught between the cogs as Mahajan's weight set them in motion. "Shit!" she cried, tugging harder, but still unable to free it. The Indian slithered beneath the foot—

The pressure on the rod was released.

Nina yanked it out—and the mechanism ground into action.

The foot descended. Realizing the danger, Mahajan reacted in fear and crawled faster...

Wrong move. The trap had fooled its victim—and the huge foot dropped like the stone it was, stamping down on Mahajan's back with a terrible snap of crushed bone. Blood spurted across the floor. The final sound from Mahajan's ruined mouth was an anguished gurgle...then he slumped, dead.

After a few seconds, the dripping foot slowly rumbled back up. Nina waited for it to stop, then shoved the rod back into the cogs. "Aw, jeez...," she said, cringing in disgust and nausea at the sight greeting her in the entrance. She pushed Mahajan to one side, then gingerly slipped under the bloody statue to do the same with his other half before hurrying back down the passage.

* * *

Eddie reached the fourth tier, sheltering in an arch as he plotted his ascent. He was cut off from his original route up the valley sides by broken balconies on at least the next two tiers, meaning he would have to climb the carved walls all the way to the sixth level.

Not an ideal plan. Even though they had been forced back by the rifle fire, Zec's men would still be likely to spot him as he ascended and pick him off. But short of making Olympic-length jumps over the gaps, he had no other way to get to the top.

The withering fire from the gunship eased off as the guardians moved into cover. None of the mercenaries were visible on the main ledge—though the Khoils' helicopter was now lowering the harness once more to pick up the chest.

Once they had their prize, they would leave—and destroy everything left behind. He had to act now. He braced himself, ready to rush out and start his climb—

A hand clamped down on his shoulder.

He whirled to smash a fist into his attacker—and stopped just short when he saw it was Shankarpa. The guardian flinched. "Jesus!" Eddie said. "What the hell are you doing?"

"I saw you fall," Shankarpa replied. He was carrying a Martini-Henry and a pouch of ammunition. "I came to find you."

"What about Nina, and Kit? Are they okay?"

"They ran into the vault—I do not know what happened to them."

Eddie looked back up. Someone pulled the dangling harness onto the ledge. "I've got to get up there."

"That is why I came for you." He pointed into the darkness. "There is a tunnel—it will take you to the bridge on the fifth level. It is the fastest way back to the vault. My men will give you cover as you cross."

"So you're helping us now?"

"My father trusted you. But these people, the Khoils—they are enemies of Shiva. They must be stopped. Come, this way."

• • •

Hunched low behind the chest, Zec secured it to the winch line. The guardians were still directing intermittent shots at the ledge, but the suppressing fire from the MD 500 was holding them off. How long that would restrain them when they realized their treasure was being airlifted away he didn't know, or care to find out. He fastened the last clasp, then spoke into his headset. "Take it up!"

The line tightened and the chest rose from the ledge, suspended in the web of netting and straps. As soon as it was airborne, the Dhruv sideslipped away from the cliff face so the chest could be winched up without fear of its swinging into the rock.

Zec ran back to the doors, another helicopter on his mind. "Chinook to recovery position!" he ordered. "We're evacuating. Ready rocket launchers!"

• • •

Kit tried to push the dead mercenary away, feeling another blinding burst of pain as the corpse's limp arm bashed his wound. For all the effort and agony, he only managed to move him a short way; the sword poking from the man's belly had wedged against the gondola's wall. Cursing, he tried to wriggle out from under the body—

The floor lurched.

For a moment he thought it was an earthquake. But then he heard a metallic scraping beneath him—and realized the gondola itself was moving.

He looked up, seeing to his shock that the hot air from the furiously blazing fire in the brazier had partly inflated the balloon. No longer a flaccid bundle of fabric, it had swollen enormously, reaching the roof of the cavern.

The gondola jolted again, harder. Kit grimaced at another bolt of pain in his leg. The balloon's envelope was taller than the vault, meant to be inflated in the open.

Trapped against the rocky ceiling, heat was building up too fast. Sparks and cinders swirled in the updraft as the fabric began to burn.

He kicked with his good leg, finally dislodging the dead man. He pulled himself upright—then fell again as the balloon left the ground, the flying palace swaying beneath it.

* * *

Nina was making her way back to the entrance, keeping to the shadows, when she heard loud noises to one side. Someone starting up one of the war machines? There was no reason for the mercenaries to do so—maybe Kit was still alive.

She climbed onto the plinth of a statue for a better view—and was startled by the sight of the great bloated grub of the balloon squirming against the ceiling. A fierce fire burned inside the elaborate little palace.

A fire that was spreading to the rest of the balloon. Glowing patches of light flickered inside the silken outer shroud . . . getting larger as she watched.

If the balloon ruptured, the burning fabric would land on top of the gondola—and Kit.

No longer concerned with stealth, she ran through the cavern to help him.

* * *

Shankarpa brought Eddie to the end of the steep, narrow tunnel, the other side of the valley visible through an archway. Eddie looked out. The rope bridge was off to one side. To his dismay, someone aboard the red-and-white helicopter was pulling the chest into the cabin. "Shit, they've got the box!"

Dark anger crossed Shankarpa's face. "They will pay," he said, opening the old rifle's breech and loading a round. He took aim at the Dhruv—then both men flinched back from the hurricane of snow and grit as the Chinook descended. The big helicopter slowly backed toward the giant statue, lines dangling from its open rear ramp.

Shankarpa fired at the Chinook. The boom from the old gun was painful in the confined space, but the only result for all the sound and fury was a clang as the round struck armor. The MD 500 had pulled away to let the larger chopper into the valley, but its gunner was still watching for telltale bursts of smoke from the rifles—a rattle of fire shattered the stonework outside the arch.

"I need you to keep that gunship busy," said Eddie. "If it catches me while I'm crossing the bridge, I'm fucked!"

"There is another tunnel that will take me to the other guardians. I will tell them to cover you as you cross."

"How long will it take you to get there?"

"Two minutes."

Eddie glanced out. The Chinook was moving into a hover—much lower than the Khoils' helicopter, the whumping blades of its rear rotor actually beneath the overhanging rock, tips less than ten feet from the statue of Shiva. The pilots were trying to get the rear ramp as close as possible to the ledge so the mercenaries could jump in rather than having to ascend the ropes. "I don't have that long. Go—get there as quick as you can."

Shankarpa started for the tunnel. "What are you going to do?"

Eddie looked back at him. "Run like buggery!"

* * *

The downwash from the Chinook's rear rotor blasted through the vault, sweeping up the dust of centuries in a blinding swirl. Nina squinted as the gritty storm stung her eyes.

The wind caught the balloon, setting the palatial gondola swinging like a pendulum. She expected it to be blown farther back into the great cave, but the combination of the gondola's gyrations and air currents gusting around the cavern's ragged natural roof instead sent it spinning toward the entrance.

Fire burst through the balloon's skin. Either there was a hot spot above the brazier or the material had torn on the ceiling, but it didn't matter—a rush of escaping air sent a huge spray of embers across the vault, falling like glowing snowflakes. Nina hurriedly pulled up her hood as they dropped around her, scorching her parka.

Rapidly losing height, the gondola hit a siege engine near the launch ramp. She glimpsed Kit as he bailed—or was flung—out the door; then the whole thing crashed to the floor, knocking over the brazier she had originally lit.

The balloon itself was being consumed with frightening speed, large parts already reduced to ash and motes of hell-fire. The air filled with smoke. Coughing, Nina weaved through the flames, hoping Kit hadn't already been swallowed by them.

* * *

Eddie looked out at the Chinook. It was hovering precariously with its rear ramp just above the lip of the ledge. He spotted Zec crouching low, waving his men into the helicopter.

He couldn't wait for covering fire. He was out of time—the mercs would soon be gone, firing their parting shots to destroy the vault.

And Nina.

He ran to the rope bridge, arms outstretched for balance as he traversed the planks two at a time. Still no booms from the Martini-Henrys. He looked for the MD 500—

The men aboard saw him, the little helicopter pivoting to bring the M249 to bear.

Laser-lines of tracer fire seared past him as he ran.

* * *

Zec heard the gunfire and glanced down the valley to see the MD 500 unleashing a barrage at a figure running across one of the rope bridges.

Chase! The Englishman was certainly a survivor, he admitted with grudging admiration. But his luck had surely run out—the gunship could use the tracers to "walk" its fire onto its target. One hit, and he would fall to his death—if the onslaught didn't destroy the entire bridge under him.

But he couldn't spare the time to watch. The last five men were jumping onto the ramp, others inside pulling them into the hold. Behind them was Tandon, but he wasn't moving to board. "Get inside!" Zec ordered.

"We have to wait for Dhiren," Tandon insisted.

"There's no time! We need to—"

Two sounds hit him simultaneously. The first was a salvo of booms from the guardians' rifles as they opened fire on the MD 500—and the second was an explosion inside the vault.

• • •

A few seconds earlier, Nina had found Kit, curled in agony as he clutched his injured leg. She dragged him away from the burning swaths of fabric draped over the treasures around him—

The next instant, they were knocked down by an explosion.

The rockets!

Stacked behind the *vimana*'s launch ramp, the burning debris scattered from the brazier had set them alight.

A second rocket detonated—then a third shot upward, slamming into the ceiling and bursting apart like a bomb.

"Jesus!" Nina cried, pulling Kit under a statue as sparks rained down. Another rocket flew past, streaking toward the rear of the cavern like an enormous firework.

* * *

Eddie had no idea what was happening as he heard what sounded like explosives going off in the vault—all he knew was that the guardians had saved him from being torn apart by the MD 500's machine gun. At least two shots had hit the gunship, which was now hurriedly ascending.

He jumped over a bullet-riddled plank and continued across the bridge. Halfway there, but he still had to go up another two levels...

* * *

Zec grabbed Tandon. "Get aboard, now!" He pulled the Indian toward the Chinook's gaping maw—

Something black shot at them on a trail of flame.

* * *

The explosion of the first rocket had flung the others in all directions. One landed between the two high walls of the launch ramp, blunt nose pointing toward the open doors... and its fuse sparking and sizzling.

The fire reached the rocket's tail—

It blasted off with a sizzling *whoosh,* the stonework on each side channeling it straight ahead. It shot through the entrance, searing past Zec and Tandon as they dived out of its way—and flew into the Chinook's hold.

One mercenary was set aflame as it passed, another almost decapitated by the cylinder as it smacked into his head. The blow deflected it upward to hit the ceiling—and ricochet down again.

Into the cockpit.

It slammed into the central instrument console, flicking around madly and blasting fire into the pilots' faces. They screamed, flailing blindly in unbearable pain—and let go of the controls.

The Chinook rolled violently, slewing away from the

ledge. The burning mercenary fell from the rear hatch; other men dashed against the cabin's unyielding metal wall. Zec and Tandon hurled themselves flat as the rotor blades scythed above them.

The backwash of fire burned through the rocket's silk-wrapped body—and it exploded, blowing out the cockpit windows. Pilots dead, controls smashed, the helicopter barreled down the valley in a death-roll—

Straight at the rope bridge.

* * *

Eddie was three-quarters of the way across, coming up fast on the plank that had broken under him on the first crossing, when he heard another explosion, nearer but oddly muffled. He looked around for its cause—

"Oh, *fuck*," he gasped.

The Chinook, smoke pouring from its shattered cockpit, rushed toward him.

He ran, not caring anymore if the planks could take his weight. All he cared about now was staying ahead of the deadly blur of the front rotor, the blades a giant circular saw carving through the air ...

29

Eddie dived as the rotor slashed through the bridge less than a foot behind him.

The severed ropes cracked like whips as their tension was released. The Chinook roared past, sucking a blizzard of loose snow into its rotors. The storm almost blinded him as he grabbed a plank with one hand, swinging with the collapsing bridge. The wall rushed at him through the whirling snow—

His other hand found a rope just as the bridge crashed against the valley side. The plank he was holding snapped, leaving him dangling by only his straining arm, swaying on the line like a human plumb bob. Chunks of smashed wood tumbled past.

A colossal boom shook the valley as the Chinook slammed into the cliff at its end and exploded. Boulders and burning wreckage tumbled down to block the passage beneath a huge cloud of dust and snow and black smoke.

Eddie struggled to find a new handhold. He managed to reach an intact plank above, only to wince as a splinter stabbed into his middle finger. He pulled himself up. The remains of the bridge had turned into a fractured ladder.

Some of the planks—now rungs—were broken, others missing entirely, but there were enough left intact for him to reach the fifth tier.

Holding the rope tightly, he pulled the inch-long splinter out from his finger with his teeth, then began his ascent.

* * *

From the Dhruv, Khoil gawped at the Chinook's blazing wreck. "What happened?" he demanded into his headset. "Zec, what happened?"

It took several seconds before the Bosnian managed a reply. "A rocket—I don't know where it came from. All my men are dead!"

"What about Chapal and Dhiren?"

"Your man Tandon is here with me. The other—" He broke off at the sound of another explosion in the cavern. "The other one, I don't know. He's probably dead."

"Pramesh, we have the Vedas," said Vanita. She tapped the chest, now safely stowed in the cabin. "Let's just go."

"Chapal is still down there—and I want to be sure Chase and Dr. Wilde are dead," he replied firmly. "Pilot, move back to the cliff. Tell the gunship to cover us." The Dhruv turned and headed back for the vault.

* * *

Eddie reached the top of the makeshift ladder, seeing footprints in the snow where the group had walked along the tier earlier in the day. More snow billowed past as the Khoils' helicopter moved overhead, lowering the harness.

* * *

Nina poked her head out from beneath the statue. Most of the rockets had fired or exploded, the remainder duds, the gunpowder in them broken down by time as Eddie had predicted.

They weren't out of danger, though. The explosions had

stopped, but fires were still burning, the vault filling with smoke. Most of its treasures would be unharmed beyond being blackened by soot, but there was still enough wood and fabric to keep the flames alive for some time. "Can you move?" she asked Kit.

"I think I will have to," he said, suppressing a cough as gray wisps coiled around him.

She helped him up. Together, they picked their way through the fires to the entrance.

They gave the area behind the ramp a wide berth in case a rocket went off—but then stopped as they saw two figures outside. "Dammit," Nina muttered, recognizing Tandon. "We can't go out there—they'll kill us." She looked for anything that might help, spotting something near the overturned gondola. "Wait here," she said, propping Kit against a frieze. "I'll be right back."

* * *

The winch line descended above Zec. "You go up first," Tandon told him. "Dhiren might still come. And if Wilde and Jindal are still alive, I want to be sure that they do not stay that way."

Zec nodded, watching the harness's descent—then movement caught his eye, someone running along a tier below. He almost laughed. "Chase! He must have woken up *very* early this morning."

Tandon was not familiar with the Bosnian proverb, but he understood its meaning. "His luck has run out. Give me your gun."

Zec unslung his MP5K and handed it to the Indian. "Here," he said as he reached for the harness. "Wait until he is closer. Then we'll see how awake he really is."

* * *

Eddie reached the next flight of steps and pounded up them to the seventh tier. He saw two men at the top of the broken stairway: Zec and Tandon, preparing to be winched up to the helicopter...

Tandon was aiming an MP5K.

The nearest archway was behind him. Eddie skidded on the snow, turning to retreat—

• • •

Tandon fired as the Englishman stumbled, trying to back up and reach cover. Even with the MP5K's short effective range, he could still hose the tier with automatic fire—

Another MP5K barked... *inside* the vault. Two shots hissed past him—but a third hit his bicep, tearing out a ragged lump of flesh. Tandon roared, dropping the submachine gun, which cartwheeled down the steps to fall to the valley floor.

Zec had just fastened the harness. He spun to see Nina emerge from the vault, holding the gun of the mercenary Kit had killed. That she had only scored a glancing hit from relatively close range told him all he needed to know about her shooting skills—and he gambled that unlike her husband, she didn't possess a true killer instinct.

"Bring me up *now*!" he shouted into the headset. "Tandon, grab me!"

Even with a gunshot wound, Tandon was quick to react. As Zec was hauled off the ledge, he leapt up and clamped a hand around the Bosnian's wrist. They swung out over the valley, the helicopter pilot immediately increasing power and banking away from the cliff.

Nina ran out on to the ledge, aiming at the two hanging men—but couldn't bring herself to fire again. Both were unarmed, one was injured, and killing them would have no effect whatsoever on the Khoils' plan. She knew that Eddie would have fired anyway, but it wasn't something she could do. All she *could* do was hiss "Son of a bitch!" as the pair were carried aloft.

Who had Tandon been shooting at? She looked across at

the neighboring tier, seeing nobody—then a familiar head cautiously peered out from an archway. Joy and relief filled her. "Eddie!"

He waved at her, then ran along the tier to leap over the gap onto the stairway. "Ay up, love!"

She kissed him. "Oh, God! I thought you might be dead!"

"It'll take more than this bunch of tossers. And Shankarpa and his boys helped. What about Kit?"

"He's okay—he's inside. But we need to get him out of there—the place is filling with smoke."

"Yeah, I can see that." A dark cloud was billowing out from the top of the doorway. "Okay, let's get him, then—"

A rising noise made them both turn. The gunship was approaching. As they watched, the M249 was drawn inside—to be replaced by another weapon.

An RPG-7 rocket launcher.

◆ ◆ ◆

Aboard the Dhruv, the winch operator pulled Tandon into the cabin. Zec followed, rapidly releasing the harness and slamming the hatch. "Wilde and Chase are still alive," he reported.

"Not for long," Vanita snarled. "Gunship! Destroy the vault! Kill them, now!"

◆ ◆ ◆

Kit limped out of the vault—only to be scooped up by Eddie and Nina as they ran back inside. "What's happening?"

"Nothing good, as bloody usual!" Eddie told him. "Nina, give me the gun." He took the MP5K as they deposited Kit behind the shelter of one of the great stone doors. The MD 500 had turned to face them, the gunner leaning out to aim the tubular Russian weapon along the aircraft's length; the backblast from the rocket would be devastating inside the cockpit.

Eddie fired first, aiming high to compensate for his gun's lack of range. The bullets arced down to strike the approaching chopper's canopy. It cracked, some of the shots piercing the Plexiglas, but they didn't have enough power behind them to cause any major damage.

The same wasn't true of the RPG-7. Smoke burst from the launcher, the dark dot of the rocket racing at the ledge—

Eddie dived back behind the door as it exploded, stone shards slashing past him. The gunship had veered just as the rocket fired, the pilot startled by the bullet hits, and the warhead struck short of the vault's entrance.

But it still caused plenty of damage. With a thunderous crack, the stub of the stairway toppled into the abyss, a swath of the ledge following it.

Eddie looked outside. "Buggeration and fuckery!"

"My favorite words," groaned Nina, joining him. "What—oh..."

It was as if a giant had taken a great bite out of the ledge. A section covering more than half its width was gone, the remains of the stairway now in fragments far below.

And with the stairs gone, there was no way to reach the tiers on the valley walls. The gap was now well over thirty feet: impossible to jump even for the greatest Olympian.

The helicopter withdrew, the gunner pulling the rocket launcher back inside to reload it. Eddie checked his gun. Only three rounds left. He would need a great deal of luck to hit anybody aboard the MD 500—and with the pilot now knowing he was armed, the next rocket would be fired from a safer distance. The RPG-7 had a range of almost a third of a mile. "You didn't find any other way out, did you?"

Nina shook her head unhappily. "What if we found some ropes and climbed down?"

"It'll take too long. We need a faster way..." He trailed off.

"Oh, no," she said firmly as she saw his gaze fall upon the *vimana* at the top of the ramp. "No way. We are *not* flying out of here on a goddamn ancient glider!"

"We know it works," said Eddie, lifting Kit and hustling him toward the ramp. "That Atlantean bloke of yours said it got those priests back down the mountain."

"That was eleven thousand years ago!" she protested.

"Well, maybe this one's not that old."

"It's old enough! And you don't know how to fly it."

"I've flown a glider," Eddie insisted as he started up the ramp. "Well, that one time. Kit, you'll have to hop to it, literally."

"Just so you know, I am agreeing with Nina," said Kit, wincing with each step. "I don't think this thing is safe."

"Neither's being hit by a fucking RPG!"

"Bad idea," Nina muttered as she hurried up the other side of the ramp. "Very, very bad idea."

"You were impressed by it before," said Eddie, reaching the *vimana*. He half helped, half pushed the unconvinced Indian onto the slatted platform under the wing, then examined the rocket.

"As an archaeological find, it's world shaking. As a plane, it's more likely to be bone breaking!"

"Those other machines still worked—maybe they built this to last as well. Give me those matches, then get aboard." He tweaked the end of the fuse as Nina produced the matches. "Okay, light the blue touchpaper and... hang on tight, I suppose."

Nina lay down beside Kit. Leather straps hung from the wing's wooden spars; she guessed they were meant to hold the passengers in place, but there wasn't time to tie them—all she could do was wrap two around her wrists and grip them as tightly as she could, wedging her feet against the framework. The ramp dropped away before her, the ski jump at its end seeming laughably inadequate to get them airborne. "Oh, crap, what are we *doing* ..."

Eddie struck the match and touched it to the fuse. It flared with a hiss, spitting sparks. "Houston, we are go for launch!" he cried, scrambling between Nina and Kit and yanking the cords to pull out the chocks from the *vimana*'s runners.

With a grating screech of corroded metal on stone, the glider lurched a few inches down the ramp—then stopped.

"Okay, that didn't work like I hoped," said Eddie, grimacing. He grabbed what he hoped were the control rods, looking back to see the fizzing fuse almost fully burned away. "Shake us loose before it fires!"

They jerked at the frame. The runners squealed, shifting slightly. "Harder, harder!" said Nina. "This is one time I *really* don't want to be stuck on the runway!"

One final combined push—

The rocket fired—just as the glider jolted free.

The flecks of corrosion spitting from the metal were replaced by a shower of sparks as the flying machine screeched down the ramp. Before they knew it, they were at the bottom, g-force pressing them down against the slats as the glider hurtled up the ski jump ...

And took off.

All three passengers screamed as the *vimana* cleared the doors, the broken edge of the ledge rushing past beneath them. The screams got louder as something else shot below—another RPG round. It hit the ramp and exploded in a shower of shattered stone. One side of the structure collapsed, crushing several of the parked gliders.

Their own glider was of more concern, however. The rocket was pushing it forward, but it was no longer gaining height—it had reached the top of its parabolic trajectory and was arcing inexorably downward. The wooden wings creaked frighteningly. Eddie pushed the controls forward, hoping the *vimana* would respond like a hang glider and level out, but it only steepened their descent.

Nina glimpsed Shankarpa and the other surviving guardians watching in wonder as they flashed past—then they disappeared from sight as the glider dropped below the uppermost tiers. "Up would be good. Up, up, *up*!"

"I'm bloody trying!" Eddie shouted. If pushing forward made them go down, maybe pulling back would do the opposite...

He hauled at the wooden levers. More alarming creaks came from the wings, the fabric rippling and flapping. But it seemed to be working—the *vimana*'s nose began to tip upward—

"Eddie, look out!" cried Kit. The MD 500 came into view directly ahead, descending toward them.

"Whoa, shit!" Not having a clue how to steer, he jammed the controls sideways in the hope it would bank the glider. It worked—the *vimana* veered left.

But now it was heading for the valley wall, the carvings on the tiers reaching out to snatch at its fragile wingtip—

He yanked the controls back the other way, pulling them to gain height. The *vimana* was buffeted violently in the downdraft as they passed the gunship. The rocket was still burning, thrusting them along the valley with ever-increasing speed.

Toward the cliff at its end.

A column of oily smoke roiled from the wrecked Chinook, but it couldn't mask the great wall of gray stone rising ahead. "Whatever you did to make us go up," Nina said fearfully, "do it more!"

Eddie strained to pull back the controls. Pops and cracks came from the overstressed wood. The snow-covered cliff top came into view as the *vimana* climbed, but the glider was losing speed, even the rocket's power not enough to overcome the weight of three people. "Come on, you bugger," he gasped. If they didn't increase their angle of climb, they would crash into the rock wall just short of the summit. "Come on, come on, fucking *come on*!"

The wings crackled, fabric stretched to tearing point—but they weren't going to make it...

Nina screamed as they hit—and kept going, bursting through the thick snowdrift atop the cliff. She spat out snow. "Jesus *Christ,* Eddie!"

"I wasn't worried," he lied. They flew over the pass through the ridge, an updraft raising them higher. Mount Kedarnath rolled vertiginously before them. With the weather far clearer than on the previous two days, they could see all the way to the distant lowland plains. "Look at that!" he whooped, laughing. "We did it, we got out of there! *Yes!*" He took one hand off the controls for a moment to pump his fist. "So my hearing's a bit knackered—so what? I don't need ears to kick arse!"

"That you don't," Nina told him, managing a quick smile.

"Without wanting to sound negative," said Kit, who had only just opened his eyes to take in the landscape wheeling below, "we are not exactly home and dry yet."

Eddie gestured to the southwest. "We're not far off, though. We can fly this thing back to Kedarnath. Maybe even all the way to Gaurikund!"

"Just like the priests of Shiva," said Nina. "This is incredible! Terrifying, but incredible."

Kit was more pragmatic. "You can fly it... but can you land it?"

"Find out soon, eh?" Eddie said, turning southwest.

The rocket popped and fizzed, then burned out. Nina looked back to make sure nothing was on fire—and saw they hadn't escaped all the threats in the lost valley. "Eddie! The chopper's coming after us!"

The MD 500 had turned to follow its unexpected prey,

accelerating after the *vimana*. The gunner withdrew the rocket launcher, the M249 returning in its place.

"Bollocks!" Eddie hissed. Even if the gunship didn't shoot them out of the sky, it could simply follow until they landed and pick them off from the air—or even force them to crash by flying overhead and using the rotor downwash as a weapon. He had to lose the helicopter if they were to have any chance of survival—but how?

The view ahead gave him an answer. He banked the *vimana* back toward the towering mountain.

"What are you doing?" Nina asked, anxiety rising as the peak filled her view.

"I've got a plan."

"Is it a good one?"

"Probably not—but it's all I've got!" He glanced back. The chopper was about five hundred yards behind, and closing. "Tell me when he points the gun at us."

Nina looked over her shoulder as Eddie's attention returned to the looming mountain. While the sky was mostly clear, the ever-changing weather of the Himalayas had formed bands of clouds around Mount Kedarnath. One in particular had caught his eye. He banked toward it.

The wings shook as another gusting updraft caught them. But even though they were climbing, they were still getting closer to the ground every second as it rose up steeply before them.

"Eddie, gun!" Nina warned. He shoved the controls sideways, banking the *vimana* to the left. Tracer bullets whipped past on their right. He swung back in that direction before the next burst was unleashed, the bullets this time passing to the left.

Nearer than before. He pulled the rods back to gain more height, heading for the wedge of cloud jutting from the mountainside. Another cry from Nina and he banked hard right as more shots seared past, getting closer and closer as the gunner tracked the glider—

Flat *whaps* from the wing as bullets ripped through it were followed by a terrifying crack of wood: a support spar had been hit. The *vimana* lurched, veering left as it lost lift on that side. Eddie forced the control levers over even harder to compensate. They were now almost beneath the cloud, a great gray mass tilting upward from the mountainside...

A flag cloud. The harbinger of a storm.

And they were heading right into it.

30

Hold together," Eddie begged the ancient flying machine as the creaks from the wounded wing grew louder.

"They're firing!" Nina wailed. More tracers streaked at them, bullets smacking against rock just ahead of the glider—

A huge surge of wind suddenly seized the *vimana* and propelled it up the cliff with a terrifying rush of speed. Gale-force air currents were sweeping upward, giving the flag cloud its distinctive appearance—and carrying them into its heart.

Visibility dropped to nothing as the screaming wind battered them. All Eddie could do was hope he was pulling the controls hard enough to keep the glider from plowing into the mountain.

The cracks from the wing were joined by an almost explosive bang as another spar gave way. The *vimana* was disintegrating—

They burst out of the flag cloud—almost close enough to reach out and touch the cliff as it blurred past. Eddie forced the glider into a steeply banking turn away from the rock face. They were losing speed even with the boost of the wind from below, threatening to stall...

A shriek of engines and whirling blades—and the MD 500 blasted out of the cloudbank after them.

It too had been swept upward by the wind, but while the *vimana*'s wings had carried it practically parallel to the steep cliff, the helicopter had emerged too close to the unforgiving rock—

Its rotors smashed into the mountainside and shattered. Instantly losing all lift, the fuselage hit the cliff face. The gunner, leaning out to find his quarry, was smeared up the rock in a long red line. Tumbling, breaking apart, the MD 500 blew to pieces, streaks of liquid flame raining back down into the storm cloud below.

One danger gone—but they were still in the grip of another. The wind howled past the *vimana*, the torn wing flapping angrily. Eddie hooked one foot over Kit's ankle to help hold him in place as he aimed the glider back down the mountain. "Okay! Let's hope this thing doesn't fall apart!" he shouted as he leveled out.

Nina looked ahead. Past the cloud, she made out the village nestling at the head of the valley. "How far is it?"

"About three miles—but I'm going to get as far down the valley as I can—ah!" The *vimana* dropped sharply, emerging from the gusty updraft into calmer air.

"You, uh, might have to rethink that," said Nina.

"After everything we've just been through, I'm not going to die in a sodding plane crash." He yanked back the levers. "Maybe we can catch an air current."

"Or we could just, y'know, *land*," she countered.

"We just need a bit more height, then we can fly right down the valley."

"The valley that was full of boulders and rivers and other things we don't want to hit?"

"Picky, picky!"

"I'm in favor of the 'landing immediately' plan," Kit piped up.

"And walk all that way on one leg?"

"Better than on no legs!"

The wind picked up as they drew closer to the valley. Eddie raised the *vimana*'s nose; it slowly began to climb. "See? I know what I'm doing—I'm not just a pretty face!"

"God, I hope you're right," said Nina.

He huffed. "Name one time when I've been wrong."

"When you went to Switzerland to rescue Sophia and accidentally ended up helping her steal an atomic bomb?"

"Yeah, I thought that might come up," he muttered, nudging Kit. "See, this is the problem with getting married. Wives remember every bloody little thing..."

"I'll remember that if I *live* to get married," Kit replied.

Eddie grinned, then turned his full attention to the delicate balancing act of keeping the glider in the air. He had to trade airspeed against altitude, risking a stall every time he climbed.

The village drifted past below, the winding line of the river heading down the valley. He made a gentle turn to follow it. "See? This is better than walking."

"We've still got eight miles to go," Nina reminded him. "And we're getting lower."

"So's the valley."

"We're going down faster."

"Thought you liked it when I go down fast?"

"Eddie!"

"We'll make it," he assured her.

But they had already lost almost half their initial height. Eddie angled upward, the wind's whistle dying away as they slowed. There was a roller-coaster feeling of weightlessness as he leveled off, then they began to drop again.

More quickly than before. A faint hiss of tearing fabric came from the damaged wing, and the *vimana* listed. Eddie quickly compensated, but it took more effort than before. "Okay, maybe only some of the way."

Nina searched for potential landing sites. They were past the relatively easy upland approach to the village, floating above rugged slopes through which the river had cut a gorge. "How long have we got?"

"I dunno—two miles. If we're lucky."

"Okay, okay," said Nina, forcing herself not to panic. "Keep over to the right, away from the river." She squinted into the distance, seeing dark shapes taking on dimensionality against the snowscape. They were down to an altitude that could support more varied plant life than tough grass. "Eddie, those bushes—if we fly into them, they'll cushion our landing."

"Hopefully," he replied. If they were moving too fast, they would tear straight through them—pitching the *vimana*'s passengers into the gorge. "Hold tight!"

They flew down the valley, the rough ground undulating beneath them—but drawing inexorably closer. The bushes were spattered across the valley floor like specks from a paintbrush. Eddie found a fairly dense patch, and judged the distance to it. If he pulled up almost into a stall, then descended sharply, it should catch them before they built back up to a dangerous speed.

Should being the operative word.

He made a final course adjustment. "Okay, here we go."

Kit regarded the approaching vegetation with an increasingly unhappy expression. "What if it doesn't stop us?"

"Then we'll find out which religion's right! Ready, ready ...*hang on*!"

He hauled the controls back as hard as he could. The *vimana* pitched up sharply, the wood groaning. They were gaining height, but slowing, slowing...

"Now!" He shoved the wooden levers forward. The nose dipped—

Too late. They had lost too much speed—and stalled, the *vimana* plunging almost vertically. "Oh, shit, *shit*!"

He yanked desperately at the controls. Something in the wing snapped. The ground rushed at them—

With a *whump*, the fabric of the wings filled with air and pulled taut one last time. The *vimana* shot forward like a daredevil bird swooping out of a dive just short of the ground. Nina shrieked and shielded her eyes as it crashed through the bushes in a burst of snow, stubby branches whipping at her face.

But they didn't stop.

The *vimana* ripped the bushes right out of the ground. For a moment it seemed that it was going to take off again—then with a huge crack the wings finally collapsed, broken spars and shredded silk trailing behind the glider as it crashed down on its runners.

And still it kept going. It had turned from an aircraft into a sledge, slithering downhill at an ever-increasing pace.

Nina hurriedly unwound her wrists from the leather straps as she saw what lay directly ahead. "We're gonna go into the river!"

"Everybody off!" said Eddie.

"What do we do?" Kit asked, eyes wide as he saw the rapidly approaching gorge.

"Just jump!" Eddie grabbed him and leapt from the back of the platform. Nina followed. Human snowplows, they bounced and skittered down the hill after their former ride. Despite Eddie's best efforts, he lost his grip on Kit. The two men separated, skidding along on their backs.

Nina, the lightest, was the first to be slowed by the mass of snow she had collected in front of her. Dazed, she lifted her head to see two white fountains continuing past. "Eddie!" she shouted as the broken *vimana* sailed over the edge of the gorge and smashed on the rocks below.

Eddie had also witnessed the glider's sudden disappearance. He spread his arms and legs wide for extra drag, digging his heels down through the snow.

He felt his soles tearing small stones from the iron-hard ground—then nothing...

It took a moment for him to realize he had stopped. He shook snow from his face, then cautiously sat up. Both legs were dangling over the edge of the gorge. Fifty feet below, the *vimana*'s remains were being swept away by the river.

He dragged himself back to solid ground. Nina staggered down the slope, while Kit lay to one side, having stopped barely a foot short of the gorge. "Everyone okay?" Eddie groaned.

Kit weakly cradled his left wrist. "My arm..."

Eddie examined it. It didn't seem broken, but he guessed it was badly sprained. Using his belt as a makeshift sling, he and Nina helped Kit stand. "We're about four miles from Gaurikund," he said, remembering the lay of the land from their ascent. "You think you can make it?"

Kit managed a feeble smile. "Well, it's downhill, at least."

"You'll be fine. You got him, Nina?"

She supported him from the other side. "Got him. Ready, Kit?"

"I'm ready." They started down the hill. "So...this is archaeology?"

"Yeah. Ain't it great?" Nina said sarcastically. "Just when you think things couldn't possibly get any worse, they do."

A rumbling chatter echoed down the valley. "Like now," said Eddie. The Khoils' red-and-white helicopter was visible in the distance—heading toward them.

"Oh, *man*!" Nina protested. "Why can't they just leave us alone?"

"Those bushes," Eddie said, pointing to a patch of snow-laden shrubs nearby. They hustled Kit over and crouched behind them, watching anxiously as the helicopter drew steadily closer. Had its occupants tracked the *vimana* as it made its descent—and was Zec now preparing to shoot the survivors? It kept coming, passing almost directly overhead...

And continued southward.

"They must be going back to Delhi," said Nina, watching it shrink into the distance.

"Great," Eddie said. "They'll be there in an hour, and we'll be lucky to reach Gaurikund by nightfall. Maybe we should have thumbed a lift with them."

Kit shook his head. "Even I would prefer to walk."

Eddie and Nina both smiled, then with Kit between them began the long trek back down the valley.

* * *

Eddie's estimate was accurate: It was dusk by the time they finally reached Gaurikund. First aid was quickly arranged for Kit, but his priority was phoning Interpol headquarters in Delhi. Unfortunately, the news he got after reporting events was bad—the Khoils had already left India aboard their private jet.

A helicopter was quickly arranged to fly the exhausted trio to the capital. After being debriefed at Interpol, Kit was taken away to have his wounds treated. Eddie and Nina also gave statements before their injuries, less serious, were checked by a doctor, but after that were left alone in a conference room, with nothing to do but wait as the bureaucratic machine ground into motion.

"You okay?" Nina asked, resting her head on her husband's shoulder. A muted television mounted high in one corner was showing CNN, images of President Cole's visit to Japan in the lead-up to the G20 summit flashing past.

Eddie fingered the bandage covering the cut he had received from the statue of Kali. "Still got all my important bits, so okay. You?"

"Fine. More or less. I was thinking about Girilal. He didn't deserve to die like that."

"He didn't deserve to die, full stop. He saved our lives, though. Twice. That's got to be good for his karma."

"I just hope his beliefs helped him at the end," said Nina morosely. "But at least he got to see his son again, and they settled some of their differences."

Eddie gave her a sharp look. "Meaning what?"

"Meaning... what it sounds like." It took her a moment to realize what he was saying. "You know, if you don't want to speak to your father that's up to you, but it doesn't mean everyone's pushing you to do it."

"Yeah, yeah, okay. Sorry." He changed the subject. "Don't know about the karma of Shankarpa and the others, though. They might have ended up on our side, but they still tried to kill us. And Christ knows how many other people they knocked off before then."

"The Indian government'll have to decide what to do with them, I guess. But at least the vault survived fairly intact. That makes a change for us."

"The Khoils still bagged those stone tablets, though," he reminded her. "So whatever it is they want to do, they're free to do it."

"Bring about the collapse of civilization, Pramesh told me. So that he can oversee the rebuilding on his terms— and push his particular apocalyptic brand of Shiva worship on everyone."

Eddie made an amused sound. "He seemed pretty upset when Girilal basically said he was being a huge arsehole."

"Pramesh is a true believer—having a holy man tell you that Shiva would be ashamed of what you're planning to do must be hard on the ego. But what *are* they planning to do? He said it involved manipulating information, but it'd need a catalyst, something that would make lots of people want answers—answers that could be twisted to enrage them..." She looked up at the TV. The piece about Cole's

Japanese visit was wrapping up, a graphic showing that the final leg of his international tour would bring him to Delhi. "It's got to be the summit. It'd explain why they were so desperate to get the Shiva-Vedas—they had a deadline. And if you want to start global chaos, killing a group of world leaders would be about as good a catalyst as you could get."

"But how would they get past all the security?" Eddie asked.

"I don't know, God damn it!" He raised an eyebrow at her snappish reply. "Sorry, I'm sorry." She let out a frustrated breath. "I'm just pissed they got away. And we've got no idea where they've gone."

"Actually, we do." They looked around to see Kit, his sprained arm in a sling, limp into the room on a crutch. Behind him were Mac, who smiled broadly on seeing the couple, and another man, thin-faced with a drooping mustache, who appeared considerably less pleased at the sight of them—or of Eddie, at least.

"Kit!" Nina cried, jumping up. "Are you okay?"

"The doctor said I will mend," said the Indian. He gave his bandaged arm a rueful look. "Eventually."

She smiled, then greeted Mac warmly before giving the mustachioed man a peck on the cheek. "And Peter. Good to see you again."

"You too, Nina," he replied, before regarding Eddie with disdain. "Chase. Hello."

"Alderley," Eddie replied, with equal antipathy.

"So," said the MI6 officer, "how was your party?"

Nina looked apologetic. "I am *so* sorry you didn't get your invitation, Peter. *Somebody*"—she glared at Eddie—"made a hash of things."

"Completely by accident," Eddie told him, not quite hiding a smile. "I was gutted that you weren't there, obviously."

"Obviously," said Alderley, stone-faced. Mac chuckled.

"In that case, you can apologize to Peter for the, uh, mix-up, can't you?" said Nina. When Eddie didn't reply immediately, she jabbed him with an elbow. "Can't you?"

"I suppose," Eddie said, with a complete lack of contrition. "Sorry that you couldn't come to our wedding do and drone on about restoring your Ford Capri, Alderley."

Another jab. "Eddie!"

"That's okay," said Alderley sarcastically. "It's the thought that counts. Anyway, I've got some information about your friends the Khoils." He put a briefcase on the desk, taking out several manila folders and a laptop. "While MI6 doesn't have any specifically actionable intelligence on them, what Mac told me was enough to raise flags. And with the G20 summit going on, any potential threat has to be investigated."

"What did you find?" Nina asked.

"A lot of financial activity—hardly surprising considering the Khoils own a multinational company, but our banking boffins are always looking for suspicious patterns. They've been setting up various . . . well, they've described them as 'protected archives,' but you could call them bunkers, I suppose. Isolated facilities with everything needed for long-term survival—exactly the kind of thing you'd want if you planned to spark off World War Three. An old salt mine in Montana, something in Australia, Mongolia—and a place in Greenland, which is, according to their flight plan, where they're going."

Nina turned to Kit. "Can you put out a warrant on them?"

"I'm afraid not. At the moment, we don't have enough direct evidence to issue a red notice. Based on our statements there is enough to issue a green notice, but that's just a warning to local police of possible criminal activity, not a confirmation."

"Why the hell would they want to go to Greenland?" Eddie hooted. "There's not a lot there."

THE SACRED VAULT 425

"That might be why they've gone," said Nina, a possibility striking her. "Pramesh said one of the reasons they stole those treasures was to protect them while everything else collapses. We saw in Iraq what happened to the country's museums—they were looted, and most of the contents still haven't been found. Imagine that on a global scale! But if you wanted to keep something absolutely safe, you'd put it as far away from civilization as possible—like that seed store in Norway, the Doomsday vault. Maybe they're hiding everything they've stolen in Greenland. Peter, do you know exactly what kind of facility they have there?"

Alderley flicked through the folders, then shook his head. "Some decommissioned Cold War ice station. I don't have the details."

"If that's their bolt-hole, there must be some significance to it." She gestured at the laptop. "Can I use your computer?"

Alderley nodded, and Nina opened the machine. "What are you looking for?" Mac asked.

"Whatever they're doing up there."

"How are you going to find that out?" Alderley asked dubiously.

She went to the Web browser—and loaded the Qexia search engine. "To quote their own commercials," she said with a grin, "just ask."

It took only a minute for the network of links to produce a result that surprised everyone in the room. "*That's* his data center?" said Eddie, reading the news article, translated from the Danish, that accompanied a picture of Khoil standing before a bizarre structure. "Bloody hell. And I thought his house was over the top."

"It says it's over a hundred miles from the nearest settlement," said Nina. "If you wanted to keep something hidden, it's a good place."

"So what do we do? Fly up there and knock?"

"If Interpol finds anything to tie the Khoils to the Vault

of Shiva, then yes—it directly connects them to the attempted theft of the Talonor Codex in San Francisco. As soon as they have something, they can issue an arrest warrant. Am I right, Kit?"

"The Indian government is flying a team to Mount Kedarnath first thing tomorrow," Kit replied. "There are two crashed helicopters there. If their tail numbers match the ones hired by the Khoils' company, we have our connection. We can upgrade the green notice to a red, and work with the Greenland police to search"—he indicated the strange building on the laptop screen—"this place."

"Will you be going?" Nina asked.

He tapped the crutch on the floor. "I don't think so. But we will still need an expert to identify any artifacts that might be found there. If you want to go."

"Absolutely," said Nina immediately.

"That wasn't what I was going to say," Eddie grumbled, only half joking. "We just got back from the Himalayas, and now you want to go somewhere even colder?"

"It'll be worth it to see the expression on the Khoils' faces when they get arrested." She turned to Alderley. "Is there anything else you can do to protect the summit in the meantime?"

"Without any specific threat, all I can do is try to persuade the Indians to raise the security alert level—and it's already pretty high. But..." He thought for a moment, rubbing his mustache. "All the countries at the G20 have intelligence officers in their delegations—my opposite numbers, you could say. I can have quiet words with them, try to get them to take a gander at the Khoils for themselves. If we pool information, we might be able to find something actionable."

"How long will it take, though?" asked Nina. "The summit starts tomorrow."

"Yeah," Eddie added. "It won't help much if whatever

Khoil's planning happens while you're swanning about at some spooks' cocktail party."

"That's not *quite* what I'll be doing," said Alderley irritably. "As a matter of fact, I was going to suggest that Mac come with me to talk to some of these people. And Mr. Jindal, too. Getting firsthand accounts from reliable sources can speed things up enormously."

"Will you be able to get us security clearance for the summit?" Mac asked.

"For an MI6 adviser and an Interpol officer? No problem. It's not as though you're disreputable types." He looked directly at Eddie, who mouthed an obscenity.

"I'm happy to help as much as I can," said Kit.

"Great. I'll make the arrangements." He took out his phone.

Mac stepped forward to speak to Nina and Eddie. "So, off to Greenland? Rather you than me. One of the best things about retiring from the Regiment was knowing that I'd never have to spend another minute on a glacier."

"Funny, I thought that too," said Eddie. "Didn't quite work out."

The Scot smiled. "Well, best of luck. And wrap up warm."

"Don't worry," Nina assured him. "I'm not planning to spend one second longer than I have to in the cold!"

31

Greenland

Nina gazed out of the porthole of the de Havilland Twin Otter aircraft at the landscape ten thousand feet below. It was an unbroken, empty swath of snow, and in the near-eternal night of the Arctic winter there should have been nothing to see... but instead, it was one of the most amazing natural sights she had ever set eyes upon.

The sky was alive with the shimmering glow of the aurora borealis, green and red and pink lights coiling across the dark dome above. The blank snowscape became a giant canvas, a piece of abstract expressionism on a grand scale as colors were poured over it from the heavens. "Eddie," she said excitedly. "You've got to see this."

Eddie paused in his discussion with Walther Probst, Interpol's tactical liaison officer, to glance through another window. "Not bad," he grunted, turning back to the German.

"That's all you've got to say? *Not bad?*"

"I've seen it before. The SAS does Arctic training in Norway. After a couple of days freezing your arse off, you stop noticing it. Actually, it's kind of a pain because it makes you easier to see."

"I married a philistine," she complained before joining the two men. "How long till we get there?"

"About ten minutes," said Probst. The de Havilland was nearing the end of its long northeasterly flight from Greenland's capital of Nuuk, traversing the vast empty wastes of the huge island's central glaciers. Its destination was, quite literally, in the middle of nowhere.

As Kit had expected, the tail numbers of the two wrecked helicopters on Mount Kedarnath confirmed that the Khoils' company had indeed hired them. As a result, he had convinced Interpol to issue a red notice on the Khoils—and now it was going to be enacted.

There were two officers of the Rigspolitiet, the Danish police service, aboard the plane, but their presence was largely a formality; Probst's team of eight men, all armed and wearing body armor beneath their Arctic clothing, would carry out the actual mission. The objectives were simple—serve the warrant, arrest the Khoils for extradition to Interpol headquarters in Lyon, and search for evidence linking them to the artifact thefts. No warning had been sent ahead; the hope was that by the time their lawyers were able to take action, the Khoils would already be on their way to France.

The final preparations were being made, the team examining pictures of the building they would be searching. "What *is* this place?" one of the men asked.

"It used to be an American radar station," said Nina, having found the background on the giant structure known only as DYE-A unexpectedly interesting, a piece of modern-day archaeological research. "Part of a chain going all the way from the Atlantic coast of Greenland across Canada to Alaska. There were four others like it in Greenland, but this one was also part of a secret operation called Project Iceworm, where they tried to hide nuclear missile bases under the ice."

"And everyone thought it was the Russians who were

supposed to be sneaky," said Eddie, raising a few chuckles from those team members old enough to remember the Cold War.

"It didn't work out at the other sites because the glaciers weren't stable enough," Nina continued. "The tunnels they built collapsed after a few years. DYE-A was the only place where they stayed intact, because it's sited above an extinct volcano; the ice is trapped inside the caldera and can't move. So they built an emergency bunker there as well, a sort of backup NORAD where they could keep running World War Three even if everywhere else got nuked. But it was never used. At least, not by America."

"You think the Khoils are planning to use this bunker as a hideout?" asked Probst.

"It's definitely a possibility. It was designed to support people for years, if necessary."

The German indicated a locker at the rear of the cabin where the team's weapons were stowed. "Okay. As soon as we land, collect arms, and we will go to the building. Our friends from the Rigspolitiet will issue the warrant—we will make sure they are not, ah, obstructed in their duties." A small ripple of laughter.

The rasp of the propellers changed as the plane started its descent. "Better strap in," Eddie told Nina. He sat on one of a pair of rear-facing seats at the front of the cabin, Nina beside him. Outside the window, the spectacular auroral display played across the wings.

* * *

Pramesh Khoil stood in the eye of a hurricane of information. The infotarium around him, its hundreds of screens flashing at a dizzying rate, was a larger version of the one in Bangalore, constructed on a scale to match the huge chamber topping the former early-warning station. The fifty-five-foot-high geodesic dome had once housed one of DYE-A's three massive radar antennas; now it was his com-

mand center. He was raised twenty feet on a circular platform, a staircase curling down to a lower elevated walkway ringing it, from where two more sets of steps
descended to the floor. Directly above him, hanging from
the domed ceiling, was a large rig housing projectors for
the biggest screens. A small lectern at the platform's edge
contained the sensors for the gestural control system.

Despite the visual overload, Khoil's attention was fo-
cused on three screens in particular. One showed mostly
darkness, the lights of a city seen from the air glinting like
gems on black velvet; beside it, the same view was repeated
with the benefit of night vision, the cityscape rendered in
ghostly shades of green. Both giant projection screens were
overlaid with the graphics of an aerial head-up display, an
artificial horizon showing the aircraft's course and speed,
altitude and attitude.

The third, smaller LCD screen was a live feed from a
news network. The president and prime minister of India
stood on a red carpet at the majestic Rashtrapati Bhavan,
the president's official residence in Delhi, greeting the German chancellor. The leaders of the world's most powerful
nations were assembling for the G20 summit, meeting for
the evening's opening ceremony and state banquet before
the conference proper began the next day.

But, Khoil knew, there would be no next day for the at-
tendees. The world was about to change forever. The corrupt and decadent Kali Yuga would end, and a new,
purified cycle of existence would begin.

Tonight.

Vanita stood beside him, trying to shut out the visual
distraction of the other screens to concentrate on the news
feed. "How much longer?" she asked. "Are they all there?"

"Not yet," said Khoil. He held out his right hand with
the palm flat, fingers slightly opened, and tilted it. On the
two main screens, the image of the city followed suit, the

speed of the aircraft's turn increasing slightly. "Be patient, my beloved."

"I *am* patient," she insisted, tight-lipped. "But it's frustrating, waiting on...*politicians*!" She almost spat the word, her earrings jingling.

Khoil lowered his hand, the artificial horizons leveling automatically. "It will not be long now. Just another—"

A trilling sound interrupted him. "What's that?" Vanita demanded.

"A security alert." A gesture, and Zec's face appeared on one of the screens. "What is it?" he asked the Bosnian.

"Radar has picked up a plane," Zec told him. "About five minutes out—and descending."

Khoil immediately raised both hands, fingers playing a silent concerto in the air as virtual keyboards flashed up. A radar tracking display appeared, showing the intruder's course. A dotted line predicted its final destination: DYE-A's long ice runway. A flick of a finger, and the aircraft's identity was revealed, its transponder code cross-checked in a millisecond against Qexia's vast database. "A government aircraft," he said. "But they would not turn up unannounced, unless..." His gaze snapped back to Zec's image. "Jam its radio! Shoot it down—and send a team to eliminate any survivors!"

* * *

The de Havilland shuddered, buffeted by the winds sweeping across the ice plain. Nina grabbed Eddie's hand. "Ow," he complained.

"What?"

"Bloody nails, digging into me!" He pulled open her clenched fingers.

"I'm just nervous—we're about to land on a glacier hundreds of miles from anywhere, and I'm pretty sure we won't get a warm welcome."

"Oh, come on. You've been to the Antarctic—this is like

Central Park in comparison. Besides, we've got all these guys and their guns on our side—and the Khoils don't even know we're coming."

Shouts of alarm in Danish from the cockpit, the plane banking sharply—

A bright flash outside the windows—then a hole burst open in the fuselage with an earsplitting bang and the shriek of shredding metal. One of the cops was hit in the head by shrapnel, a splash of blood flying across the cabin.

The plane dropped, loose items tumbling in free fall as a freezing wind screamed through the rent in the hull. One of Probst's men had not fastened his seat belt—he was dragged through the torn hole, the jagged metal ripping his clothing and flesh before the slipstream snatched him away.

Another light outside, the orange flicker of flames. The engine was on fire. The de Havilland lurched, the rasp of its remaining propeller rising as the pilots increased power. "What the hell's happening?" Nina shrieked.

Eddie clutched his armrests. "A missile! Those fuckers are trying to shoot us down!" He twisted to look into the cockpit. The copilot yelled into his headset, declaring a Mayday—but from his expression was getting no reply. Beside him, the pilot struggled with the controls. The plane was dropping fast, nose angled downward. Through the cockpit windows, Eddie saw a light in the distance, a glowing blue sphere on the snow.

DYE-A. The Khoils' base. They would crash within sight of it.

A loud whine and a shrill grind of metal ran through the cabin as the pilot extended the wing flaps. The de Havilland's dive started to level out. "Can you land?" Eddie shouted.

Panic cracked the copilot's mask of professionalism. "We can't make the runway! Crash positions! Brace for impact!"

"Oh, shit," Eddie gasped. He faced the cabin, relaying the instruction to the others before turning to the terrified Nina, who was leaning forward with her hands on the back of her head. "No, no!" he said, pulling her upright. "We're facing backward—crash position's different. Sit up straight, keep your back against the seat. Sit on your hands so they don't flap about." He demonstrated.

She followed his example. "Eddie, I'm scared!"

Eddie tried to think of something reassuring to say, but all he could manage was "I'm not fucking thrilled about it either!" He glanced sideways, seeing the aurora-lit landscape rising to meet them. A cluster of lights rolled past the windows—they had passed the radar station. He looked back at Nina, meeting her frightened eyes. "Stay with me—"

"Brace! Brace! *Brace!*" screamed the copilot. The engine's snarl echoed off the ice as the plane reached the ground...

The de Havilland hit. Hard.

The landing gear, fitted with skis for a touchdown in snow, collapsed. One of the struts stabbed upward into the cabin and impaled an Interpol agent. The shock of impact pounded through the seats as the plane slammed down on its belly, skidding across the glacier in a huge spray of ice. Another agent's seat belt snapped, flinging him across the cabin to crack headfirst against the wall.

Deceleration pressed Nina and Eddie into their seats, vibration battering them. Metal cracked, something wrenching away from the hull's underside with a horrible screech—

The entire fuselage was ripped in half behind the wings. Two men, strapped helplessly into their seats, were yanked backward as the floor was torn out from beneath them— and the tail section mowed them down. Its jagged leading edge gouged into the ice, making it tumble as it fell away behind.

More seats broke loose and spun into the trail of debris, another man screaming as he was thrown into the night. Nina gripped her seat as tightly as she could, eyes closed in terror.

The front section tipped over as it continued its uncontrollable skid, the undamaged wing dropping toward the ice—and stabbing into it. The sudden drag spun the fuselage around—then the entire wing was abruptly torn away at its root, wrenching a huge chunk of the ceiling with it. The weight of the remaining wing dragged that side down. Another slam of impact as the wingtip hit the ice, a crunching groan of metal as the wing buckled ... and the plane finally bumped to a stop as the wrecked engine dug into the ice like an anchor.

The silence was so sudden that for a moment Nina, eyes still squeezed closed, thought she was dead. It wasn't until she managed to draw a breath that she convinced herself otherwise.

Even that breath told her she was not out of danger. The air was bitingly cold—and laden with the heavy stench of aviation fuel. She opened her eyes. To her surprise, some of the emergency lights in the remains of the cabin were still glowing.

The scene they illuminated, however, was not one she wanted to see. A member of the Interpol team was sprawled over a broken seat, a jagged metal rod impaling his neck. Probst was still alive, breath steaming from his mouth, but from the unnatural angle of his foot it was certain that he had broken his ankle. The agent beside him was also breathing, apparently unconscious. The surviving cop was strapped in his seat facing her, a deep cut on his cheek. He groaned softly.

No sound from the seat beside her, though, no billowing condensation in the cold air. Nina almost didn't dare turn her head to see what had happened to her husband—and when she did, she felt a sharp stab of whiplash pain. But she forced herself to look...

Eddie was slumped in his seat, eyes closed, blood around his mouth.

Not breathing.

"Eddie?" she said, voice quavering. No answer, no movement. She reached out to touch his face, but stopped just short, afraid that she would find no warmth. "Eddie? Are you..."

Still no reply. More frightened now than she had been during the landing, she touched his cheek—

"Buggery bastard *fuck*!" he yelled, exploding to life and thrashing against his seat belt. Nina shrieked, flinching back. He clawed open the buckle and jumped up, fists clenched in fury.

"Eddie, Eddie!" Nina cried. "Jesus! Are you okay? Eddie!"

A plume of frozen breath hissed out through the gap between his two front teeth as he grimaced. "No, I'm fucking not! God! A plane crash! A fucking *plane crash*! That nerdy little bastard Khoil, when I get hold of him..." Another, longer exhalation, then he took a deep breath before speaking again, more calmly. "Buggeration and fuckery."

"So...I guess you're okay?"

"Nothing broken. Feels like someone whacked me with a bat, though." He put a hand to his chest, finding that his coat was torn where some piece of flying debris had struck him. "What about you?"

"Hurt my neck, but apart from that, I think I'm all right."

The surge of rage fading, Eddie took in the other survivors, and hurriedly crouched beside Probst when he saw his foot. "Shit, that looks bad."

The German's eyes fluttered open. "*Was ist pass...*," he began, before switching to English on seeing Eddie. "What happened?"

THE SACRED VAULT 437

"We were shot down," Nina told him, shakily standing. She heard electronic warbles from the cockpit and investigated. Her hopes that the pilots were still alive were quickly dashed; one man was bent over with his head twisted at an unnatural angle, eyes staring blankly at the ceiling. There was no sign of the other, but blood smeared across a broken window suggested he had been thrown out of the plane.

Eddie quickly checked the other two survivors, waking Probst's associate as the cop groggily sat up. He looked back at Nina. "Is the radio working? We need to send an SOS."

"I don't know. Something's still switched on, though—there's a weird noise."

"It...it's a radio jammer," said Probst. "It must be at the radar station."

"Oh, great," Nina moaned. "That means the only people we can call for help are the ones who tried to kill us." She spotted a yellow box marked with a red cross under the empty pilot's seat and pulled it out, finding not just first-aid gear but also survival equipment—packaged food, a Very pistol and flares, foil blankets, various tools. "Walther, I've got some bandages and a splint," she said, bringing the box to Probst. "We'll try to fix your foot."

Eddie moved to the torn end of the fuselage and looked out across the plain. They had landed on a slope, the long, wreckage-strewn gouge torn by the front section as it slid downhill clearly visible in the aurora's ghost-light. The wing that had been ripped away was standing almost vertically, poking out of the ice like some strange flag. Beyond it, some distance away, he saw the broken tail section half buried by snow.

There was another source of illumination, something more than the auroral display. Over the crest of the hill was an unnatural glow. The radar station. The building itself was out of sight; the plane's uncontrolled slide down the ice had carried it a mile past the base.

But they wouldn't be alone for long. Two bright white lights appeared on the horizon.

Snowmobiles.

32

They're coming," Eddie said. "We need guns. Who can move?"

The cop stood, grunting in discomfort but still able to walk. The other Interpol officer tried to get up, only to drop painfully back into his seat. "Okay," Eddie told the cop, "come with me."

"I'm coming too," said Nina.

"No," he said firmly, indicating Probst. "Do what you can with his foot. We'll take these bastards out before they get to you." He put a hand on the cop's arm. "You ready?"

The Greenlander was only young, in his twenties, and his fear was clear. "I—I'm okay," he said.

"You'll be fine," Eddie reassured him. He pointed to the wreckage of the tail. "We get to the gun locker and kill any fucker who comes down that hill. Sound good?" The cop nodded. "Okay, let's go."

He jumped out of the fuselage. The surface snow was surprisingly hard-packed, his feet only sinking a few inches before ice crunched beneath them. He started to run up the slope beside the ragged, debris-strewn gouge, kicking up a crystalline spray with each step. The cop followed.

The snowmobiles were speeding toward the crash site, rooster tails of snow swirling in their wakes. Eddie pushed harder, skirting the severed wing. The stink of fuel filled his nostrils as he passed it. More debris lay in his path, as did a dark splash of blood across the whiteness. He kept running. The tail section loomed ahead—

One of the snowmobiles veered toward the two men. The aurora's light had betrayed them.

Eddie cursed and leapt into the channel, hunching down as he scrambled over the churned ice. He looked back at the cop—who froze as the headlight pinned him. "Get down!" he shouted. The cop broke from his paralysis and jumped after him—

Gunfire spat from the snowmobile, bullets ripping into the young man's head and chest. Blood splattered across the ice as he crumpled.

Anger surging, Eddie ran on, head down. Ice sprayed over him as more gunshots smacked into the snow.

The half-buried tail section was not far ahead. Its interior was dark, a black mouth surrounded by jagged metal teeth. He vaulted a large hatch lying on the ground and sprinted into the shadows. The open end of the fuselage was packed with snow, seats jutting through the mound—but beyond it the central aisle was more or less clear, the gun locker at its end.

He scrambled over the drift. No emergency lights here, but there was enough illumination from the aurora for him to find the locker. He grabbed the handle—

It turned—but the door only opened an inch before banging against something. He pulled harder. It flexed, but still refused to open. "Shit!" He groped in the darkness... and found that the floor had buckled upward in front of the locker.

He kicked at it, trying to bend it back down, but it was too solid. A harsh light shone through the portholes—the snowmobile was almost on him. The other vehicle roared on down the slope toward the plane's front section. Two men on each machine.

The passenger on the one approaching leaned out from behind the driver, gun raised—

Eddie dropped flat as bullets riddled the wreck. A shot clanked off the seat frame just above him. Spears of light stabbed across the cabin through each new hole in the fuselage.

If he stayed put, he was a dead man—he would be pinned inside the hull. He slithered on his belly over the piled snow as more shots punctured the plane's skin. Emerging into the faint auroral glow, he pulled himself around the torn edge of the fuselage to take shelter behind it.

The snowmobile's snarl dropped to an idling stutter. The gunfire also stopped. Eddie risked a peek at his attackers. If the gunner were reloading, that would give him a few seconds to take action...

He wasn't reloading. He was pulling the pin from a grenade.

Eddie sprang up and ran for the rear of the wreckage as something small but heavy clanged off metal behind him—

* * *

Nina had forced herself to keep bandaging Probst's ankle even through the sound of gunfire—but she jumped up in horror at the explosion, seeing debris showering down around the tail section.

One of the snowmobiles was still barreling straight for her. The other had stopped farther uphill; a man hopped off, the driver revving up and turning to ride after his comrades.

No sign of Eddie. Had he been inside the tail?

She didn't have time to consider the horrible thought. A man on the nearer snowmobile opened fire. "Jesus!" she gasped, ducking. Bullets kicked up snow and peppered the fuselage.

The other Interpol agent yelled in fright as a round struck the forward bulkhead. He lurched upright, clambering into the open and starting to run across the ice.

"No, wait!" Nina shouted, but it was too late. The gunman had spotted the fleeing figure and shouted for the driver to angle after him. Flame flashed from his gun's muzzle as he opened fire on full auto—

The running man tumbled bloodily into the snow.

The snowmobile swerved back toward the plane, driving alongside the trench. Nina crouched beside Probst, desperately searching for an escape route, any form of defense. But the wrecked fuselage offered no protection and no hiding places, and they had no weapons—

Yes, they did. She pawed through the survival kit. The orange-painted Very pistol might not have been designed as a weapon, but it was still a gun. She opened the breech and inserted a flare, then snapped it closed.

"You'll never hit them with that," Probst warned her weakly.

"I'm not aiming at them," Nina replied, jaw set. She raised her head, judging the distance to her target. Waiting for the right moment.

The gunner fired again. Shots cracked against the seats. Nina flinched, but held her position.

Waiting . . .

Now!

She pulled the trigger.

With a *thump*, the flare sizzled away on a trail of red-lit smoke toward her target—not the snowmobile, but the severed wing, and the ruptured auxiliary fuel tank inside it? . . .

And fell short.

She had overestimated the projectile's power, not aiming

high enough. The flare landed, sending up a plume of steam as the intense heat melted the snow. Nina ducked, fumbling for a second flare, but she knew that by the time she reloaded, the snowmobile would be past the wing.

She had missed her one chance.

* * *

Eddie was being hunted.

The gunman had quickly realized that his grenade had not caught anyone inside the fuselage. Now he was circling the tail section, MP5K at the ready. There were no tracks in the surrounding snow, so his quarry was close by . . .

Eddie heard the crunch of his footsteps as he approached the stern. He was crouched on the other side of the high tail, unable to move—any sound would reveal his position. And at such close range, a burst from the Heckler & Koch would go straight through the plane's aluminum skin. The other man didn't even need to see him to kill him.

His only chance was a surprise attack as the gunman rounded the tail. But he could tell his hunter was cautious, unlikely to fall for such an obvious ploy. The icy crackles came closer, pausing. Listening.

Eddie tensed, ready to spring—but he knew that without a diversion, he had no chance of reaching his enemy before being shot . . .

* * *

Nina loaded another flare. But it was too late—the snowmobile had passed the wing—

A new light, brighter than the aurora. Startled, she looked between the seats—and saw flames spreading outward from the sputtering flare.

The fuel!

It had trickled downhill—and now the fire was rushing back up the line of flammable liquid to its source—

The wing exploded, metal shards scything in all directions. The blast tore apart the engine, sending one of the propeller blades spinning away—to slam into the snowmobile. The driver's upper body was reduced to a red pulp by the heavy piece of metal, his hands and the stumps of his forearms left clinging to the handlebars. The vehicle swerved out of control and crashed into the trench, flinging the other man into a pool of burning avgas.

* * *

Eddie heard the explosion—and the crunch of ice underfoot as the gunman whirled to see what had happened.

His diversion—

He threw himself bodily at the rudder, slamming it into the gunman on the other side. Swinging around the tailplane, he launched himself at the staggering figure and tackled him at chest height. The gun went off—but the bullets went wide. He pressed home the attack, driving a powerful blow into the man's stomach.

The gunman crashed against the battered fuselage. Eddie grabbed for the MP5K, but only managed to get a hold on the other man's wrist.

His adversary smashed his free hand down on the Englishman's head. Another harsh blow to the base of his neck dropped him to one knee. Eddie was still gripping his attacker's right wrist, but could feel him twisting the gun around at him—

He punched the gunman's stomach again. From his awkward position it didn't cause any real damage, provoking only a gasp and a flinch—but that was all he needed.

His hand slid up from the man's wrist to the MP5K's butt, finding his opponent's forefinger...and squeezing as he yanked the weapon downward.

The gun blazed on full auto. Its remaining bullets slammed into the ground between the two men, fire meeting ice—and lead meeting leather as the last bullet tore through the gunman's boot and blasted off his big toe. He screamed, hopping as blood spurted from the neat nine-millimeter hole.

Eddie wrested away the empty gun—and viciously smashed it into the wounded man's face. Nose crushed, the gunman fell on his back. Eddie dived on him, pushing the gun down hard against his neck. The man struggled, spitting blood and thrashing at Eddie's face . . . then there was a wet crunch deep inside his throat. With a final gurgling breath, he fell still.

◆ ◆ ◆

The other snowmobile's passenger was also breathing his last, flailing blindly in the pool of burning fuel before slumping, flames roiling over his body.

The force of the explosion had knocked Nina to the floor. Wincing at the unexpected wave of heat, she staggered upright. A swath of the ice channel was now a lake of fire; the Twin Otter's main fuel tanks were in its belly, and had ripped open when the fuselage broke in half, spewing out the volatile liquid. "Guess we don't have to worry about freezing to death," she told Probst—before realizing the danger was not over.

The second snowmobile was still coming. And she had dropped the flare gun when she fell.

Defenseless.

◆ ◆ ◆

Eddie found a spare magazine on the dead man's belt. He slapped it into place and pulled back the MP5K's charging handle with a clack, then ran around the broken fuselage to see the remaining snowmobile's red taillight passing the burning wreckage of the wing.

The rider was well out of the submachine gun's effective range. He had to get down the hill fast to save Nina—but how?

The auroral glow shimmered over an intact piece of the plane on the ground. That was one way...

• • •

Nina dragged Probst into the cockpit. The bulkhead wouldn't give them much protection, but it was better than nothing.

The snowmobile skidded to a stop. Nina cautiously looked around the doorway, seeing a shadowy figure climb off the idling machine. He had a gun in his right hand... then switched it to his left to take something from a pocket.

A grenade.

"Oh, shit," Nina whispered. She backed into the cockpit, but there was no solid door that could be closed, just a flimsy sliding partition. No protection. She could flee through the broken window, but that would mean abandoning Probst to his death—and even if she did, there was nowhere to run, nothing but bleak ice for a hundred miles in every direction.

The man hooked a finger around the pin, pulled it out—

And whirled at a noise from behind.

Eddie hurtled down the slope, riding the de Havilland's cabin hatch like a sledge and howling like a banshee. The startled man fumbled with his gun and the grenade, trying to switch the two weapons between his hands without releasing the latter's spring-loaded spoon and arming the fuse. He brought up his MP5K—

So did Eddie. The compact weapon spat flame. Bullets twanged off the wreckage behind his target, but one shot hit, a puff of blood bursting from the man's thigh. He screamed, instinctively dropping what he was holding to clap both hands to the wound as he fell...

On his own grenade.

Eddie dived off the hatch, covering his head with his arms. "Grenade!" he yelled—

The explosion this time was considerably more muffled.

Pieces of the luckless gunman splattered down around the steaming crater in the ice.

Eddie stood and circled the starburst of red to the broken fuselage. "Nina! You all right?" She appeared in the doorway, face alight with relief, and embraced him. He kissed her, then saw Probst in the cockpit. "Are you okay?" The German nodded. "What about the other guy?"

"He's dead," Probst said flatly.

"Dammit . . ." He noticed that some of the lights on the instrument panel were still active—including the radio. "Is that jammer still running?"

Probst listened to the electronic warbling. "Yes. This radio won't have enough power to break through it, not on the emergency battery."

"Then we'll have to shut it off." He regarded the glow on the horizon, then his gaze moved to the puttering snowmobile. "Think I'll meet our new neighbors," he said, checking his gun's remaining ammo.

"I'm coming with you," Nina said.

"No, you stay here with him."

"Eddie, I am coming with you," she said defiantly, taking more items from the survival kit—a pair of foil blankets, a small roll of duct tape, and a compact oil heater. She started to tape one of the blankets over the broken cockpit window. "I think there'll be more people than just Pramesh and Vanita in that place. You'll need all the backup you can get." The makeshift windbreak in place, she helped Probst into the pilot's seat and draped the other blanket over him, then propped the heater on the control yoke. "Walther, as soon as we take out the jammer, you send an SOS."

"How much time will you need?" he asked. A glass tube set in the little heater's side revealed the oil level; considering the small size of the tank, it was unlikely to last long.

"If we haven't done it in an hour, we probably won't be doing it at all." Pulling the partition across the doorway as she exited, she faced Eddie. "Okay, let's go."

"Seriously. You're not coming," he said as she pushed past him and headed for the snowmobile.

"Oh, I seriously am."

"You don't have a gun."

Nina picked up the exploded snowmobiler's MP5K. "I do now." She trudged through the snow to the waiting vehicle and straddled it. "Whose turn is it to drive?"

33

They rode up the icy hill, Eddie at the controls. In the aurora's ever-shifting light, it was easy to follow the trails of the two snowmobiles.

Not that there was any doubt about where to go. The glow grew brighter as they neared the hill crest. "So, do you have a plan?" Nina said.

"Let's see what we're dealing with first." They reached the summit...and radar station DYE-A came into view.

Internet photos had not truly prepared them for the sight. The main structure, the "composite building," was huge, an enormous black block more than 120 feet high—and that was without the radome elevated on the building's central core atop it. The dome itself was lit from within; when Eddie had glimpsed it from the plane it had been a vivid blue, but now other colors pulsed inside, an amped-up electronic version of the aurora overhead. Communications masts festooned with dishes sprouted beside it.

Brilliant spotlights illuminated the surrounding ground, revealing that the composite building stood within a crater-like depression in the ice. The black walls absorbed what little heat came from the sun at this latitude, raising the air temperature around them just enough to slow the accumulation of snow. The main block was supported by eight massive legs—hydraulic jacks, able to lift the station higher if the drifts became too deep.

The radar installation was not the facility's only structure. Several smaller buildings were clustered to one side, and at the end of the long ice runway was an aircraft hangar. A path marked by a line of lights on poles ran from it to the edge of the depression beneath the composite building, where a covered walkway extended across the gap to its lowest floor.

"Looks like they've made themselves comfortable," said Eddie, taking it in. He indicated a line of large cylindrical tanks. "Those'll be full of diesel—enough to keep them going for months."

"However long before they feel it's safe to poke their noses out of their rat-hole after the apocalypse," Nina guessed. "What do we do?"

He scanned the area for signs of life. "Do you see anyone?"

Nina squinted into the wind. "Nope." She looked up at the windows, which in the interests of preserving heat were small and few in number; all were lit, but nobody was silhouetted in them. "Windows look clear too."

"Okay, let's look for something to break."

"Did I ever tell you that I love you for your subtlety?" Nina joked as they warily headed for the walkway. It would surely not be much longer before somebody realized the men sent to finish off any crash survivors were overdue. "Whoa, wait. Look at that."

A broad ramp descended into the depression beneath the main building, where a path had been dug to a boxy metal structure extending down from the base of the radar station—and into the ice below. The path led to a pair of large sliding doors. "It's an elevator shaft," she realized.

"Big elevators," Eddie added.

"Very big elevators. Big enough to take all the equipment for a Cold War bunker...or Michelangelo's *David*, you think?"

"Easily." There was a hatch beside the two doors. "We might be able to get in there. Maybe there's a ladder."

"Or we could just, y'know, use the elevator," she said as they descended the ramp.

"That might be a bit of a giveaway that we're here. See? I'm being subtle."

They reached the hatch. "Is it locked?" Nina asked as Eddie tried the handle.

"Who's going to break in, Nanook of the North?" He rattled it until the crust of ice over the jamb broke away. Opening it, he jabbed his gun inside.

Nobody lay in wait. The entrance led to an emergency ladder running parallel to the elevator tracks. He stepped onto the walkway inside, about to climb the ladder when he looked down through the gridwork floor. The shaft dropped into blackness, a line of small maintenance lights shrinking to pinpricks in the dark. "Bloody hell. How deep is it?"

"I don't know, but they would have built the bunker deep enough to survive a nuclear strike..." She trailed off.

"What's the matter?" Eddie began, before some form of spousal telepathy—or realization of the inevitable—gave him the answer. "Oh, for fuck's sake. You want to climb down there, don't you?"

"If the US military's built you a mini-NORAD, you might as well make use of it. Whatever the Khoils are doing, that's probably where they're doing it from."

"It's a bloody long climb!"

"Well, we *could* take the elevator..."

Eddie made a disapproving sound, then grudgingly mounted the ladder. "All right. But for God's sake don't slip." He began to descend, boots clunking on the metal rungs.

Nina followed suit. The descent was easy at first, but after a few minutes her muscles started to ache—and the bottom of the shaft didn't seem any nearer. "I just had a depressing thought."

"Yeah, that's what I want to hear right now," Eddie said. "What?"

"What if they dug the bunker out of the actual bedrock? The Greenland ice sheet is over two miles thick in places."

"If we have to climb down a two-mile fucking ladder," he warned, "I'm going to throw you down the quick way!"

"I, uh, don't think it'll be *quite* that far," she said. All the same, she looked down the shaft with increasing frequency, hoping for some sign of the bottom.

It came after another few minutes—still some distance below, but a dimly lit rectangle of gray was now visible at the end of the trail of lights. The sight rejuvenated them, and they increased the pace of their descent.

Finally, they reached the bottom. Eddie stepped onto another walkway and went to the hatch at its end. The bottom of the shaft proper was about six feet below, a concrete block covered by icy water. As Nina climbed off the ladder behind him, gratefully resting her arms, he opened the metal door a fraction of an inch.

More drab gray concrete greeted his eyes as warm air blew past him; a wide corridor, lit by sickly fluorescent bulbs. The hatch opened into an alcove in its side, blocking his view down the passage. Gesturing for Nina to stay still, he took hold of his gun, then stepped through and peered around the corner.

The corridor was about thirty feet long. At its far end was a huge metal door, painted a dull institutional green. Another, larger alcove on the opposite side contained a desk, the sleek laptop on it in marked contrast with the Cold War clunkiness of the surroundings. An Indian man was passing the time in exactly the same way as any bored worker in a regular office: surfing the Internet.

"There's one guy," Eddie whispered to Nina, "and a huge bloody door. We've found the bunker." He brought up the gun. "Wait here."

He checked that the man was still fixated on the laptop, then slipped around the corner and advanced quickly along the corridor. Unless the guard had the peripheral vision of a boiler-suited sentry in a Bond movie, he would spot the intruder at any moment...

Eddie made it almost halfway before the man's eyes flicked sideways. He jolted in his seat, startled, then lunged for a control box on the wall—

"I wouldn't," Eddie said, MP5K fixed on the man's head. He froze, outstretched palm stopped a few inches from a large red alarm button. "Sit back down. Hands in the air." The guard obeyed. Eddie came to the desk, keeping the gun locked on him. "Okay, Nina," he called.

Nina hurried to him, pointing her own gun at the guard as Eddie frisked him. "I see what you mean about the door," she said. "It must weigh ten tons! How are we going to get inside?"

"Let's ask Chuckles here," said Eddie. He shoved his gun's muzzle under the guard's chin. "How do you open the door?"

"You—you push that button," the guard stammered, indicating the control panel.

"Which one?"

"The one that says *Open*."

Nina examined the panel, finding that one of the buttons on it was indeed marked OPEN. "Huh. Whaddya know?"

"You do the honors, love," Eddie told her. She glanced at the guard for any signs of treachery, but the only thought in his head appeared to be the very real concern that a bullet might go through it. Shrugging, she pushed the button.

Yellow warning lights flashed, and a low mechanical drone filled the corridor. With surprising speed for its size, the door smoothly swung outward, revealing that it was more than two feet thick. Beyond it, oddly, was darkness: Nina had expected to see some sort of control room. "That was ... kinda easy."

"It's a bunker, not a bank vault," Eddie replied. "You don't want to wait five minutes to get inside while there's a nuclear missile on its way."

"Good point." She looked at the guard. "What about him?"

Eddie cracked him sharply on the forehead with his gun. The man slumped to the floor. "What about him?"

"The subtlety phase was pretty short-lived, I see." She stepped through the door into the chamber beyond.

Even without lights, she could tell it was large, her footfalls soaked up by the space. A small bulb beside the doorway illuminated another control panel. A bank of what looked like light switches was topped by a button marked MAIN L; she pushed it. With a clack, the overhead lights came on. She turned ...

Her assumption that the Khoils were using the Cold War bunker as an operations center had been wrong. They had found a more spectacular use for it—the chamber had been turned into their own personal museum, a display of some of the world's greatest treasures. Eddie moved past her to investigate some doors in the far wall, but Nina's eyes were only on its contents.

The statue of David dominated, but the marble figure was surrounded by other artifacts of equal—perhaps even greater—value. A quartet of terra-cotta warriors stood guard on each side, stolen from the vast archaeological dig at the tomb of the First Emperor in Xi'an. Before them, mounted on a stand, was a sculpted piece of polished silver standing roughly four feet high. At its center, an oval orifice contained a large piece of what appeared to be dark glass. The Black Stone, the sacred Muslim artifact set into place in Mecca by Muhammad himself.

She recognized numerous other treasures as she entered the bunker. The Standard and Mantle of Muhammad stolen from Topkapi Palace in Turkey, the Antikythera mechanism from Athens... There were even artifacts she didn't recognize, which the Khoils had presumably decided met their personal criteria for "protection"—a painting on silk of a woman in feudal Japanese dress; some kind of stone altar carved with an unfamiliar script—

"Holy shit!" she gasped.

Eddie returned from his explorations, having found extensive living quarters beyond one of the doors. He regarded the incredible collection. "Took the words right out of my mouth. Not a bad lot at all."

"No, I mean—look at this," she said, hurrying to one item on the periphery of the display. A crude figurine, carved from an odd purple stone...

"They nicked Prince out of your office?" asked Eddie. "Cheeky bastards!"

"It's not the same one," Nina said. The figure was in a different pose from the primitive sculpture discovered in the Pyramid of Osiris. There was nothing to indicate why the Khoils considered it important enough to steal, or even from where it had been taken. It seemed as out of place among the incredible treasures around it as its near-twin had in the Egyptian god-king's tomb... yet the mere fact of its presence suggested there was more to the figurine—to both figurines—than met the eye.

But it was clear which treasure the Khoils thought most valuable. The centerpiece of the fantastic display was the chest from the Vault of Shiva. It was closed, but Nina found when she lifted the lid that all the stone tablets were still inside. No doubt the ancient texts had already been scanned, translated, and analyzed by Qexia. The Khoils had what they needed to spread their own warped interpretation of their god's word.

She backed away. "We found everything—so now we need to make sure they get back to where they belong."

"We need to wreck that radio jammer first," said Eddie.

"Sounds like your area of expertise. We'd better get moving." They left the vault, heading back past the unconscious guard. "Although I'm really not looking forward to climbing back up that ladder."

Eddie gave her a weary smile. "Have to admit, I'm coming around to the idea of using the lift—"

Someone had beaten them to it.

One set of elevator doors rumbled apart—revealing Zec and Tandon. Both men pointed handguns at them, fingers tight on the triggers.

Neither Eddie nor Nina had a weapon raised. They froze. "Cock," Eddie muttered.

"Drop the guns," said Zec. A half smile as they obeyed. "You are really incredible, Chase. What does it take to kill you?"

"A bullet to the head should do it," Tandon said, kicking the fallen MP5Ks away. He pushed his gun against Eddie's temple. The Englishman tensed, Nina drawing in a sharp breath of fear. "But...Mr. Khoil wants to see you first."

"Lucky us," said Eddie as the gun withdrew. "How'd he know we were here?"

Zec nodded toward the laptop. "It has a webcam connected to the security office. As soon as I saw the guard was not at his station, I rewound the stream. And there you were."

"Move," Tandon ordered. "Into the lift."

The elevator was a wide square platform, surrounded by railings but otherwise worryingly open. Nina and Eddie unwillingly stepped aboard. While the Indian kept them at gunpoint, Zec dragged the unconscious guard into the lift. Once both men were inside, Tandon pushed a button and the doors rattled shut. With a whine of motors, the elevator began its long journey to the surface.

* * *

The ride ended at the lowest floor of the composite building. Two more armed men were waiting as the doors opened. One picked up the guard and carried him away as Zec and Tandon ushered Nina and Eddie out. "Up the stairs," said Zec, gesturing to a staircase.

The utilitarian, military-drab environment of the bottom level gave way to considerably more high-tech surroundings as they ascended. Two entire floors of the old radar station had been gutted and replaced by massive data centers, rank after rank of computer servers processing information.

"Christ," said Eddie as they kept climbing. "All this just to play *Tetris*?"

"It's part of their plan," Nina realized. "Pramesh said he had archives storing information so it wouldn't be lost when civilization collapses. This must be one of them. He's recording every bit of data that passes through the Internet."

"Yeah, 'cause that's what the world'll need after the apocalypse—funny pet videos and porn."

"I'm sure he'll be very selective about what survives and what 'accidentally' gets lost to history."

Zec gave them an odd look. "What do you mean, the apocalypse?"

Nina and Eddie exchanged glances. "Taking a dump during the briefing, were you?" Eddie asked. "Or did they just not tell you that part?"

"You've been told everything you need to know," Tandon said firmly to Zec as they continued upward. The next level appeared to be living areas; the one above was the same, but more expensively appointed—the Khoils were apparently reluctant to give up the comforts of wealth, even in the Arctic.

The stairway ended here, but they still had higher to climb. Nina and Eddie were escorted along a short hallway to another set of stairs, this one spiraling upward through the building's central core to the giant dome. It took them via a distinctly industrial level, large—and from their appearance, Cold War vintage—electrical transformers emitting menacing hums. They had once fed power to the giant radar antenna; now they supplied energy to the 360-degree light show that had replaced it.

"Dr. Wilde!" called a familiar voice as they trooped into the infotarium. "And Mr. Chase too." Pramesh Khoil stood with his wife atop a circular platform at the dome's center.

Vanita regarded them with disgust. "Why are they still alive?"

"They have gone through a lot to be here, Vanita," said Khoil. Smug pride blossomed on his face as he waved a theatrical hand at the giant projection displays. "Bring them to the walkway. We may as well let them witness the end of the Kali Yuga."

"You are showing off," she said in a scolding tone as Zec, Tandon, and the guard marched Nina and Eddie up to the circular walkway. "We should just kill them."

"Soon, my beloved, soon," he replied, looking up at the two screens displaying the view from the aircraft. The city lights drifted across the picture as the plane continued its long circle. His gaze shifted to the news feed. "But it is almost time to begin—the G20 leaders have all arrived."

"That's your plan?" Nina asked, appalled. "You're going to crash a plane onto the summit?"

"You won't have a chance," said Eddie. "Twenty world leaders in one place, including the American, Russian, and Chinese presidents? If there's a fucking *sparrow* in the air over Delhi, it'll have a missile locked on to it."

"That *is* Delhi," said Khoil, nodding at the screens. "My drone is circling on automatic pilot fifteen kilometers west of the Rashtrapati Bhavan. Nobody knows it is even there."

"You've got a *stealth* plane?" Eddie said in disbelief.

"There are advantages to owning a stake in a military aircraft company. Stealth is a major area of research. I have access to that research, and have put it to better use than any government project."

Nina remembered what she had seen at the Khoils' palace. "Wait, this plane of yours—dark gray, propeller at the back, weird looking?"

"Yes. I was test-flying it at night." He raised one hand, palm flat, and tilted it to the left; the airborne images followed suit. "It takes a little getting used to, but I have mastered the controls. A shame this will be its last flight. It is fun." He lowered his hand. After a moment, the horizon tipped back. "As you see, when I am not controlling it directly it follows its default programming, which currently is to fly a standby orbit. Once I fly it past a certain point, though, it has another program."

"A kamikaze run," guessed Eddie.

"Correct. Even if I lose communication, it will still carry out its mission. But for maximum effect, precise timing will be needed." He indicated the news feed, which showed a floodlit stage. As yet, the only people on it were technicians making final preparations. "I do not know exactly when the G20 leaders will assemble for their photo call. As soon as they start to appear, I will begin. The computers can guide the plane to the right spot, but only I can choose the most devastating moment."

"You finally admit there are things humans can do better than computers, and *that's* your example?" said Nina.

"There is an irony to it. But after the explosion, everyone in the world will seek answers—and Qexia will provide them."

Her voice filled with scorn. "The *wrong* answers."

"Qexia does not lie," Khoil replied, displeased at the implied insult. "It simply weights the results according to user expectations. In India, it will seem that Pakistani militants carried out the attack. In Pakistan, India will be seen as falsely accusing an Islamic power that has been pointedly excluded from the G20."

"Anger will rise," continued Vanita. "People in both countries will demand action—they will demand blood! War will start between India and Pakistan, and it will escalate into a nuclear conflict. Once that happens, the violence will spread. Country against country, East against West, Hindu against Muslim, Muslim against Christian. The world will burn." Her face twisted with a terrible smile of satisfaction.

"Not everybody gets their information from Qexia," Nina pointed out. "And not everybody's driven by rage and vengeance, either—however corrupt and decadent you think they've become. You won't start World War Three from just one event, even something this big."

"We do not need to," said Khoil. "A global nuclear war is only a forty-two percent probability...but there is a ninety-nine percent probability that the networks of finance and trade vital to modern civilization will collapse. The effect will be the same." He took position at the virtual controls. "You are a historian, Dr. Wilde. But this is the end of history. The start of a new age. *Our* new age. Enlightened...purified. A new Satya Yuga."

On the news feed, the technicians cleared the stage. The camera panned across to a doorway, from which officials emerged. Camera flashes lit up the area like strobes.

"They're coming out," said Vanita excitedly, grabbing her husband's arm.

He lifted her hand away. "Vanita, my beloved, I need you to clear the platform so I can fly the *vimana*. It would be unfortunate if you nudged me and made it crash short of the target." She was annoyed by his undercurrent of sarcasm, but descended the steps to the circular walkway, where she stood beside Tandon.

Khoil raised both hands, paused for a moment like a conductor preparing to cue an orchestra...then clenched them as if gripping invisible controls. The view from the cameras tilted sharply as the stealth plane banked. The artificial horizon matched the move, a green line indicating the course to the presidential residence swinging into sight.

Text also appeared at the bottom of the screens. TIME TO TARGET: 04:02. The number counted down. 04:01, 04:00, 03:59...

34

Nina stared at the screens in horror as the Indian president and prime minister made their way to the stage. "If you do this, millions of people will die—and a lot of them will be in your own country!"

"They will be reborn in the next cycle," Khoil said, eyes fixed on the view from the aircraft. "And they will be born into a better world."

She had no counter to that. Khoil was a man set in his beliefs, and there were no words she could use to change his mind. Only action would make a difference now. "We've got to stop him," she whispered to Eddie.

"Yeah, I got that." If he could reach the upper platform, he could disrupt the plane's flight by punching out Khoil and taking over the virtual controls, crashing it somewhere safe—or at least forcing it to return to its fail-safe orbit until the world leaders were back indoors.

Getting onto the platform, though, was the problem. There were three men with guns there to stop him.

Unless he could make it *two* men ...

"You're Bosnian, right?" he asked Zec in an almost conversational tone, to the mercenary's surprise. "The country's pretty much half and half Christians and Muslims, isn't it?"

"Yes," said Zec, suspicious. "Why?"

"Well, that part of the world's had some...well, problems between different ethnic groups. It might have calmed down now, but this'll start it right back up again." He indicated the Khoils, both fixated on the big screens. "Your bosses just said that's what they were after."

"That is not my concern," Zec said, but the idea, having taken root, was clearly troubling him.

"It'll be your wife and son's concern, though. You said they live in Sarajevo. That's not exactly high on the list of cities people associate with peace and harmony and good times." Eddie's expression hardened. "They're going to die. And you'll have helped it happen."

Vanita glared angrily at them. "Enough! Zec, go back to security." She addressed the guard, jabbing a red-nailed finger at Nina and Eddie. "You. Shoot these two."

The guard pushed past Zec, raising his gun—but Tandon intervened. "Please, let me." He smiled coldly. "I have been looking forward to this."

"All right," said Vanita. "But quickly."

Eddie gave Zec a look. "Last chance for your son to be proud of you."

Tandon advanced, pocketing his gun...and raised his hands to deliver a lethal martial arts strike. "It will be quick," he assured Vanita, "but *not* painless."

"Good," she said. "Do it." The countdown on the screen reached three minutes.

Tandon stepped closer. Nina gripped Eddie's hand—

A spray of blood and brain matter splattered across the dome as Zec shot the guard in the back of the head.

Eddie pushed Nina down, crouching to give Zec a clear shot at Tandon as the dead guard fell. His MP5K clattered to the floor ten feet below, skidding away to end up near the spiral staircase.

Zec fired again—and Tandon *dodged*, twisting aside. The bullet missed him by less than an inch. Zec tracked him, releasing another shot as the Indian dived under the railing, grabbing the edge of the walkway as he fell and flipping himself underneath it. Eddie heard soft clanks from below; Tandon was hanging from the catwalk's underside, effortlessly swinging parkour-style along its supporting scaffold. Zec backed up, gun darting from side to side in expectation of an attack.

Eddie ran past Nina. Vanita hurriedly retreated, but he ignored her, instead pounding up the curved stairs to the upper platform. "Ay up," he said to Khoil. The billionaire's plump face filled with fear. "Can I play?"

Nina jumped up, raising her fists as she charged at Vanita. While no expert at unarmed combat, she had still received enough training from her husband to throw a good punch—and this one would be particularly satisfying. Vanita turned and ran, Nina pursuing her around the walkway.

Tandon's head briefly popped up into Zec's view. He fired, but the Indian had already ducked out of sight with snake-like speed. The Bosnian shifted his aim, shooting at the floor. Four bullets punched holes through the metal plating with shrill spangs—but Tandon was too fast. A clank of something falling as he swept hand over hand along the scaffold, then in an acrobatic, almost gravity-defying move, he swung back up feetfirst under the railing—and drove a crunching kick into Zec's stomach. The mercenary flew backward, crashing against the outer railing—

It gave way. Zec tumbled over the edge. His neck cracked horribly as he landed headfirst, flopping limply to the floor. The broken length of railing clanged down beside him.

Khoil backed away as Eddie approached. He reached the edge of the platform and cowered, with nowhere to run. On the big screens, the view of Delhi tipped sharply, the drone swinging back around toward its standby orbit now that it was no longer receiving control signals. "You— you can't stop—"

Eddie punched him hard in the face. Khoil spun off the platform, landing with a crash on the walkway below, smooth skin now marred by a smear of blood from his split lips.

Wiping his knuckles on his coat, Eddie moved to the center of the platform and raised his hands. "Okay, let's see how this works..." He spread his fingers as he had seen Khoil do and tilted one hand experimentally. The horizon on the screen followed his movement. "Yes!" He looked for somewhere among the city's lights that would be safe enough to crash the drone.

A black line ran across both images. A river.

"Let's make a splash," he said, tipping his hand forward as if pushing an imaginary joystick. The drone began to descend.

Tandon ran to help Khoil, but the billionaire shouted, "No! Up there, stop Chase!"

Nina was fast gaining on Vanita, who was trying to run on two-inch heels. "Get your ass back here!" she shouted. They had completely circled the walkway, reaching the broken section of railing. Vanita jumped through the gap, landing beside Zec.

Nina leapt after her, aiming to knock her down—but Vanita scrambled clear, one of her shoes flying off. Rolling as she landed, Nina jumped up—

To see Vanita going for the dead guard's MP5K.

She dived at her, tackling the sari-clad woman just before she reached it and slamming her to the floor.

The river grew steadily larger—but Eddie was forced to abandon the controls as Tandon rushed at him. The drone climbed steeply back to its fail-safe altitude.

Eddie and Tandon circled each other. The Englishman

raised his fists. Tandon brought up his own hands, fingers together like ax heads—then a flash of triumph crossed his face as he remembered he had a gun. He reached for it—

Finding nothing but an empty pocket. It had fallen out when he was swinging from the walkway.

Eddie lunged, a powerful punch steaming at Tandon's jaw.

The Indian whipped his head back, the blow only grazing his chin. He snapped up an arm to hook Eddie's as it passed, then whirled, simultaneously slamming an elbow against the other man's head and painfully twisting his shoulder.

Eddie staggered as Tandon released him, turning to face his enemy—and a roundhouse kick crunched into his sternum. He reeled backward...

And fell off the platform.

Like Khoil, he landed with a bang on the metal walkway—but unlike the software mogul, his plunge didn't end there as he slid under the railing and dropped another ten feet to the chamber's floor. Pain coursing through his shoulder and chest, he lay on his back, winded.

Nina grappled with Vanita, thumping a punch into her kidneys. Vanita shrieked, lashing out with one hand—and slashing Nina across her left cheek with a ring. Face stinging from the cut, Nina flinched back as the red talons clawed at her eyes.

Her retreat gave the other woman the chance to twist and kick her in the stomach. Nina gasped, doubling over. "You think I'm weak?" Vanita snarled, another strike catching the side of Nina's head. "I know how to fight—I grew up in the slums!" She scrabbled for the gun—

Nina grabbed her trailing sari and yanked her back, stamping down hard on her bare foot with a heavy boot. Vanita screamed as her little toe broke. Nina swung her around, drawing back her fist. "And I'm from *New York*, bitch!"

She slammed a punch into her face. Spitting blood, Vanita fell beside Zec. Shaking out her aching hand, Nina stood and turned to find the gun. It lay about ten feet away. She started toward it—

The broken length of railing cracked against her knee as Vanita swung it like a baseball bat. Nina stumbled, almost falling. The metal tube whooshed at her again as Vanita limped after her.

Khoil hurried up the steps, a hand to his bloodied mouth. Tandon moved to help him, but was waved back. "Kill him, kill him!" the billionaire screeched. His bodyguard jumped down to the walkway as he took his position at the invisible controls once more.

Eddie was struggling upright when he heard a crash from above as Tandon landed. The Indian vaulted the railing—flying straight at him. With a yelp, Eddie rolled sideways. A heel slammed down where his head had just been.

More world leaders were on the stage, the smaller nations being introduced first. The president of South Korea shook hands with his hosts, flashing cameras recording the moment. The countdown had been rewound by Eddie's hijacking of the controls, but it was still ticking away as Khoil brought the drone back on course.

Three minutes, thirty-two seconds to impact.

The railing clanged dully against Nina's forearm as she shielded her head from Vanita's attack. She held in a cry of pain, retreating from another blow—and backing into the enormous video wall. Unlike the one in Bangalore, which was divided into segments to allow access, this infotarium formed an unbroken 360-degree circle inside the dome. The aluminum framework rattled with the impact, one of the LCD screens flickering as it was jolted.

Teeth bared, Vanita swiped the makeshift club at her—

Nina dived sideways. The railing smashed one of the screens behind her, its backlight panel blowing out with a bang and a sputter of sparks. The broken display crashed to the floor, exposing the geodesic fiberglass panels of the radome behind it.

Tandon kicked Eddie hard in the side, bowling him across the floor to the stairs leading up to the walkway. Wheezing, Eddie used them to clamber to his feet—as his attacker thrust a killing blow at his chest.

Even battered and winded, he had enough strength to jerk aside. The blow missed the lethal pressure point, but still hit his rib cage agonizingly hard. He staggered backward as Tandon struck again, and again, aiming for his throat, his heart. Each time, he was just barely able to parry the blows, but all that did was shift the pain to his arms. And Tandon wasn't even breaking a sweat—the bastard was playing with him, wearing him down little by little until he was unable to defend himself.

Khoil glanced at the two fights playing out below, but remained fixated on the screens. The Japanese prime minister walked to the stage. Three minutes, ten seconds.

Vanita swung the railing again, knocking Nina against another screen. She raised the club high over her head, about to smash it down on Nina's skull—

Nina grabbed one of her earrings and pulled. Hard.

The piece of jewelry tore away from Vanita's ear—with a chunk of lobe the size of a thumbnail still hooked on it.

Vanita screamed as blood gushed down her neck. Nina seized her by her sari and yanked with all her strength, slamming Vanita face-first through the gap between the screens—and into the triangular panel behind it.

The fiberglass broke apart with a splintering crack. A freezing wind blasted through the hole, frost and condensation instantly forming on the inside of the dome and the nearby screens. Vanita pulled back—and screamed even louder as the panel's razor-sharp edges ripped into her cheeks like bear claws. The railing clunked to the floor.

"Vanita!" Khoil cried. But he didn't move to help her,

his mission the higher priority. He adjusted the drone's course slightly. The countdown reached 02:50.

Nina snatched up the railing and was about to clout Vanita with it when she realized there was someone who needed it more. "Eddie! *Catch!*"

She hurled it across the dome like a javelin.

Eddie fended off another blow, looked up, saw the railing arcing toward him—and caught it. He spun and swung it at Tandon's head. Suddenly on the defensive, Tandon jumped back, protectively whipping up an arm. The railing cracked painfully against his wrist.

Eddie swung his new weapon again, the reversal of fortune filling him with a surge of energy. "That's more fucking like it!" He forced Tandon toward the wall. The Indian tried to dart away, but Eddie hit his shoulder, knocking him back into the support frame. It shook, rattling the video screens. "Oi! I'm not finished with you!"

"Yes!" Nina cried triumphantly as her husband turned the tables—only for Vanita to throw herself at her with a shriek, overcome with rage as blood ran down her ruined face. She slammed the American back against the video wall, driving a knee up into her stomach. Nina groaned, winded—and Vanita clamped her hands around her throat. The fingers tightened, taloned thumbs digging deep into her neck.

Eddie attacked again, the metal pole thudding against the Indian's ribs. He grinned nastily as his opponent's face twisted in pain. A couple more blows would knock Tandon down, and then he could deal with Khoil. He pulled back the railing for another swing—

Tandon leapt—and grabbed a horizontal cross-member above. He pulled himself sharply upward, swinging his legs up like a trapeze artist as the pole whipped past an inch beneath him. He hooked one foot around a strut, using the support to haul himself around, spider-like, and climb higher.

Eddie swung again, but Tandon was just out of reach. The railing smashed a video screen, which fell to the floor with a bang. Tandon glared down at him as he clambered across the framework. Its aluminum joints squeaked and juddered under his weight.

The projector rig at the top of the dome also shook, causing the images on the big screens to wobble. Khoil glanced around to find the cause of the disruption. 02:25 remaining on the countdown.

The framework had been designed to support the screens and the overhead rig, Eddie realized—nothing more. The extra weight of a grown man was straining it to its limit...

He swung his makeshift bat—not at Tandon, but at the exposed metal structure where the screen had fallen away. A vertical strut broke at the joint with a sharp snap of metal. A whole section of the framework jolted violently, screens flickering. The projector rig lurched. Khoil looked around again, this time in alarm as Eddie kept bashing at the weakened frame. Another screen broke from its mount, swinging on its power cord before shattering on the floor. "Chapal! Stop him!"

Tandon dived at the Englishman from above, deadly hands outstretched like claws—

Eddie whipped up the pole.

Fear flashed in Tandon's eyes—but too late.

The broken end of the railing punched through his chest, spearing out through his back with a gout of blood. Even impaled, though, he still knocked Eddie down, literal deadweight slamming him to the floor.

Both Khoils stared at the length of metal jutting from their bodyguard's back in disbelief. "Chapal!" Vanita cried, for a moment the woman she was choking forgotten—

Nina drove the heel of her palm up against Vanita's chin. The Indian woman's open mouth snapped shut—catching the end of her tongue between her teeth. Vanita spat out blood, half an inch of muscle hanging only by a few threads of mangled tissue.

"Bite *your* tongue!" Nina gasped, throwing a punch. It only caught Vanita a glancing blow on the cheek, but it was enough to make her stagger backward and slip on the film of frost that had formed on the metal floor as the icy wind shrilled through the hole in the dome. She stumbled . . .

Landing beside the MP5K.

Vanita grabbed the gun and jumped up—

Nina dived at her, skidding on her stomach along the frost. She wrapped both arms around Vanita's ankles and twisted. Already unbalanced by her missing shoe, Vanita staggered and fell . . .

Down the stairs.

She screamed—then the cry was cut off abruptly by an echoing bang as she hit hard metal. More *thump*s followed as she tumbled down the steps. The MP5K fired at each impact, bursts of bullets clanging off the machinery. A fierce eruption of sparks came from one transformer as a round shattered an insulator, the resulting short circuit causing an angry, sizzling hum to rise within it. Several screens in the dome above flickered. But Vanita didn't hear the sound or see the flashes as she crashed to the floor, unconscious.

Nina heard and saw them, though. "Oh, crap," she gasped, crawling to the stairs and looking down. Vanita was sprawled at the bottom, the gun beside her . . . but the spraying sparks and ominous crackling noise changed Nina's mind about going down to get it. The short circuit was causing the mineral oil used to cool and insulate the old transformer to boil—to ignition point. It could explode at any moment.

Eddie kicked away Tandon's corpse and looked up at the platform. Khoil broke through his shock, whirling to check the still-trembling images on the main screens. The drone was closing on its target: 02:05 to impact. He made several rapid hand gestures; no longer controlling the flight of the stealth aircraft, but calling up a menu screen.

Nina realized what he was doing as commands flashed up on the giant video wall. The game was almost over—and the billionaire was trying to fix the result. "Eddie!" she yelled, voice rasping in her bruised throat. "He's locking the controls!" Even without anyone guiding it, the drone would still carry out its pre-programmed mission.

Eddie sprang up, but knew that by the time he reached the upper platform Khoil would have completed his task. He needed a faster way to stop him. *Shoot him*—but the guard's fallen gun was nowhere in sight.

Which left—

He stamped a foot down on Tandon's ribs and grabbed the length of railing, yanking it out of the dead man's chest. He spun to smash the metal pipe against the dented framework—

The aluminum strut he hit broke in two. The effect on the rest of the weakened structure was instantaneous: A chain reaction rippled upward as the weight of the video screens caused the horizontal supports to collapse one after the other. Eddie ran as the larger screens above him fell, smashing on the floor and blowing out with gunfire cracks and sprays of sparks and smoke.

The breakdown reached the top of the dome. The images on the two big screens jolted crazily as the projector rig shook—then tipped sharply as one side broke free, swinging above Khoil with a shrill of tortured metal. He looked up—

The rig tore loose. It dropped the thirty feet to the platform before Khoil could manage more than a startled scream, pounding him to the floor like a pile driver.

Nina winced. "Guess you really *can* be crushed by the weight of information."

Eddie went to her. "Jesus! You okay? Looks like you got bitten by a vampire!"

Nina was confused until she put a hand to her neck and realized that Vanita had broken the skin with her sharp thumbnails. She wiped off the blood. "Yeah, but we need to—"

A loud bang cut her off. Smoke swirled up from the stairs. The crackling sizzle from the transformers below grew louder, more agitated. More of the screens flickered. "Not keen on that," Eddie muttered. He looked back up at the dome. With the projectors gone, the two largest screens were now blank—no way of knowing how close the drone was to its target. "Come on!"

He ran for the platform, Nina following. They reached the upper level to find that Khoil was still alive, groaning weakly under the projector rig. "How do we stop the plane?" Nina demanded.

Despite his pain, Khoil somehow managed a twisted smirk. "You can't," he gasped, blood on his teeth. "The autopilot is set. In less than two minutes, the Kali Yuga will end..."

35

A large patch of dark blood was swelling across the chest of Khoil's Nehru jacket. Eddie jammed his heel down on it, making the Indian scream. "Tell us how to unlock the controls!"

"No," Khoil rasped as Eddie eased the pressure.

"You're not going to live much longer no matter what, but I can make every second of it really hurt."

"It... doesn't matter. I will be reborn in a new golden age..."

"As a dung beetle, if there's any bloody justice." Realizing that Khoil was utterly committed to his plan, he gave him one more jab before turning to Nina. "What the fuck do we do now?"

"I don't know," she said, scanning the active screens in desperation. Maybe Khoil had made a mistake, leaving some way they could divert the drone. But she saw nothing helpful...

Her gaze flashed back to one screen in particular. The display showing the live news feed from the presidential palace was still active. The British prime minister was shaking hands with his hosts. Only a few more world leaders still to appear, the last being the president of the United States, and everyone would be in place for the drone's suicide strike—

"Peter!" she exclaimed, the sight of the British politician reminding her of one of the members of his entourage. "We can call Peter Alderley; he can warn them!"

"Well, yeah, we could," Eddie said, "if we had his number. And a phone."

"We've *got* a phone. If I can remember how to work it..." She thought back to the smaller infotarium in India, then raised one hand as if holding an invisible handset and brought it to her ear.

Nothing happened. The screens remained unchanged. "Dammit!"

Eddie gave her a look of disbelief. "This isn't a good time to play charades!"

"I saw him do it in Bangalore—like a virtual phone." She moved closer to the slender lectern housing the motion sensors and tried again, slowing and exaggerating the move...

The screens changed, a keypad overlaid on the images. "Yes!" she cried. "What's the number?"

"How the hell would I know Alderley's number?"

"Not his number—*Mac's* number!" She raised her other hand, forefinger extended; a glowing circle appeared over the keypad as the sensors tracked her fingertip. "He's with Peter, and you know *his* number, don't you?"

Eddie quickly recited the digits, Nina tapping at thin air to enter them into the virtual keypad. "Just hope he remembered to charge his phone."

The animated CONNECTING... icon appeared, but nothing seemed to be happening. Nina and Eddie exchanged worried looks—then a hollow hiss came from speakers overhead. Another tense moment, and the ringing tone echoed around the dome. Twice, three times...

"If the world ends because we got sent to voicemail, I'm gonna be very unhappy," Nina muttered. "Come on, Mac, pick up—"

A click, then a familiar Scottish voice, slight puzzlement evident at being called from an unfamiliar number. "Hello?"

"Mac!" Nina cried. "Thank God! It's us, Nina and Eddie!"

The background noise suggested that he was in a large room, a hum of conversation audible. "What's going on? I thought you were in Greenland?"

"We are," said Eddie, "but the shit's about to hit the fan in Delhi. Khoil's got a stealth drone full of explosives about to do a kamikaze run on the G20 photo call *right now*—you've got to get them out of there!"

Silence for a second. Then an urgent shout of: *"Peter!"*

"What is it?" called Alderley.

"We have a situation. Over here, now! Kit, you too."

"Where are you?" Eddie asked.

"At the Rashtrapati Bhavan—we've been dealing with the head of the Indian security service."

"Useful."

"Not really—he doesn't believe the Khoils could be a threat."

A new voice: Kit. "What's happening?"

Mac quickly summarized the situation for his companions. "Chase," said Alderley, "is this intel good?"

"Straight from the arsehole's mouth," Eddie told him, with a quick look down at Khoil. "I don't know how long until it hits ground zero, but it's less than ninety seconds. You've got to evacuate everyone—or at least get them under cover."

"Eddie!" said Nina urgently, indicating the news feed. On the screen, President Cole was emerging from the palace, striding along the red carpet to meet the Indian leaders. Now that all the G20 leaders had arrived, they would gather for their group photo...and become the highest-value target on the planet.

"Shit!" said Eddie. "Mac, get them out of there! *Now!*"

"We're on it," said Mac. A muted *thump* came from the speakers as he disconnected.

"It's too late," Khoil said from the floor. "You can't stop it."

All Nina and Eddie could do was watch the news feed as the world leaders began to congregate.

· · ·

Mac and Alderley hurried across the crowded room, Kit following as quickly as he could on his crutch. The majority of the guests were high-ranking Indian politicians and civil servants, the remainder diplomats and officials from the other countries attending the summit.

There was only one person the trio were interested in, however. They spotted the portly, gray-bearded man near the doors leading to the expansive courtyard where the leaders had assembled. "Mr. Verma!" Alderley called, barging past a cluster of Russian delegates to reach him.

Arivali Verma, the head of India's Intelligence Bureau, looked around in annoyance from his discussion with his Chinese opposite number. "Mr.... Alderley, yes?" He recognized the taller, older man with him. "Colonel McCrimmon? What is it?"

"There's about to be a terrorist attack," Alderley said urgently. "We have to get the delegates into cover."

"What?" Verma looked to one of his subordinates standing nearby. The man's bemused expression told him that he had heard nothing of the sort through his earpiece. "Where did you hear this?"

"Does it matter?" Mac snapped. "Just evacuate the courtyard!"

"What kind of attack? I need more information! The entire world is watching—if I call an alert and nothing happens, we will look like fools!"

"Better that than doing nothing until a plane crashes into them!" said Kit, catching up.

Verma huffed. "If an unauthorized plane came within fifty kilometers, I would be told immediately."

"Not if it was a stealth plane," said Mac.

"A stealth plane?" Verma echoed in disbelief. "This is absurd!"

"We don't have time for this!" Kit growled. He tried to push past Verma to the door, but his assistant moved to block him—

Mac suddenly planted both palms squarely on Verma's chest and shoved him backward. Arms flailing, he crashed against his subordinate. Both men fell to the floor in an ungainly heap.

Everyone nearby was shocked—then several of the Indian contingent rushed at Mac . . . including the men guarding the courtyard doors. The Scot winked at Kit, the slight flick of his eyes toward the exit giving the younger man a clear instruction. Alderley, hemmed in by the charge, realized what he was doing and swung a punch at one of the men trying to grab Mac before he too was swarmed.

Leaving the doorway clear.

Kit hopped over the outraged, flapping Verma and into the courtyard. Ignoring the resurgent pain in his injured leg, he hurried forward, pulling out his ID and holding it above his head. "Interpol!" he cried. "Everyone inside—there's a terrorist—"

A pair of black-suited US Secret Service agents dived at him, slamming him to the ground. The world leaders looked around in surprise at the commotion, some reacting with alarm at the last word.

The agents grappled with Kit, forcing him onto his chest and pulling his arms up painfully behind his back. He struggled but couldn't break free: the only thing that could escape was his voice. "They're going to crash a plane!" he cried. "A suicide flight—*9/11*! Get out of here! Get out!"

Those two numbers got everyone's attention. One agent released Kit's arm, putting a hand to his earpiece to listen to an incoming transmission over the hubbub—then jumped up and pulled Kit to his feet. The other American agents mobilized as one to surround Cole and clear a path for him to get indoors. To the Secret Service, any hint of a threat to the life of the president was treated as confirmed until proved otherwise; the potential consequences of underreacting were infinitely worse than the opposite.

The security details of the other leaders took their cue from the Americans. The courtyard had several exits, all of which led inside the palace; the group split up to run for them.

The two agents bustled Kit back toward the door. Over the shouts and screams, he heard another noise—a high-pitched buzz, the rasp of an aircraft propeller.

Getting louder...

◆ ◆ ◆

Nina and Eddie, watching the news feed, saw the camera pan sharply to catch Kit being tackled by a pair of agents. His mouth moved as he shouted, but the screen had no sound.

The picture jolted as the press corps panicked, someone bumping the camera. Its operator valiantly tried to cover the action, aiming it at the world leaders, but by now they were scattering in all directions. "Oh, shit," Nina whispered.

"Any second," Khoil croaked. "Any second now..."

The image tipped downward as the cameraman abandoned his post and fled, only flagstones and a section of red carpet visible. Running shadows flickered across the screen.

A flash—

The picture jolted, then broke up into stuttering pixellated squares for a moment before cutting out entirely. The screen went black.

Eddie looked frantically at the remaining screens in the hope that one would reveal more information, but nothing was forthcoming. "What happened?" Nina asked. "Oh, God, what happened?"

Khoil managed a bubbling, coughing laugh. "The Kali Yuga has ended, Dr. Wilde. That is what has happened. The global collapse is inevitable . . . Lord Shiva will destroy the old age to begin a new one."

"We can still tell everyone what you've done," Nina told him, helplessness turning to anger. "There won't be any war if they know you were behind it—no matter what you've rigged Qexia to say."

"This is no longer a time for reason," the billionaire said. "Emotion will rule—anger, fear, vengeance." His gaze moved to a screen above her. "Look. There it is . . . the image that will change the world."

The live news feed was back, displaying a view from a different camera—this one in the grounds of the Rashtrapati Bhavan, shaking as its operator was jostled by people around him. The enormous palace, lit by banks of floodlights, stood out sharply against the black sky—as did a rising column of smoke and dust, drifting across to obscure the huge dome that was the building's centerpiece.

"You see?" rasped Khoil, with rising triumph. "They are dead. Qexia is already blaming Pakistan. I . . . I have won!"

"The only thing you've won is a kick in the bollocks," Eddie snarled, drawing back one foot. Khoil flinched, but Nina grabbed her husband's arm before he could deliver the strike.

She pointed up at the screen. "Eddie, look!"

The picture had changed again, to another handheld camera. The image jerked as the cameraman ran down a corridor, glimpses of ornately decorated walls briefly visible through a pall of swirling smoke. The broadcast was coming from somewhere inside the palace...but how far from ground zero? People staggered past, half-seen ghosts with clothing and faces caked in dust.

Nina and Eddie stared up at the screen, barely daring to breathe. The camera entered a large room. A ragged hole in the far wall was briefly visible before the cameraman turned his attention to the people around him. Those nearest the broken wall were covered in rubble, clearly dead. Others were still moving, dark blotches of blood standing out through the pale dust.

But despite the carnage, the cameraman was following his journalistic instincts. The image steadied, fixing on individual groups of people. Searching for the surviving world leaders.

If there were any.

Black suits, turned gray by the covering of smashed stone and plaster. Secret Service agents. Clustered around someone. The camera shakily zoomed in.

An agent, blood on his neck and shoulder, slumped back—to reveal the dirtied face of President Leo Cole. But he was still, a pale statue. Nina gripped Eddie's hand, unable to speak for fear. Was he alive or dead? She couldn't tell...

He moved, mouth widening in a silent cough. Opening his eyes, he wiped his face and spoke to one of the agents.

"Yes!" Nina exclaimed, squeezing Eddie's hand tightly. "Never thought I'd be so happy to see a politician talking!"

The image moved away from Cole, reacting to something off screen. It hunted through the drifting smoke before settling on another leader: the Indian president, leaning against a wall as two men hurried to help him. "The bigwigs got out okay, then—some of 'em, anyway." Eddie watched the screen as the camera searched for more survivors. "What about Mac, though? And Kit?"

"And Peter," Nina reminded him, getting a noncommittal grunt in reply. The cameraman continued through the room, people rushing past to help the injured. More powerful faces appeared, the Indian prime minister and Russian president being guided toward clearer air. Behind them—

"Mac!" Eddie cried, catching a glimpse of the Scot limping toward an exit. His suit was torn, blood smeared over one arm, but he didn't appear badly wounded. Following him was Kit, supported by a Secret Service agent. An overweight, bearded Indian man jostled through the crowd to speak to him, then the cameraman moved on.

Nina turned to Khoil, whose expression was slowly collapsing into dismay. "They survived. We managed to warn them in time. I guess Qexia *couldn't* predict everything. So the question is: What now?"

"We still need to shut down that jammer," said Eddie. "Soon as we do, Probst can send an SOS."

"Or we could do it here." Nina moved back to the sensor unit, raising her hand to her ear to make another virtual phone call. The keypad reappeared on the screens. "We'll just call—"

An earsplitting bang came from below, a shower of sparks spitting up from the stairwell with a fierce electrical crackle. Smoke spewed into the dome as all the remaining screens flickered, then went dark.

"What the hell was that?" Eddie yelled.

"A transformer's blown!" As a child, Nina had once been evacuated from school when a faulty transformer on a neighboring building exploded, starting a fire and knocking out the power for three blocks. The same was happening here, only on a much larger scale—and flames rose higher as she watched. "We've got to get out of here."

"How? That's the only exit!"

She looked across to where she had slammed Vanita into

the outer wall. "Not anymore. Come on!" She hurried over to Khoil.

"What're you doing?" Eddie demanded.

"He's got to stand trial—"

He pointed at the blood pooling around the billionaire's broken body. "He'll be dead in five minutes without a medic, and nobody's going to run through a fire to help this little turd. Especially not me! Besides, he believes in reincarnation, right? He can find out if he was right."

"But we can't just leave him," Nina protested.

Khoil's breathing became more labored. "You . . . you have condemned the world to remain in the Kali Yuga," he spat. "Shiva will reward me in the next life. He will punish *you* for eternity!"

Another loud detonation from below shook the dome, a screen dropping from the support frame and smashing on the floor. The flames in the stairwell rose higher. "If we don't get out of here, we'll die with him!" Eddie shouted. He grabbed her arm, pulling her to the steps.

She looked back at Khoil, seeing that his blank, expressionless android mask had finally been completely stripped away, leaving nothing but anger and hate. Then he was gone as they descended to the walkway, then hurried to floor level. They started for the hole in the dome wall—

"Chase . . . ," said a low, straining voice. Eddie whirled. Zec. The mercenary was still alive—just. He had broken his neck in the fall, his head twisted around alarmingly, but the break was at a vertebra low enough for him to keep breathing. His body was limp, however, still splayed as he had landed. Paralyzed.

Eddie hesitated, then went to him. "What're you doing?" said Nina, reluctantly stopping halfway to the hole in the dome. "If we don't have time to get Khoil out, we don't have time for him either!"

She was right, he knew, but the situation was different. Zec had helped them—*saved* them. Abandoning him felt wrong...even though attempting to get him out of the dome would probably result in them all being killed.

Zec also knew the score. "No, leave me," he whispered before the Englishman could pick him up. "Just tell my family...that I did the right thing. Tell my son he can be...proud of me."

"I will," Eddie promised.

"Thank you." A feeble smile. "I hope...Hugo will not be disappointed when I see him. Now go. Go!"

Eddie backed away, giving him a nod of silent thanks before turning to follow Nina. She was already at the exposed section of dome, kicking at the fiberglass panels. He joined her, slamming his sole against one of the geodesic struts. Metal bent, then snapped under a second blow. The panels shattered, freezing wind gusting around them.

The resulting hole was now large enough to fit through. Nina went first, finding herself on a narrow ledge, looking down at the composite building's roof close to thirty feet below. "Whoa! It's higher than I thought."

There was no sign of a ladder. "We'll have to jump," said Eddie.

"Are you kidding? We'll break our legs!"

Another explosive crackle of electrical fury came from behind them. "Well, we could just stand here and watch the aurora, but we won't have long to appreciate it." He ran to one corner. "Here!" he said, pointing down. Though the heat from inside the radar station had melted most of the snow off the sloping roof, the elements had still maintained a hold on some areas, a steep drift having built up against the north-facing wall.

"It's not very deep."

"Better than nothing!" He clambered over the rail, hung from it...then dropped. There was a flat *whump* as he hit the piled snow, followed by a string of expletives.

"Are you okay?" Nina called as he crawled from the drift.

"You were right—it's not very deep. Come on, jump down."

She reluctantly dangled from the railing, muttering darkly before releasing her hold. The drift exploded around her as she landed, the mound of snow doing little to cushion her landing. "God *damn* it!" she gasped, spitting out ice.

Eddie helped her up. "It's going!" He indicated the little windows above them. Actinic flashes from the sparking, overloading transformers stabbed through the orange flicker of flames. "Come on!"

Nina couldn't see any skylights or other ways back into the building, only the jutting tops of the station's eight blocky support legs. "Where?"

"Behind that!" He pointed at the nearest leg. "Get down and cover your ears!"

They rounded the structure, finding another snowdrift on its exposed side. Eddie practically threw Nina into it, diving after her—

The remaining transformers, hulking Cold War relics filled with hundreds of gallons of mineral oil coolant, exploded.

The floor of the dome erupted with liquid fire, the blast from below ripping the geodesic structure apart. Zec was killed instantly; Khoil, higher up, screamed and thrashed as the flames consumed him in his own personal funeral pyre. The walls of the central core collapsed onto the roof and smashed through it into the floors below, the burning remains of the dome tumbling down on top of the devastation.

Shielded by the support leg, Eddie and Nina were still pounded by the force of the explosion as the colossal building shook. Flaming fiberglass fragments hailed down around them. Eddie hurriedly brushed cinders from his scalp and crawled to peer around the leg, seeing the communications masts topple and crash to the ground like great steel trees. "I think that's the jammer sorted out, then."

"And everything else," Nina added. "This whole building's going to burn—we've got to..." She trailed off.

"What?" Eddie demanded, suspecting that he wouldn't like the answer.

"The vault," she gasped. "We left the vault open—if the building burns down, the debris'll fall down the elevator shaft and destroy all the treasures!"

"So let me guess—you want us to go down there and save everything? We'll have a sod of a job carrying that statue back to the lift!"

"We don't have to take anything out, just make sure they're protected. Eddie, we *have* to," she went on, pleading. "We can't let them be destroyed, not now. You saw how thick that door was—all we have to do is close it. Even if the building collapses, someone can still recover everything later."

"Yeah, and they might recover what's left of *us* if we're down there when it happens!" But he saw her point. The war the Khoils had hoped for might have been averted, but if their private collection of stolen cultural treasures was destroyed, they would still get one last laugh from beyond the grave. "Okay, okay. But we'll have to be quick. I don't know how long this place'll hold together."

Nina stood. "First thing we need to do is get off this roof." She gingerly made her way to the edge and looked across the aurora-lit plain. Far below, several people were running for one of the smaller structures at the base's periphery. "Where are they going?"

"Emergency shelter, probably," said Eddie, more interested in the building on which they were standing. At one end of the roof, metal stairs led downward: access so that the flat expanse could be checked for weather damage. "C'mon."

Skirting pieces of burning debris, they ran for the stairs

and descended to a short catwalk. At its end was a door; Eddie kicked it open. A narrow stairwell led down through the composite building. The air was already hazy with smoke.

They hurried down the stairs, Eddie wincing at the pain from Tandon's beating. At the bottom, he held Nina back, feeling the door for heat on the other side, then cautiously opening it a fraction in case anyone was still in the building. But the corridor was empty. The way clear, they headed for the elevators.

Both of the cage-like cars waited at the top of the shaft. Eddie regarded them dubiously. "Bad idea, using a lift when there's a fire...but I'm not climbing down that bloody ladder again." They entered one of the elevators, which began its rumbling descent into the glacier.

"Now that the jammer's down, how long before help gets here, do you think?" Nina asked.

"Couple of hours, probably."

"I hope Walther can hold out that long."

"I hope *we* can hold out that long. The Khoils are dead, but some of their staff're still around, and they seemed pretty big on loyalty. I don't want to have got through all this and then get shot by their pastry chef. When we—"

They both looked up sharply at a noise from above, a deep metallic groan punctuated by ominous *thumps* and bangs. The elevator shook, the vertical tracks rattling as the building's weight shifted on its support legs.

"So," said Eddie, hovering a hand over the EMERGENCY STOP button, "are some bits of old junk *really* that important to the world?" Nina glared at him. "Yeah, thought so." He stepped back—then froze as he spotted something in the adjacent shaft. "Shit!"

The cables of the other elevator were moving. They looked up again—and saw that the second car was descending after them. It was moving at the same speed as theirs, meaning it would arrive at the bottom some thirty seconds later. Someone leaned over the guardrail.

Vanita.

Holding a gun—

Nina and Eddie dived in different directions as she opened fire with an MP5K. They were far enough below her to be beyond the range at which the compact weapon could be aimed effectively—but she was unconcerned about accuracy, spraying the lower elevator with bullets. Rounds clanged off the metal floor like hailstones, stray shots striking the girders between the two elevator tracks.

"Jesus!" Nina cried, wedging herself tightly into a corner in the hope that the car's frame would give her some protection. "I thought she was dead!"

"No such luck," Eddie growled, doing the same on the other side. He winced as a shot ricocheted off the guardrail above him. "But she'll be out of ammo any second—"

The firing stopped. Nina cautiously raised her head. "Yes!"

"Unless she's got another mag..."

The gunfire resumed.

"Why do you always have to tempt fate?" Nina shrieked, cringing back into what little cover she had as more bullets ripped into the elevator.

"You were the one fighting her! You should've hit her harder!" Eddie fired back.

The onslaught stopped. Eddie had been counting the shots; Vanita had only used about two-thirds of the gun's thirty-round magazine. That suggested she didn't have any more mags—but she still had more than enough ammo remaining to kill them.

They were almost at the bottom of the shaft. "She'll be right behind us," he warned, "so get ready to run."

The elevator stopped. Eddie rolled through the gate as it opened. Nina sprinted after him, a three-round burst of bullets riddling the floor just behind her.

The vault door gaped at the other end of the corridor just as they had left it, the stolen treasures visible beyond. Eddie went to the alcove containing the security station and pressed himself against the wall, planning to ambush Vanita when she arrived, but Nina waved furiously at him from the vault entrance. "No, get inside!" she shouted. "I'll close the door!"

"And she'll just open it again!"

"At least it'll slow her down! Come on!"

Eddie hesitated, then ran for the vault. Another rumbling boom from high above roiled down the shaft as the second elevator reached the bottom.

The gate opened. Vanita stepped out, the gun raised. The left side of her face was burned, hair singed away where flames from the exploding transformer had caught her as she fled. The other half was twisted into a snarl. She shrieked in Hindi as she fired, a blood-spitting outburst of rage and vengeance.

Eddie dived through the open door as the shots seared over him. One of the terra-cotta warriors was hit, a hole exploding in its chest. "Shut the door!" he yelled, scrambling out of Vanita's line of fire.

Nina hit the button on the inner control panel. With a thrum of powerful motors, the massive door began to close.

Vanita broke into a run. "You can't hide! Shiva will find you! *I* will find you!" She fired again, another burst striking the thick metal door as it swung shut. Reaching the control panel, she raised her hand to push the OPEN button—

A much louder noise from the surface, the sharp boom of an explosion—followed by crashes as debris plunged down the elevator shaft, clanging off the girders as it fell. Vanita whirled, seeing an orange light through the open gates, rapidly getting brighter—

Burning wreckage smashed into the elevator cars and

burst apart on impact, a wave of fire and shrapnel surging down the confines of the concrete corridor. It hit Vanita, slamming her violently against the door as shards of wood and metal stabbed into her like flaming arrows.

Even inside the vault, the pounding sounded like an animal clawing at the metal. Nina jumped in shock, then slapped her hand firmly back on the CLOSE button. But the door showed no signs of moving. Eddie stood and went to her. "I don't think she's coming in."

"Was that something falling down the shaft?"

"Half the radar station, by the sound of it—" They both flinched as the lights went out. Darkness for a moment, then from the depths of the bunker came a rattle of machinery. The lights flickered, then came back on. "Emergency generator," he said. "Must cut in automatically if the main power goes off."

"You mean we're stuck down here?" said Nina in alarm.

"For the moment. I wouldn't open that door for a while, anyway—there might be a fire outside. But we've got power, we'll have air—if this place was built as a bunker, it'll have scrubbers like on a submarine—and I saw supplies in the living quarters. The Khoils must have set things up so they could stay down here if they needed. We've just got to wait for someone to come and dig us out."

She still wasn't happy. "That could take ages."

"So? Is there something else you were planning on doing?"

Her gaze went to the collection of antiquities. "You know, I could actually use the time to check the treasures. Find out if any of them have been damaged, try to catalog everything..."

She started toward them, but Eddie put his hands around her waist and pulled her back. "For Christ's sake, it's always bloody work, work, work with you!"

"Well, what do *you* think we should do with the time?"

He pointed at the door leading to the sleeping quarters, a smile spreading across his bruised face. "Seeing as we've finally got some time to ourselves, I've got a few ideas."

Nina grinned. "Just so long as they don't involve props."

New York City

Nina stood before her office windows, staring out across Manhattan. Despite the December cold, it was a clear day, sunlight glinting dazzlingly off the skyscrapers. But her mood was anything but bright.

Eddie stood beside her. "If you're not feeling up to it...," he said quietly.

"No, I'll be okay," she insisted. "I have to see him. I *need* to see him." More loudly, to the open intercom: "Bring him through, please, Lola."

Eddie squeezed her hand in reassurance, then stepped back at a tap on the door. Nina took a breath. "Come in."

Desmond Sharpe entered.

Nina felt a resurgence of the emotions that had stricken her at Rowan's death. Desmond was shorter and stockier, hair gray rather than black, but his eyes were just like his son's. She tried to greet him, but the words froze in her mouth.

He saw her distress, and spoke first. "Hello, Nina," he said softly.

"Hello...Desmond." Nina hesitated before using his first name, almost falling back on a formal *Mr. Sharpe*. But she had been on familiar terms with him while dating Rowan, and afterward.

She introduced him to her husband, who shook his hand. "I'm sorry for your loss," Eddie said simply. Desmond thanked him. "I'll be outside, give you some privacy."

He left the room. Nina tried to assemble her thoughts before speaking, but found herself only able to begin with a superficial pleasantry. "Thank you for coming. Although you didn't have to come all the way from Bridgeport. I wanted to see you at home. And—and I'm so sorry that I wasn't able to be at Rowan's funeral. I should have been. I'm sorry." Her eyes turned down to the carpet between them.

"Nina, it's okay," Desmond replied, stepping to her. "I know you've been . . . busy. I still keep up with the news."

She lifted her head, seeing his small, sad smile. "I'm still sorry. I should have seen you, or at least called you, much sooner. I didn't because . . ." He gaze dropped again, as did her voice. "Because I was afraid to."

"Why?"

"I thought you'd blame me."

"Oh, Nina." He put a hand on her shoulder. "Why on earth would I blame you? You tried to help him; you . . ." His voice became choked, hoarse. "You were there with him. At the end. And, do you know, of all the people he could have been with, I think Rowan would have been happy that it was you."

Nina looked back up at Desmond, hot lines of tears trickling down her cheeks. "Thank you," she whispered.

* * *

Desmond left Nina's office several minutes later. Eddie was waiting outside; the older man paused to speak to him. "Thank you."

"For what?" Eddie asked.

"For dealing with the people who killed my son. I didn't say this to Nina, and I hope you won't tell her I said it, but you gave them what they deserved. I call that justice. The world needs more people like you."

Eddie wasn't quite sure how to respond to that, settling for a noncommittal nod as he shook his hand again. He reentered the office as Lola escorted Desmond out, finding Nina back at the window. "You okay?" he asked, moving behind her and putting his arms around her waist.

"Yeah." She sighed. "Desmond and I talked about Rowan, how much we're both going to miss him. But it's going to be so much harder for him." She leaned against him, wiping her eyes. "I heard you talking to him—what did he say?"

"Just...saying thanks," he said, honoring Desmond's request to keep his bitter outburst private. "Sure you're all right?"

"I will be. Thanks." She put her hands on his. They stood in silence, looking out across New York together.

The moment was broken by the trill of the intercom. "Nina?" said Lola. "Mac and Mr. Jindal are here."

Nina extricated herself from Eddie's arms, surprised. "I didn't know they were in town."

"Mac was with Alderley down in Washington for some intelligence debrief—he told me he'd see us before he flew back home. No idea Kit was here, though."

The familiar Scottish and Indian voices reached them before the visitors themselves: "...with both of them on the team, they would easily be able to stand up to India," said Mac.

"But how can you know? Scotland have never played in a Test match," Kit replied. He tapped on the open door, entering as Nina waved them in. "Hello! Good to see you both again."

"And you," said Nina. She noticed he was limping. "How's the leg?"

"Better, thank you. I can walk without a crutch now, which is a great relief! It still hurts, but it will heal completely soon."

"Already back at work at Interpol, are you?" Eddie asked him as he shook hands with his old friend and mentor.

"Yes—which is why I am here. But I will tell you in a minute. After Mac admits that I am right about Sachin Tendulkar being the greatest cricketer of all time." He grinned at the Scot.

Eddie shook his head. "Not more bloody cricket."

"You should learn from this lad, Eddie," said Mac. "He's very sharp and capable. And polite and respectful, too. Even if his grasp of the facts about sport is somewhat tenuous." Now it was Kit's turn to shake his head.

"So what brings you here, Kit?" asked Nina.

"Well, the first thing is that I wanted to tell you I have been promoted! I am now the Chief Investigator of the Cultural Property Crime Unit."

Eddie patted him on the back. "Nice one, mate. Congratulations!"

"Well deserved, I think," Nina added.

Kit smiled. "Thank you. But the other thing is that I will be working with you again in the future. I have been appointed Interpol's official liaison with the IHA in matters of cultural property crime. I just came from a meeting with the UN's Mr. Penrose—he will give you all the details, but I wanted to tell you in person. And I also wanted to bring you our first new joint case."

He took a box from the briefcase he was carrying and opened it—to reveal the purple statuette Nina had seen among the Khoils' collection of stolen treasures. "Most of the other treasures have been returned, but Interpol has not been able to identify its true owner, and so far we have found nothing in the Khoils' records about it either. It's possible Fernandez's gang killed its owner, so its theft was never reported."

"Or," Eddie suggested, "maybe it wasn't reported because whoever they nicked it from didn't want anyone to know they had it in the first place."

"Why would anyone want to keep it a secret?" asked Nina. "Nobody knows anything about it."

"The Khoils must have known, otherwise why would they have stolen it?" said Kit. He looked across the room to the statuette's not-quite-twin in the display case. "But now that you have two of them to examine, perhaps you will know too. I persuaded Interpol that you and the IHA were the best hope of identifying it." He handed the box to Nina and closed his briefcase.

"Uh, thanks," she said, slightly taken aback by the unexpected "gift."

"Are you staying in New York?" Eddie asked.

"I'm afraid I can't," Kit told him. "I have to fly back to Lyon right away—my new job somehow has a large pile of paperwork waiting for me already!"

"I know how that feels," said Nina, putting the box on her desk. "Well, congratulations on the promotion, Kit. Hope we see you again soon. Okay, not *too* soon, as that'd mean some archaeological treasure's been stolen . . . but you know what I mean."

"I think I do," he said with a grin. "Good-bye, my friends." He shook everyone's hand, then departed.

"What about you, Mac?" said Nina. "Do you have to rush off too?"

Mac gestured toward 44th Street beyond the window. "Only as far as the Delacourt hotel." He gave Eddie a wry look. "I thought after the trouble last time I was there, I should give them the custom as compensation. But after that, I'd rather hoped you'd both join me for dinner tonight."

"We'd love to," said Nina.

"I'm always up for some good nosh," Eddie added.

"Superb. In that case, I'd better go and check in. If there's anywhere you particularly recommend, give me a call. After all"—a smile—"I know you have my number. Since that's how you saved the world!"

"Again," said Nina. "We really should start billing for services rendered."

Mac laughed, then his smile became even warmer as he shook Eddie's hand. "You know, I thought when I first met you—God, what is it, almost sixteen years ago now?—that you had far more potential than met the eye. People like Stikes thought you were just a troublemaker, but sometimes we need somebody who'll stir things up. I'm proud, I'm *honored*, that you proved me right. Well done, Eddie. Damn good work."

Eddie stood straighter, beaming. "Thanks, Mac. That means a lot."

Mac released him, then kissed Nina's cheek. "And you've done a fantastic job of civilizing him. I wouldn't have thought it possible—"

"Oi!" Eddie protested.

"—but achieving the impossible seems to be one of your talents. Keep it up." He went to the door. "I'll see you both later."

Nina waved as he departed, then turned to her husband, smirking. "Aw, look at you. You're so happy and proud. It's sweet. It's like you just got praise from your dad."

She had meant it in a humorous way, the tactlessness only striking her after the words left her mouth. But rather than responding with irritation as he had before, Eddie appeared contemplative. "What is it?" she asked.

"You just made me think about Shankarpa and Girilal—about them getting to talk to each other one last time. And about Zec, wanting his son to know he'd done the right thing." He picked up the phone. Nina saw that the first two digits he dialed were 44—the international code for

the United Kingdom. "Hi, Elizabeth," he said when he got
an answer. "It's me. Yeah, yeah, I'm fine; I'll tell you all
about it later. Just a quick call—can you give me Dad's
phone number?"

The surprised response from the other end of the line
was loud enough even for Nina to hear. Eddie listened with
rising annoyance to his sister's gloating at his change of
heart. "No—no, I'm *not* saying I'm gonna call him," he interrupted. "Just that I wanted his number. In case I need it.
Which I don't right now, okay? So, you got the number?"
He took a pen from Nina's desk and wrote it down. "Okay,
thanks. Talk to you again soon. Give my love to Holly and
Nan, will you? Bye."

"So *are* you going to call him?" Nina asked with a sly
smile.

"Don't you bloody start." He pocketed the paper.

"What about dinner, then? Italian? French? Thai?"

He grinned. "I could murder an Indian."

           ❖ ❖ ❖

Kit walked through the gates of United Nations Plaza onto
First Avenue's busy sidewalk. He took out his phone,
glanced around to make sure nobody was paying him any
particular attention, then entered a number and made a
call.

A brusque, impatient response. "Yes."

"Sir, it's Jindal," he said. "I've just left the United Nations. Pushing to be assigned to the case paid off—the IHA
now has the two statues. As the new liaison between Interpol and the IHA, I will be in a position to monitor their in-
vestigation."

He had hoped to receive some praise, but was unsur-
prised when none was forthcoming. "You think Dr. Wilde
will be able to find the third?"

"If anyone can, she can. I'm sure of it."

"I hope so, Jindal." The implication of threat was understated, but clear. "Is your cover still secure?"

"Yes, sir. Nobody at Interpol or the IHA suspects that I'm working for the Group. If anything, the events in Delhi have given me more freedom to operate."

"Good. Keep us informed of Dr. Wilde's progress. As soon as she locates the third statue...the plan can begin."

The call ended. Kit double-checked that he had not been overheard, then disappeared into the crowd.

**HANG ON FOR A NEW
ADRENALINE-FUELED RIDE
WHEN NINA WILDE AND EDDIE
CHASE RETURN IN**

EMPIRE OF GOLD
by Andy McDermott

Deep in the jungles of South America, an incredible trea-sure has been hidden for centuries, and archaeologist Nina Wilde possesses the key to finding it. With her husband, Eddie Chase, her goal is to find the legendary last outpost of the Inca Empire—which could point the way to an even greater discovery long thought to be just a myth: El Do-rado, the lost city of gold. Corrupt soldiers, ruthless mer-cenaries—led by a man with a personal grudge against Eddie—and murderous rebels will stop at nothing to ob-tain the unimaginable fortune for themselves. But even as they all battle to find the treasure, Nina and Eddie's great-est enemy may turn out to be someone much closer to home....

Coming to a bookseller near you in Fall 2011

DIVE INTO AN EPIC QUEST FOR
THE WORLD'S ULTIMATE TREASURE!

An ancient warrior.
An incredible treasure.
A lethal enemy.

It's the opportunity of a lifetime: the chance to prove that a tomb containing the remains of the legendary hero Hercules actually exists. If American archaeologist Nina Wilde can locate it, it will be the most important historical find ever unearthed. But as Nina and her ex-SAS bodyguard, Eddie Chase, begin their search, it's clear that others want to find the tomb—and the unimaginable riches within—and will do anything to get there first.

Who will find the tomb of Hercules first, and what fantastic treasure does it hold? From New York to Shanghai, from Switzerland to the diamond mines of Botswana, Nina and Eddie must stay one step ahead of their enemies in a race to solve a mystery as ancient as civilization itself. But when a beautiful woman from Eddie's past joins the hunt, all the rules change—and in this life-and-death game, their next move may be the most dangerous one of all.

DARE TO OPEN...

THE TOMB OF HERCULES
by Andy McDermott

Available now

UNEARTH AN ADVENTURE
CENTURIES IN THE MAKING!

A legendary weapon.
A ruthless assassin.
A perilous hunt.

Excalibur... Legend has it that he who carries King Arthur's mighty sword into battle will be invincible. But for more than a thousand years, the secret to the whereabouts of this powerful weapon has been lost... until now.

Archaeologist Nina Wilde is hoping for a little R&R with her fiancé, former SAS bodyguard Eddie Chase. But the couple's plans are dashed when a meeting with an old acquaintance propels Nina and Eddie into a razor's-edge hunt across the globe—battling a team of elite mercenaries who will stop at nothing in order to claim a prize every treasure hunter has coveted since the final days of Camelot. Nina and Eddie must do everything they can to keep the legendary blade from falling into the wrong hands, because the truth behind the sword's power—and those who seek it—will not only shock the world but plunge it into a new and more devastating era of war.

THE ONE WHO DRAWS THE SWORD
HOLDS A TERRIFYING POWER IN...

THE SECRET OF EXCALIBUR
by Andy McDermott

Available now

DISCOVER AN ACTION-PACKED
THRILL RIDE THAT WILL KEEP YOU READING
LONG INTO THE NIGHT!

An incredible discovery.
A merciless foe.
A deadly race for the truth.

Off a remote stretch of the Indonesian coast, archaeologist Nina Wilde has made an astounding discovery: an artifact that will rewrite everything that's known about human history. But before she can return to tell the world of her find, her ship is brutally attacked, her crew is ruthlessly murdered, and the artifact is stolen. Someone wants this secret to stay hidden—and will do anything to keep it that way.

From the depths of the ocean to the Australian outback to the halls of the United Nations, Nina and her fiancé, ex-SAS bodyguard Eddie Chase, embark on a quest to stop the all-powerful Covenant of Genesis, a clandestine group sworn to keep Nina's discovery a secret. Nina and Eddie have faced tough adversaries before, but the relentless Covenant is always two steps ahead of them—and more than willing to kill again. Who will be the first to expose the truth—and claim the most valuable archaeological prize of all time?

THEY WILL STOP AT NOTHING TO PROTECT
THE WORLD'S BIGGEST SECRET....

THE COVENANT OF GENESIS
by Andy McDermott

Available now

JOIN THE RACE TO STOP
A DEADLY CONSPIRACY!

A buried Egyptian temple.
A secret kept for 6,000 years.
A treasure worth killing for.

An international TV audience waits breathlessly as archaeologists prepare to break into a long-hidden vault beneath the Great Sphinx. But student Macy Sharif has already made her own shocking discovery: a religious cult raiding the site. Their prize? A map that will lead to something far more astounding: the lost pyramid of Osiris. Framed by corrupt officials, Macy goes on the run, trying to reach the only people who can save her before she is silenced—permanently.

American archaeologist Nina Wilde, once a renowned scientific explorer, now all but blacklisted by her colleagues, is trying to rebuild her reputation. But Macy's plea for help will send Nina and ex-SAS bodyguard Eddie Chase on the ultimate treasure hunt. From the streets of Manhattan to a yacht off Monaco to a buried desert site, they'll follow an elusive trail stalked by a killer determined to uncover a six-thousand-year-old secret. And beneath the forbidding desert, they'll enter a forgotten world both wondrous and horrifying, where the ancient God of Death has kept his secrets—until now.

A SHOCKING SECRET IS HIDING IN...

THE PYRAMID OF DOOM
by Andy McDermott

Available now